TIDES OF DUPLICITY

COVENTRY SAGA BOOK 2

ROBIN PATCHEN

JDO PUBLISHING

Copyright © 2021 by Robin Patchen

All rights reserved.

No part of this book may be reproduced in any form or by any electronic or mechanical means, including information storage and retrieval systems, without written permission from the author, except for the use of brief quotations in a book review.

Cover designed by Lynnette Bonner

*For the ladies of the Quid Pro Quills:
Susan Crawford, Kara Hunt, Jericha Kingston, Candice Sue
Patterson, and Pegg Thomas.
I couldn't do this without you.*

CHAPTER ONE

Tabitha Eaton smacked a bug crawling up her neck. Had she lost her mind? Sure, she'd craved adventure. Safe adventure. The kind of adventure with trained guides taking her to pretty places and keeping her away from all of this...

Smack.

Whatever had landed on Tabby's calf flew away unscathed. All she had to show for her defensive effort was a red mark in the shape of her palm.

This was insane.

Every brush of a leaf, every drip of sweat, she was certain was the bite of some tiny exotic creepy-crawly thing that would give her malaria or worse.

She glared at the back of the man in front of her. This had been his idea.

Of course, in Fitz's defense, it wasn't as if even trained guides could keep crazy jungle bugs away from her. If the insect repellent she'd practically bathed in wasn't cutting it, nothing would. Also in Fitz's defense, until now the hike had been amazing. This wild, untamed jungle was like an amusement park to someone who'd always craved adventure. Or who'd claimed to, anyway. Now that Tabby was here, she wasn't so sure.

Fitz had promised a vista like nothing she'd ever seen, but what did she really know about this guy? She'd met him less than two weeks before, just another hotel guest. For all she knew, Fitz was a serial killer, and she was climbing to her own grave. Maybe he was some sort of fancy-resort murderer. They showed up everywhere, those killers, didn't they? There'd been a serial kidnapper in Coventry, her hometown. If they could show up there, why not in Belize? Why not here?

Maybe she should climb back down and run, run...to her own death, no doubt. She hadn't the slightest inkling where she was. She didn't speak Spanish. She didn't know how to survive out here.

On the other hand, this place... It was fascinating. She'd seen more wildlife—and she did mean *wild*—in the last two hours than she'd seen her entire life in New Hampshire. Birds of every color, shape, and size imaginable, brightly colored against the green, green world. Full bushes and undergrowth, dark trees with dripping bark, and a canopy so high and thick that the hot, bright sunlight, which had traveled millions upon millions of miles to reach earth, could not penetrate. Though it wasn't raining, there was so much moisture in the air that she was soaked with sweat. The foliage, the flowers, even the earth was different here than anything she'd ever experienced. The scents weren't familiar—at times sweet to the point of cloying, at other times rich and dark like manure and bracken. But not. Not like home. Not what she was used to.

It was as if, when they'd motored away from the resort to the mainland that morning, they'd left behind all she'd ever known.

The shriek of a howler monkey skittered down her spine. And the... the gubnut... Was that what Fitz had called it? No, gibnut. A jungle rodent. A twenty-pound jungle rodent that, unlike what was always said about such creatures, was not nearly as afraid of her as she was of it. She was sure that, if she turned around quick enough, she'd see the little stalker behind her, hoping, as Fitz had explained, that she might drop a bit of food. As if she had a free hand for a sandwich. Her hands were quite busy smacking bugs and gripping handholds to keep from plunging to her death.

The incline was only getting steeper. Fitz, in front of her five minutes ago, was now *above* her on this slope. Where was he taking her?

He'd promised she'd like it, but right now all she wanted was to be back at the resort on the little island off the coast, her toes in the sand, her gaze on the ocean, surrounded by waiters in khaki shorts and golf shirts, carrying trays with tall drinks clinking with fat ice cubes.

She gripped a skinny, slippery limb and pulled herself up another step.

Fitz turned back to face her, an easy smile on his face. "Almost there."

She would have snapped at him, let out all the thoughts swirling in her head, but she was out of breath, the thick air seeming to clog in her lungs.

Crazy. Her thoughts had gone as wild as this place.

She climbed, ignoring the man above her. When she looked up, Fitz was standing at the top, looking down at her. His lips quirked in a mischievous expression she'd seen more than once. "You're four feet away, Tabby. Don't have an anxiety attack on me now."

How did he read her so easily? She'd barely met the guy, but he could see through her like clear glass on a sunny day.

He reached down, palm open. "Come on, babe. I've got you."

Babe. She'd always thought it sounded smarmy when guys

called her babe. From Fitz, though, the word was affectionate, tender.

Not that she could ever really be his babe.

When she was close enough, she reached toward him.

He grabbed her hand and hoisted her the last few feet as if she weighed nothing. When she felt the solid forest floor beneath her feet, he said, "You did it."

"This had better be good."

His smile broadened, filling his whole face and making the skin around his eyes crinkle. She really liked that smile.

Surely it wasn't the smile of a serial killer.

Now that she'd reached the top, she could admit that her thoughts had gone a little far afield.

Still holding her hand, he tugged her forward. "It's just this way." After a moment, they broke through the thick underbrush.

Her breath caught in her throat.

They were standing at the top of a cliff overlooking a lush valley. Her vision snagged on a waterfall at the far end. The water splashed into a pool so clear she could follow the schools of brightly colored fish from where she stood high above. Surrounding the valley was the greenest world she'd ever seen.

"It's magnificent."

His smile—oh, that smile—seemed delighted. Delighted with her delight.

Despite the harrowing hike he'd led her on, she still liked him. Too much.

He squeezed her hand. "I did this hike the second day Shelby and I got here, all by myself. She had no interest."

Fitz's teenage sister seemed like a great kid, but it didn't surprise Tabby that she'd foregone the hike with her big brother, not when there was so much to do back at the resort. Tabby didn't doubt that the boy Shelby had taken to spending so much time with had contributed to her decision.

"How did you learn so much about the local attractions, plants and animals and"—she gestured to the landscape around them—"all of it?"

He shrugged. "Read the brochures, did a few internet searches."

This world... it was the most beautiful thing she'd ever seen. The colors so bright, they seemed almost unnatural. The sounds, the smells.

"Was it worth it?" he asked.

"Five minutes ago, if you'd asked me if anything could be worth what we just endured, I'd have said absolutely not. But now"—she turned to face him—"definitely. This will be the highlight of my trip."

His brows lowered over pale blue eyes. "I can't believe you're leaving tomorrow."

She couldn't either. Tomorrow she'd go back home, back to her boring human resources job at Hamilton Clothiers. Back to her small house in snow-covered February in New Hampshire. Back to her parents and her brother, her responsibilities and commitments.

Two weeks she'd been in Belize. Two glorious weeks, a vacation she'd spent a year saving up for, even though hardly anybody back home had understood.

Two whole weeks? her boss had asked.

By yourself? her coworker had asked.

Only Chelsea, her oldest and dearest friend, had understood. *Belize will be perfect. You'll love it.* Chelsea had been in this part of the world. She'd even recommended the resort. Of course, Chelsea had also cautioned her to stay on the property, where she'd be safe.

This was not safe. This hike, this beauty, this man beside her. Nothing about this was *safe*.

Tabby was sick of safe.

Fitz was gazing down at her. He lifted her hand and kissed her knuckles. His gaze flicked to her eyes, her lips. "Tabby."

"Don't."

"I don't think I'm going to be able to live with myself if I don't kiss you at least once."

"I can't, Fitz. It'll be too hard."

"Why?" The sadness in his expression almost had her changing her mind. But she couldn't. She took a few steps back. "You know why."

"We could just try—"

"It won't work."

"It's a couple hours' drive, no more."

"It won't work." She'd spoken the words too many times in the previous few days. "Long-distance dating. I can't leave Coventry, and you've got your sister. You can't leave Providence."

"She graduates in—"

"You're a city boy, Fitz. You don't belong in my world, and I don't belong in yours. One or both of us would end up with a broken heart." Her. It would definitely be her. Because this handsome, gentle, charming man must have women falling all over themselves to be with him. Tabby was the one with no options. Tabby was the one who'd met and passed on—or been passed on by—every eligible man in her little town. "This is going to be hard enough without making it worse."

"A kiss would be worse?"

Much worse.

Much, much worse.

Because it was going to be agony saying good-bye to Fitz tonight.

Two weeks. Two weeks with this man and he'd somehow wrapped around her being. He'd made a place in her life she'd never be able to fill without him. But she could still get over it. She could still recover, as long as she stayed smart. As long as she didn't let him get any closer.

But if he kissed her? Remembering his lips on hers would make leaving him pure torture.

She turned back to the vista, her thoughts quivering with sadness, with desire. "So, do we go down there, or—?"

"Yup." His voice had lost its life. "Come on." He didn't take her hand this time, just marched forward. They'd swim. They'd laugh. Fitz would shake off his frustration and have fun for her sake. He'd pretend he didn't mind, pretend that all was well in order to make her happy.

She loved that about him, too.

CHAPTER TWO

Fitz McCaffrey stood about ten feet behind where Tabby sat at a table for two on the patio of the resort's casual restaurant. The blue sky faded into sunset while she tracked a sailboat gliding across the horizon. That was Tabby, though. He'd known her for two weeks, and he felt like he could read her mind already. Right now, she was thinking about whatever exotic locations that sailboat would reach and about the adventures the people aboard would experience. Fitz wouldn't tell her that it was one of the many sailboats rented from a marina just a mile down the beach. He wouldn't tell her that the folks on that boat were vacationers just like her. That would ruin all her fun.

He snapped a few pictures with his camera. He'd probably taken a hundred of her since they'd met, mostly with her glaring at him. He loved taking pictures, and she hated to have her picture taken. Their one point of contention.

A woman at the neighboring table said something to Tabby, and she responded. After a moment, the two were laughing. How did Tabby do that, make friends with everybody she met? That was her, another thing he loved about her. Fitz's suspicious nature kept him from trusting easily, but Tabby was as trusting as anyone he'd ever met.

He snapped another photo, this time getting the stranger in the picture. The two of them laughing with the pink-and-orange sky in the background created a beautiful image.

He was glad Tabby had chosen this more casual restaurant. He'd offered to take her to the steakhouse tonight, but she preferred the outdoor seating and the view. Now, the evening breeze lifted her long brown hair. She brushed it out of her face.

She looked stunning in the pale peach top he'd bought her at the resort shop a few days earlier—bought because he'd known it would look great on her. It did, too, the skinny straps showing off shapely shoulders covered with a smattering of freckles, the clingy fabric hugging all her curves. Tabby had a girl-next-door look. Unpretentious, honest, and downright gorgeous.

She was leaving the following morning, going back to the work she wouldn't admit she hated. Back to the loneliness she swore didn't bother her.

And he was no better, preparing to return to his own private hell.

If only they could stay in Belize forever.

Tabby turned and caught his eye, her expression shifting from surprise that he was standing there to pure pleasure. When he approached, she said, "I think they expect you to sit before they serve you."

He slipped into the chair across from her. "This is my last chance to gaze at you."

She smacked his arm playfully. "You're a smooth talker, Fitzgerald."

He winked as if he hadn't meant the words. As if it were all some colossal joke. But they both knew it wasn't. They both knew they'd formed a bond these last two weeks that could be something more than just a vacation fling.

But she was willing to accept that this would be their last night together. Maybe he should too. It wasn't as if he had anything to offer her. Everything he'd had, everything he'd ever wanted, had been stripped away. He was left with a job he despised, a photography hobby he could hardly afford to pursue and frankly didn't even enjoy that much, and a teenage sister who depended on him for everything. A sister who, despite her dependence, was pretty sure she didn't need him at all.

He couldn't blame Tabby for not wanting a relationship with him. Nearly thirty years old, and his life was a mess.

"There you are."

They both turned as Shelby snaked her way among the tables and approached, the skinny boy who'd occupied nearly every moment of her time here in Belize just a few feet behind. Twice, Fitz had caught them lip-locked. The second time, he'd seen that boy's hands sliding across Shelby's bare back between the top and bottom of a skimpy bikini he hadn't authorized as if they were on an expedition into the unknown. It had taken all of Fitz's self-control not to beat the kid senseless. As it was, he'd gripped the skinny shoulder a little too hard when he'd yanked him away. But he'd directed his comments to Shelby. "Change out of that bikini and throw it in the trash. Now."

Normally, she'd have put up a fight, but she must've seen something in his gaze because she turned and scurried back to their suite.

Only when she was out of sight did he press the kid up against the rough brick and threaten to break every bone in his body if he so much as touched her. The kid had sworn nothing had, or would, happen.

Right. Fitz had been a teenager once. All those raging

hormones. He knew what Shawn was after probably better than the kid himself did.

Of course, the bikini hadn't made it into the trash. Fitz found it shoved in the back of Shelby's drawer. He'd taken it to the beach that night and had a little bonfire.

He had no idea what his father would have done. No doubt he'd have handled it better, but Fitz was doing the best he could.

Now, Shelby stopped beside him. "I'm going to dinner with Shawn and his parents. They're taking us to some fancy place up the beach."

Fitz had met the kid's mother, a forty-something bottle blonde who'd been nipped and tucked into the body of a much younger woman. But she'd seemed nice enough, responsible enough. "What time will you be home?"

Shelby rolled her eyes. "I don't know, *Dad.*" The word was tossed like an insult. Fitz was no Colin McCaffrey, and they both knew it. "After dinner, I guess."

"No later than midnight. Stay with their family. Don't go wandering on your own." He caught Shawn's eyes and added, "And remember what I said." With his eyes, he tried to impart his meaning—*I will have you begging for mercy if you so much as touch her.*

"I won't forget, sir."

Sir, like he was an old man. Fitz caught Shelby's second eye-roll in sixty seconds just as she turned to leave.

He grabbed her forearm an instant before she was out of reach. "You want me to find you some oatmeal?"

Oatmeal—their code word that meant *get me out of here* or *I'm not safe.* He reminded her of it often, but she'd only used it once. She'd been at a party when a bunch of kids had shown up uninvited carrying bottles of liquor and bags of drugs. For all Shelby's teenage attitude, she was a well-behaved kid. She hadn't wanted to make a big deal out of leaving. So, she'd called him right there in the middle of her friends and, after chatting about nothing for a few seconds, asked him to put oatmeal on the grocery list.

He'd been there to pick her up ten minutes later. She'd probably complained loudly to all her friends about her overprotective brother on her way out the door, but once she'd climbed in his car, she'd been grateful.

Unfortunately, Shelby didn't need his rescue tonight. "I think I'll skip breakfast tomorrow." She sent him a wink, telling him she wasn't angry. "Thanks anyway."

"Be safe," he called as she walked away.

Her hand lifted in a wave, but she didn't turn back.

"She's in good hands," Tabby said.

Fitz settled against his chair again. "Yeah. I know. It's just... Every day, I beg God's forgiveness for the hell I put my parents through. If I'd had any idea..."

"That's the thing about teenagers, though. They don't know anything. I mean, I'm six years out of my teens, and I still feel like I don't know anything."

He took her hand and kissed it. "You're delightfully naive."

"Hey, you're not that much older than I am."

"True." He kept her hand in his. He needed the connection, even if she didn't.

His lovely Tabby was gentle and optimistic. She'd lived a sheltered life. Maybe not one without tragedy, but certainly nothing like his. She'd gone to college, returned to her hometown, gotten a job, and worked. Simple. Normal.

So unlike Fitz's own experience.

"She's going to graduate in just over two years," he said, broaching the subject she'd forbidden more than once.

"I have a friend." Tabby's voice had taken on a conversational tone, but it sounded forced. "I was a few years behind her in school, so I never knew her back then. She was a foster kid."

"I would never let my sister—"

"I know. I know. You're devoted to her. I lo... I admire that about you."

He pretended she'd finished her first thought. Pretended Tabby had the courage to use the L-word with him. Not that he wanted her to love him, maybe, but to admit to deeper feelings than admiration—he'd take that.

"This friend... It's a long story, but she found herself on her own at seventeen. No family at all. I mean, no parents, no siblings, no cousins. She was really and truly alone in the world. It shaped her. It changed her in ways... I never understood how important family was. The way Cassidy puts it, she feels like she's lived her whole life on a tightrope with no safety net. One small slip, and it would be over. Even now, with a town that loves her and a man...she just got married. But she still struggles to believe she's safe, that she has a home." Tabby leaned toward him, her gold cross necklace dangling above tanned skin. "You're giving your sister a safety net, a home. You're going to need to do that long after she graduates and goes off to college. You've taken on a serious responsibility with her. Her graduation isn't going to change—"

"I know that." He pulled his hand away from hers. "Don't you think I know that?" He took a breath, tempered his words. "But I get to have a life, too, don't I? I mean, why can't I support Shelby and have us too?"

"I'm not leaving New Hampshire. You can't leave Rhode Island. It's as simple—"

"Fine."

"Don't do that, Fitz."

"It's fine." He settled back in the chair to get a handle on his emotions, his tone. Tabby was right, he couldn't leave Rhode Island. He wouldn't uproot Shelby's life. Their parents' deaths had done enough of that. But Tabby could leave her mountain home if she wanted to. If she cared enough about him.

Which was what it came down to. She didn't. Simple as that.

Her voice was tentative when she said, "If I could—"

"I know." He didn't know. But he wasn't going to ruin their last night together talking about it. His faith, young as a preemie and just as fragile, told him to trust God with this. He'd learned not to count on anybody, learned nobody could be trusted. Putting faith in God felt as natural as letting Tabby go.

It seemed he had no choice on the second, so he might as well try practicing the first.

CHAPTER THREE

Fitz knew he was dreaming. He knew the arms pulling him closer were phantom arms, the lips exploring his were phantom lips. The thick brown hair between his fingers was phantom hair. But he held his phantom Tabby close, knowing it was as near as he'd ever get to the real woman.

The ringing of the phone yanked him from the bliss.

He slid his cell off the nightstand and noted the time. Nine fifteen a.m.

But the ringing wasn't coming from his cell. Who would call on the hotel phone?

Tabby? Had her flight been cancelled? His heart soared at the thought. Maybe they could have another day together. Even just a meal. He'd have happily accompanied her to the airport, but she'd refused that offer like she'd refused his every attempt at lengthening their time together. The night before, he'd walked her to her door, kissed her forehead, and told her good-bye, hoping she'd initiate a kiss—a real one. But she had only squeezed his hand and disappeared into her hotel room.

She'd made saying good-bye look so easy.

And anyway, she'd call his cell phone. Whoever was on the

line wouldn't be Tabby.

Shelby was surely asleep in the other bedroom. She hadn't woken before noon since they'd arrived.

But the phone continued to ring. He snatched the handset.

Before he could speak, the voice on the line said, "Fitzgerald McCaffrey?"

Fitz sat up in his bed. "Who is this?"

"We need to talk. It's about your girlfriend. I'm in room six thirty-nine. Be here in fifteen minutes."

"Why would I—?"

The phone slammed in his ear.

He sat back on the bed. About his *girlfriend*? The closest he'd come to a girlfriend in years was Tabby, and that hadn't been nearly close enough.

But who else could the caller have meant?

Father, should I go?

His faith was new, like a stiff pair of leather shoes he hadn't broken in yet. Maybe faith was like that. Maybe it never got comfortable. That it had occurred to him to ask God's input was a miracle in itself. Talking to someone who wasn't there? He couldn't tell if he was practicing faith or just showing the beginning signs of insanity.

If the word *girlfriend* referred to Tabby, was she in trouble? The thought of her propelled him out of bed.

He dressed quickly, then paused at his sister's closed door. He resisted the temptation to look in on her and risk her wrath. Her privacy had become sacrosanct in the last few years. He tried to respect it and look after her at the same time. No easy feat. But she'd made it home the evening before—seconds before the midnight curfew—and gone to bed. She was safe.

He wrote her a quick note explaining exactly where he was going and left it on the kitchen counter. He could take care of himself in most situations. But just in case something terrible happened to him, at least the note would give the police a place to start looking.

He left their suite, feeling naked without his gun. He'd almost gotten used to not wearing it, to not needing it. With the uncertainty of the odd phone call, he wished for the protection.

He and Shelby were on the third floor, and logic would dictate that he go to the elevator. Instead, he headed toward the stairwell on the far end of the balcony-like hallway. Like many resorts, the hallway and stairs were not enclosed but outside. The weather was warm and muggy.

He opened the heavy stairwell door, closed it softly behind him, and made his way up three flights. He stepped out of the stairwell as quietly as he could and did a quick sweep of the hall before walking silently. It was empty of vacationers. A maid's cart rested in the hall beside a room being cleaned by at least two women, based on their chatter. Behind a couple of doors, he heard voices, but nothing unusual. It felt like any morning at any resort on any beach in the world.

Fitz reached room 639 and listened, back pressed against the wall beside the door. His gaze flicked along the hallway and caught sight of a shiny black something wedged against the ceiling just a few feet down. That something made him lift his hand in greeting. He added a smile aimed at the camera for good measure.

The door beside him opened, and a man stepped out. Gray beard, slender, long stringy hair, beady eyes. He wore jeans, a black T-shirt, and a baseball cap. The guy looked like a young version of Willie Nelson. "Glad you made it."

"If I'd had more time, I'd have put on my good suit."

The guy's lips angled up slightly, but the smile seemed tight, little stress marks at the corners.

Fitz stepped into a suite set up like his and Shelby's, with a kitchen on the right, a table and chairs on the left, a small living area beyond, and bedrooms on each side. Seated at the glass table were three more men. The two on the sides seemed like the kind Fitz had spent his short law enforcement career trying to put behind bars. Cropped brown hair, tattooed forearms, and tight T-shirts covering biceps bigger than their brains. The slimmer one had a goatee. The other had a little more chub in his clean-shaven cheeks.

They looked enough alike to be brothers, Tweedle-Dee and Tweedle-Dum. Goofy names didn't make them seem one iota less threatening.

The fourth man sat at the far end as if it were a long shiny conference table and not a small glass-and-nickel number. He had silver hair styled in a fashion that would have gone better with a brown plaid suit and a wide tie than it did with the tangerine golf shirt. His skin was dark—tanned, not swarthy. He had hazel eyes and wore a predatory smile. And, though Fitz didn't remember ever having met him, something about him seemed familiar.

The man said, "Have a seat, Mr. McCaffrey."

Guards on two sides, the Willie Nelson wannabe behind. He didn't have a lot of choices, and he didn't have to see them to know at least three of the men in the room had guns beneath their oversized T-shirts. Whatever this was, and despite the steaming coffee mugs on the table, it wasn't a friendly invitation to breakfast.

Fitz slid into the chair opposite the guy in charge. "What can I do for you?"

"Name's Ronnie," the silver-haired man said.

"That supposed to mean something to me?"

The guy chuckled, but there was no humor in it. "I need you to do me a favor."

"Why would I do that?"

"Tell me about your girlfriend?"

"If I had one, I might consider it."

"Tabitha Eaton."

Fitz let out a scoff. "Not a girlfriend. We just met."

The man—Ronnie—seemed to be waiting for him to add more words to his short statement.

Fitz sat back and draped his arm over the back of his chair. All ease and confidence, though his mind spun. What could Tabby have to do with anything? Tabby, the innocent New Hampshire girl, couldn't possibly be tied up with these people.

"Surely you two talked," Ronnie said.

"It wasn't exactly about *talking*." Fitz emphasized the last word, hating himself for the lie. But he added for good measure, "You know how it is."

He watched Ronnie's reaction, but the man betrayed nothing.

And then it came to him where he'd seen this guy.

He'd been by the pool wearing board shorts, tanning his hairy chest and flabby belly. He'd been seated beside Shawn's mother. This man was on the old side to be the parent of a teen but too young to be the grandfather of one. Was this Shawn's father? Fitz might guess he was the mother's boyfriend, but now that Fitz had placed him, the resemblance to the teenager who followed Shelby around like a puppy was obvious.

Fitz's heartbeat raced. He should have looked in on Shelby before he'd left. He dropped the arm and leaned forward. "You're Shawn's father? Did something happen to the kids?"

The night before, Shelby had gone into her room and closed the door. A half hour later, he'd seen her light go off. Surely, she'd gone to sleep. Surely, she was still safely tucked in their hotel suite.

"Tabitha Eaton," Ronnie said. "What can you tell us about her?"

"Does this have anything to do with my sister?"

"We'll get to Shelby and Shawn. First—"

"No." His voice was too loud. He took a deep breath. He'd get his answers faster if he cooperated. "I can tell you almost nothing about Tabby. She works for Hamilton, the clothing company. She lives in New Hampshire. What do you want with her?"

"She stole from me." The man's genial façade cracked, and Fitz saw clearly the fury behind it.

Tabby? A thief? "I can't believe that's true. She's no criminal mastermind."

"You just told us you hardly know her." Ronnie shifted his oversize bulk in the chair. The man had the look of someone who used to be built like a truck but hadn't seen the inside of a gym since the Clinton administration. "What do you really know about her?" He leaned forward and rested too-thick arms on the table.

Fitz didn't know enough about Tabby to defend her. He only knew what she'd told him. And yeah, he had always thought he was good at reading people. But recent experiences had proved he wasn't as good as he'd thought. His ex-partner had proved that. The fact that Fitz was currently unemployed, or might as well have been, proved that. And no, he didn't consider his current gig a real job.

Maybe, like almost everybody else in his life, Tabby had lied to him. Maybe that was why she didn't want to get involved with him. Maybe that explained everything.

Much easier to think that than to think that she just didn't like him enough to take a chance on their relationship.

He closed his eyes. Tabby, a thief? It didn't make sense. Nothing about Tabby had seemed dishonest. If anything, she'd been too honest. But that could have been a ruse. Didn't people use honesty, or the illusion of transparency, to deceive? Wasn't that how con men worked?

He was so stupid. He'd been sucked right in.

"You're right," Fitz said. "I don't know anything about her. I don't know what you want, but I can't help you." He pushed back in his chair, but Willie pressed his bony hands into his shoulders.

Fitz turned and looked at the man behind him, one eyebrow raised in a look that clearly spoke, *do you mind?*

Willie backed off.

"Nevertheless," Ronnie said, "you are uniquely qualified to do us this favor. You have a relationship with her, and we need you to use it to get my items back."

Fitz focused on Ronnie again. "Look, I'm sure whatever she stole is really valuable and all that, but why would I get involved? It has nothing to do with me."

Ronnie shrugged his wide shoulders. "I got a couple reasons for you. First, either you get the stuff back from her"—he nodded with his chin to the goons—"or these guys do. I have a feeling your methods will be a little more palatable."

What kind of thug used the word *palatable*?

But then the threat registered. Tabby in these men's hands... No, he couldn't have that.

Not that it was his business. They'd had a vacation fling—barely even that. A real fling would have involved a kiss or more. The old Fitz would have expected more, but he was trying to bury that part of himself now. Obviously, what he felt for Tabby—scratch that, what he *had* felt for her before she'd left him without looking back—shouldn't be enough to compel him to protect her.

But... was he really going to leave her to these men?

He swore under his breath. He would run to her aid in a heartbeat, but he couldn't exactly traipse off to New Hampshire —or wherever the con-woman who called herself Tabitha Eaton was really from—with Shelby in tow. He didn't want his sister anywhere near these people. In fact, though they were supposed to stay another couple of days, they'd be packing up and leaving on the first available flight. And Fitz would be deleting Shawn's number from Shelby's phone. He would not have his sister associating with this family.

But... Tabby.

"She didn't do it."

Ronnie nodded to Tweedle-Dee, who stepped into a bedroom. "We have proof," Ronnie said.

Proof was a strong word, but Fitz would stay to see what evidence they held. Not that he had much choice.

The guy returned with a laptop, opened it, and turned it to face Fitz. On it, a video had been paused. A small office lit by what had to have been a very dim light off-camera. A wall of cabinets stood on one side, and a desk was opposite the camera. The room was empty.

The man pressed a button, and the video began.

A moment later, a woman stepped into the office and closed the door. Careful to keep her face averted from the camera, she slipped off her sweatshirt and laid it between the bottom of the door and the floor before flipping the light on. She was taller than the average woman and had brown curly hair she'd secured in a ponytail. She wore a peach top with spaghetti straps. In the bright light, he could see the freckles on her shoulder.

Tabby?

She pulled a lower cabinet open to reveal a steel safe and crouched in front of it.

She pressed an apparatus—probably a listening device—against it. She turned the dial a few times, then slowed down and did it again. It was a painstaking process.

After a few minutes, though he couldn't see the screen, Ronnie said, "Skip the boring part."

The thug fast-forwarded while Fitz's heartbeat raced.

Though intellectually he knew Tabby had gotten out without getting caught, his heart was terrified somebody was going to burst in.

"Not like in the movies," Ronnie said. "Either she's not very good at safecracking, or the movies make it look too easy."

Safecracking wasn't easy. Fitz had worked enough robberies to know that. A very small part of him was impressed by Tabby's skill.

If it was Tabby.

Twenty-five minutes after she'd entered the room, the thief opened the safe and pulled some kind of box out. She peeked inside, then closed the safe and cabinet. She flipped off the light, slipped on her sweatshirt, tucked the box under her arm, and left.

The video stopped.

After a moment, Ronnie said, "So you know, that's the office behind the check-in desk. Now, I don't know that woman from Adolph's nephew, but what you don't see in the video is that her wallet fell out of her sweatshirt, or so we assume. It was found on the floor behind the counter this morning. The clerk didn't realize the theft had taken place. When your girlfriend came to the counter frantically looking for her wallet, the clerk gave it back to her. She grabbed an Uber to the airport and left."

Fitz's mind was spinning. If he hadn't seen it with his own eyes, he wouldn't have believed it. Except...

"Obviously," Fitz said, "the woman in that video is an experienced thief. Not everybody knows how to crack a safe. But she didn't disable the camera. Why make such a rookie mistake?"

Ronnie lifted one shoulder. "She didn't see it."

"But she'd done her homework enough to know exactly where the safe was and the light switch. She'd been in there before. Is the camera hidden?"

Ronnie's eyes narrowed slightly. "It's in plain sight."

"Doesn't make sense."

"Maybe she thought she'd disabled it or something." Ronnie sipped his coffee and set it back down. "Doesn't matt—"

"And another thing... Why bring her wallet? A key card, maybe. But—"

"All questions you can ask her when you find her."

"How am I supposed to do that?"

"Shouldn't be too hard."

The goon minimized the video and pulled up a website—the Hamilton Clothiers corporate website. The tab labeled, "Our Team" was open, and there was Tabby's photo.

"Wait." Fitz pushed back in his chair. "You're saying she really is Tabitha Eaton, she really does live in New Hampshire, she really does work for Hamilton?"

"Seems that way."

The thieves Fitz had known were smarter than that. Why wouldn't Tabby have used a different name? Or stayed at a different hotel if this was the one she planned to burgle?

She was somehow both a criminal mastermind and a bumbling idiot.

The Tabby he knew was neither.

"I can see you're torn," Ronnie said. "I do have another, shall we say, inducement, if protecting your girlfriend from my friends isn't enough to compel you to do the right thing. But I'd rather not go there. I'd rather you and I work together like friends."

"We're not friends, and I don't care what was stolen from you and, despite your *proof,* I don't buy that Tabby stole it." And even if she did, he wasn't about to help this guy. "You're barking up the wrong tree, and I am not the monkey who's going to climb it for you."

Ronnie looked over Fitz's head at Willie. "Monkey. That's funny. I like that." Ronnie's amusement was gone when he met

Fitz's eyes again. "I did a little research on you. Fitzgerald Colin McCaffrey. Former detective in the Providence PD. Fired for corruption."

Fitz worked to keep his expression neutral. "I resigned. No corruption."

"I heard the story. Let's be honest. You're not so snowy white that you can't work with a guy like me. And I'm not so heartless that I wanna hurt your little girlfriend." Ronnie's lips twitched, and he spread his hands, palms up. "Cards on the table. If I thought hurting her would get my property back and keep me out of trouble, I'd do it. But I can't go in and out of the US within a couple of weeks without raising flags I don't want raised. But you can do it." There was his predatory smile again. "If I send my guys after her, she probably won't live to tell about it. We can do that if that's what you want. But I think once you hear about my inducement, you'll decide to work with us."

Fitz was processing the threats, the images that came to mind at the thought of what could happen to Tabby. He had to figure out a way to protect her, or at least to warn her.

And then everything else he'd said registered. "What inducement?"

"Shelby, of course."

The bottom dropped out of Fitz's stomach. He stood, shaking off Willie's grip.

The two others stood as well. Only Ronnie remained sitting.

"What about her?" Fitz's voice was low, threatening, but Ronnie didn't seem intimidated.

"My son talked her into an early morning sail to see the sunrise."

Fitz snatched his cell from his pocket, but Willie grabbed it before he could dial.

"It's too late," Ronnie said. "Don't worry. My wife is playing chaperone, and my crew will take them where I say. Now,

Shawn thinks he's in love with your sister. I don't want to hurt her. But..." He shrugged. "It's better if she thinks she's on a trip voluntarily. Better if she thinks you've given your consent for a longer cruise."

Fear blasted in Fitz's brain like a foghorn. "If anybody lays a hand on my sister—including that pimply kid of yours—I'll kill him. But first, I'll kill you. I can land a bullet between your eyes from five hundred yards. You'll never see me coming, and nobody can protect you. If anything happens to Shelby, I'll have nothing to live for. You've taken her, which means you've taken responsibility for her. If she comes back to me with so much as a bruise, I will take you out."

The man brushed off his words like a pesky mosquito. "When you have my stolen goods, I'll return her to you. As long as she doesn't know she's a prisoner, she'll have the time of her life. But if you warn her, if you try to tell her what's going on or ask her to tell you where they are? We'll find out. And then, we'll have to lock her up. My yacht is big, but there aren't a lot of comfortable places to confine a person. There's a hold under the deck. No windows. No communication. That's where she'll spend the rest of her tour. Better if she believes she's taking a cruise."

They had her. Shelby was probably already miles away. Was she having fun? Or was she nervous that she was going to get in trouble? Or did she already know she was a prisoner? Shelby was smart but trusting. Would that she would stay innocent until he could get her back.

The problem was, that yacht would never be found if the crew didn't want it to be.

"She won't believe I gave my permission," Fitz said. "She'll get behind on her schoolwork. She knows I'd never—"

"Convince her."

"She won't believe me."

"Sit down, Mr. McCaffrey."

"She's not going to—"

"Sit. Down."

Slowly, Fitz took his seat again.

The goons remained standing.

Ronnie nodded to one of them, and he snatched a bundle of papers from the counter and slid it facedown on the glass table.

"Have a look," Ronnie said.

Reluctantly, Fitz flipped over the paper and saw the image of a necklace. In the top corner was the logo for Sotheby's New York. Receipts...he flipped through them. There were six items—two necklaces, a bracelet, and two rings that sported jewels so big and garish, nobody would ever think they were anything but costume jewelry.

The last item was an antique hand-carved wooden box. He recognized it as the one the thief had taken from the safe. He assumed the jewels had been inside.

All the items had been purchased three weeks earlier by someone named Gail Seder at an auction for just over five hundred thousand dollars. The receipts had been emailed to a man named...

Ronald Mullins.

The name registered.

This man was part of the Irish Mob operating out of Boston.

Ronnie Mullins had bought the jewelry and box and then smuggled the pieces out of the country. The jewelry had probably been on the neck and fingers and wrist of his nipped-and-tucked wife. The box had probably looked like a cheap souvenir in the suitcase.

An antique box and a half a million dollars' worth of jewels. The man would stop at nothing to get them back. Even if that meant threatening an innocent woman from New Hampshire.

Even if it meant kidnapping a teenage girl.

CHAPTER FOUR

From the sixth-floor balcony, Fitz glanced at the shimmering pool below, ignoring the man just beyond the sliding glass door behind him who, Fitz was certain, was staring his way.

He'd stormed outside moments before, not even attempting to exit the suite into the corridor. Four against one—he wouldn't have gotten far. And walking away from this situation wasn't an option anyway.

He leaned against the metal railing and stared out to sea at what had seemed like paradise the day before.

Tabby by his side, his sister happier than she'd been in years. He'd come to Belize on a job to get pictures of a guy who'd claimed to be permanently injured at work. Both the guy's employer and the insurance company figured the guy was faking the extent of his injury. They'd hired the private investigation firm Fitz freelanced for, and Fitz had discovered the claimant's plan to come here on vacation, thanks to his old-fashioned detective work. He'd found a discarded note in the guy's trash with flight numbers and the name of the resort.

Sure, he could have hired a local to get the shots, but he and Shelby had needed a vacation. They'd needed the time away from rumors and pressure. After he'd resigned from the department, she'd talked him into letting her enroll in an online private high school, so she'd mostly kept up with her work while they were here. And they'd had time together, time to heal —again.

The fraudster showed his hand on day one, and Fitz had snapped the pictures to prove it. He was pretty sure somebody with a debilitating and permanent back injury wouldn't be able to surf. After that, this trip had been pure pleasure.

Shelby had enjoyed the freedom and anonymity of being away from everyone who knew Fitz's shame, and she'd spent as much time with Shawn as Fitz would allow, giving him time to work on his photography and time to spend with Tabby. It had been perfect. Paradise.

His paradise had turned into hell on earth.

He should never have trusted that the pimply kid and his parents wouldn't harm Shelby.

He should never have trusted Shelby to obey his rules.

He should never have trusted Tabby to be who she said she was.

How many times would he have to learn the same lesson? Nobody could be trusted. Ever.

At the top of the list of people Fitz knew he couldn't trust— Ronnie Mullins. Fitz's work on the anti-gang task force in Providence had taught him about many of the high-level mobsters in New England, and those in Boston were of particular interest, the Boston and Providence mobs being incestuously linked. Ronnie Mullins's name had come up in more than one investigation. Now that Fitz had placed the face, he was ashamed he hadn't recognized him before. But Ronnie Mullins had taken a backseat to newer members of the organized crime family. He'd thought the man had gotten out of the business.

Apparently not.

What was Fitz supposed to do now? He no longer had friends in law enforcement, nobody who trusted him and nobody he trusted. He could call his former chief, but Collins would love the chance to make a name at the federal level. He'd call in the FBI or the DEA for sure. They'd jump on the possibility of bringing Ronnie Mullins to justice. Saving Shelby wouldn't be anybody's priority.

No. Fitz had trusted the authorities. He'd been burned for it.

Fitz was the only person he trusted with his sister's care.

And Tabby's.

He was going to have to take off the aspiring photographer hat, take off the private investigator hat, and even take off the old police detective hat. If he was going to work with Mullins, he'd have to find an entirely new person beneath his own skin.

To save Shelby, he'd do whatever it took.

He turned and yanked open the sliding glass door so quickly that Mullins stepped back in surprise.

Fitz stepped past him and forced levity into his voice. "This is gonna be fun." He sat at the table. "I need to talk to my sister."

Mullins took his time settling into the chair opposite. "Sure, sure. You got a plausible story?"

"Yeah." One that should work, anyway. "She's going to be suspicious. We've already been gone from home for two weeks. She needs to keep up in school, so the only way this works is if you give her access to a laptop. I'll tell her she can stay with your family if she promises to get her schoolwork done. Otherwise, she's gonna have to go stay with our grandparents. If she believes she has to do school while she's on the ship, then she might, *might*, believe I'd allow this."

Mullins regarded him a long time. "Access to a laptop gives her access to you."

Fitz thought back to what he'd learned about Mullins. The man hadn't been much of a player in the years Fitz had been on the force, but stories about him abounded from the late nineties and early two thousands. Mullins's fingers had been deep into gambling and prostitution rings. He'd been suspected of having more than one rival taken off the street—always in a body bag. He'd been ruthless but never reckless. That he was still alive and operating was a testament to his cunning. He would do whatever was necessary to get his money back.

None of that mattered now. All that mattered was getting Shelby home.

"I love my sister enough to do my best to protect her from you and from the knowledge that she's in danger." Fitz kept his voice low and steady despite his fury. "I'm going to play my part, and I expect you to play yours. If you hurt her, I'll dedicate the rest of my days to making you pay."

"Let's stop with the threats."

"You started it. I'm just telling you—I'll finish it."

The older man heaved a sigh and adjusted himself on the chair. "You do your part, you'll get her back."

Fitz held out his hand. "I'm going to need my phone."

One of the goons plopped it in his palm, and Fitz pushed back in his chair, stood, and started toward the balcony.

Mullins followed and laid a meaty grip on his shoulder.

Fitz turned. "What?"

"One week. You have one week to get my stuff. Not a day longer."

"And then what? You kill my sister and live the rest of your life looking over your shoulder?" He shrugged off the man's hand. "It'll take the time it takes."

"I already have a buyer, and we're making the deal a week

from today. If that deal falls through"—he spread his arms wide—"all is lost. My life, my business, my family... and your sister."

Fitz's mouth went dry. A week?

What if he couldn't do it in a week?

He turned, tried to leave the self-doubt in the living room, and headed outside.

Behind him, Mullins said, "We need to hear—"

"I'll be on the balcony. You wanna stand at the glass and eavesdrop, that's on you." He stepped into the muggy morning, closed the door behind him, and dialed, praying for help in lying to the only person in the world who truly loved him.

It sounded like Shelby was laughing when she answered. "I hope you're not too mad at me," she said. "I didn't want to wake you, but I figured you'd find my note."

She'd left him a note? If he knew his sister—and he did—the note was on her bed, only to be found if he discovered she'd left.

"Where are you?" he asked, because it was the next logical question.

"On Shawn's yacht. They flew here, but their crew sailed it down. Isn't that so cool? They have a crew!"

Crew. Goons. Tomato, to*mah*to.

"This thing is wicked long, too. Like fifty feet or something."

"Sixty-five." The boy's voice carried in the background.

"Dainty little thing," Fitz said.

"Omigosh, it's so cool. Shawn tells me it sleeps ten people. I wish you could see it. Maybe when we dock, Shawn'll let you come on for a tour."

"Yeah, that'd be great." He tried to infuse his voice with enthusiasm. "Listen, Shawn's dad and I have struck up a bit of a friendship here."

"Really?" Her voice sounded more than skeptical, and she lowered it. "He kind of scares me."

Fitz gave his sister points for good instincts. "Yeah, I can understand that. He's got sort of a mobster vibe." Fitz laughed as if it were all some big joke. "Thing is, he wants to hire me to do a job for him, but the job is down here—in the jungle, if you can believe that. I guess he owns some property, and he thinks the people operating it are swindling him. I don't mind the idea of recouping some of what we spent on this trip, but I can't very well leave you at the resort by yourself. I was thinking of sending you to Grandma and Grandpa's—"

"Please, no." She groaned. "I'll just stay at the resort. I promise I won't get into any trouble, and I'll get all my schoolwork done. How long will you be gone, anyway?"

"A few days, a week at most." He hoped.

Mullins stepped onto the balcony. His next words proved he had indeed been eavesdropping. "Why doesn't she hang with Shawn and Lena on the boat?"

"Was that Mr. Mullins?" Shelby asked. "I could stay on the boat? Omigosh, Fitz, that would be awesome. Can I?"

Fitz sighed. Shelby was making this far too easy. Of course, she trusted Shawn and the boy's mother. Why wouldn't she? At least Fitz hadn't passed on his own suspicious nature to his sister. At least he'd done that right. "I guess that'd be okay." He met Mullins's eyes. "But your stuff—"

"Just pack it up," Mullins said. "I can get it to her."

"That'll work," Shelby said.

Another problem solved. "As long as you promise to keep up with your school—"

"I promise." She squealed, the high pitch painful in his ear. "Thank you, thank you. This is going to be so much fun!" She started to fill Shawn in on what was happening, and the kid sounded just as excited as she was.

This was insane. Fitz was trusting his sister's safety to a mobster and a teenage boy with wandering hands. He closed his eyes as images of everything that could go wrong hit him.

The problem was, he *didn't* trust them to take care of Shelby. He just had no choice.

She was still chattering to Shawn.

"Shelby," Fitz said.

"Oh, sorry. Yeah?"

"I think you are going to be headed farther offshore, so your cell service might not be what you're used to."

A pause, then, "I hadn't thought of that."

This worried her. All the danger Shelby was putting herself into with these people, and she was concerned about not being able to get on Instagram and Snapchat.

He needed to pass a little more suspicion on to her. When he got her home, they were going to sit down and have a long talk about making good choices and not putting herself in compromising positions. He'd taught her to shoot a gun, but apparently all his lectures about dangerous strangers had been lost to her.

"Just trust Mrs. Mullins and stay with them."

"Where'm I gonna go?" The *duh* in her statement was understood. "We're on a boat."

"Call me whenever you can."

"You'll be in the jungle, though, right? Will you have service?"

A fair question that proved she'd been listening—a rare event. "If I don't answer, leave a message. I'll want to know you're safe. And do your school work. And—"

"I gotta go. Thank you, thank you. Be careful doing...whatever it is you'll be doing. Love you, brother."

"Love you, too, sis." He added, "Be safe," but knew she hadn't heard. The line was dead.

It took a moment before he could face Mullins without swinging his fist. He swallowed the fury that rose. "If anything happens—"

"Yes, yes. You'll kill me. But that's not going to happen. You're going to get my jewels, I'm going to make my deal, and everything is going to be okay. After this, we'll never have to see each other again."

Somehow, Fitz didn't think it would be that easy. "I'm going to need cash, and I'm going to need that video."

CHAPTER FIVE

A couple more hours of sleep didn't seem like that much to ask, but the alarm blared on Tabby's bedside table. She smacked her cell to silence it and rolled over, ignoring the sunlight coming through her closed eyelids.

Didn't matter what time it was. Tabby needed sleep.

The next sound that rocked her quiet room wasn't the alarm but somebody banging on her door.

Grudgingly, she slid her feet to the floor and shuffled to her closet, where she donned a thick robe and fuzzy slippers. She didn't bother glancing in the mirror over her bureau. Whoever dared wake her so early deserved what they got.

She trudged down the stairs, vaguely aware that the world was unusually bright beyond the windows.

She yanked open the front door and glared, first at the man, then at the fresh snow blanketing everything. Sometimes, she thought it was beautiful. Sometimes, she loved the snow. Right now, all she wanted was sand and salt spray and warmth. "Seriously? It's the crack of dawn."

Her father's typical grin widened. "Hate to break it to you, Tabby Cat, but it's almost noon."

Noon? Her reaction must have shown on her face because Dad chuckled. "You've slept half the day away."

She pushed open the storm door, letting in a burst of freezing air along with her too-cheerful father, and then headed for the kitchen, where she set to making a pot of coffee.

"Your mother can make you a cup," Dad said.

What did Mom have to do with anything? Tabby filled the carafe with water, poured it into the reservoir, and pressed the button to start it brewing.

"If I call her now, she can have it brewed by the time we get there."

Tabby leaned against the countertop in her small eat-in kitchen. "What are we talking about?"

"She's making lunch." Dad settled in a kitchen chair, one of her garage-sale finds. "Don't you remember?"

Obviously not. Tabby rubbed her eyes, tried to wake herself up, and willed the coffee to brew faster.

"You agreed before you left on your trip to come over today and tell us all about it. When you didn't show up or answer your phone, Mom asked me to check on you."

Asked. More like nagged until he surrendered. Easier to drive across town on snow-covered roads than to argue with Marion.

"Any chance you could tell her I'm sick?"

His bushy eyebrows lowered over his dark brown eyes—the color of the ones she saw in the mirror every day. "Are you?"

"I could be. I was in an exotic location and then on a plane for a million hours." Or felt like it, anyway. "I could have all sorts of dangerous diseases. I'd better stay home."

"And feed your mother's fears?"

Bad idea, she knew. But her head ached and her stomach grumbled, probably from lack of eating anything the day before except the two gingerbread biscotti cookies she'd gotten on the airplane and the bag of chips she'd grabbed from the vending machine in Boston the night before. She rubbed her temples. "I'm really not up for it, Dad. Just tell her I'm not feeling well."

"If you say so." He pushed back in his chair and stood.

Tabby allowed a little jolt of happiness. She could crawl back into bed and sleep until work tomorrow.

Dad headed for the door but stopped before he stepped outside, looking back over his shoulder. "I'll tell her. Of course, you know what that means."

Tabby was too tired to figure out his riddles. "What?"

"She'll be worried. I'll tell her you seemed fine. Maybe she'll believe me and be offended that you blew off the lunch she made—she put a ham in this morning. Smells delicious. And she fixed those yummy potatoes you like, the ones with the bacon and sour cream. It'll hurt her feelings, but she'll get over it. You know how easygoing Mom can be."

"Your sarcasm is showing."

One side of his mouth tugged up. "More than likely, though, she'll think you've come down with something. If I know her, we'll be back over here in an hour to take care of you. Ham, potatoes, and probably your brother in tow." He looked around at her tidy space. "I'm sure we won't stay long. Maybe just until after the evening news."

Tabby groaned. Dad was right about all of it.

"I need a few minutes."

Dad sat on her sofa and put his feet on the coffee table. "Grab me a cup of coffee, and I'll be happy as a pig in—"

"Dad." She poured two cups of coffee, gave him one, then sloshed hers over her fingers as she hurried up the stairs. No time for a shower, but she changed her clothes, brushed her hair, and braided it quickly. She splashed some cold water on her face and headed back down.

A half hour after she'd awakened, they arrived at the house

where Tabby had grown up. The moment she stepped inside, Mom came from the kitchen. Her short graying hair perfectly coiffed, she wore slacks and a blouse beneath a long apron as she rushed across the family room.

"I was so worried!" She wrapped her in a hug, which Tabby tried to return despite the insulated coffee cup in one hand and the purse in the other.

"I'm fine, Ma."

Her mother backed up and took Tabby's shoulders, studying her face. "What happened to you? Were you hurt? Injured? Did you get sick?"

"I had a great time and came home alive."

Mom's concern morphed to irritation. "Well, forgive me for caring."

Tabby forced the corners of her mouth up and hoped the smile was convincing. She kissed Mom's cheek. "Nothing to forgive. I'm sorry I worried you."

Mom backed away, brushing her hands against the apron. "We expected you earlier."

"My flight landed late, and the drive from Boston took forever. I overslept."

Dad took her coat and purse and laid them on the sofa. "You should've seen her at the door in her robe and fuzzy slippers."

Tabby cringed, seeing immediately what Dad only realized after the words had come out.

Mom's face paled. "Tabitha Lynn Eaton, you know better than to open the door when you're not properly dressed. What if it had been a rapist? Or a neighbor! What would they think?"

Only Mom would worry about what a rapist might think—and be more worried about neighbors' judgments. Tabitha shot her father a *thanks a lot* look before addressing her mother. "Who else would show up uninvited on a Sunday but Dad?"

"Still," Mom insisted, "one of the neighbors might have seen."

"It's fourteen degrees outside, Ma. There were no neighbors out."

Mom's chagrin faded. "Well, I suppose... You know I only want what's best for you." She swiveled and led the way to the kitchen.

When Tabby stepped in, her brother turned his wheelchair toward her, arms outstretched. "You're alive. It's a miracle." His lips twitched at the corners.

She leaned down and hugged him, whispering, "Don't encourage her."

His chuckle came from deep in his belly.

Tabby propped a hip against the chair beside him. "What'd I miss here? Anything to report?"

Before Chris could respond, Mom said, "Well, mostly we've been worried about you."

"Yeah," Chris agreed. "We've just been sitting here praying the rosary every night since you left. I'm pretty sure Ma lit a couple of candles at the church."

"Stop that," Ma said. "We're not even Catholic."

Chris turned so their mother couldn't see and rolled his eyes.

Tabby smacked his arm, and he feigned injury. "Ma, she hit me."

Mom stopped tossing the salad long enough to smack his other arm. "It's the price you pay for sarcasm."

Chris's laugh, sounding so much like Dad's, warmed her heart. There'd been years after his accident he'd hardly smiled, let alone laughed. But he was coming out of it, learning to live with it. Slowly, though. So slowly. She wondered if she'd ever get her real brother back.

Tabby and her mother got the meal on the table, and Tabby

tried to snatch bites of ham and potatoes while telling her family about her vacation and all the things she'd seen and done. She tried to make it sound as if she'd had a great time—which she had—but was glad to be home. Which she wasn't.

No. That wasn't true. She loved her house. She loved her family. She loved New Hampshire. It was just...

Fitz.

No matter how she'd tried to keep her distance, somehow that man had wormed his way into her heart.

She was trying to refuse her mother's apple pie when she berated herself for about the hundredth time that day to stop thinking about the man she'd likely never see again. "I can't eat another bite."

But Mom slid a plate steaming with a slice of pie in front of her anyway. "Ice cream?"

Chris was already digging into his helping, as was Dad. They were both watching the showdown between the women.

"It's snowing," Tabby said.

One hand holding the pint of vanilla, the other wielding the scoop, Ma said, "So?"

"So normal people don't eat ice cream in February."

"Nonsense." Mom doled out a scoop and plopped it on the warm pie. "Normal people eat ice cream with pie. I'm starting to think you got too much sun down there."

Defeated, and not too sorry for it, Tabby tried a bite of the dessert. Who was she kidding? She'd eat the whole thing. Why not extend her vacation calories one more day? She'd start her diet tomorrow. She had to go back to work, so she'd be in a bad mood anyway.

"Did you make any new friends?" Ma asked.

As if she'd just gotten home from the first day of third grade. "A couple," Tabby said.

"Any boys?" Dad asked.

At least he treated her like a teenager, not a grade-schooler. "Not really."

Dad accepted the answer, but Chris's eyebrows hiked.

She glared at him, and he held out his plate. "Get me another slice, would ya?"

Ma jumped to do his bidding, dumping another slice of pie on his plate along with another couple scoops of ice cream. How Chris managed to stay slim without the use of his legs and eating Ma's cooking all the time, Tabby couldn't understand.

After lunch, Tabby started to help clear the table, but Mom shooed her away. "You're the guest of honor. Go on into the family room. Why don't you and Chris pick out a movie to watch?"

Tabby didn't argue, but she wouldn't be staying for a movie. She needed to get home and unpack.

She followed Chris, not offering to help him with the wheelchair. Mom and Dad had refitted the house after his accident. He could get around fine without her help. In fact, she was pretty sure he could do a lot more than he did without help, but with their parents too eager to jump in whenever he needed anything, Chris might not ever know that.

That was an old argument she'd had with all of them more than once. But nobody listened to her. She was just the little sister. What did she know about anything?

She sat on the sofa beside her brother's wheelchair. They were quiet at first, knowing Mom was listening. After a moment, though, the water came on, and she started barking out orders...suggestions...for ways Dad could help. "Take the pan out of the roaster and bring it here. No, no, dump the juices into a Tupperware first." Ma huffed. "Do I have to do everything?"

Dad's quiet, "I can manage," barely carried over the din.

"Ah, the sweet sounds of home," Tabby whispered.

Chris's smile was tight.

"I don't know how you stand it."

"They grow on you."

"Like mold on cheese?"

His smile only grew a little. "It's not like I have a lot of choices."

Another argument with him Tabby'd had more than once. But she dove in anyway. "You do, Chris. You could..."

He held up his hand to silence her. "Let's don't do that today. Tell me about this *boy* you met."

She glanced toward the door, but her parents were busy cleaning up and bickering. At least the bickering was friendly. They seemed to have no other way to communicate. "His name is Fitz. Nice guy. We spent a little time together."

Chris leaned forward. "A little time. Translated from Tabby-speak to English, I'd say you're in love."

"Don't be ridiculous."

"How much time?"

She shrugged, not wanting to tell him the truth. And not wanting to lie. "My last day there, he took me to the mainland, and we hiked into the jungle. It was amazing." She took out her phone and scrolled to the pictures she hadn't shared at lunch. She didn't need a lecture on personal safety after the fact, thank you very much.

Chris scrolled through the images. "Wow." A few pictures later, he said, "Wow," again, and then, "I had no idea there was any place so beautiful."

"It was gorgeous." If she closed her eyes, she feared she'd be transported right back to that spot. But it wasn't the memory of the view that had her keeping her eyes wide open. It was the memory of Fitz holding her close, wanting to kiss her.

She should have let him.

But then she'd be a puddle of mush, unhappier in her life than she already was.

Chris scrolled further and stopped. "This him?"

She glanced at the screen, at the shot she'd gotten of Fitz and Shelby on the beach on one of the rare occasions the girl had joined them. They'd been playing in the waves, splashing each other like the siblings they were. "Yeah. With his little sister. Their parents died when he was in college, so he's her legal guardian."

Chris whistled. "Rough cards."

She reached to take her phone back. "We all have rough hands to play in life. You know that better than anybody."

Chris's palm slid over hers. "They're the cards we're dealt, though. What I'm learning—too slowly, I'll admit, but it's getting through this thick skull—is that lamenting the cards is useless."

Tabby smiled at her brother. He'd come so far. "I'm proud of you."

He squeezed her hand. "I'm also learning that everybody has tough cards, like you said, and looking around and thinking about how other people have harder cards and feeling guilty is no better than seeing how other people have easier cards and feeling sorry for yourself. You have to play *your* cards."

She snatched her hand away. "I know that."

He shook his head. "You need to live your own life, sis."

"I'm doing that."

"Yeah? So you and this Fitz guy, you're a thing now?"

She looked at the TV on the far side of the room. Sports news, muted. She watched basketball highlights as if she gave a rip about the score of the Lakers game. If it were the Celtics, maybe.

"I'm guessing that's a no," Chris said.

"He's not from here."

Chris's eyes softened at the corners with sympathy. "Does he live in Belize? He didn't look like a local, but—"

"He's from Rhode Island."

Chris threw up his hands. "Oh, Rhode Island. I can see how that would be a barrier. You'd hardly ever be able to see him. I mean, Rhode Island is a twelve, fourteen-hour flight? Or wait... that would be a walk. We could probably *walk* to Rhode Island in twelve hours." He tapped the giant wheel of his chair. "Well, I'd roll and probably beat you."

"It's farther than that. And we both have jobs and lives, and he has his sister..."

Chris was ignoring her as he pulled his cell from his lap and started tapping. After a minute, he said, "Two hours and forty-eight minutes from here to Providence. One hundred sixty-nine miles."

"It might as well be on another planet."

Her brother huffed out a breath and sat back. "Did you like the guy?"

"Yeah, he was nice, but—"

"Did he have any interest in seeing you again?"

She shrugged, but Chris saw through her. "So you blew him off, probably gave him some story about how you could never leave New Hampshire, about how your life is here, everything you love is—"

"It's not a story. It's true."

"The real truth is that you feel responsible for us. For me."

"Not you. Mom and Dad. You know how she is. Imagine me driving to Providence to visit *a boy*."

He almost smiled. "She'd worry, but you know, she only wants—"

"—what's best for me."

They said the last few words in unison, and Tabby giggled and slapped her hand over her mouth. Hopefully, Mom hadn't heard. She'd be offended for sure.

"You know Mom would worry every moment I was gone."

Tabby did her best Ma impression. *"And here you go, traipsing off to Providence to meet some strange man you hardly know."*

"She'd get over it."

"Would she? I don't know. I mean, if something ended up happening with this guy, if we got serious... I just don't see the point in dating someone I can't marry, and I can't marry him. His life is down there. Mine is here. They're here." *You're here.* But she didn't say that. The last thing Chris needed was a helping of guilt that matched his helping of pie and ice cream. "My job is here."

"You hate your job."

She shrugged. "I think you should move in—"

"I'm a grown man." Chris's teasing tone was gone, replaced by anger and frustration. "I don't need my baby sister to take care of me."

"I know that. I just think you need out of this house. My place—"

"I will *never* move in with you. Never."

She sat back, pressed her hand against her chest. She'd asked him more than once, and he'd refused politely before. But the words he'd just spoken hadn't been polite, not even close.

"If I did that," Chris said, "you'd never get your own life."

"I have my own—"

"Lie to yourself if you want to, but don't lie to me. If you're too scared to take a chance on this Fitz guy, fine. But don't use me as your excuse."

"I just got back from two weeks in Central America. I'm not scared."

"At a resort on the beach. That isn't exactly a life-altering adventure."

It was the only kind Tabby would ever get to have. She wouldn't say that, though, not to Chris, whose adventure had cost him the use of his legs. Not to their parents, whose lives had been inextricably altered the day of his accident. No, Tabby's job was to support her brother and her parents. To help them pay Chris's exorbitant medical bills. To try to encourage Chris to get a life outside this house.

Chris had been dealt paraplegia. Tabby had been dealt having a family that needed her support.

And Fitz had been dealt Shelby.

They all needed to know their roles, and they all needed to stick with them. Which meant Fitz and Tabby could never have anything beyond a vacation fling.

No matter how much that truth hurt.

CHAPTER SIX

Tabby's first day back to work was about as enjoyable as she'd figured it would be.

Her coworkers had made zero effort to keep up with her tasks, just stacking files on her desk for two weeks. Eleven hours of work under her belt, and the pile looked just as high as when she'd begun.

After managing the roads—slick, thanks to two fresh inches of snow—Tabby finally stepped inside her little Cape Cod-style home and draped her down jacket over the sofa inside her front door. She dumped her bag beside it and continued to the kitchen at the back of the small house, where she opened her refrigerator.

She really should have gone to the grocery store the previous day, but who'd had the energy?

Fortunately, Mom had given her some leftovers, so she slapped a piece of ham and a spoonful of potatoes on a plate and shoved it into the microwave, trying not to think about the scrumptious blackened grouper and coconut shrimp she'd eaten Friday night. And the man who'd shared the meal with her.

The microwave hummed, and Tabby sat and yanked off her

boots, then slid her feet into her fuzzy slippers. She probably shouldn't store her shoes in the kitchen, but who was going to complain?

Maybe in the spring, she'd get a dog so she'd have someone to come home to.

No, dogs were too much trouble. The last thing she needed was more responsibility. A cat, the kind that could forage for food if she left it outside.

Just as the microwave dinged, the doorbell rang. Probably some kid selling something. It was February, Girl Scout cookie season. Forget the diet she was supposed to start today. She'd gladly take a box of Thin Mints—or three.

Ignoring the voice of caution in her head about who the stranger could be—which sounded way too much like her mother—she headed to the door and yanked it open.

Not a Girl Scout.

Her breath caught in her throat. She realized her jaw had dropped and snapped it closed.

Fitz, arms crossed and shivering in the frigid breeze, still managed to look casual as he leaned against the wrought iron railing that lined the concrete steps. "Surprise."

"What in the world are you doing here?"

"At the moment, turning into a freeze-pop."

She pushed open the storm door. She could hardly think what to say but tossed out, "I guess you should come in."

He slid past her. "Thanks for that gracious invitation." He stopped in her living room and looked around, not that he could see much in the dark. She turned on the lamp by the door, then passed him and turned on the one near the sofa. Fitz took in the space, and she couldn't help but wonder what he thought about it. She'd bought the off-white sectional new, but the coffee table and end tables she'd found at a garage sale and stained a dark coffee color. The sixty-five-inch flat screen was new, but she'd owned the TV stand since college. The lamps, the decor—it was all vintage New Hampshire, meaning sturdy and functional and practical. Meaning, mostly used.

She'd thought the space cozy and warm, but watching Fitz take it in, she saw it differently. It screamed backwoods country girl.

Well, that was what she was. She might as well own it.

"How did you find me?"

He tossed a smile her way. "This amazing new invention called Google. I typed in your name and the city where you live, and voilà! There was your address."

"It shouldn't be that simple."

He shrugged but added nothing else.

"I was just about to eat."

"I thought I'd take you out."

She couldn't help the laugh. Trying to sound stern, she said, "What are you doing in Coventry?"

"I told you I'm a nature photographer." His lips quirked up at the corners. "Turns out, New Hampshire has nature."

She tried to glare at him but feared herself too fatigued and confused to make it work. She spun and stalked to the kitchen. "I'm too tired to go out."

"Fair enough. Smells good in here. Whatcha eating?"

She crossed to the counter and pulled her dinner from the microwave. "Leftovers from the meal my mother made yesterday."

He walked closer, barely glancing at the food. She was thankful for the plate between them when his gaze caught and held hers. "Looks good."

She shoved the plate into him. "Fine, then. You eat it." Her voice hinted at her anger. What was he doing here? How was she supposed to forget about him when he showed up on her doorstep?

Seeming unoffended by her tone, he took the plate. "Is this all you're going to eat? This isn't enough to feed a squirrel." He tried to hand the plate back. "I'll get something later. Don't worry about me."

She ignored him and swiveled to the fridge. "There's more. Just set that on the table while I make you a plate."

"Then your meal will be cold."

"The magic of the microwave."

She piled his plate with ham, potatoes, and corn casserole. While it heated, she grabbed a zipper bag of salad Mom had sent with her and fixed them each a bowl.

While she worked, Fitz silently watched her. Whenever she glanced his way, she saw a slight smile on his face as if he found catching her off-guard amusing.

She was seriously annoyed, though she couldn't say why. Maybe just hungry. And tired. And...

Why was he here?

The microwave dinged, and she practically tossed his plate to the table before snatching her own and warming it again.

Finally, she slid into the seat beside him.

"You okay?" he asked.

She stared at her food, hands shaking, eyes burning. She was just tired. Her reaction to seeing him made no sense. She should have been happy, not angry, not emotional. She should have been touched that he'd go to such lengths to see her again. She shouldn't have felt... how did she feel?

Frightened.

Worried.

Because he wanted more from her than she could give.

Which made her... sad. A pathetically small word for such a huge emotion.

"Do you mind if I pray?"

She shook her head, feeling ridiculous.

Fitz offered a quick and simple blessing over their meals and then dug in. Three bites later, he said, "This is delicious. Your mom made this?"

She swallowed a bite of ham. "It's nothing fancy."

"Who needs fancy? I'll take a simple home-cooked meal over fancy any day."

Right. Exactly the words to make the country bumpkin feel better. "Where's Shelby?"

Worry passed over his face, an expression she'd seen often enough when he discussed his sister in the previous two weeks. Though it seemed... sharper, somehow. "I sent her to our grandparents' house for a week. We had a little tiff." His smirk told her it was more than that, but she didn't push. "We needed a break from each other."

"About the young man... Shawn?"

"And his family, yeah. I got a bad feeling about them and told her I didn't want her communicating with him after we went home. She lost her mind. Teenage girls... Seriously, how do parents survive? How does anybody know how to handle this stuff?"

"I'm sure you did fine."

"I'm sure I didn't. I sent her to her grandparents' house in Pennsylvania. They live in the Poconos, and their cell service is spotty. It should give her plenty of time to get caught up on school and forget about that boy."

Right. Because all that was needed to forget about a vacation fling was a little time and no internet. Yet, here Fitz was, and here she was, actively *not* forgetting about each other.

"Anyway, it's nothing you and I need to talk about. Hopefully, Shelby will cool down and want to come home in a week or so. I figured, as long as I wasn't saddled..." He shook his head. "Wrong word. But..."

"I know what you mean."

Seeming to forget his meal, he stared at Tabby across the table. "As long as I had some time on my hands, I thought I'd come here to see you. And get some shots. It's beautiful here. You're—"

"Different from Belize, but pretty in its own way." She cut off whatever he'd been about to say, guessing it would have been some compliment to charm her.

He sliced a bite of ham and added some potatoes to the fork, then said, "We always went to Pennsylvania for vacation when we were kids. The mountains there are nice, but these are grander." He ate the bite, uttering a little *mmm-mmm* while he chewed.

Drinks. She'd forgotten drinks. She stood and snatched two glasses. "I wish I had something else to offer." She spoke over her shoulder as she filled the glasses with water. "I need to go shopping."

She set the glasses on the table, and he sipped from his. "This is perfect." He set it down and leaned back in his chair. The chairs were new. The circular wooden table old but refinished. She was proud of the job she'd done on the table and how well the grouping looked with the pretty silk flower centerpiece, which she'd shoved aside. Did that say country bumpkin?

It definitely didn't say city girl.

Oh, what did she care? This was who she was. Why was she ashamed of it?

"I wanted to surprise you," he said suddenly. He'd been watching her. What emotions had shown on her face? "Obviously, that was a bad idea. When you first answered the door, you looked almost... angry. I thought for a second I was about to be dispatched by a jealous husband or boyfriend or something."

He seemed to wait for her to say something, but she wasn't sure what. She ate some salad, barely tasting it.

"Anyway," he continued, "I should have warned you I was

coming. I didn't mean to... offend you or invade your space or anything."

She sat back. "It's fine. I'm..." She wiped her hands on her napkin, then balled it in her fist. "You threw me off. You and Belize... it feels like a different world. It's weird to have you here."

"Weird... bad?"

She didn't know how to answer that. She didn't know how to explain how she felt. "It's fine."

"'Fine.' That's what I was going for." Before she could answer with an apology, a clarification, he took her hand, raised it to his lips, and kissed her knuckles. "I'm sorry I surprised you, and I'm sorry you don't know how to feel about my being here. I'm not sorry to be here, though. Even if you're angry, even if you're trying to figure out how to get rid of me, even if you've tripped some silent alarm and the police are about to come haul me off to jail for invading your life, it will all be worth it for another five minutes with you."

She pulled her hand back, fighting a smile. "You're such a charmer, Fitzgerald McCaffrey."

"Just don't confuse *charmer* with *liar*."

"If you say so." She decided not to worry about it. Tomorrow, she'd have to deal with Fitz and whatever he thought was going to happen between them.

Like the diet she kept putting off, she could start forgetting about Fitz tomorrow. Tonight, she'd just enjoy his company.

CHAPTER SEVEN

Ignoring the clatter and chatter in the busy diner, Fitz sipped his Dr. Pepper and replayed the events of the night before for the hundredth time. Tabby's home had surprised him. Because she'd admitted to having loved going hunting and fishing with her brothers, he'd pictured some northwoods cabin complete with bear heads and fish mounted on the walls. He'd pictured rough pine paneling and plaid couches. The way she'd talked about herself and her life, he'd imagined her house would scream *country*.

Instead, it was charming, the decor fashionable and eclectic. It reflected the woman he'd thought he'd known—down-to-earth and yet wonderfully complex.

Nothing about the little Cape Cod screamed *international jewel thief.* Nothing about the woman herself did, either.

He replayed their conversation, studying Tabby's words from every angle, searching for duplicity, for dishonesty. As when they'd been in Belize, he'd detected none. She seemed as honest and down-to-earth as ever.

As he'd been doing since Saturday, he told himself she couldn't be a thief.

As he'd been doing since Saturday, he reminded himself that he'd seen the video.

She was a thief, and a liar, and a very, very good one.

That and the fact that his sister's life was in danger because of what Tabby had done made it okay that he'd lied to her, though his words convicted him whenever he thought of them. *Just don't confuse charmer with liar.*

He hated himself for how the lies had flowed as smoothly as the gentle surf back in Belize. He'd lied about Shelby's whereabouts. Lied about why he was in New Hampshire. But his feelings for Tabby, despite everything, hadn't changed.

At least he didn't have to fake that part.

A man stepped into the narrow restaurant and gazed around the room. About forty years old, he wore a sweater vest over a light blue button-down and jeans and didn't exude the *gumshoe* vibe at all. Looked like he was going for the yuppie look. He matched his photo on the website, so Fitz waved him over.

The man slid his trim frame into the booth opposite him and held out his hand. "Tad Vogler, Neely Investigations."

"Fitz McCaffrey. Thanks for meeting me."

"Not a problem." When the waitress approached, Tad ordered a soda. On the phone, he'd declined to join Fitz for a meal, and Fitz had already finished his uber-healthy breakfast of French toast with real New Hampshire maple syrup, sausage, and eggs. Delicious, but not nearly as good as Tabby's leftover ham and potatoes. She'd scoffed at the simple meal, but that was because she didn't miss home-cooked food. He wasn't much of a cook himself, and Shelby eschewed anything that seemed like a chore. The two of them ate frozen dinners or takeout most nights.

Tad opened a laptop and dove in. "Tabitha Lynn Eaton. Twenty-six. Graduated from Plymouth State."

Tad told Fitz what kind of car she drove—a brand-new Ford

Bronco—and where she did her banking. He told Fitz her employment history and even guessed at her salary.

Not bad, if the guess was accurate. Plenty of money to afford the house and the car, especially since she had nobody to support. So why take up a life of crime?

"Everything about her checks out," Tad was saying. "Nothing fishy in her past. No arrest record."

"What can you tell me about her movements since she got home?"

"Her flight landed Saturday at Logan late, nearly two a.m."

"Was she wearing any jewelry? Anything noticeable?"

The man's eyes narrowed the slightest bit. "Nothing I noticed. Why?"

"Never mind." Perhaps she'd worn the jewelry until she got through customs and then put it away. More likely, though, she'd just stowed the stuff in her suitcase. He doubted any customs agent would have questioned the jewelry or the antique box. They could all easily be passed off as fakes.

The P.I. continued. "She got the shuttle to her car and drove straight home. Sunday, an older man picked her up at her house about noon and drove her to another house." He read the address, another one in Coventry. "It belongs to Stanley and Marion Eaton, her parents. After a couple hours, the father drove her home. She didn't leave again until work Monday. Stayed there all day. And then—"

"I followed her home from work and was at her house until about ten."

"My guys were back then. She didn't leave again until she went to work this morning. I got a guy watching the business, but so far, no movement since she arrived this morning."

Fitz had really hoped this would be easy. All he had to do was figure out where Tabby had put the jewels and steal them from her. No reason to tell her he knew her crime. No reason to tell her anything. If she'd gone to a bank and put them in a safe deposit box, he'd be in trouble. But she hadn't gone to a bank.

"You sure she hasn't met anybody else?"

"She's at work all day. She's probably meeting people. It's not as if we can get in there."

Frustrating but true.

"What kind of bag did she carry in yesterday?"

"Big purse." Tad held his hands about eighteen inches apart. "Big enough for a laptop."

He'd seen her carrying it home from work the night before. "Was it...bulging or anything?" Because it had been flat when she'd left the building. Maybe she'd made the handoff at work.

Tad smirked. "Pretty flat. Normal, I guess. If you'd tell me what we're looking for, we could be of more help."

He ignored the remark. This guy didn't need the details.

The jewels could have been in her bag, but not the antique box. Maybe she planned to keep that. Maybe she passed off the jewels to someone she worked with.

But why keep the box, which would prove her guilt? Seemed she'd want to get rid of all the goods immediately. And what kind of stolen-goods fence lived in Coventry, New Hampshire?

The whole thing felt...off.

"Could she have met somebody when her flight landed?" Fitz suggested.

"I watched her from the time she left security until she got home. She didn't talk to anyone. Didn't even go to the restroom. Could be somebody was on the flight with her."

"Or she handed off the stuff during her connection. She flew through Dallas, right?"

He clicked a few keys on his laptop. "Connecting flight was late going out, but she couldn't have planned for that. The plan was for a forty-minute layover. She didn't have enough time to go out of security and back through and make the flight. But her connection could've bought a ticket to meet her at the gate."

Fitz heaved a deep sigh. He'd spared no time—or money, though that had come from Mullins, so he wasn't too broken up about it—in making sure Tabby was under surveillance. But the woman could have done anything with the jewels. She could already have sold them, or she could have them hidden somewhere in her house.

Fitz needed more information. It was already Tuesday. If he was going to have the goods back in Belize by Saturday, he had to fly out Friday. Three days. How had a week turned into three days so fast?

"You want us to keep watching her?"

"Yeah, until I tell you differently. And I need you to do some more digging. I need to know who she spends time with. Friends, friends of friends. Maybe somebody she goes to visit out of town or someone who comes to visit her. I'm going to do some investigation of my own, so I might need help with that as well."

One eyebrow quirked. "We don't do anything that's not on the up-and-up."

"Not asking you to." Not directly, anyway. He hoped the subtle difference would be lost on Neely Investigations.

CHAPTER EIGHT

Fitz had told the investigator to let him know immediately when Tabby left the office. The man's eyebrow had quirked again—Fitz wondered if it was a look he'd practiced in the mirror as a gawky kid—but agreed. Tad had probably guessed what Fitz planned to do, but he hadn't called him on it.

Now, Fitz parked his rental, a dark blue sedan, on the street around the corner from Tabby's place. As he'd done a thousand times since Saturday, he dialed Shelby's number. As with every other time, the call went straight to voice mail. Was she at sea, too far from cell phone towers to get a signal? Or had she figured out that something wasn't right and started asking questions?

He pictured his sister locked in a closet, the floor rolling beneath her, the hum of the engine drowning out her cries.

As he'd done a thousand times since Saturday, he lifted a prayer for her. God would have to take care of Shelby while Fitz found the stolen goods. He climbed from the car and started walking as if he were out for a stroll, as if anybody would take a stroll in a strange neighborhood when the temperature hovered in the low twenties. It was warmer than it had been the day before, but the word *warm* was a misnomer in this case. Central New Hampshire and Rhode Island might both be in New England, but there was a big difference between the two.

The trees were tall, the undergrowth thick, and the houses decades past new. He'd guess they'd been built in the sixties, maybe early seventies. Most were split levels, but there were a couple of Colonials and a few Cape Cods like Tabby's. Each sat on a pretty large parcel of land—at least an acre, maybe two—and was separated by enough space and forest to make them all seem private.

During Fitz's reconnaissance mission the night before, he'd learned that Tabby wasn't as concerned about security as people who lived in the city. Foolish. If he cared about her—which he didn't—he'd lecture her about it. No security panel inside the front door. No video doorbell. She didn't even have a peephole to see who was standing on her stoop. She could look through one of the two front windows, but based on her reaction to seeing him the night before, she didn't make a habit of that.

Wouldn't an international jewel thief keep her own property better protected? The thought had him worrying that there were hidden cameras, but he'd seen nothing to indicate that. And he was pretty good at this.

Not as good as Abe. Fitz could use his ex-partner's senses right about now. The man was practically an encyclopedia of information about New England's organized crime families. And his ex-partner saw things Fitz missed. Whereas Fitz had been exceptional at gaining people's trust and getting them to talk, Abe had been a master at seeing the unseen, ferreting out the hidden. The man, with those ugly black-framed glasses, had better vision than any cop Fitz had ever worked with.

If only Fitz had Abe's vision. Maybe he'd have seen the man's duplicity before it had cost Fitz everything.

He and Tabby had been halfway through last night's movie

when he had excused himself to use the restroom. She'd paused the romantic comedy and gone to the kitchen to make popcorn—in an old-fashioned air popper like his mother used to use. With the sound of popping in the background, Fitz had visited the bathroom, then silently gone into the dining room and unlocked one of her windows before joining her in the kitchen just in time to watch her drizzle butter and sprinkle salt on the warm snack. He'd grabbed a handful. It was deliciously savory, much better than the microwaved stuff.

Tabby had been completely unsuspicious.

Wouldn't an international jewel thief be less trusting?

Now, Fitz walked up Tabby's driveway, thankful it'd been plowed so he wouldn't leave footsteps, hearing Abe's voice in his ear. *Just because you don't see a camera—*

Yeah, yeah, yeah. He'd heard Abe's warnings often enough in their years working cases together. He still couldn't believe his old friend was corrupt.

First Abe, now Tabby. Was anybody in the world *not* corrupt?

He took the walkway, stepping on the footprints he'd made the night before. When he neared the steps that led to the door, he hopped to the edge of the house and walked to the dining room window, glancing around to ensure he was alone. He didn't see a soul. He raised the glass storm panel—no easy feat with its old metal locks—before pushing up the window itself.

No alarm sounded.

He climbed inside, then closed the window.

He started in the dining room, searching through the china cabinet. Based on the design and the way the doors stuck, it was an antique or close to. But it had been beautifully kept, or perhaps refinished. Had Tabby done that? Was she really an HR manager, a decorator, a furniture refurbisher, and a jewel thief?

She was an enigma.

In the glass-fronted display cabinet, he found a set of cream-colored dishes with pink and green flowers. The set looked like it might have been popular a half a century past or more. Maybe Tabby's grandmother's china. Definitely didn't match the decor. In the cabinets below, he found a white tray with the raised image of a turkey on it, a green Christmas-tree shaped platter, and various serving dishes. In the drawer between the cabinets were different styles of placemats, all of which looked unused. The Christmas version still had the tags on them. As if Tabby hoped to someday host meals. As if she were preparing for the family that had never come.

She had a family, though. Much more of one than Fitz had with only his little sister and his elderly grandparents.

Though Fitz wasn't in the habit of buying placemats and dish sets for the family he didn't have, he understood Tabby's craving. He craved family, craved support and normalcy. He tried to give those things to Shelby, but how could he give what he didn't have?

After checking the china cabinet for hidden compartments—and finding none—he sat back on his heels. No priceless jewels. No carved box.

A quick search of the centerpiece on the dining room table yielded nothing. He moved into the kitchen. Dishes, pots, pans, food. Not much of the last. Seemed Tabby hadn't gone shopping since the trip. A good reason to take her to dinner tonight.

His stupid heart beat double time at the prospect. *She's a thief,* he told it, but that didn't slow its pace.

Tabby's cabinets were well-organized. In fact, some shelves had nothing on them at all. He liked that about her, liked that she didn't feel the need to fill every inch of her life with stuff.

He searched the drawers and found silverware and serving spoons and cooking utensils. He searched the refrigerator and found condiments, a couple types of cheeses, butter, a nearly empty half-gallon of milk that had expired a few days past, a container of cream, and what remained of the leftovers they'd eaten the night before.

The freezer—maybe this would be the place. Perhaps she'd frozen the goods in a block of ice. But he took out the few items and examined each. One seemed to be homemade spaghetti sauce, a discovery that once again made him wish for more with this woman. A woman who could make her own marinara sauce scored points in his book. There were a few uncooked chicken breasts in a zipper bag. Some pecans. Who froze pecans?

Weird, not nefarious.

After a thorough search of the living area, he headed upstairs.

He started in the emptiest room, which held a twin bed and empty bureau. The closet, too, was empty.

He stepped into the next room and froze. *Bingo.* Her office. This was where he'd find what he was looking for.

But after an exhaustive search of each drawer in the desk, he still found no jewels, no carved box. In the file cabinet, he discovered her bank statements, which she kept in a file marked *bank statements*—organized girl that she was. They revealed how much money she made and where she spent it.

She earned more than enough to cover her mortgage payment—which was very affordable. In Providence, even a house this size would cost a pretty penny, but in Coventry... The numbers probably made sense.

He also discovered that her car payment wasn't as much as he'd guessed for a brand-new Bronco. Had she made a sizable down payment? Where'd she gotten the money for that?

Did it come from proceeds of goods she'd stolen?

He looked through her credit card statements.

She seemed to only have one card. The statements went

back twelve months. He could imagine her sliding the new one into the file every month, then discarding the one from the year past. He pictured his own desk at home, the foot-high pile of bills he should probably throw out but rarely did. If she ever saw it, would she itch to organize it or itch to run? He'd have to deep clean if she ever visited.

Which she never would. He needed to keep his head in the game.

He looked through each credit card statement and discovered that Tabby didn't use the card much and paid it off monthly, avoiding interest charges while earning cash back. Wise woman. He looked for large payments and found very few. She'd spent a couple hundred dollars the previous month at a place called Wayfair. A quick search on his phone told him it was an online home store—furniture, decor, that kind of thing. Tabby'd gone to Wildcat Mountain and Cannon Mountain a few times the previous winter and back in December. They were local ski areas.

He'd half expected to see airline charges. Wouldn't an international jewel thief have to travel occasionally? That seemed a prerequisite for the job. But it looked like Tabby had been honest with him when she'd told him she rarely ventured farther from home than Manchester, an hour and a half south of Coventry. Aside from the airline tickets to Belize, he didn't see charges for anyplace outside New Hampshire—not including online retailers—in the last twelve months.

He didn't understand. Maybe she had another credit card, another file cabinet, another life.

She must. There was nothing here that pointed to Tabby being a criminal.

Tempted as he was to dismiss the notion, he couldn't do that. He closed his eyes and let himself remember the video he'd seen of the thief in Belize, sneaking into the hotel's back room, cracking the safe, stealing a half a million dollars' worth of goods. Because she'd done that, Shelby's life was in danger.

He lifted another prayer for his sister.

The sound of a car door slamming had his eyes popping open. Quickly, he put the paperwork back and slid the files into the cabinet and closed the drawer.

How could she be home? Why hadn't Tad told him she'd left work?

Downstairs, the door creaked on the hinges.

Fitz straightened the desk so it looked as it had when he'd found it. Tidy. There was a notepad with nothing written on it. If he'd had time, he could've taken a pencil to the top sheet to reveal what she'd last written, but he doubted she'd jotted anything like *hide stolen goods under the floorboards*. This wasn't a Hardy Boys Mystery, after all.

Fitz crept to the window. A pickup was parked in the drive.

Was that somebody coming to collect the goods? Tabby's buyer—or fence, maybe?

Footsteps sounded on the creaky hardwood staircase.

Fitz slipped into the office's closet and pulled the door mostly closed. He watched through the crack into the hallway as a guy with bright red hair, wearing jeans and a parka, reached the top of the stairs and turned the other way, toward the master. He was carrying a cardboard box.

A few seconds passed.

Was this guy searching as well? Would he find Fitz in the closet?

Fitz pulled the handgun he'd bought the previous day in Manchester from the holster at his waist. He didn't want to come out shooting, but he needed to be prepared. Five hundred thousand dollars' worth of goods were at stake. People had been known to kill for less.

A moment later, the guy walked down the hall, empty-handed, went down the stairs and out the door.

Fitz hurried to the window and watched the guy jog to his truck. He carried nothing in his hands. The pickup backed out of the driveway and drove away.

Fitz collapsed into Tabby's desk chair. Who in the world was that?

Whoever it was, he hadn't come in through the dining room window. No, he'd had a key. A family member? She had a bunch of brothers, didn't she?

But Tabby'd told him that two of her brothers lived out of town, and the third was a paraplegic. That was some other man, a man who was welcome in Tabby's bedroom.

Maybe that man was the reason Tabby'd been so shocked—and angry—to see Fitz on her doorstep. Maybe Tabby wasn't just an international jewel thief. Maybe she was also a two-timing liar.

Angry at Tabby for her lies, angry at himself for the jealousy that flooded his blood, Fitz concluded the search of the office and moved into her bedroom.

The room shouldn't have surprised him. He should have expected the quiet elegance... And he hated that he'd used the term *quiet elegance* like some kind of design magazine writer, but that was what came to mind. A white upholstered headboard supported more pillows than any human being could use, all artfully arranged over a thick pale-pink comforter. Sheer curtains in a matching shade of pink framed the two windows. A white fluffy area rug hid most of the hardwood floor, and a crystal chandelier hung from the center of the room. Cream-colored end tables and bureau held photographs, which pulled his attention.

If he had to guess, most of these were family members. There was an older gray-headed lady, but the men had the same brown curly hair as Tabby's. All were tall like Tabby. In fact, except for the man in the wheelchair, the men towered over her five nine frame. None of these had red hair. None of these was the man who'd come in earlier.

There were women in other photos. One with straight blond hair who looked vaguely familiar. After a second glance, he realized this was Chelsea Hamilton, though she'd married recently, and Hamilton was no longer her last name. She was the CEO of HCI. Tabby had said they were friends. Another woman in the photo had dark brown straight hair and striking green eyes. The three of them were pictured at a lake and laughing.

There were some photos with women he guessed were Tabby's sisters-in-law and a few kids who were probably her nieces and nephews.

A cardboard box lay in the center of the bed. By the way it pressed down on the cushy blankets, it was heavy. Was that why the man had carried it up here?

He glanced at the return address label. Some company in North Carolina. What could it be? Did it have anything to do with what she'd stolen?

Had the man taken the stolen jewelry and left this? What a simple and effective way to transfer the stuff to the fence.

Too many questions, not enough answers.

He'd ask Tad to dig into Tabby's friends, see if any of them had bright red hair and ties to criminal activity.

He almost preferred to think of the redhead being her fence than to think he might be a boyfriend. Jealousy was pulsing even as he named himself every kind of idiot. She was a thief. He didn't want her anyway.

He needed to get Shelby back. Nothing else mattered.

With that in mind, pushing away the guilt and shame for going through her personal things, he searched every inch of her private space. And found nothing.

CHAPTER NINE

The employee babbled on while Tabby nodded, hopefully politely. Somehow, she'd become the designated collector of all complaints at HCI, and this particular employee had a new one every day. Her grievances were always minor, usually easily managed, and generally followed by ten or fifteen minutes of chitchat. Tabby assumed the woman, a widow whose kids had moved south years before, was just lonely. Most days, Tabby listened patiently, but the stack of work loomed, and she had to clench her fists and her jaw to keep from interrupting the diatribe.

She pushed back in her chair and rounded her desk, snatching her water bottle on the way. "Walk with me. I need a refill." This was definitely a good time to use the *let's go to the break room, where I'll get my drink and then politely excuse myself back to my desk* routine. She had to do it about once a week with someone. She caught the eye of Kelly, the payroll manager in the office next door, who gave a knowing smile. Yeah, those in HR all knew Tabby's tricks, but fortunately the most annoying and talkative employees hadn't caught on yet.

She got her water, made an excuse, and returned to her desk

alone, but the moment she opened the next file, her phone rang. She snatched the receiver and barked, "Tabitha Eaton" a little too sharply.

"I'm bothering you." Chris's voice had her pulling in a deep breath.

"Just one of those days."

"Rough going back after a two-week hiatus."

Furlough felt like the right word. The kind the state might give a convicted felon.

Stupid thought, but there it was. "What's up?"

"You're gonna kill me."

She gritted her teeth but forced a smile she hoped came through in her tone. "Uh-oh. What happened?"

"I accidentally scheduled my PT for today instead of tomorrow."

Chris had been going to PT for years. At first, it had been daily, then bi-weekly. Now, they only had to get him to Concord once a week. Dad usually handled the appointments. As a professor at Plymouth State, he could take the time during the day that neither Mom, a secretary at the grade school, nor Tabby could manage.

"Why can't Dad do it?"

"He has a class."

"And Mom—?"

"They've got some kind of testing today. She said she can't leave. I could just skip this week and—"

"No. No, it'll be fine. I'll just..." They'd learned the hard way that skipping PT was not good for Chris. If he didn't go, he'd skip his exercises too. And skipping exercises usually led to depression. Chris needed the once-a-week connection with his therapist.

Tabby could take some files with her, she supposed. The

appointments usually lasted an hour or longer. The afternoon wouldn't be completely wasted. Just mostly.

"I can do it," she said.

"I know it sucks." Chris sounded defeated, a tone she hadn't heard from him in months.

"Don't be silly. I'm dying to get out of here."

"Yeah, but—"

"Normal time?" she asked.

"We need to leave here about eleven."

The clock on the far wall told her she had forty-five minutes before she had to leave. She wouldn't be back to the office until three. She'd lose a half day.

Tabby stopped by her boss's office to give her the news. The woman sighed. "Your brother needs you. We're all about family here at HCI."

The familiar line didn't carry the weight it had before one member of the founder's family had murdered another member the summer before. They'd learned that family could be the most dangerous people in the world. But Tabby's boss had gone to high school with Chris and still had a soft spot for him. And anyway, nobody could accuse Tabby of shirking her duties. She put in more hours than anybody besides Chelsea herself.

Most of the time, she had nothing better to do. "I'll be caught up on my work by the end of the week," Tabby assured her.

The woman shooed her away, and Tabby returned to her desk. She'd barely read the first sentence of the complaint on the top of her pile when her phone rang again, this time her cell.

She was about to deny the call when she saw who it was. After a deep breath, she swiped to connect.

"Hey, you," Fitz said, his voice as rich and deep as espresso.

Her pulse slowed, and the jagged edges of her anxiety

smoothed. His voice was as comforting as warm surf between her toes.

"Hey yourself. Did you get some work done today?"

He chuckled. "Not all of us report for duty at eight a.m. I'm having a lazy morning."

"Color me jealous. I could use a little lazy."

"How about a lazy lunch? I thought I'd come by and take you—"

"I wish I could. I have to take Chris to Concord for physical therapy."

"Oh." The single word carried a world of disappointment. She knew how he felt. She'd like nothing better than to sit across from Fitz and share stories and laugh and pretend they were back in Belize.

Two weeks away had planted a seed of discontentment in her heart that she needed desperately to yank out. And maybe dump a little weed killer on. She loved her life.

Well, she liked it.

Mostly, she liked it.

And, if she were being honest, the discontentment had been planted long before Belize.

"Can I come?" Fitz asked.

"To physical therapy?"

"I guess not." He sounded so dejected, she nearly laughed. "Your brother probably doesn't need your"—his pause had her holding her breath—"friend tagging along."

Friend. Yes, that was the right word. Never mind that her heart seemed to stutter at it. What would be the harm if Fitz came? It might pull Chris out of the funk he seemed to have fallen into. Chris needed people in his life besides his sister and his parents. Thanks to the anger and depression that had dogged him for a decade, he'd lost most of his friends. Their brothers rarely came home. A dose of Fitz's charm might be just the thing to cheer Chris up.

Who was Tabby kidding? She could use a little cheering herself.

"We would love that," she said. "Can you swing by the office? We'll drive over to get Chris together."

"I'm on my way."

Tabby pulled into her parents' driveway, shooting a glance at Fitz at her side. It was odd having him there. In his khaki shorts or swim trunks and casual T-shirts, he'd seemed to fit in Belize. Now he wore jeans and boots and sweater and jacket, and yet he fit here too, relaxed and casual as could be. As if it weren't strange that he'd dropped everything and come to New Hampshire to see her.

She'd felt out of place in the exotic paradise until he'd rescued her that first day, sitting beside her as if he belonged there and then making her laugh before she could pretend she wanted to be alone. He'd made her vacation magical. She'd thought some of that magic was due to the location, but here he was, in cold, boring New Hampshire, and everything outside the windows seemed to sparkle just for him.

He'd been uncharacteristically quiet during the ride, gazing out the windows at the passing scenery. Nothing exciting out there, though. Just trees, trees, and more trees. Now, he regarded the house she'd grown up in, a red garrison with a breezeway between the garage and the main house.

"Nice place." Fitz turned his attention across the street. "You ever skate on that?"

Her house was the last one on dead-end street and across from a body of water the neighbors generously called a pond. In the spring when the snow melted and the waters rose, "pond" seemed right. But when the waters receded and the vegetation poked out, the truth poked out with it. It was a swamp.

An ugly name for a beautiful place, a place that hummed with life in the summers. Birds and bullfrogs and beavers and thousands of other species made their homes here. When she was a kid, she'd look from her second-floor bedroom to what she thought of as her little corner of heaven. She'd thought Coventry the most magical place on earth back then. Not the place of drudgery it seemed today.

Thanks to the overabundance of rain that fall, it looked more lake than swamp right now. "I wasn't much of a skater, but my brothers did sometimes. They and their friends would go out and shovel the snow off to create a little hockey rink."

"Fun."

She parked, and he came around as if to help her from the truck. She was on the driveway before he got there.

He smiled when he reached her. "You let me play the gentleman more in Belize."

She had, hadn't she? But that wasn't who she was. She was a northern girl, the kind who could build a fire and shovel a driveway and maneuver a four-wheel drive truck through a snowdrift. The kind who kept snow boots and a spare parka in her backseat, just in case. The kind who used to love to race her brothers on snowmobiles, back before the accident. Before Mom had eradicated all dangers from their home.

Fitz slipped her gloved hand into his, hanging on when she tried to pull away. "I might slip," he said. "I might need you to hold me up."

She glanced up at him, loving that he was taller than her lanky frame. Loving that he wasn't put off by her, no matter how hard she tried to push him away.

The garage door opened as they neared it, and Chris rolled

toward them, eyebrows hiked.

"Chris, this is my friend Fitz." She'd meant to warn him Fitz was coming. She'd lost track of time.

Fitz dropped Tabby's hand and shook Chris's. "Great to meet you. Your sister told me all about you."

"She's way too nice for that."

Fitz chuckled. "You'll have to fill in the blanks then."

Chris gave her a narrowed-eyes gaze before returning his focus to Fitz. "You're coming along?"

"If you don't mind. I came to see Tabby, but she's hardly had any time for me."

Chris looked from one to the other as if trying to solve a puzzle, finally saying, "Sounds like her. They work her too hard at that place."

As if Chris would know. He hadn't had a job since he'd bussed tables at The Patriot when he was in high school. Tabby headed for the van in the driveway and yanked open the rear doors.

Fitz stood back while she lowered a ramp and Chris rolled himself into the car. After she'd folded the ramp and stowed it, she turned to him. "Ready?"

"As rain." Since Chris was in the back, he took the passenger seat.

Tabby backed out of the driveway, wondering if this had been a mistake. She was accustomed to her brother and all the work it took to transport him from one place to another, but who knew what Fitz was thinking.

She'd barely started down the narrow road when Fitz turned toward the back. "Sucks you have to sit in the back."

"No big deal. Sometimes, when I have help, I can get into the passenger seat."

"I could've—"

"It's fine. I'm comfortable in my chair, and it's easier this way."

"On the way home," Fitz said, "we'll switch."

"On the way home, I'll be in wicked pain. I won't want out of my chair."

"Is that why Tabby's driving you?"

Tabby winced and glanced at her brother in the backseat, but Chris's face showed no distress.

"One of these days, I'll get a car of my own. Haven't quite gotten the money for that yet."

At the stop sign, she caught Fitz giving her a look that seemed almost... suspicious. But that made no sense. The look passed before she'd had adequate time to analyze it. And did she really need to be analyzing Fitz's looks?

"Do you like to talk about what happened?" Fitz asked.

"Actually, yeah."

He did? Chris never talked about the accident with her. But then she never asked him about it anymore.

"For years, I wouldn't," Chris said. "But I'm learning to have peace with it."

Tabby turned onto the state highway that would take them to I-93 and settled in to listen.

"I was fifteen," Chris said. "My brothers and I went skiing."

"And left me at home," Tabby added.

Fitz smiled at her. "Were you jealous?"

"They were always leaving me out."

"Well, you were a *female*, so—"

"Still am," she said.

In the rearview, Chris waffled his hand as if he weren't sure about that.

Fitz said, "Your brother doesn't see what I see."

From the backseat, Tabby heard a gagging sound and tried not to smile. When Chris was done with his little show of disgust, he continued. "Russ and Rich were showing off. They were better skiers than I was. I was irritated and jealous." His voice took on a bitter note. When he spoke again, the bitterness was gone. "It was the last run of the day, and they were way ahead of me, so I decided to take a different route. I wasn't trying to beat them—no way I could do that. But we used to ski through the woods sometimes, take unmarked trails, hit jumps. You ski?"

"My grandparents live in the Poconos, so we used to go there when I was a kid."

"So you know what I mean."

"I wasn't that good. I stuck to the groomed trails."

"Smart guy," Chris said. "I saw a path we hadn't tried and decided to take it. I figured, if nothing else, at least I'd have done something they hadn't. And since the lifts were closed, they wouldn't be able to.

"The trail started easy, just narrow and winding, but no problem. They were better than I was, but I was pretty good."

"He was excellent," Tabby said. "He'd have eventually been better than them."

"Anyway, the sun was going down, and I couldn't see very well. I got going too fast and hit a jump I wasn't ready for. For a split second, I felt that weightless feeling you get, that feeling I used to live for. And then I hit the snow and tumbled. My fall was stopped by the trunk of a pine tree."

"Ouch," Fitz said.

"You'd think, but I don't remember pain. I remember thinking I was glad my brothers hadn't seen the fall. And then it occurred to me that it probably looked really cool, and I wished they *had* seen it. I realized I was an idiot for going off on my own. And then I tried to move. When I couldn't... That's when I panicked."

Fitz shifted to better see Chris. "I can't imagine."

"My brothers... I figured they'd just think I was being a brat or something and go into the lodge and wait for me to show up. And then it would get dark, and nobody would find me. But Russ told the ski patrol right away. It still took a couple hours before I was found, but it could have been much worse. It could have been the next day. I could have frozen to death out there. Would have if Russ and Rich hadn't known something was wrong."

"That was God," Tabby said. "Russ and Rich were eighteen and seventeen, definitely not the most compassionate guys in the world. Russ says that when he turned around and Chris wasn't there, he knew immediately something was wrong. He said he felt it"—she tapped her stomach—"in his gut."

"Wow." Fitz turned his attention back to Chris. "That's amazing."

"Yeah. God's good. But not good enough to keep me from this." Bitterness carried on his words. Before Tabby could interject, he added, "But He didn't make me take that trail. I know that."

Fitz nodded, still facing behind. "How long's it been?"

"Thirteen years." Chris's voice held a hard edge. "Thirteen crappy years of me feeling sorry for myself. But no more."

"Turning over a new leaf?"

"Trying to. I always liked woodworking, so I started my own business, sell my stuff on Etsy and places like that."

"What kind of stuff?"

A minute later, Chris handed Fitz his cell, and Fitz was scrolling through pictures. "Wow, you're talented."

"It's bringing in a little money, but it's not enough to support myself. I'm taking online classes. I'm a little late to do the college thing, but..." His voice trailed.

Tabby wanted to pipe in with all the reasons he needed to

stick with school, to follow the dreams he'd had before the accident. But she held her tongue. Chris didn't need her to lecture.

"What are you studying?" Fitz asked.

"I want to be a financial planner."

"Ah, numbers," Fitz said. "My nemesis. If I had any finances, I'd hire you."

Chris's chuckle sounded genuine. "I'm hoping I can get a job at the end of this. I thought I'd love working for myself, but I've discovered the flaw in the plan."

"What's that?" Fitz asked.

"When you work for yourself, you're your own worst employee."

That brought a laugh. "I hear that."

When the laugher died, Chris filled the next empty space with, "So, what's going on with you and my sister?"

CHAPTER TEN

Ten minutes after they delivered Chris to the PT office, Fitz pulled out a chair for Tabby at a restaurant down the street. The two-story place looked like an old house on the outside. The inside was composed of differing tones of wood—wood floors, wood paneling on the walls, wood beams on the ceiling, wood tabletops, wood chairs. A fire glowed from the fireplace in the corner and filled the room with the aroma of Christmas mornings and cold winter nights. Their table was near the window, where they looked out from the cozy warmth at the snowy wonderland beyond.

Nice place for lunch, not that he had time to waste on this meal. He needed her to reveal something about herself that would help him find the stolen goods. He needed to keep in mind why he was here. Not to get to know her, not to deepen their already too-deep relationship, but to dig into her secrets.

"Very homey," he said.

She shrugged.

He reached across the table and took her hand, feeling attraction and desire, guilt and frustration. Why did this woman have to be so captivating? "I'm coming to appreciate everything about this state. Especially you."

She snatched her hand away, unrolled her silverware, and laid her napkin across her lap. He'd made her uncomfortable. Good. He needed her off balance.

No reason he should be the only one.

"I haven't heard Chris talk about his accident in a long time," she said.

"How come?"

She looked past Fitz, her lips pressing together.

The server came and took their drink orders.

When he left, Tabby said, "We don't talk about what happened. My mother can't stand to hear it mentioned, and, at first, Chris didn't want to either. It upset him. I guess he wants to talk about it now, but..." She bit her lip, then sighed. "I didn't know that. I should have. We've all sort of...sort of danced around him. He was angry. For years after it happened, living in the same house with him was like living with nitroglycerine. You never knew what would set him off. We learned to be careful about what we said around him, how we acted. He's finally climbing out of that pit, but I guess the rest of us are still tiptoeing like he might blow."

"I didn't know," Fitz said. "Maybe I should have—"

"You did exactly the right thing, which I knew you would." Her smile and her confidence in him had his defenses falling away. He needed to build up an immunity to her. "You've got a knack for knowing how to deal with people. It's a gift, I think."

She perused the menu, and he pretended to do the same. But her words, intended to be kind, cut him. He did have a knack for people. He'd used it well as a cop. He'd used it with Chris, and he was using it with Tabby. Using it to get her to trust him so he could save his sister. A good cause, but the deception made him sick.

Tabby had put Shelby in danger. Not on purpose, but she had. Still, lying to her felt wrong in every way.

She peered over the menu. "Have you ever thought about photographing people instead of nature?"

Another thing to feel guilty about. He'd lied to her about his work. He never told anybody when he was on a job. One mustn't run around telling strangers they're investigating someone. For all he'd known when he'd first sat with Tabby, she was a friend of the guy he'd been paid to watch. Secrecy was essential.

He'd sat beside her because she was attractive and because he figured he'd look less conspicuous at the beach if he weren't alone. He hadn't dreamed they'd get close. He'd taken to telling people he was a nature photographer because it was true, even if it was barely more than a hobby.

"I've done some portraits." Also true. Like everyone in the world, he sometimes took pictures of people.

"I just think that, with your knack for making people feel comfortable, you'd be able to get quality shots other photographers wouldn't get."

He lifted his phone and snapped a photo of her. In the picture, she was giving him a look he'd seen often in Belize. It said, *Please, not another picture.*

He turned the screen to face her, and she laughed.

"Presumably, your subject would *want* to have their picture taken. And presumably, you wouldn't catch them off guard."

"Presumably," he said. "But I like nature. Like you, it doesn't have to be coaxed into beauty."

"You're such a charmer." She tapped her menu. "Do you want to split something?"

Despite his giant breakfast, his stomach was growling. "Aren't you hungry?"

"I really need to start a diet. After two weeks in Belize—"

"Are you crazy? You're perfect."

Her cheeks turned a pretty shade of pink. "I put on a couple of pounds. I probably need—"

"*Mangi, mangi.*" He affected an Italian accent. "Eat, eat. You're too skinny."

She giggled. "I guess I can start my diet tomorrow."

"Tomorrow or the day after never. You don't need to diet. Now, what are you going to get?"

"I think this salad—"

"Nope. I'm buying, and I forbid it. Something that'll put some meat on your bones." He skimmed the menu. "The burger. That's what you really want, right?"

Her smile. Oh, that smile. He loved that he could make her smile like that. Hated himself for loving it.

"You know me too well."

After the server took their orders—a burger for her, the signature pot roast for him—Fitz brought the subject back to Chris. "Is there any hope your brother will regain the use of his legs?"

"They're coming up with new therapies and surgeries all the time. Many are experimental. All are expensive."

"Insurance doesn't cover it?"

"Nope." She sipped her coffee and set it back down. "There's one that's really promising for his kind of injury. I wish we could come up with the money. Between my parents and my brothers and me…"

"That would be life-altering for Chris."

"Yeah. Except… Until recently, honestly, I didn't think it would be a good idea. Obviously, if he could regain the use of his legs, that would be awesome. But how much a person recovers, how well the therapies work, is very much dependent on the person's emotional state. Chris has done a lot of sorry-for-himself. He needs to come to terms with what happened. Otherwise, no matter what therapies he gets, the bitterness isn't going to go away, and bitterness makes us weak, not strong. It isn't caused by circumstances. It's caused by our reactions to circumstances. If he doesn't get a handle on that, nothing anybody does is going to help him."

"I didn't get a sense he was bitter."

"He's working on it. The woodworking, school... And he's finally going back to church. God's working in his heart. But he's still very angry, mostly at himself. He'll take that bitterness with him wherever he goes."

"So, if you had the money, you wouldn't help him get the use of his legs back?"

"That's not a fair question." She sipped her drink, studied it as if the answer were floating on the water. "I think we don't have the money in our family because God has a different plan. Maybe, someday, we can raise the money for one of those treatments. And maybe the treatments will be even better, give him more mobility than anything they can do now. But until then, Chris has to learn to deal with the life he's been given." She leaned forward and reached across the table.

It was unusual for Tabby to reach for Fitz, to close the distance she'd carefully kept between them. He slid his hand into hers, hating the way his body responded to the simple touch.

"You understand what I mean, right?" She sounded almost pleading. "You lost your parents in a tragic accident. You're putting your life on hold to raise your sister."

"Not on hold exactly,"

"You've made Shelby a priority, as well she should be. I'm just saying, life is hard, but we have to grow in the difficulty, not let it defeat us. Chris has let his accident define him. He's let it ruin him. I've watched my parents do everything they possibly can to help him, and it's only made it worse. They expect nothing from him, and for years, that's exactly what they've gotten."

Fitz hung on Tabby's words, marveling. He'd experienced what she was describing. After their parents died, he'd been forced to go on in order to care for Shelby. But Shelby... she'd retreated into herself. Only when he'd quit putting up with her moods and her poor grades and her laziness had she started to come out of her funk.

Tabby looked at their joined hands as if only then realizing the connection, then pulled away and sat back. "Maybe I'm a terrible person. I don't know. They just... My family sort of ranks people by age. The oldest is the smartest, the youngest is the dumbest. I'm the youngest, so I've always been"—she waved the air between them—"adorably naive. That's how they see me. But I'm telling you, the more we do for Chris, the less he'll do for himself."

"I'm sure you're right."

"I'm glad you think so. Russ is starting to come around. Rich..."

"He's the oldest, right?"

"Yeah. I think he feels guilty, as if Chris's accident had something to do with him. He wants us siblings to go in to buy Chris a van. He thinks if Chris has some freedom, he'll feel better. Maybe that's true, maybe not. I think his issues are a lot deeper than lack of a vehicle. I said I'd pitch in if Chris pitched in too. Chris should have to earn some of the money for his own car. It'll make him feel independent. It'll give him ownership in his own life."

"That's really smart," Fitz said.

"Rich thinks I'm selfish."

"You're anything but selfish." His words felt sincere. They weren't, but they felt it.

That was one of Fitz's gifts, the ability to believe what was coming out of his mouth in the moment. It was why people trusted him. It was why he wasn't trustworthy.

He used to be. Back before his life fell apart, he'd been honorable and good.

Nothing about this situation was either.

They ate their lunches and laughed as they had in Belize, as if all were right in the world. Though, here in New Hampshire, Tabby was no longer the carefree soul he'd first come to care for. Worry lines tightened her face when she talked about her brother. If he tried to steer the conversation to her job, she changed the subject.

Did she hate it that much?

Did she hate it enough to become a thief? Why not just choose a different career path? Seemed wiser than risking prison. But then, he'd put enough criminals behind bars to know people weren't logical or wise.

He'd paid the check when her phone dinged with a text. "Chris says he'll be done in fifteen, so we need to leave in five."

He'd spent hours with her, but he'd learned nothing that could help him find the stolen goods. He wasn't sure what he'd hoped to learn, but something. Most of the time, if he got people talking, they let important facts slip, but Tabby had revealed nothing.

Either she was that good, or she wasn't guilty.

Again, he reminded himself of the video evidence.

He'd seen her crack that safe. He'd seen her take the box of jewels.

They were back in the van when he raised a topic that she'd shut down over and over in Belize. Back then, he'd meant it. Now, he meant it to soften her defenses.

Or so he told himself.

"We could make this work. I know it's a long distance—"

"Please don't." She shifted gears and backed out of the parking spot.

"Why won't you even discuss it?"

"Let's just enjoy our time together while you're here."

"And then... what? Pretend we never met?"

She turned onto the road and said nothing.

"Will you be able to do that?"

"I'll have to, won't I?"

He thought of the redheaded man in her bedroom that morning. "There's someone else, isn't there?"

"What?" Her gaze snapped to him. "There's nobody in my life. Nobody."

"Right. Sure." But the idea was growing, metastasizing like cancer. "You didn't want to go out to dinner last night or to lunch—"

"We just ate."

"In Concord. Far away from where you live. Maybe you don't want to be seen with me. Maybe there's another man, and you're afraid he's going to find out."

"Yup. That's it." She hit the gas too hard as she took a corner. "I went on vacation for two weeks, by myself, even though I have a boyfriend. No, no a *husband*. Yeah, I have a husband. I keep him hidden in the attic, only bring him out for special occasions."

"I'm just trying to understand."

"What's to understand? I live in New Hampshire. You live in Rhode Island. Long-distance relationships never work."

"Have you ever had one?"

"No. And if you have, then the fact that you're sitting here with me proves it didn't work."

"I never have, but at least I'm not afraid to try."

She said nothing.

Anger rolled over him. He didn't want to fall in love with a thief and liar.

Not that he was being honest with her, but that was different.

And he didn't want her. But there was something special between them, and that she'd discard it as if it happened every day, as if it didn't matter...

It didn't matter. Nothing mattered but getting Shelby back.

But the frustration pulsed anyway.

CHAPTER ELEVEN

That afternoon in his hotel room, Fitz paced from the door to the window. This building had probably been standing since the forties or before. A yellow Victorian just a block from downtown, it looked like it belonged right in this spot. Though the outside screamed turn-of-the-century, the inside was clean and tidy, the walls painted a blah beige, the bathrooms refinished with new, if not fancy, fixtures. He could've stayed at one of the many hotels on the outskirts of town, but Fitz had wanted to get a feel for Coventry, thinking it could help him understand Tabby and her actions.

He shoved in his earbuds and called the PI, who answered on the second ring. "This is Tad."

If Fitz's name had been Tad, he'd have answered with his surname. Of course, a guy named Fitz probably shouldn't throw stones. "You got anything for me?" He'd called after he'd left Tabby's that morning and asked him to be on the lookout for a redhead in Tabby's life.

"Since we met a couple of hours ago? Not much."

"What'd you learn about her friends? The redhead specifically?"

"As far as we can tell, there's only one redhead in Tabby's life, and he's married to her best friend. Name's Dylan O'Donnell. Wife's Chelsea Hamilton O'Donnell, CEO of HCI."

"You got a picture?"

The photo came through on his cell a moment later. The man's hair was bright red. His size and shape matched the man who'd been at the house that morning. "Any idea what he drives?"

"Green Dodge Ram."

A pickup. That tracked. So, was Tabby having an affair with her best friend's husband?

Fitz seriously doubted it.

"Any chance O'Donnell has criminal ties?"

Tad chuckled. "Aside from the fact that he used to be a police detective? Cards on the table, I've met the guy. He's as straight as the blade in your razor. He's a PI, but he specializes in finding lost people. Mostly homeless people and addicts whose families love them and want to help. He's a good guy."

Despite the fact that he'd been in Tabby's bedroom, despite the fact that he'd delivered a mysterious package, Dylan O'Donnell didn't seem like the missing piece Fitz was searching for. "Anything else?"

"We're still looking into friendships, but we're finding nothing suspicious. I don't know what you're looking for on this woman, but I think you're on the wrong track."

He was beginning to think so too. "Keep looking. Let me know what you learn."

He ended the call and dialed Mullins, who answered on the second ring. "Tell me you have my stuff."

"Not yet. Listen, we need to go about this a different way. Who else knew about the jewels?"

A short pause preceded the man's raised voice. "What

difference does it make? We know who did it. We've got the woman on video."

"I've had her under surveillance since she landed in Boston. She hasn't gone anywhere but to work and her parents' house without me at her side. No clandestine visits. She hasn't even gone grocery shopping. I searched her house, and your stuff wasn't there."

"I should've sent my associates. They'd have the information by now."

The implication that Fitz wasn't doing the job well grated. "Your guys are all brawn and no brains. If you want your stuff back, you're going to have to trust me."

"You don't know them. Don't let the muscles deceive you. I don't surround myself with idiots. And I don't trust you at all. I trust that you care about your sister. I trust you don't want me taking out my anger on her."

The threat brought a wave of fury Fitz had to breathe through. He kept his voice low and measured. "We're trusting each other. Right now, I need to know everybody who knew about the goods. You bought them at auction. Was your name associated with the bids?"

"I had a surrogate bidder, so nobody could have known I was the buyer."

He remembered the name on the receipts. "Gail Seder?"

"I've used her a bunch of times. She used to work for Sotheby's and knows her stuff."

"Contact information?" Mullins told him, and Fitz wrote the woman's address and phone number down. "Who else?"

Mullins blew out a long breath. "My guys, of course. They know everything I know."

"I need names."

"Joey and Marco Novak."

"They were seated at the table with you?"

"Yeah."

Brothers. They'd looked enough alike that Fitz didn't doubt it. He wrote down their names. "Where are they from?"

"Jersey, I think. Or maybe Long Island."

"It warms the heart the way you take an interest in your employees. What about your Willie Nelson-wannabe. What's his name?"

There was a slight chuckle on the other end of the phone. "Name's Wilson Dunbar."

"Wilson? He's actually a Willie?"

"And proud of it."

That was obvious. "Where's he from?"

"Providence." A short pause was followed by, "Grew up next door to me."

Willie was an old, old friend of Ronnie's. Did that mean he was loyal? Not necessarily. "Who else?"

"Lena."

Ronnie's wife. "I assume she wore the jewels on the plane?"

"Yeah. We put the antique chest in the suitcase in bubble wrap and slapped a *Made in China* sticker on the bottom, just in case. Nobody gave it a second glance."

"Why'd you buy the box?" Because of its size, the box was the riskiest thing they'd carried. The risk had bothered him since he first saw it.

Mullins sighed. "Gail picked it. After we got here, I'd decided to hold onto it to give as a gift. I wish I'd left it in Boston."

"Who's it for?"

"Doesn't matter."

"Mistress?"

"I'm loyal to my wife." The words were low and threatening. "It's a gift for one of my kids. Obviously, since the box was a surprise, she didn't know about it."

"No need to get testy. Just trying to figure this—"

"We know who did it."

"Did you run into anybody while Lena wore the jewelry?"

A loud sigh filled a gap. "Nobody."

"Ask her, just in case. Maybe she saw somebody in the bathroom."

"You think I'd let her go to the bathroom by herself wearing a half a million dollars' worth of jewels? She didn't leave my sight."

"You don't trust your wife.?"

"I trust her with my life. I love my wife. I didn't want her to get hurt."

Fitz didn't point out that, as a mobster, Ronnie's very presence at her side put her in danger. "Somebody knew, Mullins. Somebody knew about the jewels, and that somebody told the thief. She didn't just *happen* to rip off the safe that night. It had to have been planned in advance. When did you arrive in Belize?"

"A month ago."

Tabby had arrived about two weeks after that. Theoretically, somebody could have hired her to steal the goods, and she could have planned the whole thing in a couple of weeks.

Theoretically.

Except she said she'd been planning the trip for a year. And he'd seen the airline tickets on her credit card statement.

"How did you get that video you showed me?" Fitz asked.

"It wasn't doctored, if that's what you're thinking. The people here at the hotel are very loyal to me and my family. Their loyalty is rewarded."

"I'm trying to figure out how close you are with the managers down there. Could you find out when Tabby's reservation was made? It should have been made months ago, maybe up to a year ago. If she made it in the previous month, that tells us we're on the right track."

"Everybody else already knows we're on the right track."

Fitz ignored the statement. "While you're at it, I'd like a list of everybody who was staying at the hotel that night. Go through it yourself, see if any names jump out at you. If Tabby did this, she didn't do it alone."

"I can get you that stuff. But here's what you need to know. You've got one more day to show me you're making headway or I'm sending Willie up there. I can't afford to take any risks. You got it?"

The thought of Tabby in that goon's hands made the pot roast Fitz had eaten for lunch rumble in his stomach. "I'll have something for you tomorrow, but get me those names."

"I'll have 'em by the end of the day. I expect to hear from you—"

"I haven't been able to get in touch with Shelby."

"They're at sea."

"I need to know she's okay. I need to talk to her. Today."

A long pause followed the words. Finally, Mullins said, "I'll see what I can do." And the line went dead.

CHAPTER TWELVE

Fitz tried to tell himself he wasn't disappointed when Tabby turned down his dinner invitation. Considering they'd had lunch together, and that she'd been out of the office for hours that day, he'd known it was a long shot.

He had research to do anyway, and spending time with Tabby was only muddling his brain. Nothing in the way she spoke or acted or carried herself indicated deep, dark secrets. She seemed genuine and sincere.

Either she was, which meant somebody had framed her, or she was an exceptional liar.

After he called the PI and gave him the names Mullins had given him, he put on his boots and jacket, grabbed his laptop and notebook, and headed outside. He needed to get away from those four walls. Maybe a new environment would give him new ideas.

It was after six, but the late lunch was still with him, so he headed for the library, a small white building a block off Main Street. Inside, it smelled like mildew and books. He found a seat, opened his laptop, connected to the internet, and looked up Ronald Mullins. He needed to dig around the man's past.

Mullins had been born into a mob family connected with the biggest names on the east coast. His specialties were protection schemes and illegal gambling rings.

The protection schemes dated back to the eighties. Businesses that chose not to pay were shut down—or burned to the ground. A couple of guys who decided to try to catch him in the act had ended up dead.

After that, accusations against Mullins had faded away. Not because he'd stopped his illegal activity but because he'd silenced his enemies.

Fitz noted the names of the people who'd been murdered. Maybe there was a connection. Maybe somebody was trying to pay Mullins back for all the damage he'd done.

His nightclub—strip club, according to the newspaper—had been busted more than once for gambling and prostitution. One of his managers had gone to prison, but Mullins had somehow wiggled out of charges.

There'd been no way to prove he'd profited from or even known about the gambling going on at the premises. About the prostitution, he'd said, "Though I do discourage moonlighting, what my employees do on their own time is up to them." Again, no proof he'd profited from their "moonlighting." But everybody from the DA to the guy who collected the club's garbage knew he had.

One article linked Mullins with the man the police believed responsible for a good portion of the drugs smuggled into Providence. The link was tenuous, though. If he had gotten involved in smuggling, he'd been smart about it.

After two hours, Fitz's phone rang. He didn't recognize the number but connected the call.

"Fitz?"

"Shelby!" He stood suddenly. "Where are you? Are you all right?"

Somebody at a nearby table shushed him.

He shoved his laptop into the case, grabbed his jacket, and made his way to the door.

"Omigosh, we're having so much fun! We're at sea, and I thought it would be awful not having my phone, but I don't even care. We've been playing board games with Lena—she asked me to call her that—and getting tanned on the deck. And yesterday, we pulled into this wicked secluded little cove and went swimming, and Shawn and I had a picnic on the beach. It was so romantic."

As his sister babbled, his worries faded. She was all right. For now, she was safe and happily oblivious. He pushed out into the cold night and stopped on the concrete landing at the top of the stairs. "I'm glad you're having a good time, though maybe I'd like to hear less about romance and more about board games."

"Sorry, bro. But I'm just saying, Shawn's a good guy. And this is such a nice family. I thought, you know, since they're so rich that they'd be, like, stuck up or whatever. But they're not. Yesterday, Shawn was taking a nap, and Lena and I sat on the deck and drank piña coladas—don't worry, mine was virgin—and had girl talk." Her voice became wistful. "It made me miss Mom, you know?"

"Yeah." Fitz could fill a lot of holes, but he'd never be Mom. "How are you calling me? You're at sea, right?"

"There's a phone in the cockpit they let me use. I guess it's a satellite phone, so I can't use it very often."

"Are you alone?"

"The captain is here."

So there'd be no private conversations, which didn't surprise Fitz. He wondered if anybody was listening in.

"If you needed to get in touch with me," Fitz asked, "can you ask the guy to call me? Or do you need Mrs. Mullins's permission? I need to know you're safe, and when I go days without hearing from you—"

"I'm safe. You don't have to worry. But yeah, if I need to talk to you, I can call." Her voice became a little distant. "Right?"

A man's voice in the background said, "Anytime."

"See, it's all good," Shelby said.

"Getting any schoolwork done?" He asked because, under normal circumstances, he would.

"I'll get caught up when we're home."

"So...no."

"There's no internet. And anyway, why take time out of a fabulous experience to study biology?"

"You make a good point. But if you get the chance—"

"Yeah, yeah, yeah. How's your case going?"

"You know." He made his voice sound relaxed, dull even. "Boring stuff."

"You're out in the jungle, right? Is it awesome? It must be wicked hot. How do you have service out there?"

He hated lying to his sister. "I'm in a little town right now. You'd be surprised at the long tentacles of AT&T."

"Thank God for that. I'm so glad I got in touch with you. When Mr. Mullins called and said you were worried about me, I felt bad I hadn't called earlier."

"You're having too much fun to worry about your boring older brother."

"That's true."

He chuckled, and it wasn't even forced. He was relieved to hear her voice.

"Marco's giving me the stink eye," she said on a laugh, "so I guess I gotta go. Love you, bro."

"Love you too, sis. Call soon."

Fitz slid his phone into his pocket and leaned against the metal railing of the library's handicap ramp. Shelby was okay. A knot of tension loosened in his belly. For now, she was okay, and Fitz could focus on getting her back so she'd be okay forever.

He glanced at the library's glass doors and the brightly lit lobby beyond. He'd spent hours there, and he'd learned almost nothing. There was too much information to sort through. He'd never been the dig-in-and-find-the-answers guy. He'd been the guy who asked questions, got people to talk.

The last thing he wanted was to ask for help, but he was out of options. And running out of time.

If Willie the thug showed up in Coventry, he'd get what he wanted from Tabby or kill her trying.

Fitz went down the steps, his feet crunching on thick granules of salt on the concrete stairway. The night was quiet, only the occasional car passing by, but the worries in his brain thundered.

He made his way back to Main Street. With every step, the truth became clearer.

He had no choice. He'd do anything to save his sister. Even this.

He turned onto Coventry's main thoroughfare. There were a number of restaurants in town, two on this block, a little pizzeria and a place called The Patriot, which was closed. He reached the pizzeria, where he ordered a small pepperoni at the counter and then stepped back outside.

There was almost nothing that could get him to make this call. Almost.

He yanked out his phone, shoved in his earbuds, and dialed the number from memory.

The phone rang three times. Fitz had almost given up hope when the man answered.

"Has hell frozen over?" Abe Bachelor's deep voice held no hint of amusement.

"Apparently."

"Should I be on the lookout for flying pigs?"

"Probably."

Silence settled between them. After a minute, Fitz said, "I need your help."

"Obviously."

If Fitz had expected more from his former partner, he'd have been disappointed. Good thing Abe could never disappoint him more than he already had. "I need all the information you have on Ronald Mullins and a few of his associates."

There was a long silence on the other end of the phone, so long he glanced at the screen to assure himself they were still connected.

Finally, Abe said, "You're kidding, right? Two years ago, you accused me of corruption."

"It was either you or me, and I knew it wasn't me."

"Accuse me of lying, accuse me, for all intents and purposes, of *murder*. Now, you call and want information, and I'm just supposed to, what? Do your bidding as if nothing happened? You can take your questions and shove 'em where—"

"Shelby's been kidnapped."

Abe, the man who'd claimed to be a Christian and then gotten in bed with the mob, uttered a single curse word Fitz had never heard from the straightlaced cop. He could picture him now, pushing his too-thick black-rimmed glasses up on his dark skin.

Whatever happened between the partners, Abe had cared for Shelby. He'd been like an uncle to her, been to every birthday party since their parents died. He'd bought her Christmas presents every year. He'd even driven her to after-school activities when Fitz couldn't do it. Fitz had trusted Abe with his sister.

He'd trusted Abe completely. No matter that Abe had

betrayed everything that had ever mattered to him, Fitz believed his care for Shelby had been real.

"Mullins has her?"

"On his yacht." Fitz related what he knew while Abe listened, occasionally asking questions but mostly just taking it in. Abe had worked on the organized crime task force before he and Fitz became partners. A decade older than Fitz, the man knew more about the mob than anybody Fitz had ever met. That he'd used that information to line his own pockets, Fitz could still hardly believe.

When he was finished, Abe said, "You think the woman—Tabby—stole the stuff?"

That was the million-dollar question. "I saw the video. I saw her do it." But Abe knew Fitz well enough to know there was more to the story and stayed silent. Finally, Fitz added, "I think it's possible she's innocent. I don't know for sure. How could I?"

"You used to trust your instincts."

"Back when I thought I had good ones, yeah." Before he'd discovered his own partner was corrupt, he'd blindly believed he could tell when people were lying.

"I assume the FBI is working it," Abe said.

"Mullins told me no cops."

"That's what every kidnapper tells every victim. You're smart enough to know—"

"I don't trust the FBI not to screw it up or to keep it quiet. If I get them involved, they'll focus more on bringing Mullins down and less on saving my sister. I can't take that chance."

"One law enforcement agency disappoints you, and you throw out the whole lot. Is that it?"

"They didn't *disappoint* me. They forced me to resign when I'd done nothing wrong. Because—" He cut off his own words. He needed Abe's help, and dredging all this stuff up wasn't the way to get it.

Mercifully, Abe let it go. "What about this woman... Tabby? What aren't you telling me?"

"I've told you everything."

"I don't think so."

Abe's self-confidence grated on Fitz's nerves. They'd been partners so long that even after two years of silence, it was a waste of time for Fitz to try to keep secrets from him. "Before all this happened, Tabby and I were kind of a thing. In Belize. We only knew each other for a couple weeks, though, so it's not like it was that serious."

"But?"

"She doesn't seem the type. I never would've suspected her of anything illegal. But if Tabby's responsible for my sister getting kidnapped, then it's irrelevant."

"Huh."

"What?"

"Known you for a long time, Fitz. Never known you to like anybody that well after just a couple of weeks. You're far too suspicious for that."

"Maybe I've changed."

"Not for the better. If you trusted this woman after just two weeks..."

Fitz had trusted her after two days. Maybe two hours. He'd trusted her from the very beginning.

"...then I suspect she's trustworthy."

Abe's words sent a flash of confidence through Fitz, but it died a quick death. If Tabby hadn't stolen Mullins's stuff, then he had no idea who had. How could he get the items back in time to save Shelby? How could he prove Tabby's innocence?

Or would he lose them both?

"Just tell her what's going on," Abe said.

The suggestion rankled. "I can't tip her off. That'd be—"

"You've always been good at reading people. You'll know if

she's lying. If she's not, you can quit wasting your time on her. And maybe not destroy your relationship with—"

"I'll handle Tabby. You just look into Mullins."

"If she didn't do it—"

"I've got it," Fitz snapped. The last thing he needed was advice from Abe, the man who'd proved affection and friendship were kryptonite to Fitz's intuition.

"I'll learn what I can about Mullins and all these people whose names you've given me." Abe's deep voice was even and unperturbed. "What will you be doing?"

"I'm working Tabby, trying to get her to confide in me. And I'm working the hotel angle. Whoever did the job wasn't working alone. I should get the names of everyone staying at the hotel tomorrow."

"Okay, good. You get any more names you want me to dig into, you send 'em to me. But here's the deal. You get nothing from me until we talk about what happened two years ago. In person."

"I'm in New Hampshire." And he had zero desire to put eyes on Abe.

"I can head that way."

"I don't have time for that. I'm trying to save my sister's life."

"You should've thought of that before you ignored my calls for two years. You and me, in person, or you get nothing."

"What else is there to say?"

"What *else*?" His deep voice thundered through the phone. A beat passed, and when Abe spoke again, his volume had lowered. "In person or nothing."

Fitz clenched his fists at his side, the chilly air not cooling his anger at all. "Fine."

"I'll be in touch."

CHAPTER THIRTEEN

Thoughts of Fitz had kept Tabby up too late. Even though she was working as hard as ever, with him in town it felt as if she'd extended her vacation. And she didn't want it to end.

She was supposed to be well into the process of forgetting about him, yet she couldn't get him off her mind.

She'd hit the snooze button one time too many and had already been running late when she left her house for work Wednesday morning to find her neighbor stepping through the trees between their yards, arm waving.

"I'm so glad I caught you."

Tabby pressed on a smile like a sticker, the first fake smile of the day but no doubt not the last. "Mrs. Pollack. What can I do for you?"

"I need to talk to you." The seventy-something woman was no more than five feet tall, marching across the lawn like Napoleon. "Did you know there were men in your house yesterday?"

Men? "Dylan O'Donnell came by. I ordered an organizer for my closet and had it delivered to my friend's house because I was on vacation. It was heavy, so he brought it inside."

"You give strange men a key to your house?"

"My best friend and her husband, yes. They watered my plants while I was gone."

Mrs. Pollack was nodding as if giving Tabby's words serious consideration. "Well, now, I know that Dylan fellow who married the Hamilton girl. You could pick out his red hair from the space station."

Tabby's fake smile morphed into a real one. "You might be right about that. Listen, I'm late, so—"

"It was the other one who concerned me, him climbing out the window and all. But I know the Hamiltons are friends of yours, so I figured there was some really good explanation. I was rather curious, though."

The other one? Out the window? "I'm sorry. I'm not sure what you're talking about."

Mrs. Pollack's eyes grew round. "Really? The dark-headed man. He left, oh, maybe thirty minutes after Mr. Hamilton."

"O'Donnell. Dylan's last name is—"

"Oh, you know who I mean." She waved off Tabby's words.

"Are you saying there was someone else in my house yesterday?"

"Yes, dear." Mrs. Pollack looked at Tabby as if she were dim-witted.

Tabby studied the older woman more closely. She wore a zip-up purple robe and soft slippers with no socks, despite the fact that the temperature hovered in the low twenties and there was snow on the ground. Her curly silver hair stuck out on one side but was pressed down on the other as if she'd just rolled out of bed.

She'd always seemed sharp, but she wasn't making any sense today. Tabby made a mental note to call Tommy Pollack and find out if her neighbor was suffering from dementia. If so, Tabby'd need to keep a closer eye on her.

"Well, nothing to worry about." Tabby squeezed the short woman's shoulder. "I thank you for keeping such a keen eye on my house while I'm at work. Speaking of"—she made a show of checking her watch—"I'm running late, so I'd better go."

"Have a good day, dear. I'll keep a lookout, see if that other fellow comes back."

"You do that. Thank you." Tabby watched as Mrs. Pollack walked among the trees between their houses. A moment later, she heard the distant sound of a storm door slamming and knew the woman had made it home safely.

Hours had gone by when Tabby looked up at the knock on her office door, dreading whoever stood on the far side. She rarely closed it, taking the whole "open door policy" to heart, but she'd needed time this morning to focus on getting caught up.

Kelly poked her head in. "You've got a visitor. I happened to be downstairs, so I brought him up."

As the door opened wider, Tabby's gaze snapped to the clock above it. How was it after noon? Before she could figure out where her morning had gone, Fitz stepped inside.

Her face warmed. Though everybody in the company had seen the cluttered space where she spent so much of her life, she wasn't prepared for Fitz to be here.

Behind him, Kelly's eyes rounded and her jaw dropped in an exaggerated look of shock. She lifted two thumbs but dropped her hands and masked the ridiculous look when Fitz turned to her. "Thanks for walking me up."

"Sure." Her voice was as calm and dignified as could be. "Nice to meet you."

When Fitz turned back to Tabby, Kelly fanned her face as if too cool it. Tabby couldn't help but giggle as her friend walked away.

Oblivious, Fitz said, "Did I interrupt something?"

"Sorry. I lost track of time." She'd agreed to meet him in the lobby at noon. He'd been waiting nearly fifteen minutes.

"We can reschedule if you want." Though the words were casual, a disappointed note resonated. He'd come to New Hampshire partly to see her, and she'd hardly made any time for him.

"I worked like a dog this morning so I'd have time for lunch, and I do. Let me just..." She closed the file she'd been updating and logged out of her computer. When she looked up, he was gazing at her space, lips pursed, arms crossed.

"What?"

He met her eyes, but the irritated look didn't fade. "Your office is a wreck."

"Thanks for pointing that out."

He wasn't wrong. Files were stacked in multiple places, some a foot high. Papers and sticky notes covered the surface of her desk and her credenza. She had two... no, three different coffee-stained mugs in various, illogical places, along with an empty paper plate that she hadn't bothered to toss out the evening before. A few notepads and crumpled pieces of paper littered what remained of her workspace so that hardly any of her brown desk showed. She'd been perusing a few books on management before her vacation, and she'd tossed them on the floor when she'd come back to make room for more files. More paper lay scattered beside the trash can. Sticky notes had been stuck to the walls beside old lists and policies she'd tacked up over the years.

When she'd first been given this office, she'd fixed it up to match her style. She'd brought in some family pictures, a scented candle, a few other decorative items. She'd brought two plants. Now, one was dead, the other following its footsteps to the grave.

Nothing about this space reflected who Tabby was.

Not that any of that should matter to Fitz.

She stood and tried to smile as if she hadn't noticed his irritation. It was how she dealt with disgruntled employees, though she usually knew what their problem was. She couldn't begin to guess what Fitz was so mad about. "I need to clean it. I'll probably come in this weekend—"

"You hate your job."

"What? No, I don't. I like it. I mean, it's not my *dream* job or anything, but—"

"You hate it." He gestured to the desk. "This tells me you hate it. This... this pit is a reflection of how you feel about your job."

"Thank you, Carl Jung. You wanna tell me how I feel about my mother while we're at it?"

"I could guess, but I guarantee you don't want to know."

"What is your problem?"

"Is this why—?" He cut off his own words, swallowed.

"Why what?"

He dropped his arms and stretched his hands. "I thought you didn't want to leave New Hampshire because you didn't want to leave your job. I knew you didn't love it, but I didn't realize"—he gestured to the space—"you hated it this much. Which tells me..." He ran a hand through his hair, then forced a smile. "It's fine. You ready?"

"It's anything but fine. Explain. Please."

He stepped into the hallway. "I'm hungry. You coming?"

What in the world?

She didn't move from her spot behind the desk, tempted to tell him where he could put his lunch and his attitude. She dealt with irritated people all day long. The last thing she needed was to go to lunch with one.

"I'm sorry." He walked back inside, stepped over a cardboard box she needed to empty, and stopped beside her, invading her space. He took her hand and spoke near her ear. "I'm like the Hulk, only it's hunger that turns me into a monster."

So she was supposed to pretend he hadn't just lashed out at her.

"Forgive me, please. I promise I'll be nice."

She was hungry. And, despite his attitude, she wanted to be with him. "I wouldn't want to inflict your wrath on my town."

"Then you'd better come and keep me in line."

He was so close, she could feel his breath in her hair. Prickles of desire skimmed over her scalp and across her skin. She didn't want to move, didn't want him to step away.

But he did, tugging her hand gently.

She followed but extricated her hand from his grip. "I'm already going to have to deflect a bunch of questions about you," she said. "Let's not add to it by holding hands."

The kindness that had momentarily filled his face hardened. "Sure. I get it."

She didn't press him to explain that remark. After he got a few bites in him, he'd loosen up, surely.

THE PATRIOT HAD BEEN in town since before Tabby was born. They served down-home American food, including breakfast, all day. Well, all day that they were open. The placed closed at two in the afternoon. Tabby and Fitz were seated at a booth on the wall opposite the coffee bar and ordered drinks. They hadn't spoken much on the walk from her building, and the silence felt chillier than the air outside as he skimmed the menu.

Angry or happy, Fitz was beautiful with his wavy, longish brown hair pushed back from his forehead and his pale blue eyes. The bit of scruff on his cheeks told her he hadn't shaved that morning. He looked good clean-shaven, but the scruff was sexy.

Despite the anger coming from his side of the table, she felt drawn to him like iron shavings to a magnet.

He looked up and caught her staring, and a little of the hardness left his expression. "Know what you're having?"

"Soup and salad."

His lips, those alluring lips, pressed into a smirk. "Why do you think you need to diet? You're perfect just the way you are."

"Obviously that's not true or else you wouldn't be mad at me because my office is a mess. You want to explain that?"

He set down the menu. "What was the most enjoyable job you ever had?"

"I worked as a ski instructor when I was in college. In the summers, I was a guide on rafting tours. That was fun."

"Tabby-sized adventure," he said.

"What's that supposed to mean?"

"You say you want adventure, but you like to play it safe. Groomed trails, safe rivers, recommended excursions, and romance that doesn't touch your heart."

"That's not fair."

He swallowed hard. "You're right. Sorry. I'm just... Why'd you quit those jobs?"

"They aren't exactly career options."

"You needed to make money."

"I mean, yeah. Not everybody gets to do their hobby for a living."

Something flicked in his expression. Confusion. Gone so fast she questioned whether she'd really seen it.

"What's going on with you?" she asked. "Why the third degree?"

"I'm trying to understand you. What else?"

"What else what?"

"What other jobs have you had?"

She didn't understand why he cared, or why he seemed so annoyed. "I worked at a convenience store in high school. Stocking shelves, checking people out. After college, I got the job at HCI."

"A convenience store?" His gaze fell to the menu, but he didn't seem to be reading it. When he looked up again, he said, "Was it dangerous? Sometimes, those places get ripped off."

"This is Coventry. There's more danger from moose on the loose than crime."

"Was there a safe where they kept the cash?"

"Um... yeah. Why?"

"Did you have the combination?"

"Why would I need—?"

"I don't know. Just curious, I guess. I mean, were you in charge, trusted with the keys, or—"

"I was sixteen. I wasn't a manager. They trusted me with the register. I put the big bills in the little slot on the safe."

He returned his attention to his menu. A few moments passed before he set it down with a little smack. "Tell me the truth. Do you like your job?"

"It's okay."

"Do you like it?"

"It's a job." What did he want from her? What difference did it make? "It pays well. My best friend owns the company, and—"

"Do you like it, Tabby? When you wake up on Monday morning, do you feel eager for the week ahead?"

Eager? She hadn't felt eager about her job in years.

"You hate it," he said.

"I didn't say that."

"I can read it in your expression. You can go in on Saturday, clean up your office, make it the kind of space you enjoy, but that's not going to change the fact that you hate your job."

His volume rose at the end of his little diatribe, and she leaned forward. "Keep your voice down. A lot of the people in this place work there."

He picked up the menu again.

"What do you want from me?"

His gaze flicked to hers over the menu but didn't hold. "I thought we couldn't be together because you didn't want to leave your job. Obviously, there's more to it than that."

"I told you I couldn't leave Coventry. I never said it was because of my job."

"I assumed. My fault. But..." The menu hit the table again. "If it's not the job, what's keeping you here? You told me you have no boyfriend, no husband you hide in the attic."

"This is my home."

"I have a home too." He folded his hands on the table slowly. "I have a house and a history and a life in Providence. But if not for Shelby, I'd risk all of that to see if—"

"Hello, my friend."

The interruption couldn't have come at a worse time. Or maybe the timing was perfect. Maybe the last thing Tabby needed was to hear more about what she could never have.

Chelsea and Dylan stopped beside their table, and Tabby stood and hugged Chelsea, then greeted Dylan. "Thanks for bringing that box by yesterday." She shifted back to Chelsea. "How are you two?"

"Quite wonderful, which is irrelevant," Chelsea said, her English accent only mildly tempered eight months after moving home from Europe. "How was your vacation? Did you love Belize?"

"It was everything you promised." She gestured to Fitz, who'd stood when they approached. "This is Fitzgerald McCaffrey. We met down there. Fitz, this is Chelsea Hamilton."

"O'Donnell," Chelsea corrected as she shook his hand.

"Right." Tabby offered an apologetic smile. "Still getting used to that."

Dylan introduced himself, and Fitz shook his hand.

"Are you from New Hampshire then?" Chelsea asked Fitz.

"Rhode Island. Just came up to see Tabby."

Tabby laughed that off, though it hardly sounded natural. "Not really. He's a nature photographer and, as he pointed out, there's nature here."

"That was just an excuse." He gave her a serious look. "I came for you."

She didn't know what to do with that.

Always the polite one, Chelsea covered Tabby's complete lack of response. "How lovely. Our Tabby is certainly worth the drive."

"I agree completely."

Dylan was studying Fitz with narrowed eyes. "How far is it?"

"Couple of hours," he said. "Not bad if you miss the traffic."

Dylan started to say something else, but Chelsea interjected. "We're practically neighbors." She squeezed Tabby's hand but spoke to Fitz. "It was a pleasure to meet you. I hope we see you again. Enjoy your lunch." She followed Dylan to a table on the far side of the restaurant.

Fitz waited until Tabby slid back into the booth before he did the same. "Practically neighbors," he echoed.

"To Chelsea, sure. The woman owns a private jet." Well, HCI owned it. But Chelsea owned most of HCI, so it was the same thing.

The server approached, a twentysomething girl with silvery-blond hair and a nose ring. "Have you decided what you want?"

"I'm going to have the soup and salad." She ignored Fitz when he cleared his throat. "Baked potato for the soup, house dressing on the side."

"You got it." The server turned to Fitz, her eyes going from dull to bright in an instant.

Nobody was immune to Fitz's good looks, or charm.

"And you?"

"Bacon burger with fries." When the server took their menus and left, he said to Tabby, "I'm eating light, hoping you'll have dinner with me."

"Light? You've obviously never eaten here."

"I was going to lecture you about the diet thing, but I guess baked potato soup isn't exactly low-cal."

"I'll start the diet tomorrow."

"Is that how you live your life, Tabby? Figuring you'll start everything tomorrow? Start the diet tomorrow. Start a job you love tomorrow. Start dating tomorrow? Because I agree on the diet—you can put that off forever. But the rest of it—"

"Can't we just enjoy each other's company? Why does it have to be more than this?"

"Because it is." His Adam's apple bobbed. He said nothing for several minutes, eyes taking in the crowded restaurant.

She wanted to cut the tension between them, but she didn't know how.

Finally, he turned his gaze back to her. "That's it, though. Maybe it's just *more* for me. It's not for you. It's that simple."

She should agree, tell him she didn't feel what he felt. It would be the kind thing to do. But it would be a lie.

She did care for him, more than she wanted to. She'd thought of him every waking hour since she'd met him. And dreamed of him every night.

Maybe, if he hadn't come, it would have been easier to break things off. Maybe, if he hadn't come, she'd already be forgetting about him.

But deep down, she knew it wasn't true. Meeting Fitz had changed everything in her heart.

Unfortunately, it had changed nothing about her life.

He watched her, seemed to read her mind. "What is it that keeps you here, Tabby? Tell me the truth."

"It's nothing."

He crossed his arms and waited.

"I mean, it's nothing nefarious or secret or even interesting. It's just my family."

"What about them?"

"I can't leave them."

His head tilted to the side. "Your brother?"

"Chris needs to get out of my parents' house, but he can't do it by himself. When he agrees, I'm going to put my house on the market and buy a one-story so he can move in. I never should have bought that house in the first place."

She flashed back to her conversation with Chris on Sunday. *I will never move in with you. Never.* He'd said something to that effect more than once. It was the words that followed that resonated now. *If I did that, you'd never get your own life.*

But she had her own life. And this was how she was choosing to live it.

"Let me understand this," Fitz said. "You're working at a job you hate and giving up on"—he gestured between them—"whatever this could be to take care of your brother?"

"Paraplegic brother," she clarified.

"Grown-man brother. He's not mentally challenged. He's

not emotionally unstable. He's in a wheelchair, not on life support. Do you really think he can't survive without you?"

"He won't thrive living in my parents' house."

"So you're choosing not to thrive because he refuses to? Does he want to live with you?"

"I haven't talked him into it yet, but—"

"That's ridiculous. And insulting."

She reached toward Fitz. "I don't mean to hurt your—"

"Not to me. To him. You were just telling me yesterday that your parents coddle him. How is what you're doing any different?"

She sat back. "I'm trying to help him."

"I think—"

He cut off his words when the server returned with their meals. She set them down, asked if they needed anything else, and left.

As if there'd been no interruption, Fitz continued. "What Chris needs is fewer people trying to help him and more people believing he doesn't need their help."

"You met him for an hour. You don't know anything about it."

Fitz glared at her, then turned his attention to his meal. He dolloped ketchup onto his plate, salted his fries, and popped one in his mouth. When he'd chewed and swallowed, he said, "I know a guy who came home from Iraq without his legs. He's an expert at cyber security. He's brilliant and completely capable of taking care of himself."

"That's my point exactly. Chris can too. But he's got to get out of—"

"Your parents' house—and move into yours. So you can take care of him. Will a one-story house be more expensive?"

"What? No. I mean, it'll cost money to have it fitted for his chair, but it shouldn't be a problem."

"So money has nothing to do with it?"

"How would it?"

He shook his head, said nothing.

Fitz didn't understand, and what did it matter? It wouldn't change anything. She dribbled dressing on her salad and cut it into bite-sized pieces.

"That's it?" he pressed. "You and I can't date because of your brother?"

"Maybe you'll be less mad at me if you eat."

He took a giant bite of his burger and set it down.

She ate some salad while she considered how to answer his question.

When he swallowed, he said, "There. Now I'm not mad. Is there more to it than your brother?"

Why not just tell the rest of it? There was nothing to lose. Except Fitz. And that was the goal. Right?

"My mother." She breathed out the words, then hurried on. "My dad's strong, but ever since Chris's accident, Mom's been... nervous." That was one way to put it. Other ways Tabby'd put it over the years? High-maintenance. Needy. Unstable. When Tabby was in high school, she'd come home from work one day to find her mother on the floor in the kitchen, clutching her chest and gasping for breath. Tabby'd called an ambulance, fearing a heart attack.

It hadn't been a heart attack but an anxiety attack that landed Mom in the hospital for a few days. She'd come home with medication and an appointment to see a counselor. Since then, the anxiety had been managed, but Tabby would never forget the sight of her mother's ashen face, the terror in her eyes.

Rich and Russ had moved away, and Tabby always wondered if they'd been escaping Mom's overbearing attitude. Chris was a source of worry for Mom, not peace. Tabby was the only one of her kids who was present and supportive. "She can't handle it when I'm gone. She probably prayed every second I was in Belize. That trip was the most selfish thing I've done in years."

"If you thought so, then why'd you do it?"

"I just... I needed to get away. I needed—"

"To live your own life?"

"For a little while."

"But not forever."

She shrugged, and he sighed. "That's it. You can't leave your family because of your needy brother and your greedy mother."

Tabby narrowed her eyes. She might not always like the way her mother hovered, but she wouldn't allow Fitz to insult her like that. "She's not—"

"If she'd rather you be miserable in Coventry than find happiness elsewhere, then she is."

"She only wants what's best for me." Tabby realized the second the words were out of her mouth that she was parroting her mother's excuse, the words she hurled whenever she demanded her own way.

She didn't want to think of her mother as selfish, but what Fitz said made sense.

Maybe Tabby was a fool to stay in Coventry, stay at a job she hated to take care of a brother who didn't want her help and a mother who thought she deserved it.

"Did you tell her about me?" Fitz asked.

"I didn't want to upset her." Tabby ate her soup but barely tasted it. Was Fitz right? Was she wasting her life trying to make sure everybody else was okay?

Was it selfish to want something more?

Fitz wasn't eating, just watching her. "Your mother wouldn't like me?"

"She'd like you. But the fact that you're not from here..." Mom had been nagging Tabby to *find a nice young man and settle down* for years. But she meant a local man, and Tabby'd already met all the eligible bachelors in Coventry. If she told Mom she'd met a man from Providence...

"Maybe she'd surprise you," Fitz said.

Tabby shrugged. Maybe she would.

Maybe the news that Tabby had started to fall for a guy who lived hours away would give her mother another anxiety attack, landing her back in the hospital.

Tabby didn't know, and she was afraid to find out.

Sitting across from this man who saw right through her, who dug into her life and soul and being and didn't make her want to clam up and send him away... this man who looked at her as if she mattered, as if she were valuable and delightful... Suddenly, she knew the truth. She cared for him. A lot. Meeting Fitz had opened her eyes to the reality of her own existence. She'd created a life to ensure everyone's happiness but her own.

And now, for the first time in... she didn't know how long. Maybe since her mother's nervous breakdown. Maybe since Chris's accident. For the first time, her happiness mattered to her.

And the thought of it scared her to death.

CHAPTER FOURTEEN

Fitz left Tabby in the lobby of her office building without even a kiss on the cheek. God forbid anybody think they were together. Though they'd salvaged the lunch, finally settling into safe conversations, the pall that had descended when he'd first accused her of hating her job had never lifted. Nor had they come to any solutions.

Not that they'd needed to, he reminded himself. He wasn't there to win her heart. He was there to find a half a million in stolen goods. And he was becoming increasingly convinced Tabby didn't have it.

He was sitting in a coffee shop on the outskirts of town a couple of hours later when his phone rang.

"It's me," Abe said, as if his James Earl Jones voice wouldn't give him away. "What are you working on?"

Fitz gave the shop a cursory glance. Four middle-aged women sat at a table not far from him, deep in conversation. At another table, a guy was pecking away at a laptop, earphone cords hanging from his ears. Other than them and the workers behind the counter, the place was empty. "Mullins sent me the names of everybody registered at the hotel last week. I'm combing through it."

"Anything stand out to you?"

"Nothing, and anyway, if I were going to steal a half a million from a mobster and frame someone else, I wouldn't be stupid enough to stay at the same hotel."

"A dead end then."

Fitz peered at the too-long list of irrelevant names. "Looks like it. He's still trying to find out when Tabby made her hotel reservations, but I know she paid for the flight a year ago. Truth is, I think she's innocent. I mean, what are the chances an expert safecracker would be staying in the same hotel as Mullins right when someone decided to rip him off."

"Maybe it was coincidence," Abe suggested. "Maybe she'd always planned to rip off the hotel the night before she left, regardless of who was staying there. People store all sorts of things in hotel safes. Expensive jewelry, gambling winnings, weapons."

"So maybe she just got lucky?"

"If you consider it lucky to slap a target on your back when the hunter is a merciless killer, then yeah, she got lucky."

Abe made a valid point.

"Until we know differently," Fitz said, "we need to assume the thief was after Mullins's stuff. Did you learn something?"

"What do you know about the family?"

Fitz had done that research the previous day. "Ronnie Mullins has been married to Lena for more than thirty years. He's got four kids. Two grown boys. The oldest is a lawyer specializing in family law. The second is a banker. The daughter is a social worker. The oldest two are married and have kids of their own. And then there's Shawn, the hormone-crazed teenager who thinks he's in love with Shelby."

"That's what my research turned up, too."

"But?"

"Remember back, oh, ten years ago now, there were rumors Mullins was trying to get out of the business."

"Obviously, the rumors weren't true."

"Or he just didn't succeed. It's not that easy to walk away from the mob."

"So?"

"Don't you think it's odd none of his kids went into the family business?"

Huh. Fitz hadn't thought about that. That insight... that was why he'd stomped on his pride and brought Abe in.

"It's one of the reasons we were convinced he was trying to extract himself," Abe said. "We all thought the oldest kid, Jonathan, would either become a defense attorney or would try to get on with the DA—somewhere he could help out his old man. But when the DA's office invited him in for an interview, he declined. Rumor has it Mullins told his son that he'd cut him and his family out entirely if he even sneezed on a case that had mob connections. We don't know what conversations took place in that house, but I can tell you that Jonathan started applying elsewhere. He handles divorces, custody battles, and adoptions."

"Nothing mob-related at all."

"And the second kid, Blake, is the same way. He's a loan officer at a bank and, from what we can tell, does nothing that involves organized crime."

"The daughter, too?"

"Helen. By the time she graduated, she knew the score. She's a counselor for underprivileged kids in Hartford."

Fitz made notes about everything Abe said. When he was done, he looked at what he'd written. "How does this help?"

"Not sure it does. It's just odd."

"I don't have time to dig into Mullins's psyche, Abe."

"I know, I know. Just telling you what I learned. I'm getting information on his financials from a guy at the Bureau."

"At the Bureau. After everything, how did that—?"

"You don't have time for that story, either. Can you meet me tomorrow?"

"How about we do this? How about you send me what you know, and I'll promise to meet with you when I'm back in Providence."

"In person. Or nothing."

Fitz didn't respond, and Abe didn't back down.

"You'd really risk Shelby's life for the sake of a conversation?" Fitz asked.

"You'd really risk Shelby's life for the sake of your pride?"

"It's not pride, it's *time*."

"Nevertheless."

Fitz blew out a long breath. "Just keep digging. We'll figure something out."

At five fifteen, Fitz returned to his hotel. He'd worried Tabby would turn down his dinner invitation after their awkward lunch, but she hadn't. That told him a lot.

It told him she wanted to be with him, even if their conversations were hard. Even if they didn't always agree. The easy, comfortable relationship they'd enjoyed in Belize was gone, but the attraction between them was not.

The connection was not.

In his room, he dumped his laptop bag on the bed, took off his sweater, and ran the water in the sink. After a quick shower and shave, he went to the closet. When he'd first arrived in New Hampshire, he'd gone to a department store off the interstate and bought himself some warm clothes—paid for with Mullins's money—since the shorts and T's he'd taken to Belize wouldn't do in the cold climate. Now, he dug through the sack in search of something appropriate for admitting to a woman that he'd been digging into her past and spying on her in hopes of discovering deep, dark secrets.

Tonight, he'd tell her the truth. He'd tell her everything. If she was the woman he thought she was, and if on the off chance she'd had anything to do with the burglary, she'd fess up. She wouldn't put Shelby in danger for the sake of money.

If she didn't, then she wasn't the woman he thought she was.

He grabbed a pair of dark jeans and yanked off the tags, then pulled on a light blue V-neck sweater.

He snatched a pair of socks from his suitcase and froze.

Something wasn't right.

His suitcase had two zipper pockets. He always kept his clean socks and underwear in one, his dirty things in the other. But the socks he'd chosen from the clean pocket were dirty.

Theoretically, he could have put them in the wrong pocket, except he'd worn these socks on the plane, days before. They should have been at the bottom of the other pocket.

That they weren't told him...

Somebody had been there.

Somebody had searched his hotel room.

Which meant...

He grabbed his cell and dialed Tabby. While the phone rang, he yanked on clean socks and shoved his feet into shoes. Then checked his handgun and slid it in his holster.

Tabby didn't answer.

CHAPTER FIFTEEN

Tabby had just stepped out of the shower when the doorbell rang, followed instantly by the sound of pounding.

What in the world?

She dried quickly and slipped on her bathrobe, growing more irritated by the second as the doorbell and pounding continued. She was shoving her feet into slippers when she heard a shout.

"Tabby? Are you in there?"

Fitz sounded terrified. He'd acted so strangely at lunch, and now this. What was wrong with him? Where was the easygoing man she'd met in Belize?

She hurried down the stairs and yanked open the door, but the porch was empty. She was about to call out for him when he rounded the house from the side. "What are you doing?"

He didn't answer, just took her porch steps two at a time and stepped in. "Thank God. Thank God. Are you alone?"

"Um—"

"Are you alone? Is anybody...?" He blinked at her appearance. "You were in the shower?"

"What's going on?"

He took her hand and stalked through the dining room, where he checked the windows. One was unlocked. How had that—?

He pulled her behind him into the kitchen, checking every door and window along the way.

"Fitz, what are you—?"

"I'll explain. Just..." His words trailed as he yanked her through the living room and toward the stairs, tugging her up behind him.

Her racing heart told her there was something seriously wrong. As much as she liked the Fitz she'd met in Belize, the Fitz she'd had lunch with that day was somebody different. He was suspicious and demanding and angry. Whichever Fitz had shown up tonight, she wasn't going upstairs with him. She grabbed the handrail. "You need to stop."

He turned to face her, his eyes filled with... fear?

"What's going on?"

His Adam's apple bobbed. "I need to search your house for intruders."

"Why?"

"I'll explain. I promise. I'd rather you stay with me because I'm worried for your safety. You could wait outside, but... No. It might not be safe out there. But if you'd prefer to wait here—"

"Should I call the police?"

His gaze flicked up the stairs, back to her. "I'd rather you didn't."

"Why?"

"I promise I'll explain. Just let me..." He dropped her hand and ran up the stairs.

As he peeked around, she bristled at the invasion of her privacy. How dare he? He seemed utterly unconcerned when he ran back down, passed her, and rounded the corner at the bottom. She followed into the short hallway between the kitchen and living room and watched as he disappeared through the door that led to the basement.

It was the only door he hadn't opened on his initial search of her downstairs. Had he known it led to the basement?

How?

Fear coursed through her. Fear of what, she didn't know.

Of him?

Something else?

A moment later, he came upstairs. Before she could process what was happening, he pulled her into his arms and held her against his chest. "Thank God you're safe."

She gripped his jacket. "What is happening?"

"I promise, I'll explain everything. I just..."

He looked down at her, and the dark fear that had pulsed between them turned to something different.

He dropped his arms. But he didn't back up.

She stared into his eyes, trying to discern what she saw. The fear was still there, but lurking behind it, desire.

His hands slid along her jaw, into her hair.

Her skin tingled to her toes.

Despite his crazy behavior, despite her own worries moments before, everything in her wanted to step closer, to lose herself in him. She stepped back, but he matched the movement. She needed distance, needed to think. She stepped back again, her foot nudging the wall behind her.

He was right there, his hands sliding from her scalp to her neck. Their warmth ignited her own, and her skin blazed hot. A tiny part of her knew she should push him away, not allow this intimacy, but she couldn't make her mouth work.

He leaned closer, so close she could feel his breath against her skin. She expected to feel his lips any moment. But instead, he spoke. "There's so much I need to tell you."

The words were unexpected. She couldn't process them.

He backed up the tiniest fraction, met her eyes. "Do you want me to stop?"

Not at all. But she was confused, afraid after his frantic search. She opened her mouth to say... something.

His gaze flicked to her lips. His hands slid off her shoulders and onto the wall behind her. His breath tingled through her hair. "Just say the word."

But she remained silent.

His lips brushed the skin beneath her ear, trailed across her cheek.

He backed away, stared into her eyes. Waited.

Though she knew this would change everything, she felt unable to move, her body blazing with need.

And then he kissed her.

She opened herself to him, and her world exploded, expanded, and transformed into something she'd never known.

When his arms came around her, when her hands reached behind his neck, when her back arched to take her closer to him, she knew she'd never be the same.

Everything she'd thought she was, everything she'd thought she needed to do... It all fell away in his arms.

For one short moment, the world was perfect.

Something pounded, pulling her out of the ecstasy.

Fitz stepped back, but his blazing eyes held hers. "Are you expecting someone?"

It had been a knock? On the door?

The bell rang, confirming what Fitz had already known.

She tried to speak, failed. Shook her head.

His eyes narrowed, flicked downward.

She was still wearing the robe. The belt had loosened. She straightened it, cinched it tighter.

"Open up. Police."

Fitz's eyes rounded. "Did you call them?"

"No." What in the world? She rushed around the corner into the living room toward the door. Maybe, whatever had brought Fitz here in such a panic had brought the cops too.

She flung open the door, and a uniformed police officer stepped inside. "Ma'am, we got a report of a prowler—"

"That's him!" Mrs. Pollack stood in the snow-covered yard, her arm outstretched and pointing at Tabby.

Her neighbor had lost her mind.

Except the police officer pushed past Tabby and into her house. "Sir, turn around and place your hands on the wall."

What was happening? She spun to find Fitz standing with his hands up. "I can explain." But he wasn't looking at the cop, he was looking at her.

She took a step toward him, unable to make sense of the turn of events.

"I was going to tell you everything," he said. "Tonight. I swear."

She touched her lips. She couldn't seem to make them do anything, say anything.

The cop grabbed Fitz's shoulder, spun him, pushed him against the wall, handcuffed him.

"Wait." She forced the word out, added, "What's happening?"

Another police officer said, "Your neighbor saw this man prowling around your house yesterday."

"Not prowling," Mrs. Pollack said from the porch. "Crawling out her window. Saw him about to go in again tonight, but she opened the door. He's a stalker, is what he is."

The police officer pulled Fitz off the wall and propelled him toward the front door, reciting Miranda rights along the way.

Fitz's gaze connected with hers. "You're in danger, Tabby. Don't stay here."

What was he talking about?

Mrs. Pollack stepped to the side as Fitz and the cop made their way onto the porch.

Fitz craned his neck to keep Tabby in his sight. "Go to Chelsea's and stay there. I swear, I'll explain everything."

Down the steps, across the walkway. The cop opened the back door of his cruiser. He was pushing Fitz in when Fitz yelled, "To Chelsea's. Trust me. Please."

Trust him. Trust him?

She didn't even know him.

Was Fitz a stalker?

She couldn't make sense of it, but Mrs. Pollack had said... And Fitz hadn't denied it.

And the dining room window had been unlocked.

"Ma'am?" Someone touched her shoulder, and she jumped.

When had she stepped onto the porch? She crossed her arms, tried to warm herself in the frigid air.

A police officer wrapped a blanket around her shoulders. It was a throw off her sofa. "Can you step inside? We need to ask you some questions."

When her gaze slid back to the cruiser, the cop added, "Don't worry. We won't let him go. You're safe now."

CHAPTER SIXTEEN

Fitz had paced the concrete floor of the jail cell for hours. Now, he sat on the thin mattress and dropped his head into his hands.

He'd screwed everything up.

He should have called the police the minute he'd walked out of Mullins's hotel room on Saturday morning. He should've called Abe back then and told him everything.

He should have been honest with Tabby from the very start.

He definitely should *not* have kissed her.

He could still taste her on his lips.

If there'd been any doubt of the chemistry between them, the kiss had wiped it away. He'd never wanted another woman the way he'd wanted her in that moment. But what he felt for Tabby was more than desire. It was more than affection. He wanted to hold her, to protect her, to care for her. He wanted her, all of her. Not like the girlfriends he'd had in the past, women who'd shared his bed but never his heart.

Tabby had burrowed deep into him, and no matter what happened now, he'd never be able to pull her back out.

But she hated him. He'd seen the disgust in her eyes as she'd watched him being handcuffed, hauled out of her house, and shoved into the police car.

It was no less than he deserved.

But Tabby had asked for none of this. Had she heeded his advice and gone to Chelsea's? He lifted a prayer for her safety, hating himself all the more for not being with her to protect her.

He couldn't protect anybody.

Thoughts of Shelby intruded. He didn't want to think about his sister right now, but he couldn't push her image away. Shelby, sailing with the family of the man who'd kill her when Fitz didn't comply with his demands. Shelby, who'd already survived enough tragedy for a lifetime. Their parents' deaths when she was only eight had been bad enough, but then she'd been stuck with a clueless twenty-one-year-old kid who hadn't the slightest idea how to raise a child, much less a girl.

A girl whose world had fallen apart.

After their parents' deaths, she'd slept on a blow-up mattress on the floor of his room for weeks. Even months later, when she'd finally gotten the courage to sleep in her own bed, she woke more than once from a nightmare and screamed for him. He'd lie down beside her and run his fingers along her long hair like Mom used to do until she fell back asleep.

They'd grieved together. In many ways, they'd grown up together. He was the closest thing to a father Shelby had now.

He could still remember the day his parents asked him if he'd be Shelby's guardian if anything happened to them.

"We know you'll take good care of her," Dad had said.

"There's nobody we'd trust more," Mom had added.

He'd agreed without a second thought. Stupid, arrogant idiot that he'd been. Twenty years old with no understanding of how cruel the world could be.

It had never occurred to him that, less than a year later, he'd have to make good on that promise.

A deer. A stupid deer had run into the road. The oncoming truck swerved to miss it but failed. The man had lost control, and his truck careened into Mom and Dad's lane.

He missed them so badly. Missed their confident guidance, their support, their love. Missed the home they'd created, the lighthearted and secure world he'd grown up in. They'd been the very best parents in the world.

He and Shelby had inherited the house. They'd received the life insurance. They had everything they needed. But money didn't make a home.

Poor Shelby had lost the foundation of her life at only eight years old. She was stuck with Fitz.

Fitz, who had tried to do everything right to make her feel secure and had somehow ended up blowing it. He'd made detective and then been forced to resign under a cloud of suspicion.

Because his partner had decided to dive into bed with the mob.

Mullins would never have asked this of Fitz if not for that resignation. So maybe all of this was Abe's fault.

Maybe that was why Fitz had disregarded Abe's suggestions. If he'd told Tabby the truth from the very start, he wouldn't be in jail, praying somebody else would protect the ones he loved.

CHAPTER SEVENTEEN

Fitz had no idea how much time had passed when he heard the heavy door at the end of the corridor open and slam shut.

A moment later, a uniformed police officer unlocked his cell. "I don't know how you did it. Let's go."

Fitz stood. "Did what? What happened?"

The man said nothing, just stood back and nodded toward the exit.

Fitz hurried out of the cell as if the guy might change his mind. He was taken to a small room, where his things were returned to him. He shoved his wallet, cell phone, and keys in his pocket. He clicked on his watch, then bent to slide his pocketknife into his socks.

Let the cop think what he wanted. There was no law against being paranoid.

The officer said, "You're free to go."

"What happened?"

He shrugged. "My guess? Your girlfriend's too stupid for her own good."

His ire rose, but he said nothing as he turned away. An electronic lock sounded, and the first cop pushed open the door.

Just like that, Fitz was free. He'd figured he'd be bailed out in the morning, but his watch told him it was just after three a.m. He stepped into the dark and frigid air, trying to figure out what to do next. A movement caught his eye.

Leaning against an eighties-model Lincoln Continental roughly the length of a basketball court, Abe waved him over. Six four, skin as dark as the night surrounding him, ugly black glasses, he hadn't changed a bit.

Beside him, Dylan O'Donnell crossed his arms and glared.

Fitz jogged their way and held out his hand as he reached Abe. He'd spent a lot of energy over the previous two years hating this man. Now he had to stop himself from embracing him. "You're here."

"Always bailing you out of trouble." But Abe's voice held humor as he shook Fitz's hand with his gloved one. "Brought Dylan along with me."

"You've got some explaining to do," the man said.

Fitz turned to him. "Is Tabby safe?"

"She's at our house. We've got excellent security."

Fitz held out his hand to Dylan. After a moment, Dylan shook it.

"Did you have something to do with this?" Fitz tipped his head toward the police station.

"Abe explained just enough that we think it's possible you're not a total creep. Tabby agreed to drop the charges, and my wife called the chief. She holds sway in this town."

"Thank her for me."

"Thank her yourself." He pushed himself off the car and yanked open the passenger door. "We're going there now."

To Chelsea and Dylan's, where Tabby was. Maybe he'd get the opportunity to explain.

Fitz slid into the backseat, thankful Abe had left the car

running. Just those few moments in the elements and he was freezing. Dylan took the front seat, and Abe pulled out of the lot.

"You still have this old boat," Fitz said.

"Your powers of observation always impressed me."

"How do you keep it running?"

Abe patted the dashboard affectionately. "She runs on love."

"And fuel. Lots of fuel," Fitz said. "Must've cost you a fortune to drive up here."

"Less than the bail I figured I'd end up shelling out."

It would have been peanuts compared with what Abe owed him, but it seemed petty to say so, all things considered.

He'd expected Dylan to pepper him with questions on the way back to the house, but the man was silent. And, though Fitz wanted to ask how Tabby was doing, the tension in the car grew too thick to speak.

They wound their way up dark mountain roads with hardly anything but trees surrounding them for a good fifteen minutes before Abe turned onto a driveway all but hidden by thick forest. The woods gave way to a giant structure. Fitz would have guessed it was a hotel, but no sign graced the building or the lawn, and Dylan had said they were going to his house.

Oddly, there were no windows on the front, just a single door and a lot of lights.

"Dainty little place you have here."

"Chelsea's house." After a pause, he said, "Our house. I'm still getting used to it."

Right. They'd only recently married. Must've been strange to marry the richest woman in town, probably one of the richest women in the state. An heiress, no less, though Chelsea had seemed down-to-earth and kind when they'd met at the restaurant.

They climbed from the car. Dylan led the way to an oversize door lit by a floodlight and yanked it open, and they stepped into a short hallway that led to a great room like nothing Fitz had ever seen. Not in person, anyway. A kitchen on the right with an island bigger than his car. A table on the left large enough to seat ten. Beyond those, an oversize formal living room. The back wall was all glass.

He turned to Dylan. "I thought you said this place was secure. That glass—"

"It's bulletproof and privacy-controlled. Nobody can see inside."

Was that even a thing? "You're sure?"

The man's smirk told him he didn't appreciate the question. He turned his back on Fitz and led the way to the living room, pointing to a sofa. "Sit. Stay here."

Fitz barely held in a sarcastic bark as the man disappeared down a hallway.

Abe settled onto a leather chair and nodded at the sofa. "You'd better do what he says, seeing as how he's the only reason you're out of jail."

Fitz fell onto the sofa. He'd used his one phone call to reach Abe. "What happened?"

"I called him like you asked me to, told him Tabby was in danger and asked him to make sure she was safe. He insisted I tell him what was going on, so—"

"He knows? Tabby knows?" The thought of her finding out about Mullins's threats like that made his stomach swoop.

"I told him you'd tell them in person," Abe said. "Figured that'd get you out of jail faster."

"Thank you."

Abe nodded but said nothing else.

"You didn't have to come."

"Did if I want to have that conversation you promised me. Because we both know you'd have wiggled out of it somehow."

Fitz wasn't going to deny it. He watched the hallway. Where was Tabby? Would she come out tonight? Did she want to see him?

Could she ever forgive him?

And would it matter? If he didn't get his sister back, safe and sound, nothing would matter.

Nothing.

"Did you come up with any more information for me?"

Abe nodded.

Fitz pushed to his feet. "I can't just sit—"

Movement silenced his words. Dylan and Chelsea emerged from the hallway.

Tabby walked behind them. She wore baggy jeans and a sweatshirt. Her curly hair was pulled into a bun on the top of her head. No makeup, and her eyes were red.

The sight of her brought a visceral reaction. His body remembered their kiss. His mind remembered the hatred in her gaze. He clenched his fists and resisted the desire to rush to her.

She nodded at him as she slid into the chair beside Abe's. Obviously, they'd met already.

Abe said, "How you doing?"

She shrugged, not looking Fitz's way.

Chelsea sat on the sofa opposite him.

Dylan perched on the arm. "Start talking."

Fitz swallowed, gazed at Tabby. "Would you look at me please?"

She did, and the hurt, the betrayal in her eyes was a punch to the gut.

"I was going to tell you everything tonight. I told you. Remember? Right before—"

"I remember." Her voice was strong, but the emotionless tone took him off guard.

He glanced at the others in the room before focusing on Tabby alone. "I'd prefer to have this conversation in private."

"Not a chance." Dylan crossed his arms.

"Why don't you let the lady make her own decisions?" This from Abe, an unlikely defender.

"Just"—Tabby looked Fitz's way—"explain. I'd tell them anyway."

Fitz crossed the space and sat on the coffee table across from her. He'd have to pretend the rest weren't there.

Dylan took a few steps toward him, but Tabby waved him off. "It's fine." She met Fitz's eyes. "Please, just..."

"The day you left Belize, I was summoned to a hotel room by a man with ties to organized crime. The hotel's safe had been burgled the night before, a number of valuable items belonging to him stolen. He believed you did it."

Her hand hit her chest. "Me? Why would he think I did it?"

Fitz pulled his cell from his pocket. The room was silent while he found the video. He got it started and handed the phone to Tabby.

As she watched, her face morphed from interest to confusion to horror. Her free hand covered her mouth. Behind it, she said, "Oh my gosh. How in the world...?" And then a moment later, "Who could've...?"

Fitz took the phone back and paused the video. "It goes on to show you cracking the safe, taking a box out, and then leaving."

She looked genuinely shocked.

Dylan crossed the space and held out his hand. "May I?"

Fitz handed the phone to him. Dylan and Chelsea watched it, but Fitz kept his focus on Tabby.

A minute into the video, Chelsea said, "It's not Tabby."

"Of course not." Dylan looked up from the video long enough to glare at Fitz. "Obviously it's not her."

Fitz turned back to Tabby.

She finally met his eyes. "I would never... I wouldn't even know how to do something like that."

"I believe you."

She studied him through squinted eyes. "No, you don't." She angled away from him. "You *don't* believe me. That's why you're here. You're this guy's... what? What do you call it? Like his muscle?" The pitch of her voice rose, along with the volume. "You work for him, this mobster?"

"It's not like that."

She leaned away. "That's what all this was about. You're trying to find this guy's stolen"—she gestured to the phone—"box or whatever. That's why you're here. That's why you... you kissed me. You lying, conniving—"

"He kidnapped Shelby."

Her mouth snapped shut.

"I have until Saturday to return the stolen goods to him or he's going to kill her. I didn't believe you did it, but I had to know for sure."

"So you broke into my house? That's what Mrs. Pollack said. She saw you climbing out my window."

He sat up straight, prepared for the blow that was surely to come. "Yes."

"You've been trying to get information out of me."

"Yes."

"None of it was real."

He leaned toward her again, but she angled away. "Tonight was real, Tabby. When I kissed you—"

"Don't."

A strong grip settled around his upper arm. "You need to back off."

He glared at Dylan, but the man was right. Tabby obviously didn't want him anywhere near her.

He stood, shook off the man's hand, and returned to his place on the sofa on the far side of the room.

Tabby visibly relaxed at the extra space between them. He'd known he'd blown it with her. But he'd hoped, once she knew the truth, she'd understand.

The look on her face told him he'd hoped in vain.

Dylan handed Fitz his phone and perched beside Chelsea again. "Tell us what happened tonight. Tabby said you thought she was in danger."

"Mullins told me he was going to send one of his goons up here later today to get the information out of her if I couldn't do it. I was going to tell her everything at dinner, find a place for her to hole up until this mess got straightened out. I thought I had time, but when I went back to my hotel, I realized somebody had searched it. Mullins must've decided to send his guy sooner." He focused again on Tabby. "The thought of you in that guy's hands... I swear, Tabby, I was trying to protect you."

She said nothing.

"You know this person he was going to send?" Dylan asked.

"Not really. He was in Belize. Hair and dress like Willie Nelson, body of a gym rat. Name's Wilson..."

He tried to remember.

Abe said, "Wilson Dunbar. I got a friend in the FBI who confirmed he landed in Manchester yesterday."

Fitz eyed the older man. How did Abe still have friends in law enforcement after what happened? He must've convinced them Fitz had been the one conspiring with the mob two years before. The thought rankled, but if it meant he'd have help getting Shelby back, he wouldn't complain.

Abe had more to offer. "Willie Dunbar is Mullins's right-hand man, been with him since grade school. He knows all the ins and outs of his business dealings, and he's no stranger to violence. My guess is that's why he's here—to get the stolen goods back from Tabby"—he held her gaze—"one way or another, if Fitz failed to get the job done."

Her eyes widened, flicked to Fitz. "Do you know this man? Why would he ask you—"

"Because he saw us together," Fitz said. "Mullins is Shawn's father. You probably saw him at the pool with the kids. You remember? Gray hair, big belly he seemed proud of?"

"I remember him and his wife. They were an odd pair."

"They knew us because of Shelby. He knew you and I were spending a lot of time together, and he figured I could get the information out of you."

Her head tilted to the side, her eyes squinted. "Why, though? Why did he think that? I mean, you're a photographer, right?"

Fitz could feel the eyes of the others in the room. There was nothing for it but to tell the truth. "I am a photographer of sorts. That's true. I've sold some photos to magazines, sold some online."

Her arms crossed. She knew what was coming. "But?"

"I'm also a private investigator. I was on a case, and when you're on a case, you don't exactly run around telling people what you do for a living." He turned to Dylan. "Right?"

Dylan glared at him a long moment before he shrugged. "There are times when it's wiser to keep your profession to yourself."

Way to hedge.

Fitz pressed. "Let's say you've been paid to watch someone who might be up to no good. Do you tell other people what you're doing? People who may, for all you know, be acquainted with the person you're being paid to watch?"

"Probably not," Dylan admitted.

"Do you tell strangers you're a private investigator when you're on a case?"

Before Dylan could answer, Tabby said, "You've made your point."

Fitz glared at Dylan another moment before sitting again and turning his attention to her.

"But we knew each other for two weeks," she said. "You could've told me later."

"Why would I have done that?"

She flipped her hand out as if the answer were obvious. "For the sake of honesty."

"You and I had two weeks together. You swore to me every single day that, no matter what, when those two weeks were over, so were we. Why would I have wasted one minute of our time together explaining my job to you? A job I hate with a holy passion? A job I'm embarrassed about." His gaze flicked to Dylan. "No offense intended." Though, maybe if Fitz were honest, a little had been.

Dylan's expression remained unchanged.

But Tabby's softened. "Why do you do it if you hate it so much?"

Who was she to ask him that, after their conversation the day before?

He dropped his head into his hands. He really didn't want to have this conversation right now, certainly not with an audience. He forced a deep breath and looked up, but before he could speak, Abe did.

"Fitz used to be a detective, youngest detective on the force, in fact. One of the best I ever worked with."

Tabby's jaw dropped. "You were a cop?"

"Yeah. But there was a"—his gaze flicked to Abe—"misunderstanding. A bust went sideways. A cop was murdered. Somebody had tipped the bad guys off."

Tabby started to say something, but Dylan interrupted. "Did you do it?"

Fitz kept his gaze on Tabby. "I was innocent. But Abe and I were the only suspects. They couldn't prove either of us had done it, thought maybe we'd been in on it together. We were both forced to resign."

Dylan watched Abe, then Fitz, seeming to wait for more explanation.

Neither said anything.

Tabby was rubbing her temples. "So you're saying this guy, Mullins, thinks you can find the stolen stuff because you used to be a detective and you know me."

"Pretty much."

"And he kidnapped Shelby to force you to do it."

"Yes."

She nodded slowly. After a minute, she said, "And I'm in danger from this...Willie Nelson lookalike."

"I think so, yes."

Dylan paced the length of the room. On the far side, he turned. "You should have told me immediately."

"I don't know you from Adam's second cousin," Fitz said. "Why would I have trusted you?"

"You needed to trust somebody. You didn't trust Tabby. You didn't trust the cops. You—"

"I couldn't bring the cops in. Mullins is part of the largest organized crime family on the east coast. He has ears everywhere. How could I trust them not to tip him off? I mean, after everything, would you have?"

Dylan glared. "Yes."

"Well, bully for you." He stood and took a few steps toward the irritating man. "After what happened, I don't trust anybody with my sister's life. Or Tabby's."

Dylan gestured to Abe, who seemed to be watching the exchange with amusement. "You trusted him."

Abe laughed. "He doesn't trust me. He thinks I'm dirty. He

just knows I care about Shelby."

Fitz didn't disagree.

The three men stared at each other.

Chelsea, who'd been silent until then, stood. "Well, then. Now that that's all cleared up, would anybody care for coffee?" Her tone was cool. She seemed completely unruffled. She met Fitz's eyes, Abe's, Tabby's. She smiled at her husband. "Or would you prefer to get some rest and resume this conversation in the morning? I have plenty of rooms for everyone."

Fitz smiled at the blonde. She was young, slender, attractive, and utterly confident. He could imagine her running a multi-million-dollar corporation. "I'll take coffee. I don't have time to sleep."

Abe stood as well. "You don't happen to have a Mountain Dew somewhere, do you?"

"You still drink that rot-gut?" Fitz asked.

"I've cut down to four a day."

Fitz shook his head. "That stuff'll kill you, man."

Abe chuckled, the deep tone bringing back good memories. "Good to know you care."

Tabby said nothing as she followed her friend around the island and into the kitchen. Dylan went that direction as well, leaving Abe and Fitz alone.

"I appreciate your help," Fitz said, voice low.

Abe nodded and walked away, down the hall and out the front door. He returned a moment later with an old-fashioned briefcase. He dropped it on the huge round table. "I got Mullins's financial information. Some of it looks interesting. Thought you might be able to help me dig through it."

Joining Abe, Fitz's gaze darted to the kitchen. Should they stay here? Did Tabby want him to leave?

"Dylan's already offered his help," Abe said.

Dylan glanced up at his name, gave one quick nod.

That didn't tell Fitz what Tabby wanted. But if she could stand Fitz's presence, he would stay at her side as long as she'd let him. He didn't trust anybody else to protect her.

Abe opened the case and lifted out a stack of papers that made Fitz want to groan. His least favorite part of police work.

CHAPTER EIGHTEEN

Tabby's mind was reeling as she searched Chelsea's pantry for Mountain Dew. Chelsea had assured her she had every kind of soda imaginable, but Tabby couldn't find it. What had Chelsea said? At the back, behind the... something.

Tabby couldn't see it. Couldn't see past the dark fear closing in.

A mobster thought she'd stolen from him.

She was in danger from a man she'd never met because somebody had framed her.

She'd seen the video. Even she'd thought the woman on the screen looked like her. Her curly brown hair. Her coloring. Her freckles. The woman even wore the same peach-colored top Tabby had worn that last evening in Belize.

Someone had gone to a lot of trouble to frame her for a terrible crime, and there was no way for her to prove her innocence. Maybe, if she went to court, she could convince a judge that she would be about as capable of breaking into a safe as she'd be capable of quantum physics. But this Mullins guy wasn't interested in justice. There'd be no police detectives digging into her story, no attorney on her side proving her defense, no thoughtful jury of her peers listening carefully to both sides. Mullins didn't care about any of that. He believed she was guilty, and he wanted his stuff back.

And he'd do anything to get it.

Kidnap Shelby.

Force Fitz to do his bidding.

Send a... a thug to get the information out of Tabby.

This Willie person... What would he do to her when he got his hands on her? Would he torture her?

Kill her?

She could feel him closing in. He was here. In Coventry. He'd been at Fitz's hotel. Had he been in her house? Had he searched it? Had he been watching her?

What if he was outside right at that very minute? Waiting for his opportunity? Was everybody in danger?

"Did you find it?" Chelsea's calm tone seemed to come from far away.

"Not yet." Tabby practically squeaked the words. She tried to focus on the boxes and cans of food all around her, but the sight seemed to blur.

A hand settled on her shoulder. "Are you all right?"

"How did this happen?" The words were still pitched too high.

"I wish I knew." Chelsea scooted past her, turned the corner at the end of the aisle, and came back with two cans of soda. "I'll put one in the refrigerator for Abe for later."

Tabby swallowed and tried to make her voice normal. "Abe seems like a nice guy."

"He has a trustworthy voice."

"So deep." He could do voice-overs. Abe's coal-black skin and bright white teeth, the thick glasses and easy smile—everything about him put Tabby at ease even as Fitz's presence set her on edge.

"He seems like a good man," Chelsea said. "Like Fitz."

"You think Fitz is trustworthy?"

Chelsea leaned against a shelf filled with canned vegetables. "He seems to be going to a lot of trouble to save his sister's life. I'm sure their parents are frantic."

"Their parents are dead. Fitz is Shelby's legal guardian. Has been since she was eight."

Chelsea's pretty brows rose on her forehead. It wasn't even dawn yet, Chelsea'd gotten no more sleep than Tabby, yet she looked clear-eyed and confident.

Based on what Tabby had seen in the mirror during her quick trip to the restroom, she was a train wreck. Eyes red from crying. Hair matted from the bed. Stupid jeans and sweatshirt, the clothes she'd thrown on when Dylan had shown up at her house in a panic and told her to grab her stuff and go with him. Because she'd foolishly ignored Fitz's warning, figuring the man was making something up to excuse himself as he'd been hauled off to jail. She'd been alone for nearly an hour. Anything could've happened.

Chelsea gripped her upper arm. "I can see your mind churning about him. Don't do that without all the information. Fitz is trying to save his sister's life. Let's give him the benefit of the doubt."

"Dylan doesn't like him."

Chelsea's slight grin was filled with affection. "Dylan is feeling protective of you. When we ran into you at The Patriot, he told me he didn't trust Fitz, thought it was odd he'd shown up so soon after your vacation. He called it stalker behavior. Now, we know why."

"Fitz is only here because of Shelby."

"Don't make assumptions about a man sitting"—she nodded

toward the kitchen—"right outside that door. Rather, let his words and his behavior tell you who he is."

Chelsea made sense, but Tabby feared...

So much.

"I take it that was some kiss," Chelsea said, amusement in her tone.

Only then did Tabby realize her fingertips rested on her lips. She dropped her hand. "Mind-blowing. Which either means he and I have an amazing connection or he's a master manipulator. I'm not ruling out the second."

"Let's not rule out the first, either. He could be sincere."

Possible. Improbable, but theoretically possible.

"Come on. Unless you plan to go back to sleep—"

"Not a chance."

"—then let's get some coffee and find out what they know. There's got to be a solution."

Back in the kitchen, while Tabby filled a glass with ice and delivered it and the Mountain Dew to Abe, Chelsea poured coffee for everybody else.

Cup in hand, Tabby headed for the kitchen table. There was an empty chair between Fitz and Abe, another one beside Dylan. She could be petty and sit on the far end of the table, but Tabby wasn't the petty sort. She left the chair beside Dylan for Chelsea and approached the one nearest Fitz.

He stood and pulled it out for her. "You okay?"

She said nothing, just slid into the seat. When she was settled, Fitz sat beside her. "We're looking at Mullins's business records, mostly bank statements."

"How do you have that?"

Fitz nodded to Abe, who said, "There was an investigation with the Bureau a few years back. These are old records from that time. My guy could get fired for sharing them with me, but he knows the stakes."

"What are you looking for?" Tabby asked.

Fitz fielded that one. "We don't know exactly. Somebody who might have a problem with him. Maybe somebody who'd be aware of his financial dealings."

Abe added, "Somebody had to know about those jewels. Whoever it was—"

"Wait. Jewels? I only saw a box."

Abe glanced at Fitz, who said, "Five pieces of jewelry plus the antique box. The box is the least valuable. Altogether, the goods are worth about a half a million dollars."

She gasped.

"Oh, my." Chelsea had set coffee cups in front of everybody and now slipped in beside Dylan. "Where did they come from?"

While he doctored his coffee, Fitz explained that all the pieces had been purchased at auction a few weeks prior.

"But they were bought by a surrogate," Abe said. "A surrogate Mullins is convinced is trustworthy. So the question is, how did the real thief know about the jewels?"

"And know where Mullins was going to be," Dylan added.

"Good point." Abe nodded thoughtfully. "Very good point. Surely they don't broadcast their plans." He turned to Fitz. "What did he say about that?"

"Only the family knew about the jewels and the trip."

"His friend knew," Dylan said. "Willie Dunbar."

"There were two other thugs too." Fitz told Dylan their names, and he wrote them down.

Tabby said, "His wife knew their whereabouts. And Shawn knew. And he was on his phone a lot, just like Shelby. He could've told somebody."

Fitz turned his gaze on her and smiled. "Right. Good thinking."

As if he hadn't already thought of that. Was he trying to encourage her? Or manipulate her?

Abe tapped his pen against the papers in front of him. "Who would the wife and kid have told?"

"That's information only they can answer," Fitz said, "but we're not going to be able to question them. Even if Mullins would allow it—which I don't think he will—they're at sea."

With Shelby. "Is your sister okay?" Tabby asked. "Have you talked to her? Are they hurting her?"

"Shelby is oblivious." He shook his head. "I'm thankful but also irritated that she doesn't have better instincts. She thinks she's on an adventure while I work a case."

"That's good news, right?" Tabby asked.

"I want her to stay ignorant. But when I get her back, I'm going to sit her down and lecture her about not being so trusting."

On the other side of Fitz, Abe's eyes filled with frustration, maybe anger. "Don't ruin your sister, man. You carry enough distrust for both of you."

Fitz turned his way slowly. "Mystery how that happened."

"You don't know the whole story." Abe's deep voice lowered even more. "Not that you ever asked."

Fitz shifted to look at the papers on the table, but Tabby saw enough of his eyes to believe he wasn't really seeing what was in front of him.

Whatever lay between them, it seemed neither of them was eager to get into it. Fitz flipped to the next sheet.

Dylan and Abe were looking through the stacks. Chelsea was peering over Dylan's shoulder.

When Fitz finished with a page, Tabby glanced at it. They were bank statements. Big dollar amounts, but nothing nefarious as far as she could see. The company paid its bills, just like everyone else. The difference was there seemed to be a lot of charges every month. Different electric companies, different internet providers. Different properties, obviously. There were so many charges, she didn't know how anybody could make sense of them.

Fitz's attention shifted back and forth between the paperwork and the laptop, where he was digging for more information.

Earlier, she'd been sure she wouldn't be able to fall back asleep, but her eyes were scratchy and heavy an hour into the search.

Fitz said, "Huh."

"What?" Abe asked, barely lifting his head.

Dylan looked up, waiting.

"He owns a number of properties," Fitz said. "There are two apartments in Manhattan, which is odd. Why two? And one is in Greenwich Village, which... I don't know. Doesn't feel like the kind of place Mullins would own."

"It's not a business?" Dylan asked.

"Nope." He clicked a tab on his browser, and the address came up from the last time the apartment had been listed for sale.

Tabby whistled. "Definitely an apartment, and not a cheap one."

"Not that there are many of those in Manhattan," Abe said.

That was true.

Fitz looked in Abe's direction. "Is this company owned by anybody else, or just Mullins?"

Abe tapped a few buttons. "It's a single-owner corporation, so just Mullins."

"Mullins owns a number of properties where they do business—nightclubs and restaurants mostly. Their home is outside of Boston. He owns a beach property on Martha's Vineyard, a place in the Florida Keys. He owns a condo in Grafton, New Hampshire." He looked at Tabby, one eyebrow raised.

"Ski resort."

"Ah. That makes sense."

"So what's the problem?" Abe asked.

Fitz clicked another button, and the image on the screen changed to a modest home in Narragansett. Modest compared to the other properties they'd seen, that was.

"This is the one that really bothers me." Fitz said. "The Greenwich Village apartment and"—he tapped the picture of the pretty country house—"this one. Why would he own a suburban property in Rhode Island?"

"He can afford it," Abe said.

"That's not a reason," Chelsea said. "People who have money and hold onto it do so because they make wise decisions with it. One doesn't just run about purchasing properties for no good reason."

Abe scooted closer to look at the screen. "So why would he need it?" Abe asked.

Fitz studied the image.

"It's a home," Tabby said. "Maybe he bought it for a family member. Can we figure out who lives there?"

Fitz turned his attention back to the paperwork. Abe did the same.

Dylan stared into space. "There's got to be a way."

"I don't know." Abe tapped the sheet in front of him. "It looks like the corporation pays all their bills."

Along with the rest of them, Tabby considered the question. They could go there, of course. Knock on the door and ask. She was no super sleuth or detective, but even she knew that wasn't the best idea. Who knew what they'd be walking into? They could wait for the mail to come and then peek...

Was it a federal crime to look at people's mail, or just to steal it?

She didn't really want to find out. But if they could get a look at the mail, then...

"I wonder if they're customers," she said.

Chelsea's gaze snapped up, and she smiled. "Good thinking."

"What?" Fitz asked.

"Maybe they've ordered from the catalog," Tabby explained.

Chelsea grabbed her phone and started dialing as she walked around the table, stopping behind Fitz's chair. She spoke into the phone. "Could you connect me to the shipping department, please?"

Fitz leaned toward Tabby. "Does she know it's the middle of the night?"

"Some departments work all night," Tabby whispered. "Shipping is—"

"Hello, Joanne. This is Chelsea Hamilton. Can you look up an address for me, let me know the name of the customer there?" Joanne was the night manager in the shipping department. If HCI had ever delivered to that address, she'd know it.

Everybody watched Chelsea's face. She winked at her husband, then snatched a pen from the table and wrote something down. "Thank you so much, Joanne. I truly appreciate you." She hung up and handed the piece of paper to Fitz.

"Ginger Hernandez."

"Who is that?" Dylan asked. "Do you know—?"

"Not a clue." Fitz started typing the name into his browser.

"Give me the laptop," Abe said. "I'll figure out who she is. You keep going through that stuff."

"I could just ask Mullins about her," Fitz said. "But I don't want him to know we're digging into him unless we have no other choice."

Abe made a note of the woman's name and address, then walked toward the other side of the room, cell in hand. "Maybe this'll lead to something."

The rest sat there and watched him as if the answer might appear over his head.

"I thought I'd order breakfast." Chelsea stretched. "I can ring James."

"They're still on their honeymoon, aren't they?" Tabby asked.

"Good thought," Chelsea said. "The manager there will accommodate us, I'm sure."

Dylan sent his wife an affectionate smile. "This is why I married you. You understand the importance of good food."

She smiled. "Imagine how you'd love me if I could cook."

"Impossible to love you more."

They were so adorable, Tabby had to look away. Ugly jealousy rose in her throat like nausea. She was happy for her friend. Ecstatic for her. Was it so awful to yearn for what Chelsea had?

Chelsea could keep the money and fame that came with being an heiress. She could keep the responsibility that came with being the CEO of Hamilton. Tabby wanted none of that.

But to be loved, truly loved...

The two were making eyes at each other like starry-eyed teens.

Tabby groaned. "I'm happy for you two and everything, but must you?"

"Sometimes," Chelsea said with a smile, "it feels we must." But she headed toward the bedrooms down the hall. "I'll order breakfast."

Dylan followed with a muttered, "I'll just help."

Fitz watched them go. "Newlyweds. We'll be lucky if they're back in an hour."

Fatigue and frustration and all sorts of other emotions filled Tabby's heart. She laid her head on her arms on the table and closed her eyes.

Fitz rubbed her back. "I'm sorry this is happening."

She sat up and angled away. "I think it's best if you don't—"

"It was real, Tabby." He kept his hand on her back and leaned closer. "That unbelievable kiss. My feelings for you. It's all real. Yes, I was trying to get information out of you. Yes, at first, I believed Mullins. The video, the wallet—"

"Wallet?"

"Yours." He backed away and dropped his hand. "I guess I didn't... Did you lose your wallet before your flight on Saturday?"

She had. She'd been double-checking that she had everything before she left her hotel room that morning and had discovered her wallet missing. She'd rushed to the lobby in a panic. "Somebody turned it in," she said now. "They had it at the front desk."

"The desk clerk *assumed* somebody had turned it in. He said he'd found it behind the desk. Mullins guessed you'd dropped it when you emptied the safe."

She let out a short chuckle. "I would hope that, if I were a thief, I'd be smart enough not to leave my wallet behind."

"Or not realize there were cameras," Fitz said. "That's bothered me all along. The woman who pulled off that job had cased the place. But somehow, she missed the camera? It never made sense."

"But how did my wallet end up there?"

"My guess? The real thief stole it. I'm thinking they broke into your room that night before they broke into the office."

The thought sent a shiver down her back. Someone had been in her hotel room?

"Because you'd have known the night before that it was gone, right?" Fitz asked. "Unless you went out after I walked you back to your room and it was stolen then."

"I didn't."

"But you had to have had it when I walked you back to your room. You had your key card."

"I have one of those cell phone cases with a—"

"Sleeve on the back. I remember." He was nodding. "Big enough for credit cards."

"I keep one credit card in it for emergencies because, you know, Mom. She gave it to me before the trip. Figured if I lost my wallet but had my phone, I'd have access to money. Anyway, I kept the room key in that."

He was nodding. "So if your wallet had been stolen earlier that night, you might not have noticed it was missing."

"Had to have been at dinner. I hardly ever carried my purse when I left the room, and my wallet was always in my purse. I only had it that night because I'd worn makeup. I wanted my lipstick."

His serious expression morphed into a look of tenderness that was far too close to the way Dylan had looked at Chelsea earlier. If only she could trust it. "You looked gorgeous."

She turned away, straightened the papers in front of her. "Anyway, the real thief must've stolen it."

He said nothing, and the silence between them stretched.

Fitz's fingers slid over hers on the table. "Tabby?"

"Please don't."

He pulled away his hand. "We need to talk about what happens now."

"Nothing is going to happen between us."

"Okay." A short pause, and then, "That conversation can wait. That's not what I mean."

She turned toward him. "Then what?"

"You're going to have to stay here at Chelsea's, where it's safe."

"I'm not putting my friends in danger."

"They won't mind. Dylan seems eager to make sure you're—"

"I'm not putting my friends in danger," she said again, this time louder.

"Fine, then. Where can you go? Do you have friends away from here, somebody who'd let you hole up until—"

"What happens to Shelby if I disappear?"

His lips pressed together until they turned white. "I'll worry about Shelby. You need to protect yourself."

"At the expense of a sixteen-year-old girl? I don't think so."

He turned toward her, pleading in his eyes. He was so near that she could feel the heat of his skin on her cheek as he whispered in her ear. "Sweet Tabitha, I need you to be safe."

Goose bumps rose on her arms. Her skin tingled at his nearness, and she lost the ability to argue. Forgot what they'd been arguing about.

She should push him away. Hadn't she just asked him to keep his distance? But the combination of raw strength and vulnerability she'd seen in his eyes... She couldn't force herself to push back.

Trust him? How could she trust him?

"I have to stay with you." What was she saying? Stay with him, this man she didn't trust, didn't believe?

But she wanted to, so badly. She wanted to believe this was real.

"If we don't find the stolen goods," she said, "we'll tell Mullins together that they're gone. I'll tell him I didn't do it and..." But her voice trailed.

His eyebrows rose. "And hope the murderous mobster takes your word for it?"

"I didn't do it."

"Irrelevant."

"It'd be a waste of time for him to kill me."

"Irrelevant."

"It'd get him no closer to his goal."

"Irr—"

"Then what do you suggest?" Her words were too loud in the quiet space.

He ran his hand along the side of her face, then rested his palm on her cheek. "I need you to be safe."

He was doing it again. Using his charm to get his way. She wouldn't have it. But she didn't know if she had the strength to keep fighting what she was feeling.

CHAPTER NINETEEN

Tabby took a shower, partly to wake herself up, partly to fix her out-of-control hair. She'd showered the night before, back when she'd thought the world was a safe place and Fitz a nice guy who'd come to New Hampshire because he cared for her. Amazing what could change in a matter of hours.

The quick shower had woken her up, and wet hair was better than the rat's nest she'd sported before. She'd come to Chelsea's empty-handed, figuring that, whatever was going on, she'd be back home soon. With no other choice, she'd planned to slip on the same jeans and sweatshirt she'd worn before, but when she stepped into the bedroom that used to be Chelsea's before her mother's death, Tabby found folded neatly on her bed a pair of underwear and socks—tags still on both—a pair of skinny jeans and a pretty teal sweater. On top of the pile was a note. *Thought you might want out of those clothes. These jeans are too long for me, anyway. And keep the underwear, please.* Next to that last line was a little smiley-face drawing that reminded Tabby of the notes she and Chelsea used to pass in fifth grade.

The sweater was slimmer than she usually wore, but not uncomfortably so. Thanks to the little bit of stretch in the jeans, they fit nicely and were long enough. All the clothes were, of course, Hamilton's brand.

She glanced at herself in the full-length mirror. Except for her paler-than-usual skin and the dark smudges under her eyes, she looked...good. What would Fitz think?

She narrowed her eyes at the woman in the mirror. "You don't care what Fitz thinks."

The truth shone from the reflection's eyes. *Liar.*

Turning her back on the too-honest face, Tabby walked on sock feet down the hall and into the great room. Chelsea and Dylan were in the kitchen talking quietly. Abe was at the table, head bowed over paperwork. She didn't see Fitz anywhere.

Outside, the sun was just turning the black sky gray.

Tabby headed toward the kitchen and coffee. She figured she'd need a lot more to survive until bedtime.

When Chelsea looked away from her husband, Tabby smiled at her. "I'll have these cleaned and get them back to you."

"That sweater looks so much better on you than me. And the jeans don't fit me anyway. You might as well keep it all."

"Thank you. For the clothes and...everything."

The doorbell rang, a surprising sound in the quiet morning.

Dylan glanced at the screen on his phone and headed that way. "It's breakfast."

A moment later, they had the different offerings set out in the kitchen with serving spoons. Chelsea had ordered enough for three times as many people. "I didn't know what everybody would want, so I got a variety."

Eggs, hash browns, pancakes, sausage, bacon, toast, and pastries. "I just hope we'll have enough." Tabby didn't even try to keep the sarcastic tone out of her words.

Chelsea's eyebrows lifted. "You've obviously never seen my husband eat."

Dylan, a piece of bacon hanging from his mouth, said, "Hey."

Chelsea giggled, and the newlyweds shared a look that had Tabby averting her eyes.

Abe tore himself from the paperwork on the table and grabbed a plate. "What a spread. I just sent Fitz a text letting him know the food is here."

"Where is he?"

"Went to get—"

"Right here." Fitz came around the corner from the staircase. His hair was wet too.

They filled their plates and sat at the table, pushing all the paperwork to the center so they could eat. Before they dug in, Dylan spoke up. "Anybody mind if I pray?"

Tabby set down her glass of orange juice.

Beside her, Fitz dropped the fork he'd already lifted. "Please do."

She closed her eyes and listened as Dylan prayed a blessing on their food and asked for wisdom and insight and protection for her, Fitz, and Shelby. It was a simple but powerful prayer that had tears stinging.

Fitz's hand slid over hers on the table. She didn't pull away. Didn't want to pull away.

Dylan ended the prayer, everybody said "amen," but Fitz didn't remove his hand.

She turned to him, and he held her gaze as he leaned toward her. For a moment, she thought he might kiss her, but he brushed her wet hair away from her face. "Good morning, beautiful."

She couldn't think of a response beyond, "Hi."

His smile was slight. After a moment, he turned to Chelsea

and Dylan across the table. "Looks delicious. Thank you. For everything."

They ate quietly for a few minutes, the only sounds those of silverware clinking against dishes. When Fitz's plate was half empty, he addressed Dylan. "I'm going to hire Tabby a couple of bodyguards. You don't mind if she stays here, do you?"

"What?" Tabby glared at him. "I told you, I'm not—"

"Don't be a fool," Fitz snapped. Gone was the kindness she'd seen in his eyes minutes before. "You need to be protected." He looked expectantly at Chelsea and Dylan.

Dylan's smile was tight. "This house is very secure. We'll keep you safe."

"I appreciate that, but"—she turned to Fitz—"I'm staying with you until you get Shelby back."

"I'm not putting you in danger."

"But you'd have me put my best friends in danger?"

Fitz glanced across the table. "Dylan can keep you safe. But if you can think of another place you could hole up—"

"I'm not hiding."

Chelsea said, "You could go to my flat in London. You'd be safe there."

Fitz said, "That's a great—"

"I. Am. Not. Hiding." She glared at him. He glared at her.

On the other side of Fitz, Abe cleared his throat. "I'm with Tabby on this one."

Everyone turned his direction. "You can't be serious." Fitz said the words in a tone that left no doubt he thought his former partner had lost his mind.

"Mullins is smart." Abe's words were measured. "I'd guess your friend Willie knows where Tabby is right now, and he's probably already told his boss. If I were them, I'd be looking into Chelsea and Dylan to see what properties they own. If they haven't already, it'd be easy enough to find out."

"Fine, then," Fitz said. "We'll find someplace else. There's got to be—"

"Here's what I think." Abe glanced at everyone before meeting Tabby's eyes. "Willie is here. He searched Fitz's place but was careful not to make it obvious he'd done it. Let's assume he was watching Fitz's hotel. What did he see?"

Tabby tried to picture the situation from the thug's perspective.

"He saw Fitz tear out of his hotel." Abe's attention turned to Fitz. "I'm guessing you weren't taking your time?"

"Rockets have launched slower."

Abe nodded once, his coal gaze back on hers. "Let's say Willie followed, even if he arrived a few minutes after Fitz. What did he see?"

"I had my blinds closed," Tabby said. "He couldn't have seen inside the house."

"Maybe not. But still, Fitz goes inside—"

"Not at first, though," Fitz said. "She didn't answer, so I was going to go in through the dining room window. But then the door opened."

"The point is," Abe said, "he saw you panic. A few minutes later, he saw you arrested."

"And maybe even heard me shouting for her to come here." Fitz faced Tabby. "Warning you that you were in danger."

Tabby didn't want to think about that man outside her house, but... "You think he was watching after the police left."

Fitz's attention shifted between her on his right and Abe on his left, but she couldn't take her eyes off the older man.

"Probably." Abe nodded again. "What else did he see?"

Dylan spoke up. "I picked her up and took her away."

"You're saying that Willie knows Fitz is trying to protect me." Tabby's voice was flat, which belied the fear that pulsed in her veins.

"If he doesn't," Abe said, "then he's incompetent."

"And if he knows," Tabby said, "Mullins knows."

"And if Mullins knows..." Abe said.

"Shelby's in danger." Fitz's hands fisted on the table as he faced his former partner. "I thought through all of that before I called you last night. It doesn't matter. I can't..." He turned to Tabby. "I can't figure out how to protect you both at the same time. Right now, I can protect you. I'll figure out how to save my sister. But sacrificing you won't do it. Don't you see?" He gripped her arm, his hand warm and tender. "Without the jewels, you and Shelby are both in danger. I don't want to lose either one of you. But I'm not going to lose both of you."

She let her gaze linger on his for a moment before looking past him to Abe. "You think that, if I disappear, it'll put Shelby more at risk?"

"I do."

Fitz turned to Abe. "When I want your opinion—"

"If you keep Tabby with you and tell Mullins what you're doing, it'll show Mullins you're not double-crossing him. But if she disappears, he'll assume you're protecting the person who stole from him. It doesn't look good. And unless she's unlike most people who try to hide, he'll eventually find her." Abe turned to Dylan. "Do you agree?"

Dylan's head dipped once. "Most people can't hide for long."

"But we want her to be safe," Chelsea said. "Won't she be safer if she goes far away from here?"

"How far away is far enough?" Abe directed the question at Chelsea. "How far away does she have to go to be out of their reach?"

Fitz said, "It doesn't matter. She just has to hide until I—"

"That's enough." Tabby pushed back in her chair and stood. "I appreciate everybody's input, but I'm not hiding." She looked down at Fitz. "I'm not willing to save myself and let your sister pay the price. I'm staying with you. End of story." She snatched her plate off the table and carried it to the kitchen, where she dumped what she hadn't eaten in the trash.

Her hands were shaking, her heart racing as if she'd just run a marathon.

The wise thing would be to hide. The safe thing would be to hide.

She could hear her mother's warnings to take care of herself. *How would we survive if something happened to you?*

But how would Tabby live with it if something happened to Shelby?

Maybe she was being a fool.

Fine, then. She'd be a fool. But she wasn't going into hiding. She wasn't going to put a teenager's life in danger to save herself.

Silence hung heavy in the room. Nobody was eating.

She slid back into her seat and met Abe's eyes. "Did you find out anything?"

"I'm waiting for my contact to get back to me."

Dylan cleared his throat. "I think I know who she is. Ginger Hernandez. The woman who lives in Narragansett."

The surprise on Fitz's face was met by a smirk on Dylan's. "I know you don't have a lot of respect for what I do," Dylan said, "but I'm pretty good at it."

"It's not that I don't respect it. It's just that..." But Fitz didn't seem to know how to end his sentence.

Abe filled the silence with, "Who is she?"

"I did some digging into Ronnie Mullins's past. In the late nineties, his nightclub was busted for gambling and prostitution."

"But he wasn't prosecuted," Fitz said. "Managed to shift the blame to his managers."

"Just one of the managers," Dylan said. "One of the women quoted in a newspaper article about the bust is Ginger Hernandez. She was an assistant manager at the time. Somehow, she wasn't charged."

"Should she have been?" Fitz asked.

Dylan shrugged. "How could she not have known what was going on?"

"So you think... what?" Fitz asked. "That Mullins gave her a house to keep quiet about something? Is it blackmail, or—?"

"Don't know yet." Dylan speared a piece of sausage and popped the bite into his mouth, looking from Abe to Fitz.

"Probably not." The tone of Abe's voice told Tabby he wasn't happy about the news.

"So you're saying," Tabby guessed, "that this Ginger Hernandez person probably doesn't have anything to do with what's going on now?"

"It's too soon to tell." Fitz's lips tipped up at the corners as if he were attempting a smile but couldn't quite make it happen.

But they might be no closer to finding out who stole the jewels than they had been before.

Fitz turned to Tabby. "When did you make your hotel reservations for Belize?"

"Oh, at least a year ago." She looked at Chelsea. "Don't you think?"

"It was after that big snowstorm late in the season," Chelsea said. "Remember, we'd walked to The Patriot for lunch, complaining that there was still snow on the ground? You were telling me that you'd been saving for a trip but hadn't decided where."

"That's right." Tabby focused on Fitz again. "I could probably find out the exact date, but it was last March."

"Good, good. That proves you'd planned to go to Belize long

before Mullins did. That should steer suspicion away from you."

"If he chooses to listen," Abe said.

Fitz glared the man's way. "You have anything helpful to say?"

Abe just smiled. "The buyer knew where Mullins would be and—"

"That he'd have the goods with him. Excellent point." He pushed his plate aside, slid his papers close, and made a note. "I'll ask Mullins about that when I call him."

"Whoever did it looked enough like me to make it work," Tabby said. "That should narrow it down."

"Was there anybody at the resort who did?" Dylan asked.

"I don't remember seeing my doppelgänger," Tabby said. "I'd have remembered that."

"Me, either," Fitz added. "Though, to be honest, once I met Tabby, I wasn't exactly checking out other women."

Tabby ignored the way her heart rate picked up at his words.

"You have the names of the people who were registered," Abe said. "We could go through that, see if we can find photos."

Fitz seemed to have to work to look away from Tabby. "As we discussed, though, any halfway intelligent thief would have stayed at another hotel. I think that'll be a dead end."

"The woman had to have been at the resort enough to see Tabby," Abe countered, "and close enough to get a reasonable idea of how to look like her."

"And don't forget the top," Tabby said.

Even Fitz looked confused.

"She was wearing the same shirt I wore to dinner that night."

"That's right," Fitz said.

"Which I bought in the resort gift shop," Tabby added.

Fitz made another note on his pad. "I'll have Mullins see if he can find out who else bought that blouse that day."

"Let's not count on getting a name," Abe said. "I suspect the woman is too smart for that."

"At least it adds to the case that Tabby was framed," Fitz said. "Maybe it'll help."

"Could somebody have altered the video?" Chelsea asked. "Perhaps the person who broke in didn't look like Tabby at all. Perhaps he or she simply put her image in, like they do in video games, right?"

"It *might* be possible," Fitz said, "but I don't think somebody could come up with something that authentic in a matter of hours. The theft took place around two a.m. It was discovered around eight. Six hours..."

"Not enough time," Chelsea said.

"So whoever it was looked like Tabby." Fitz turned to face her. "Tall and slender and beautiful."

She felt her cheeks warm at the compliment.

"Maybe not beautiful," Abe said. "Remember, we never saw her face."

"We're assuming it's a woman," Chelsea said, "but it could have been a thin man, couldn't it? I mean, Tabby is quite tall. And like you say, we never saw the person's face."

Tabby hadn't considered that.

"Send the video to me," Chelsea said. "Let's get it on a larger screen."

Five minutes later, Tabby and Fitz were in the office with Chelsea watching the video on her thirty-inch computer monitor. Fitz paused it when the person started cracking the safe and blew up the image.

The thief's hands were long and slender with pretty, manicured nails.

"Looks like a woman's hands," Chelsea said.

Tabby agreed. "And her wrists are really thin."

"Probably a woman," Fitz said, "but let's not completely rule out the idea."

They were halfway down the hall toward the great room when Fitz froze. "I'm an idiot."

Chelsea must not have heard him because she continued on, but Tabby stopped. "What?"

"I took all those pictures—of the guy I was surveilling, of you, of Shelby, of the landscape." He opened his phone and started scrolling. "Maybe we can find the person we're looking for in the background."

"We could use Chelsea's monitor again."

"Yeah." They continued toward the kitchen to ask but found Chelsea, Dylan, and Abe all standing in front of a laptop screen.

"Did you find something?" Fitz asked.

Dylan looked over the screen. "Maybe."

They joined the crowd. On the screen was an image of a driver's license. Ginger Hernandez's driver's license. The woman was attractive, forty-five years old with brown hair and eyes.

"Would you look at that," Fitz said.

Tabby didn't know what he was seeing. "Am I missing something?"

"Her height," Fitz said.

Tabby read it. The woman was five eight, a hundred thirty pounds. Just an inch shorter and a little bit heavier than Tabby.

"That could be her." For the first time all morning, Fitz's voice held enthusiasm. "Maybe we've found her."

Abe asked, "Does she look familiar? Did you see her down there?"

Shaking his head, Fitz turned to Tabby. "Did you?"

"I don't remember her," Tabby said.

Abe tapped the screen. "Narragansett's only a couple of hours away. I say we head out ASAP."

"Good idea." Fitz asked Tabby, "Is there any place nearby to have photos printed fast?" Fitz explained his idea to the rest. "We'll go through them on the drive."

He was taking her with him. Until that moment, she'd wondered if he'd refuse. "The drugstore in town, but"—she glanced at her watch—"I doubt they're open."

"Have them sent to Manchester," Dylan said. "You can pick them up when you drive through." He tapped on his keyboard. "I'll find someplace."

"I'll need to get some things from home," Tabby said.

It felt so good to be doing something that Tabby didn't let herself think about what would happen next. Maybe this Ginger person was the real thief. Maybe they'd somehow get her to confess or find the stolen goods at her house. Maybe it would all work out.

Maybe she was delusional, but for Shelby's sake, she prayed this was real progress.

CHAPTER TWENTY

Fitz waited not-so-patiently at the door while Tabby and Chelsea chatted on the far side of the room, about what, he had no idea. He'd thought they were just saying good-bye, but it seemed their conversation was more than that.

Abe stepped inside the house. "Car's warming up."

"Knowing that thing, it'll be warm by the time we get to Boston."

Abe's eyes darkened. "You keep your thoughts on Peggy Sue to yourself. She can hear you."

Fitz chuckled. "Peggy Sue. She's from the eighties, not the fifties."

"She's an old-fashioned girl."

Dylan had disappeared down the hall but returned now, passing the ladies and joining Fitz and Abe at the door. "Listen, why don't I come with you guys? I think I can help."

Fitz said, "That's not necessary."

At the same time, Abe said, "That'd be great."

The men looked at each other. Back when they were partners, they were almost always on the same page. Now, they couldn't agree on anything.

Abe flashed his bright smile, but Fitz recognized the falsehood in it. "He was a cop, man. He can help."

"We don't need his help," Fitz said. Because Dylan had left the job to work for himself. Maybe the guy was doing noble work. Maybe he wasn't. Fitz didn't know. He figured Dylan was on Tabby's side since she was his wife's best friend, so he had that going for him. Even still, Fitz wasn't about to trust him to be anything but a burden.

Dylan let out a short burst of laughter. "You two are like an old married couple."

"An old divorced couple, more like," Fitz said.

Dylan's smile faded, and he met Fitz eyes. "If you don't want me to join you, fine. I'll help from here. Surely you can trust me to do that."

"It's not about trust, exactly," Fitz said.

"Yeah, it is." This from Abe, who spoke to Dylan, effectively ignoring Fitz. "He's never been what you'd call trusting, but ever since the scandal in our police department—"

"Which cost me my job," Fitz added.

"—he hasn't trusted a soul, even people he's known for years."

Fitz didn't trust Abe, but he needed him. He needed all his focus to make sure Abe didn't double-cross him. He wouldn't have any to spare to keep an eye on Dylan.

Fitz couldn't explain all that, so he held out his hand to Dylan. "It's nothing personal, and frankly I think you'll be better served here helping us with research."

Dylan's grip was firm. "If you change your mind, just say the word and I'll be there. Tabby means a lot to us." His grip tightened on Fitz's hand. "You be sure to keep her safe, or you'll have a lot to answer for."

Fitz barely resisted the urge to get into a squeezing match with the guy. "I'm the one who wanted her to hide, remember?"

Dylan let go of his hand, though because of Fitz's words or because the women were approaching, Fitz wouldn't guess.

He turned his attention to Tabby. "You all set?"

She gave a quick nod. "We were talking about work. I'm so far behind already, but—"

"Don't worry about it," Chelsea said. "I'll encourage your boss to make sure you don't have more work stacked up when you get back."

"Thank you." Tabby hugged Chelsea, squeezed Dylan's hand, and turned to Fitz. "Let's go."

AFTER A QUICK STOP at Fitz's hotel for his things, they pulled into Tabby's neighborhood. Cars were warming up outside houses, white exhaust pumping into the cool air. Snow covered the lawns, but the roads were clear and dry this morning. Schoolchildren waited at a corner for the school bus, and more than one person was out walking a dog despite the frigid temperature.

Tabby's house looked just like all the rest, cheerful against the bright blue sky and deep green pines. Fitz stepped out of the car and opened the door for Tabby in the backseat. He'd offered for her to sit in front, but she'd refused. Now, she stepped past him and toward her front door, though not with eagerness but nervousness.

"You think it's safe?" she asked.

"We'll be with you."

Abe joined them, and they walked to the base of the steps.

"Why don't you let me go in first?" Fitz asked.

She handed over her keys, and he climbed the steps and

worked the lock. He took out his gun, just in case, and pushed the door open. But when he did, it got caught on something.

He shoved harder and stepped inside.

The place had been searched. Not just searched but destroyed.

Sofa cushions torn open, stuffing everywhere. Tables overturned. The contents of drawers dumped on the floor, the drawers themselves tossed aside, some broken to splinters.

Beside him, Tabby gasped.

He turned, pulled her to his chest. "I'm so sorry."

She said nothing, just lingered in his arms as Abe walked through the rubble, gun drawn. Fitz kept his eyes on the room, imagining Willie there, digging through her personal things.

And Fitz allowed the guilt that came with having done the same thing. But at least he hadn't destroyed anything.

Quickly, Abe cleared the downstairs while Fitz stayed with Tabby, gaze flitting around the room in case Willie was still there.

Abe went upstairs. After a moment, Fitz heard, "Clear," and then Abe came back down. "Nice place you have here, Tabby."

Fitz would have expected her to sob or lash out, but she laughed, pushing out of his arms. "As you can see, I'm a fabulous decorator."

"Yeah," Abe said. "This place should be in magazines."

"Sort of a treasure-to-trash theme," she suggested. "You've heard of shabby-chic? This is sloppy-swank."

Abe chuckled, his deep voice resonating in the quiet space. The laughter died quickly. "I'm really sorry about this. He did a real number on it."

Tabby wandered forward, picking her way around overturned furniture, books, and decor strewn across the floor. Standing by the door, Fitz gave her a minute to process it.

She stepped into the kitchen at the back of the house.

Fitz leaned down to set an end table on its legs, getting it out of the path. He was reaching for a lamp, careful not to step on broken pieces of bulb, when a bang came from ahead.

He looked up and barely caught sight of a man bolting across the kitchen.

Tabby screamed.

Fitz ran that direction, reached the kitchen doorway, and froze.

The back door was open.

Tabby was lying flat on her back on the kitchen tile in front of the doorway leading to the dining room.

Willie straddled her. He held a gun to her forehead. "Tell me where you put the stuff and you might get to live." He glanced in Fitz's direction. "We tried it your way. Now it's my turn."

"Get off her." Fitz moved deeper into the room until he could see Tabby's face. Her eyes were wide, her mouth open in a shocked O.

Willie turned away from Fitz, unconcerned, and leaned low until his face was barely an inch from Tabby's. He whispered something that made her cringe.

Fury colored Fitz's vision. That Willie didn't even care that he was standing there, watching this madness...

As if he'd just let Willie do as he wished.

If Fitz managed a headshot to the brain... but it was too risky. What if he missed. What if the shot caused Willie to squeeze the trigger?

Too risky.

If Fitz tackled him, the gun could go off. Also too risky.

"I swear." Tabby's voice shook. "I swear, I didn't steal anything. I don't know—"

Willie jabbed the gun into her temple. "No more lies."

Acid filled Fitz's stomach. He didn't move. Just waited. Any second now...

Lightning quick, Abe stepped into the entryway and kicked the gun out of Willie's hand.

Fitz yanked Willie off Tabby from behind, then dumped him on the floor and knelt on his back.

The man struggled, so Fitz cold-cocked him with the butt of his gun. "Be still."

Willie quit fighting.

Fitz turned to see Tabby pushing herself up. "You okay?"

Her eyes were wide. Her lower lip trembled. She nodded but couldn't seem to speak as Abe helped her stand. She was nearly too shaken to keep her feet.

"Take her upstairs," Fitz said.

Willie called, "You and I aren't done, sweetheart."

Tabby's eyes widened with fear as Abe ushered her out of the room.

When the sound of their footsteps faded, Fitz flipped Willie onto his back and punched him in the nose. "That's for the damage."

Willie seemed too stunned and disoriented to move.

Fitz punched him again. "That's for tackling a defenseless woman."

He searched the man's pockets for his cell phone, which he tossed onto a pile of spilled mayonnaise. Petty, maybe, but it seemed the least the man deserved. Fitz stood and stepped away, barely resisting the urge to kick him in the ribs for good measure.

"If you weren't Mullins's friend, I'd shoot you now."

Willie tried to sit up.

"Stay down."

The man looked like he might argue but then gave up and

collapsed on the filthy tile. "You kill me, and he'll kill your sister."

Fitz didn't doubt that was true as he scanned the floor for something...

There, beneath an overturned drawer and scattered among pens and paperclips and pads of sticky notes, Fitz spotted a roll of packaging tape. It wouldn't hold Willie for long, but it would give them time to get away.

He snatched it, keeping the gun aimed. "Not all gunshots kill. And anyway, he'd have to know what happened. Dead men tell no tales, right?"

"He'd know."

"You two that close? You think he'd feel a shift in the universe if your heart quit beating?" Fitz forced a chuckle he didn't feel. "On your stomach."

Willie glared at him. "He's not gonna like this."

"I'll take my chances."

Willie held his eye contact before finally flipping onto his stomach.

Fitz didn't want to risk Willie getting away if he put down his weapon. "A little help here!" he shouted.

A moment later, Abe's heavy footsteps sounded on the staircase, and then he stepped into the room.

"Bind his hands and feet for me." Fitz held the gun steady while Abe did as he'd asked.

"Aren't we calling the police?" Abe ripped a long strip of tape.

"I told Mullins I wouldn't bring the cops into it." Fitz nodded toward the doorway. "How is she?"

"Shaken but getting what she needs." He wrapped the tape so tight that Willie's hands paled. That ought to hold him.

"Remind her about the credit card statements," Fitz said.

"Something that proves she made her Belize reservation a year ago."

"She's on it."

"Good, good."

When Willie was bound good and tight, Abe stood. "You need me for anything else?"

"Go back and help her. Willie and I need to have a little chat."

Abe's gaze flicked from the man on the floor to Fitz. "Don't do anything stupid."

Fitz raised his eyebrows with feigned innocence. "Me?"

Abe just shook his head and walked out.

Once Abe was upstairs, Fitz crouched in front of Willie. He wrapped more tape around the man's thighs. No sense giving him the opportunity to get away. Then he dragged him toward the kitchen sink and strung tape from his hands to the pipes beneath it.

When he was done, he got into Willie's face. "Tabby didn't steal your boss's jewels."

"Just because they're not here—"

"She didn't do it, and we're going to prove it. And I'm going to find out who did and get them back. And Mullins is going to release my sister, and you're going to stay out of my way. You got that?"

"I'm just doing my job, man." His voice was garbled, nasally, thanks to the broken nose. The sound of it gave Fitz a sick little thrill. It was nothing compared to what Willie deserved.

"This was your job? To destroy a woman's home? I don't think so." He pulled out his phone and took a photograph of Willie, blood all over his face, lying in a sea of wreckage. Then Fitz backed up and got the whole room in another shot. "I'm sure your boss will be very impressed."

Willie glared. "If you send that, you'll be sorry."

"Let's be honest here, Willie. You're the man's trained monkey. You're not gonna do anything to me he doesn't let you do. And since you have zero idea where his jewels are and I do, you're not gonna hurt me. And you're not gonna hurt Tabby, either. If you want your boss to get his stuff back, you'll stay out of my way."

Tabby and Abe came downstairs, and Fitz walked toward them, not wanting Tabby to see what he'd done. Not that he felt guilty—not even a little. But she was too innocent for her own good. He stopped when he reached the doorway and turned to face the goon. "Don't worry. When we're out of town, we'll let someone know you're here. Just sit tight."

CHAPTER TWENTY-ONE

Tabby couldn't stop shaking.

Somehow, she'd managed to pack some clothes, though she couldn't remember now what she'd grabbed.

Abe had directed every step, going so far as to remind her to pack underwear and socks.

Her face would warm at the memory if she weren't so cold.

She sat in the backseat of Abe's car beneath a blanket Fitz had snatched from her couch—it had been undamaged, maybe the only thing in the house that was. Fitz sat beside her, arm around her shoulder, rubbing her arms.

Abe kept glancing at her in the rearview mirror. She tried to reassure him and Fitz that she was all right, but neither man was buying it.

She wasn't all right.

Surely somewhere in the stack of credit card statements, she'd find evidence of having planned the trip to Belize a year earlier. But she didn't know. Couldn't be sure.

She couldn't even think straight.

Her house... She thought she'd handled it well, the carnage.

It had been terrifying to walk in and see it, but with Abe and Fitz, she'd felt safe. It was only stuff, after all. Nothing had been damaged that couldn't be replaced.

But then that man had come through the back door.

Tackled her.

Straddled her.

Lowered his face to her ear and said the most horrifying words. *Don't worry, sweetheart. I'm not going to kill you.*

Not until I get what I came for.

The jewels for my boss, everything else for me.

She'd been sure she was going to die.

She'd been too stunned to move.

But Fitz was there.

And Abe was there.

She'd survived. A few bruises from the fall, a bump on her head, but otherwise, she'd be fine.

Except she'd never quit hearing that man's whispered threats.

She relived the whole thing now, telling herself she was all right.

But her body wouldn't quite believe it.

"You're okay now. You're safe."

Fitz's voice penetrated her fog. He said the words again and again. How many times had he spoken them that she hadn't noticed?

His voice was louder when he said, "I think we should go to the hospital. She's in shock."

"Good idea," Abe said. "Tell me where—"

"Let me look it up." Fitz started to shift away from her, but she gripped his arm.

"I'm okay."

He kissed her forehead. "Shock can be very dangerous, Tabby. I'll feel better if—"

"I'm okay." She sat up, took deep breaths. "I'm okay. Just... That was..."

"You handled it really well."

Her quick burst of laughter wasn't amused. "Hardly. I'm a mess. I'm..."

He shifted to meet her eyes. "We're trained, Tabby. We're cops. We've seen worse."

In the front seat, Abe added, "Heck, Fitz has *caused* worse."

"Watch it, Bachelor."

The man's deep chuckle settled her nerves a little. Fitz's tender smile settled them more.

"I don't need a hospital."

"Maybe something warm to drink?" Fitz suggested. "You like tea? My mother used to tell me tea is better at heating a person up than coffee. Abe, you see someplace, stop and let's get her something warm."

"You got it," the man said.

They were both being so kind to her, so gentle.

She settled against Fitz's side. "Tell me something else your mother used to tell you."

Fitz tucked the blanket around her again. "Hmm. Whenever I would procrastinate—"

"Which was often, I promise," Abe added. "It's a wonder we ever solved anything."

Fitz ignored him. "She'd tell me, 'sooner begun, sooner done.'"

"That's good advice," Tabby said.

"And she used to lecture me about being a contributor, not a consumer. I can still hear her saying that. Telling me the world wasn't created to serve me but that I was created to serve the Lord and, through Him, serve the world. At the time, I agreed it was better to serve than be served, but I wasn't sure about her faith."

"What changed that?" Tabby asked.

When Fitz didn't answer immediately, Tabby tried to think of a different question, one that wasn't quite so personal, anything to keep him talking. But before she did, Fitz spoke.

"When they died, I thought, what kind of a God would take them from us? How... capricious the world seemed, to lose our parents in a car accident, a stupid car accident that could've been prevented so easily. If there was a God, He could've steered the deer a different direction. He could've kept the truck in its own lane. He could've turned my parents around or sped them up or slowed them down. A million ways He could have protected them, but He didn't. I was angry, angrier than I'd ever been. But I had Shelby, so..."

Tabby's heart broke for him, twenty-one years old, grieving his parents, responsible for his sister.

"There was no sense in it," Fitz said, "but I couldn't dwell on it. I wouldn't have been any good to my sister or to anybody. I let the anger go. I let the questions go. I just... went on."

"That can't have been easy," Tabby said.

"It wasn't. But for Shelby..." He took a deep breath and blew it out. "I graduated, went to the police academy, and got hired with the Providence PD. I took care of my sister, and I never let those questions haunt me. Whenever they surfaced, I just pushed them away. Life was random, I decided. Life would never make sense. And then I met Abe."

The man in the front seat said nothing.

"I swear, every single day, he mentioned Jesus. It was annoying."

"I didn't think you were listening," Abe said.

"I was trying not to, but that high, squeaky voice is hard to drown out."

Abe chuckled, the sound low and soothing.

"I was trying to raise my sister, but I had no idea how. She hit puberty, and I swear the little girl I'd loved so much was replaced by a snarky, hateful she-monster. No matter what I did, she was angry with me. She needed Mom and Dad. I did too. We were so alone in the world, just the two of us. I tried to get help from family, but the only ones even a little interested in us were my grandparents. They offered to let us live with them, but neither one of us wanted to relocate to their tiny mountain town in Pennsylvania. I had my job, and Shelby had school and her friends. And then I lost my job, more proof the world was random and horrible. It was all really public, my name in the papers, and kids gave Shelby a hard time at school. It got so bad she begged me to let her go to school online. Poor girl. She was loyal to me when nobody else was. She believed in me, but because she defended me, she lost friends, and..."

His voice trailed. Tabby desperately wanted to turn toward him, to watch his facial expressions as he spoke. But maybe it was easier for him to speak without anybody watching.

"Somehow," he said, "in the midst of losing my job, being accused of a crime I didn't commit, trying to figure out how to steer my sister through the minefield that had become our lives while also wondering where I belonged and what I was supposed to do next..." She felt his shoulder lift and fall beside her. "Last summer, Shelby and I went on a road trip into the Blue Ridge Mountains. We were hiking, I was taking photographs, and she was complaining about the climb and the bugs and the heat. Typical sister-brother time. We reached the top of this one peak, and I looked out at the view. Tree-covered hills, a layer of mist in the valley, and I swear the Lord just... spoke to me."

After a long moment, Tabby whispered, "What did He say?"

"He said, 'Come home, son.'" Emotion filled Fitz's voice, and he cleared his throat. "Anyway, mad as I was at Abe for everything that happened, his words had gotten through to me in the years we'd been partners. At that moment on the mountain, I remembered some of what he'd told me. Enough to formulate a prayer in response to God's invitation. I got down on my knees and prayed. Shelby thought I was nuts. I didn't care. What I learned was that I don't have to raise her alone. I don't have to do any of this alone. I have God on my side. I still don't understand why He let my parents die or why I lost my job when I hadn't done anything wrong. But none of that mattered then. What mattered was that He was with me."

"He still is." The words, breathed out in the solemn moment, felt truer than anything Tabby had ever spoken. She looked up at him, resting her hand on his cheek. "He's with you, He's with me, and He's with Shelby. He'll lead us where we need to go."

"I pray you're right." He kissed her temple. "Are you okay?"

She no longer felt cold. Her hands no longer trembled. Her fears no longer churned. "I am."

CHAPTER TWENTY-TWO

When they hit the interstate in Plymouth, Fitz called Dylan and told him what happened at Tabby's house. "We left the thug tied up. Go over there and let him go."

"I take it you don't want me to call the police?" Dylan asked.

"Mullins said no cops. I'm not trying to make an enemy of the man. Just take him to the hospital and dump him. Let him figure out how to explain his wounds."

"What about her house?"

Fitz gazed at Tabby, who was leaning forward and chatting with Abe in the front seat. He lowered his voice. "Hire someone to clean it, would you? Just send me the bill. I don't want her to go home to that."

"I'll take care of it," Dylan said.

It was just after ten when they reached the pharmacy in Manchester. Abe ran inside to get the photographs while Fitz stayed with Tabby in the backseat.

"Why don't you move to the front now?" she suggested. "I hate for Abe to be up there all alone."

"He'll survive."

She tilted her head to the side while she studied him. "What happened between you two?"

"That's a long story."

Before she could say anything else, the door opened and Abe slipped in, handing a packet over the seat. "Here you go."

Fitz took it before opening his door. "I gotta make a call. Be right back."

"Wait." She grabbed his forearm. "Who are you calling?"

"Mullins."

Her gaze flicked to the front seat. "Why does that conversation need to be private?"

It didn't, he supposed, but she'd finally calmed down. The last thing he wanted to do was upset her again, and this would not be an easy conversation.

Abe turned toward her. "Let's just let him take care of it. He knows what he's doing."

Before Tabby could argue, Fitz slipped out of the car and headed across the busy parking lot toward the far corner, where there'd be less traffic noise and no shoppers.

Mullins answered on the first ring. "You'd better have a good explanation for what happened this morning."

Rage bubbled up like water in a pasta pot, and it took all Fitz's self-control to temper his words. "You gave me a task, Mullins. You tasked me with finding your stuff, and that's what I'm doing."

"By nearly killing my man?"

"He had it coming. He's lucky he didn't end up with a bullet to the chest."

"He was trying to locate—"

"He was trying to take advantage of a defenseless woman. What does that say about where his loyalties lie?"

"He told me from the beginning it was a mistake to send you, and after this morning, I'm starting to think he's right."

"He's not right. He's a rabid dog who took great pleasure in destroying an innocent woman's home. And he didn't find anything because Tabby didn't steal from you."

There was a beat of silence. When Mullins spoke, he sounded incredulous. "You saw the video."

Fitz squeezed his hands into fists, thankful for the chilly air that cooled his temper. He spoke with measured words as if talking to a child. "Somebody framed her. The woman who pulled off that job knew the camera was there. She didn't disable it because she wanted to send you on a wild goose chase. I'm done chasing geese. Tabby isn't guilty. She's not a thief. If she were, she'd also have to be a prophet because she made her reservations for Belize almost a year ago."

"If she didn't do it," he barked, "then who did?"

"I'm working on that." He tried to keep his anger out of his voice. "We're working on it. Tabby's with me, and we're trying to figure it out. I'll let you know what we learn. Meanwhile, I need you to make a list of everybody who both knew about the jewels and knew about your trip to Belize."

Mullins was quiet on the other end of the phone, and Fitz feared what the man might be thinking. That he'd wasted his time getting Fitz involved? That Shelby was more a liability than an asset?

What would happen if he decided Shelby wasn't worth his effort anymore? Would he release her?

Or kill her and dump her body in the Gulf of Mexico?

Finally, Mullins said, "Okay. I'll play along—for now. But it's a short list. Myself, my wife."

"Shawn?"

"You think I told my teenage son we were smuggling a half a million in jewels out of the country?"

Good point. "Willie and the Novak brothers," Fitz said. "They knew."

"They're loyal to me."

"Someone isn't. Someone isn't loyal to you. Somebody stole a whole lot of money from you. You should have a conversation with your thugs. Find out who they might've told."

"If one of them were guilty, he'd be gone. He wouldn't be foolhardy enough to linger and wait for me to figure it out."

"Maybe if he thinks you're on the wrong track. Lean on them. See if one breaks."

"I would, but my most *persuasive* friend is in New Hampshire."

"He's lucky he's not in the morgue." And Willie was just as likely to be guilty as the others, though Fitz didn't bother to say that. Mullins wouldn't listen anyway. "Who else?"

"Knew about both the jewels and the trip? Nobody."

"Your buyer knew."

"He doesn't know where I'm staying."

"You said he'd be there—"

"Here as in the hemisphere. Not here as in the hotel. We're not meeting at the resort or even in Belize."

So much for that lead. "He could've found out, though. He could've—"

"You're grasping at straws, McCaffrey."

One of those straws had to lead to somebody. "Maybe someone you do business with? Maybe someone with a grudge?"

"There are plenty of guys who hold a grudge against me, but none of them could've found out about the jewels."

Fitz hadn't thought this would help, but he was disappointed nonetheless. "One more question. Can you check with the resort gift shop? The blouse Tabby wore that night—the same one the woman wore in the video—came from the shop. Find out who else bought it. See if you can get a name."

"You can't be serious."

"I'd make the call myself, but I doubt they'll tell me anything. They'll tell you. Whoever pulled off that job must've seen her wearing the blouse and bought it after dinner that night, or at least after she bought it earlier that day. Look into it for me."

Mullins didn't say anything. When the silent moment stretched, he added, "You want to find your stuff or not? This is the next step."

"I don't like wasting time."

"Trust me. I'm moving as fast as—"

"You need to stop asking me stupid questions and focus. You're running out of time. If you don't get my jewels back—"

"I know what the stakes are. There's nobody in the world more important to me than my sister, and I'll do anything to protect her." Fitz's gaze crossed the parking lot until he caught sight of Tabby in the backseat of the Lincoln.

Tabby might not be more important to Fitz than Shelby, but she was running a close second. Very close.

Before, he'd been willing to betray Tabby to save his sister. Now, if it came to that?

It wouldn't come to that. Because his responsibility was to Shelby, not Tabby. He'd do his best to protect them both, but if he had to choose one…

He looked heavenward and prayed he wouldn't have to make that choice.

BACK IN THE LINCOLN, Fitz gave Tabby and Abe a quick rundown on his conversation with Mullins while Abe got them on the road. When he'd answered all their questions—there really wasn't much to add—he slid the stack of photographs out of the folder. "You look at these yet?"

"Waited for you, since they're your pictures."

He'd only glanced at them enough to disregard the landscape shots before he'd sent the rest off to be printed. Now, he took each photograph out, one by one, and held it so both he and Tabby could see. He looked beyond the subjects of the photographs—always Shelby or Tabby or both—and studied those in the background. It was amazing how often Shawn was pictured, usually with a moony-eyed expression on his face as he watched Shelby from afar.

Much as Fitz disliked the kid, he seemed smitten with Fitz's sister. Honestly, that was why Fitz didn't like him. That and his roaming hands.

The thought of them, of Shelby, had his focus turning toward heaven again, praying the Lord would protect his sister not just from the mobsters but from the teenage kid who thought he was in love.

They flipped through photographs. There were shots at the beach, at the pool, in the poolside grill, at the fancier restaurant. There were people of all shapes and sizes but, after flipping through more than half, nobody who fit the bill. No woman tall and slender enough to pass for Tabby.

"It's funny how long ago it seems." Tabby traced the line of the beach with her finger. "It almost feels like a dream."

"Dream turned nightmare."

She bumped his shoulder. "We're going to figure it out."

Where her newfound optimism came from, Fitz didn't know. And as photo after photo was set aside, he didn't share it. That woman had to have come from somewhere, but it seemed she'd been wise enough to avoid being seen. Or at least to avoid being photographed.

The closer they got to the end of the stack, the more helpless the situation felt.

He flipped the second-to-last photo facedown on the pile at

his side and lifted the final one. He'd snapped it at dinner their last night in Belize. Tabby had been chatting with the woman at the next table. He gazed at Tabby's image, her long curly hair, that blouse that had looked so beautiful against her tanned skin. She'd been stunning then. She was stunning now.

How was he going to protect her? How could he keep her and his sister safe?

She'd become very still beside him, so he glanced her way to find her staring at the picture.

He looked again. "What?"

"It could be her."

The stranger. He'd barely glanced at the woman that day, not wanting to take his eyes off Tabby. The stranger's face wasn't pictured, and all he could see above her chair were her shoulders, neck, and the back of her head. She had spiky blond hair. Fitz lifted the photograph to look closer. She was tanned, maybe sunburned. Freckles dotted her skin.

"Any chance it's Ginger Hernandez?" Fitz asked, hopeful.

"No. Too young."

Figured. But maybe this woman was involved. Maybe, somehow, they were both involved. "Tell me about her," Fitz said.

"She told me her name was Vera. I remember because it's such an unusual name. She was tall. Maybe not as tall as I am, but I didn't see her standing up. She looked maybe in her early twenties. She was attractive, and she seemed really sure of herself."

"Did you start the conversation with her, or did she—?"

"She started it. Said something about it being a beautiful view. We chatted a minute. I didn't even know you were there."

"I was enjoying the view too."

Tabby picked up on his meaning, and her lips tipped in a shy, very kissable smile.

Fitz forced his gaze back to the photograph. Tabby's purse was hanging from the back of her chair, very near the stranger at the next table. He tapped it now. "Maybe this is when your wallet was stolen."

Tabby was nodding. "I was really distracted, thinking about leaving, and… It's possible she stole my wallet while I was sitting right there."

"Whoever pulled off this job is a pro. So, who is this woman? How did she know about the jewels and Mullins's trip to Belize, and why would she target him?"

He found the photograph on his phone, blew up the woman's image, and sent it to Ronnie. *Do you know her?*

The dancing dots on his phone told him Ronnie was responding. A moment later, the text came through.

Are you asking me if I recognize the back of some random person's head?

Fitz took it that was a no. Another text came through. *Focus, McCaffrey. Your sister's life is at stake.*

CHAPTER TWENTY-THREE

The more Fitz thought about the woman at the resort, the more he wondered if their drive to Rhode Island was a waste of time. What could that girl have to do with some lady in Narragansett?

But since he had no better idea of what to do now, he said nothing. He'd done enough police work to know to follow every lead. It was often the weird ones, the seemingly insignificant ones, that led to breakthroughs.

Beside Fitz, Tabby still stared at the back of Vera's head in the photograph as if the stranger might turn around and show her face.

Fitz had pulled out his computer and was skimming through his notes, looking for connections and anomalies. So far, nothing stood out.

"So." Tabby spoke the word into the quiet, shooting him a look he could hardly decipher. Was it apologetic?

"What?" he asked.

She directed her attention and her question toward Abe.

"What happened that caused you to lose your jobs?"

Fitz started with, "Let's not—"

"We were working on a case," Abe said.

"I'd really rather we not get into this." Fitz tried to infuse his voice with warning. He had no desire for Tabby to hear this. No desire for her to wonder about him the way everybody else did. He'd seen the narrowed-eyes expressions on people's faces enough. He didn't want that uncertainty to mar Tabby's opinion of him.

But Abe either missed or ignored Fitz's warning. Probably the second.

"A drug case," Abe said. "We'd arrested a girl for possession with intent to distribute. Mary, eighteen years old. The girl was scared to death. We had an inkling..." Abe met Fitz's eyes in the rearview. "Honestly, Fitz had an inkling the girl was connected."

Tabby turned to him. "Was she? How did you know? Connected to what?"

Fitz blew out a breath. "Connected to someone higher up in the drug operation. She was. I'd been surveilling a suspect for another case a year or so before, and I'd seen this girl. Or I thought I had. Mostly, it was a guess."

"Not a guess," Abe said. "Intuition and observation and great police work. Mary was scared spitless, going on about how her life was over, how she'd never get into college, how she'd never amount to anything. You remember eighteen—old enough to be held accountable for your actions but young enough to think you never will be."

Tabby's smile wasn't knowing but indulgent.

"I don't think Tabby ever stepped a toe out of line." Fitz bumped her shoulder. "Am I right?"

"I was a pretty good kid," she admitted.

Abe nodded and continued. "Anyway, rather than book her, we leaned on her, offered to let her go in exchange for information about her supplier. We brought in someone from the DA's office, mostly to make it feel official to her. She gave us a lot more information than we'd hoped for."

Abe paused, and Fitz took up the story. "She told us who her supplier was. Not the guy I'd been surveilling, which was what I'd expected, but another kid, this clean-cut twentysomething master's student at Brown." He shook his head. "Who does that? What kind of stupid must infect a person to risk an Ivy League education and your entire future for a couple of bucks?"

Tabby just shrugged. "Arrogance in action, I guess."

Fitz agreed entirely. "Arrogance and ignorance—a deadly combination."

"So this guy," Tabby said, "this really smart, really stupid guy—"

"Corbin," Fitz supplied. "Can you think of a more hoity-toity name?"

She giggled. "He could've been Thad."

"Excellent point."

"We'd thought this Corbin was maybe..." Abe glanced her way in the mirror. "You work for a big company, right?"

"Pretty big."

"So, think of it like that. Mary was like a secretary—small potatoes."

"Administrative assistant," Tabby corrected, "but I get your point."

Abe rolled his eyes. "Semantics always get me in trouble. Anyway, she was that. We figured her supplier was some low-level manager. You know, the next rung up on the ladder. But once we started watching him, we realized he was more like a..."

"Department head?" she supplied.

"Yeah. That works. Not a V.P., but not without his resources and power."

"So," she said, "this Corbin was a department head in a big

drug operation. And department heads know a lot more than administrative assistants." She lifted a sardonic eyebrow. "Though, where I work, that's not always true."

"In secretive organizations," Fitz said, "criminal organizations—"

"I see your point."

"We watched Corbin for a few weeks." Fitz remembered those days well. The more names he and Abe collected, the more information they dug up, the more eager they'd become. "We got names of the people who came and went from his life. We figured, if we just kept watching, eventually we'd get a hint at his supplier. We never did. After a month, we decided to bring him in and lean on him like we had Mary."

"We arrested him," Abe said, "and did the same thing with him we'd done with Mary. Brought in the same prosecutor from the DA's office, leaned on Corbin, and eventually got a name."

"He didn't roll over as easily as the girl, though," Fitz said. "He was pretty sure his daddy could hire a lawyer to get him out of trouble. I had a little conversation with Daddy and Mommy about where their kid would end up if they helped him. They were convinced, and the kid turned."

"He gave you good information?" Tabby asked.

"Excellent information," Abe said. "Corbin might've been a department head, but he was being groomed for VP. He knew a lot more than we'd guessed."

The next part made Fitz's stomach swoop whenever he thought of it. He ignored the feeling and kept on with the story. Much as he hadn't wanted to talk about it, now that he was, he realized he needed to. He needed to walk through it again with Abe, see where it had all gone wrong. "While Corbin was still in custody, Mary was roughed up. Ended up in the ICU. We figured she told somebody what she'd done, but when Abe pressed her—"

"She hadn't told a soul." The certainty in Abe's voice still confused Fitz. If she had, it would explain a lot. Not everything, but it would be a start. But Abe still maintained that Mary hadn't broken their agreement.

"So wait," Tabby said. "You're saying somebody knew Mary told you guys all about the organization, but she didn't tell anybody. Did you guys tell—?"

"There were people in the department who knew." Fitz related the words automatically. He'd gone over this time and again in his head. "Our captain, a few uniforms who'd helped with the surveillance. We didn't suspect anybody was working against us. We thought somebody'd been careless. You know, somebody said something to somebody who knew Mary. An offhand word, an accidental name... Somehow, somebody found out Mary'd given them up."

"And maybe it wasn't even that," Abe said. "She got arrested but wasn't charged. We helped her craft a story about how she got released, something the dealers would buy. But she quit dealing for them at that time. When Corbin was brought in, maybe they suspected. Maybe she just didn't sell her story well. Maybe they didn't believe her."

"The point is," Fitz said, "we didn't know how they found out. Like I said, though, we didn't suspect anything nefarious was going on. We just figured—"

"Department leaks, teenage lips..." Abe shrugged. "We didn't know."

"But we weren't stupid," Fitz said. "We'd finally gotten the name of the supplier, and we knew when his next shipment was coming in. This time, we kept the circle small."

"Very small," Abe added.

"Just us and one uniformed officer." His stomach did that swooping thing again. "Young guy fresh out of the academy. Andrew."

"And the ADA and the captain," Abe added. "They knew."

"Right. They were in on the planning. We brought in other uniforms the day of the bust, but they didn't know where we were going or who the target was until we got there."

Tabby was nodding along. "In other words, there shouldn't have been any leaks."

"Exactly." Fitz's gaze flicked to Abe, who remained as cool and collected as always.

"Okay," Tabby said. "What happened?"

Fitz said, "We got there early, got in place."

"We'd been told the shipment would come in on a boat, so we were hidden, waiting. We even had the Coast Guard on alert, just in case they got away. The dealer drove up and sat there, also waiting. We spotted the boat in the distance. It looked like it was going to be a clean bust. We'd arrest two dealers and keep a huge shipment of cocaine from getting onto our streets. It would have been the biggest bust of both of our careers."

Fitz glanced at his former partner in the front seat, saw his lips pressed together, his eyes narrow. Gone was the calm confidence of a moment before. The man was angry.

"What happened?" Tabby asked.

"People started firing," Fitz said. "From all sides. It was an ambush."

"We barely made it out alive," Abe said. "Managed to fight back enough to flee."

"Andrew didn't survive," Fitz said. "He had his whole life in front of him, and in the time it takes to squeeze a trigger..." He'd been just a few feet from the kid when it happened. Fitz had pulled his body to cover, but it was too late. Andrew had died instantly.

"Another one of the uniformed officers was critically injured but hung on."

"When the dust settled," Fitz said, "we had one dead, one critically injured. Abe and I walked away unscathed."

Tabby rested her hand on his forearm. For a moment, he'd forgotten she was there. Forgotten he was there. Now, her presence, her touch, shamed him.

"The dealer and the boat?" she asked. "The shooters?"

"The shooters got away. We think they had a dinghy stashed nearby but could never prove it or identify who'd been on it. The Coast Guard stopped the boat but found no drugs. The dealer was stopped before he got home, claimed he'd been out for a late-night drive. The bust was a setup. They'd lured us in and murdered a man. It's a miracle Abe and I walked away."

"How did they know?" Tabby asked

Fitz's gaze bore into the back of Abe's head. "That's the million-dollar question. Internal Affairs investigated. The only uniform who'd known about the bust in advance was Andrew, and he was dead. Though it's possible he'd betrayed us, all the digging into his life, his background, turned up nothing. IA was convinced he didn't betray us. They cleared the captain too. That left Abe and me. And I know I didn't do it."

The silence in the car suddenly felt oppressive. They'd managed to drive through Boston during the conversation, and traffic whizzed by on both sides of Abe while he maintained his steady fifty-five miles per hour as if they weren't in a hurry. As if none of this mattered.

Tabby's grip tightened just a bit, and he met her eyes. He saw kindness there, gentleness.

But those same emotions were still in her gaze when she glanced at Abe.

"You know what the difference between Fitz and me is, Tabby?" Abe asked.

"I can think of a few things."

Abe's low chuckle clambered through Fitz like the screech

of metal against metal. What could he possibly find humorous right now?

"Besides the fact that I'm obviously wiser and much better looking," Abe said.

"Besides those things." Tabby looked Fitz's way quickly. "What else?"

"The biggest difference between us is that when Internal Affairs told Fitz they'd narrowed their suspects down to him or me, he immediately assumed I was guilty. You've heard him say it over and over, right? He knows it wasn't him."

She nodded slowly, her glance again catching Fitz's. But it didn't linger there.

"And you?" she asked. "What did you think?"

"I knew Fitz wasn't the leak. I knew my partner well enough to know he'd never have betrayed me, betrayed our department, and betrayed everything he believed in. To this day, I still don't believe he did it."

"That's because I didn't." Fitz's words were low and seething. Was he admitting his part?

"And I knew I wasn't the leak." Abe found him in the rearview, his coal black eyes blazing. "Unlike you, I didn't take IA's word for what happened."

"What are you saying?" Fitz snapped.

"If that was IA's conclusion, their conclusion was wrong."

Fitz sat back. "That doesn't even... There was nobody else it could've been."

"You, me, the captain, and Andrew, right?"

"Right," Fitz said. "There was nobody—"

"The ADA knew."

Fitz blinked. "She didn't have any details, though. She wasn't involved—"

"She knew about Mary. She knew about Corbin. She knew everything they told us. She knew enough."

He thought back to the woman. Forty-something, heavyset, frizzy hair, and darn good at her job. Fitz had worked with her on a number of cases and never got any vibe from her except authentic. More than authentic, she was enthusiastic about putting bad guys away. "You're saying you really think Karen Smithfield, a woman who made a career out of putting drug dealers and mobsters in prison, sold us out?"

"No. But I think she was the leak."

"What do you mean by that? Do you have proof?"

"Not proof, but evidence," Abe said. "I've been working on proving it for two years. And I could've used your help, but seeing as how you haven't returned any of my phone calls—"

"I thought you betrayed me."

"Yeah." Abe's voice hummed not with anger, not with frustration, but with sadness. "I know."

At one point during the conversation, Tabby had taken her hand away from Fitz's arm. He hadn't noticed, hadn't been thinking of anything but Abe's words. Now, she laced her fingers with his, giving him a squeeze, offering her support, her confidence.

But Fitz felt anything but confident.

Abe hadn't done it?

Fitz had wasted so much time hating the man, and now to find out...

Fitz had been the betrayer. Maybe not of the department, but of their friendship. Abe had consistently and unashamedly shared his faith with Fitz for years, ultimately leading Fitz to a relationship with God, and Fitz, in his arrogance and anger, had cast him aside on the words of a few IA officers. Humans, like the rest of them, who sometimes got it wrong.

Shame rolled over him, hot and heavy. He shook off Tabby's hand and shifted away from her, needing to process it. To accept his own horrible self.

She folded her hands in her lap and looked down at them.

Abe caught his attention in the rearview, held his gaze for a moment before looking at the road again.

Fitz couldn't think it through. They'd both lost their jobs. If Fitz had fought for Abe the way Abe had apparently been fighting for both of them, maybe neither of them would have been forced to resign. But Fitz hadn't fought. He'd simply brushed the dust off his feet and moved on.

Good riddance, Providence PD.

Good riddance, Abe.

Good riddance, dreams. Future.

All because he'd refused to let himself trust. Refused to be shown a fool.

He was a fool. The very worst kind.

But no more. No more.

He reached into the front seat, clamped a hand on Abe's shoulder. "I'm sorry." There was so much more to say, but emotion clogged his throat, and if he kept talking, he'd end up making a bigger fool of himself than he already had.

Abe patted the hand. "All is forgiven."

Just like that.

Who did that?

Abe. Calm, collected, faith-filled Abe. Who'd never quit believing in Fitz even when Fitz quit believing in him.

Fitz sat back again, glancing at Tabby. She smiled as if nothing had changed.

But everything had changed. Except himself, the one thing that needed to change the most.

CHAPTER TWENTY-FOUR

Tabby wasn't sorry she'd asked Fitz and Abe to tell the story of their past, even if that meant the car was quieter now, the conversation more strained. The story had needed to be told.

Poor Fitz. He'd believed the worst of his friend. A man had died right beside him. No wonder he hadn't been thinking straight.

Anybody could've made that mistake. Especially someone like Fitz, someone who didn't trust easily. He'd doubted her too.

What did that say about him? Did it reveal some deep, horrible flaw? Or did it say he was human, just like the rest of them? Yes, Fitz was flawed, a fairly new Christian who was only beginning to trust God. That he didn't trust people wasn't foolish. It was often wise, especially for someone who worked to catch criminals for a living.

She could understand what he'd done. She knew why Abe had forgiven so easily. Hopefully, Fitz would be able to forgive himself. By the look of pure agony on his face, he wasn't there yet.

Rather than reach out to him again when he so clearly

wanted to be left alone, she watched the world pass by her window. They'd left the interstate and were winding along narrow side roads not too different from those back in Coventry. The country road had neither sidewalks nor shoulders, but the lack of traffic told her neither was necessary. Snow covered the forest floor, though not nearly as much as back home. Clapboard, brick, and aluminum-sided houses were spaced acres apart. They sat on deep lots surrounded by low rock walls that were so common in New England. Though the leaves were off the trees, she could imagine what the lawns would look like in the summertime, all lush and gorgeous, graced by hydrangeas and rhododendrons and rose bushes.

Though the homes weren't overlarge, the luxury cars and boats parked in their driveways and their proximity to the coast told her it was no low-budget neighborhood. And... was that a lake she spied through the trees?

Yes, this neighborhood was miles out of her budget.

Abe turned into a narrow driveway and parked in front of a two-story brown clapboard house designed like her own Cape Cod. At first glance, it looked hardly larger than hers, but she spied a good-sized addition off the back.

Abe climbed from the car and opened her door for her. She stepped out. "Thanks."

"Sure."

Fitz met them without a word, and the three walked toward the front door.

She slipped her hand in his on the way, and he smiled at her. The melancholy that had wafted off him in the car lingered, but the smile gave her hope. He'd figure out how to get past this with Abe.

He leaned down and spoke low in her ear. "Let us do the talking, okay?"

As if she had anything to add. "Of course."

He held her gaze a moment longer than necessary.

When she turned back to Abe, she saw him studying a rock just off the path. About the size of a dinner plate, somebody had painted on it. She leaned closer to see the words, faded as if it'd been there a long time.

Welcome to Folly's Fortune.

It was odd to name a house anyway, but to name it that? She glanced at Fitz, who shrugged. They walked up the three wooden steps to the front door, and Abe rang the bell.

No answer.

A moment later, he knocked, hard.

From inside, they heard, "I'm on my way."

The door swung open, and a woman stood on the other side, adjusting a scarf over a bald head. Her skin was pale and had a gray pallor. She wore no makeup and had no eyebrows. She was hunched over. At first glance, Tabby would have guessed she was in her seventies or older.

But the second glance was the one that mattered.

Her skin was gray but not wrinkled. She was hunched, but not with osteoporosis. Tabby guessed the woman was in pain, or just very weak, as she gripped the doorframe, her knuckles white with strain. "Can I help you?"

"I hope so, ma'am." Abe swung the storm door open and took the woman's arm. "If it's all right that we come inside, why don't you let me help you to a chair?"

"Probably a good idea." She turned and, leaning on Abe's arm, led them deeper into the house.

They walked through a formal living room, then through the kitchen and into the addition on the back, a family room.

Abe helped her settle into a leather recliner. "My name is Abe Bachelor. These are my friends, Fitz McCaffrey and Tabby Eaton. Fitz and I are private investigators, and we want to ask you a few questions."

Mrs. Hernandez didn't seem surprised to find two PIs in her family room. "Have a seat," she said. "How can I help you?"

Fitz settled on the sofa closest to Mrs. Hernandez, and Tabby sat beside him. Abe chose a club chair on her opposite side.

Tabby had expected Abe to do the talking. His soothing voice and gentle nature seemed to encourage people to trust him. But it was Fitz who spoke.

"You have a lovely home." Fitz's gaze seemed to take it all in.

Tabby did the same. The view out the oversize windows on the back wall showed stark, leafless trees shading a yard dotted with snow. Beyond that, a pier jutted into the lake.

Inside, an oversize TV console filled one wall. A few photographs, most of the same little girl at different ages, graced the shelves around the set. On lower shelves were a video game console and stacks of board games and puzzles.

The wall opposite was covered with overflowing bookcases. Not fancy leather-bound books but well-loved, well-worn paperbacks. The bottom few rows held children's books that seemed to be grouped by age going from board books for babies to titles teenage girls would like.

"How long have you lived here, Mrs. Hernandez?" Fitz had been brooding since the conversation with Abe, but his voice gave none of that away. He seemed as laid back and casual as if he were visiting an old friend.

"Ginger, please. I know I don't look it, but I'm not that much older than you."

Fitz smiled. "Okay, Ginger."

"I guess I've been here..." She paused to consider the question. "Going on twenty-four years now."

"This must've been a wonderful place to raise children." He nodded to the photographs on the console. "Is that your daughter?"

"That's Veronica. My only child."

"You and your husband must be very proud," Fitz said.

The woman's smile didn't slip. "No husband, just Veronica and me."

"I guess she's at school today."

"Oh, no. She's in her twenties now. Lives in New York." Ginger reached for a cup on the table beside her, one of those plastic ones with the bendy straw sticking out like hospitals gave to their patients. Her hand was shaking with the effort.

Fitz snatched it and started to hand it to her, then stopped. "Could we get you some more? Is it water?"

"I'd appreciate that."

Before Tabby could move, Abe jumped up. "You want ice?"

"No, thank you. I prefer it tepid, even on the warm side."

Abe walked toward the kitchen and disappeared to the far side of the counter. A moment later, the faucet turned on.

"New York," Fitz said. "At least that's not too far a drive. I hope she comes home a lot."

"More so lately." She adjusted her headscarf. "It's funny how a little cancer can help us remember what's important."

"I'm sorry to hear that," Fitz said. "Do you mind if I ask—?"

"It's funny, really. All the stupid, reckless, and foolish things I did as a young person. Drinking, drugs, not to mention men." She looked past Fitz to Tabby. "Don't make my mistakes, honey. The ones who look dangerous probably are."

"I'll keep that in mind," Tabby said.

Fitz took Tabby's hand. "Hopefully Tabby's found a guy who's not *that* dangerous."

Ginger's eyes danced. "You two are together?"

Tabby said, "Not really."

At the same time, Fitz said, "We are," and glanced her way with raised eyebrows.

After firing a look at him, Tabby said, "We're still in negotiations."

Ginger laughed, which turned into a cough. Abe hurried in and handed her the cup of water, and Ginger took a long sip. When she'd regained her voice, she met Tabby's eyes. "He seems like a nice enough man, but they all do at first. Take your time, make sure he is who he says he is."

Tabby regarded Fitz a long moment before nodding at Ginger. "Good advice."

Fitz groaned. "You're not helping."

Ginger didn't seem a bit chagrined. "Anyway, all the stupid stuff I did... I figured one of those things for sure would be the death of me," Ginger said. "But no. It was the cigarettes." She shook her head. "If I'd thought for a minute I was going to live this long..."

"Lung cancer?" Fitz asked.

"A very aggressive form. Ever since I was diagnosed, Veronica has come home as often as she can. She travels a lot, though. Which is fine. She has a life. I want her to live it."

"What does she do?"

"She's a personal stylist." Ginger sat up a little straighter. "Isn't that a funny job? She worked at Bloomingdale's all through college. It started as a way to earn extra money. I try to be generous with her, but that girl can spend money like nobody's business. I had to impose some limits. Well, she loves to shop and met a lot of people through her work, so when she graduated, she somehow figured out a way to make a business out of it."

"How does that lead to travel?" Fitz asked.

She lifted her bony shoulders and let them drop. "I guess she meets clients wherever they are." Ginger waved away the words. "Honestly, I haven't the foggiest idea. She's making her way. That's all that matters to me."

"May I ask..." Fitz leaned a little closer to Ginger. "What's the prognosis?"

Ginger's smile dimmed. "Not good. Veronica has been researching trials. There's one in particular she's trying to get me into, but it's expensive, and there's no guarantee. They might be able to extend my life by a few years, but, honestly, I'm tired. I'm ready to be done. She has a life. She doesn't need me anymore. There's nobody else worth hanging on for. I'm ready to go back to dust. To just...not exist."

What a sad belief. And how much pain must Ginger feel to yearn for that?

Fitz took the woman's hand and leaned toward her. "I'm so, so sorry."

Tabby understood now why Fitz was the one doing the talking. He had a way of connecting with people, of making them feel loved and valued. Of seeming trustworthy. Maybe not just *seeming* it, but did he really care about this woman?

He made her think he did, just like he'd made Tabby think he cared about her. Maybe it was all a lie.

Ginger patted the top of Fitz's hand before pulling away. "Tell me. Why are you here?"

Fitz sat back. "We're investigating a man named Ronald Mullins. Have you heard of him?"

Her lips twitched as if she were fighting a smile. "We're acquainted."

Fitz said nothing, just waited.

After a moment, she added, "I used to work for him."

The silence in the room deepened, like a dark cloud passing over the sun. Tabby was tempted to fill it, but they'd asked her to keep quiet. It was no easy task. If she felt uncomfortable, how must this woman, the poor sick woman, feel?

Why didn't anybody say anything?

She was just about to when Ginger spoke again.

"I assume you already knew that."

"You were the manager of his nightclub," Fitz said. "Back in the day."

The woman's lips, cracked as they were, stretched into a smile. "I assume you also know he owns this house."

Fitz leaned forward. "I'm sure there's a good reason for that. We're curious as to what it is."

"I'm sure you are." Her bright eyes sparkled against her gray pallor. "I suppose it doesn't matter that much anymore, the secret. Everybody who matters knows the truth."

"Which is?"

"Why do you want to know?"

"It's sort of a long story. Mr. Mullins has asked me to find something for him."

"*Asked* you?" The skin over her eyes lifted, though there was no hair there to act as raised eyebrows. "Do you work for him?"

"Not exactly."

Ginger's gaze flicked to Tabby, then to Abe. "You're all looking for this...thing? Why?"

Fitz spoke for them all. "Like I said, it's—"

"A long story," she supplied. "And you would like me to tell you who I am to him because somehow, this could help you find that something?"

"At this point," Fitz said, "I think mostly you'll help us eliminate this line of thinking, maybe even provide a clue for us. You used to work for him. Somebody stole from him. We're trying to figure out who."

"If you don't work for him, then why...? " She tapped her nose with the tip of her finger, then dropped the hand. All amusement was gone from her voice when she said, "What does he have on you? Do you owe him money? Did you double-cross him? Why—?"

"He took my little sister." Fitz remained calm, though that muscle in his cheek twitched. "She's safe. She thinks she's having an impromptu vacation with her new boyfriend and his family."

"Shawn." Ginger's lips pressed closed, and she turned her gaze to the wintery scene outside the window. Again, silence filled the room. Another beat passed before Ginger focused on Fitz again. "How old is he now?"

"Seventeen, I think." Fitz didn't seem taken aback by the question like Tabby was. "My sister just turned sixteen."

"Did Ronnie ask you to come talk to me?"

Fitz shook his head, maybe too fast. "He'd probably be angry if he knew we were here. He thinks he knows who stole from him, but he's wrong. I'm trying to find out who really did it."

Ginger sat back, took a deep breath. "If he didn't ask you to come, then I wouldn't tell him if I were you. He prefers to pretend I don't exist."

Again, Fitz said nothing, just watched and waited.

"I assume you've guessed why he owns the house."

"Veronica." Fitz didn't explain, just let the name float in the room. But Tabby understood. She'd had a friend in college named Veronica who went by Ronnie.

Ginger's daughter was named after her father.

"He and I had been seeing each other for a year—this was back when I managed the club. He swore upside-down and backward he was going to leave his wife. There was always some good reason why he couldn't do it yet. The holidays, one of the kids' birthdays, some business deal he needed to get wrapped up. And I believed him. Every time. I was so young and reckless and… I thought I was in love. I realize now I was more attracted to his power and his money than I was to him. I loved the free-flowing drugs, the respect people showed me because they knew I was with him.

"From the very start, he's considered Veronica to be an accident. His little *oops*. I've never told him the truth, that I quit taking my birth control. I thought, if I got pregnant, it would hurry the process along. He loved his other kids so much, and I figured..." The way her lips stretched might technically be a smile, but it was nothing like those she'd given earlier. If those had been lamp-bright, this was more nightlight-wattage, as if the very thought of how her daughter had come to be dimmed her joy.

"Rather than leave Lena, which I realized later he'd never planned to do, he fired me, dumped me, and sent me on my way. I moved home to my parents' house, got a job waiting tables, and swore I'd win him back. I schemed and plotted. I even considered telling his wife about us, but a wise friend suggested I might not survive that foolishness, so I decided against it. When he offered to pay me off, I was indignant, swearing I wanted nothing from him. I thought he'd miss me. I thought he'd come to his senses. As the baby grew in my belly, so did my desperation. I'd have done anything to make him mine. And then, when Veronica was a few weeks old, I looked into her beautiful eyes, and everything changed. Whatever feelings I'd had for him, the love, the hate, the attraction, the bitterness"—she flicked her wrist as if waving them all away—"they all faded when I looked at my daughter's innocent, trusting face.

"I didn't want him or his drugs or his dangerous lifestyle anywhere near my child. I swallowed my pride, called him up, and asked him to help. He bought me this place, and I agreed to leave him and his family in peace."

Fitz looked around. "Not a bad deal."

"He didn't do it for me. Think whatever you want of him, he loves his children, even the illegitimate one. He wanted her to grow up somewhere safe, away from the city, away from his enemies. He's taken very good care of us over the years."

"You said everybody knows. Did his wife—?"

"After Veronica was born, he told Lena everything. Despite what happened between him and me, it seems he's very devoted to her. I wondered for a time if she would forgive him, if they'd ever be able to get over it. And then Shawn came along. Not that I was still pining, but maybe on some level, I'd hoped... Shawn's birth was good for me, for my mental health. I was finally able to let go of the fantasy."

"How old was Veronica then?"

Ginger's eyes flicked toward the ceiling. "Six, I think. Maybe seven by the time I heard the news."

"Does Veronica have a relationship with her father?"

Ginger's head dipped, then lifted. "That was the deal. He'd provide for us, and I'd give him access to his daughter. Not custody, not even joint custody. There were no weekend visits or summers at his house. But he made an effort to know her over the years. He'd come see her, usually about once a month, always bearing gifts. She used to adore him. When she was in high school, some of that adoration faded as she realized what happened between us. I think she's come to terms with it now."

"Her spending time with him—that must've been hard for you."

Again, the bony shoulders shrugged. "According to Veronica, he lectured her about living her life on the right side of the law. Told her in no uncertain terms that if he ever heard of her stepping a foot out of line, he'd cut us both off. Veronica was angry, thought he was a hypocrite. Maybe he is, I don't know. But if he's trying to keep his kids out of the business, I'm all for it."

Once again, Fitz reached out and patted the woman's hand gently. "Thank you for trusting us with that story."

Ginger sipped her drink, then sat back against the recliner. She looked even more tired than when they'd arrived.

"You knew him a long time ago," Fitz said. "Is there anybody you think would have it out for him? A woman, perhaps? Were there any other women?"

"I don't think so, but it's not as if he'd have confided in me. And as to enemies... I haven't been a part of that world in so long."

"Okay, then." Fitz glanced at Abe. "Did you have any questions?" When Abe shook his head, Fitz turned to Tabby.

"I think you covered it," she said.

Fitz shifted back to Ginger. "We appreciate your time. Is there anything we can get for you before we go?"

"My home healthcare worker will be here soon to fix me lunch. But thank you."

Fitz started to stand, then settled again and leaned toward Ginger. "One more thing. Earlier you said you were ready to no longer exist. Is that what you think is going to happen when you die?"

"How should I know?"

"Do you believe in God?"

Her head tipped to one side. "I never had much use for God," she said. "Always wanted to live my life on my terms. And that's how I'm gonna die too. On my terms."

Fitz took her hand. "You might not have use for Him, but He has use for you. He loves you. Loves you more than you can possibly imagine. He loves you enough that He sent his Son to die a terrible death so He could spend eternity with you."

Ginger pulled her hand away. "You obviously weren't listening."

"There's no sin so great that God won't forgive. He wants to give you peace for today and eternity for tomorrow. I know this because I've done some terrible things myself, things I'm ashamed of, but He forgave me."

Abe leaned toward Ginger. "And me," he said.

"And me," Tabby added.

"Maybe that's why we're here," Fitz said. "Maybe our coming here has nothing to do with saving my sister and everything to do with telling you the truth. That there is a God, and He loves you, and He wants you to know Him. Now, before it's too late."

She shook her head. "Did you see the rock when you walked in?"

Fitz sat back. *"Folly's Fortune.* What's it mean?"

"It means I'll never be good enough for your God. I took sin a step too far." She gestured to her bald head and wasted body. "And I'll pay the price."

CHAPTER TWENTY-FIVE

Fitz had never tried to tell anybody but his sister about Christ before. There Ginger was, on the brink of death, and she wasn't even willing to listen to words of hope. Fitz had made a mess of it.

As they said their good-byes and walked to the car, he replayed what he'd said, trying to think how he could have phrased it in a way that helped Ginger to understand. No solution came to him.

What he did know was that Ginger wasn't capable of flying to Belize, much less breaking into a safe. She could hardly walk across the house by herself. When he'd begun to believe they were wasting their time, he'd convinced himself God had led them there to tell Ginger about Christ. But nope. That had been a bust too.

And they were no closer to finding the stolen goods and saving his sister.

He yanked open the passenger door and climbed in, only thinking of Tabby in back by herself after she'd slipped in behind him.

"You want to sit up here?"

Tabby didn't respond. When he turned to face her, her eyes were bright, excited, and Fitz couldn't figure out why. He was about to ask when Abe spoke.

"I'm impressed." Abe backed out of the driveway and turned the way they'd come. "All those years working with you, I never thought I'd hear you tell somebody about God."

"Lot of good it did," Fitz said.

"It usually takes more than one conversation. I mean, how many times did you have to hear it from me before the truth got through your thick skull?"

The man made a point.

"You never know," Abe continued. "Seeds get planted. Seeds get watered. Did you plant today or water?" He flipped his hands up on the steering wheel, a *who knows?* gesture. "But you told her about God. What happens now is between Him and her."

Maybe Abe was right. And maybe that didn't have to be his last interaction with Ginger Hernandez. "I could call her sometime." Fitz considered that, tried to think what he'd say. "Or send her a book. She seems to like to read. I just hate to think of her dying without knowing, you know?"

Abe turned his way. "I do know."

"Yeah. I guess you would, all those years of—"

"We need to talk about Veronica." Tabby's voice was too loud in the small space.

Fitz turned toward her. "Why? Did you—?"

"It's Vera."

Abe asked, "Vera is—?"

"The woman from Belize." Tabby leaned toward them. "The one who—"

"Talked to you at dinner. I remember now." Abe pulled the car over and swiveled to face her.

"I saw her portrait on our way out," Tabby said. "The one hanging in the entry by the staircase."

"The one in the cap and gown?" Fitz had seen it, too, and considered how different the grown-up Veronica looked from the little girl's images in the family room.

"It was her." Tabby's voice was pitched higher than usual, and her words came out fast. "I think, I'm almost positive, Veronica is Vera. And Vera is the thief."

Twenty minutes later, they were seated in a booth at a deli off Route 1, a place Fitz never would have chosen. He was more a burger-and-fries kind of guy, but Tabby'd suggested it, and Abe had agreed, and Fitz hadn't wanted to be the dissenter. Fitz sat beside Tabby, his laptop open, Tabby leaning close to see what he saw. He was almost completely focused on the mystery they were trying to solve, though a tiny part of him couldn't help but notice the warm, beautiful woman beside him.

Across the table, Abe was looking at his own screen.

An image of Veronica Hernandez stared back at them. "Is that her?" Fitz asked.

"I'm almost positive," Tabby said.

Mullins's daughter had long brown hair and wide-set brown eyes. He could see more of her mother in her than her father. Though Ginger looked sickly now, he imagined she'd once been a beautiful woman, and her daughter took after her. Very high cheekbones gave her an exotic look. Unlike Ginger's more Latin complexion, Veronica's skin was pale, though not quite as pale as her father's. She even had the Irish freckles.

"Her hair was short and spiky and blond," Tabby said.

"A wig, maybe."

"Maybe. And she was tanned, but so was I after two weeks in Belize."

"Okay. So, Veronica could have learned about the trip to Belize from her father. He told me himself his family knew he'd be down there, and she is family."

Abe looked over his laptop. "But how did she know about the jewels?"

"Mullins said Lena wore them the day they left," Fitz said. "Maybe she saw them?"

"How, though?" Abe was looking up, trying to work it out. "They live in Boston."

Fitz considered that. "But Mullins would've had to get the things he'd bought at the auction house, which is in Manhattan. Maybe they stayed at one of the apartments in Manhattan. Maybe they flew out of Kennedy." That could all work, but... "The thing is, the jewels are so big, they don't look real. She'd have to have gotten a really close look at them to know they were authentic."

"Unless someone told her," Abe said.

"Who, though?" Tabby seemed as perplexed as Fitz was. "I doubt Lena and Veronica are friends. His wife and his illegitimate daughter?"

"Unless there's more going on there than we know. Maybe they're conspiring against him."

Felt like a stretch. Lena had seemed content beside Mullins whenever Fitz had seen them at the resort.

"Maybe the boy," Abe said. "Maybe somehow, the teenager and Veronica are friends."

"Shawn didn't know about the jewels, though." Mullins had made that clear. "He'd probably thought what his mom wore was fake."

"If he even noticed them," Tabby added. "I promise my

brothers wouldn't have noticed my mother's jewelry when they were teenagers. They probably don't notice now."

The three were quiet a moment. Fitz studied the image and his notes and tried to put it together.

Across from them, Abe said, "She wasn't easy to find online. She goes by Veronica Dawn. Maybe her middle name? Her website says she's a personal stylist, just like Ginger told us. Maybe Lena was a client."

"Even so." Tabby sounded as frustrated as he felt. "Surely Lena wouldn't have told her personal stylist about her husband's plans."

"You're right." Fitz barely lifted his attention from the notes he was staring at. "She's the wife of a big shot in a huge crime family. He didn't stay out of prison for all these years because his wife runs her mouth. No, she's too smart for that."

The quiet returned until their lunches were delivered. Oversize sandwiches and chips for himself and Abe, a salad for Tabby. He gave her meal a pointed look before meeting her eyes.

"It's delicious." Her chin lifted, daring him to argue with her.

She was so adorable, he couldn't help leaning close. He lowered his voice, whispered in her ear. "So are you."

A tremor skidded over her skin. Fitz loved that his words had caused it.

Across the table, Abe said, "I'll just sit here and eat. You two go ahead."

Tabby's cheeks turned the faintest shade of pink, and she focused on her salad.

It took Fitz a moment longer to get his thoughts right again.

After a few bites, Abe pushed the plate aside and focused on his computer screen. "I'm looking at her business website.

No address, just a post office box in Manhattan. I'm going to try to find out where she lives."

"Probably in that second apartment," Tabby said. "Don't you think? The one in Greenwich Village."

Again, Fitz turned her way. "You are brilliant."

Her slight blush deepened. "She is his daughter. And remember what Ginger said—that he'd threatened to cut off *both* of them? He must be supporting her to a degree."

"Got it here." Abe tapped a few buttons, then rattled off an address.

MacDougal Street. Why did that sound familiar?

There was something... Fitz bit into his roast beef. The sandwich was delicious, much better than he'd expected. While he ate, he studied his notes, flipping through the last couple of pages. Nothing. He flipped back until... "Got it."

Tabby leaned closer, and the scent of her mixed with the thrill of finding the connection and created an alluring concoction that nearly had him losing the thought.

"What'd you find?" she asked.

Next time, he'd have her sit beside Abe so he could focus. "Gail Seder, the surrogate bidder. The one who bought the goods at auction."

Abe swallowed a bite of his sandwich. "What about her?"

"She lives at 122 MacDougal Street."

Abe sat back. "They live in the same building."

"There's the missing piece," Fitz said.

"I wonder if..." Tabby speared a bite of salad but didn't eat it, just stared past Abe. "Maybe Gail told Ronnie about the empty apartment. Maybe Mullins chose it for his daughter."

"Or maybe," Fitz said, "Veronica learned of her father's connection with Gail and chose that building herself because Gail lived there. Maybe she's been planning this for a long time."

"Or maybe it's a coincidence," Abe said. "Whatever the reason, that's got to be how Veronica learned about her father's purchases at the auction house that day."

"But Mullins trusts Gail. Why would she betray that trust?"

"Maybe she didn't." Tabby looked from Abe to Fitz. "Veronica's obviously a professional thief. Maybe she simply broke into Gail's apartment—"

"And found the information herself," Fitz finished. "Very possible."

Abe was giving Tabby a rare look. His old friend was impressed with her.

Fitz had brought Tabby along to keep her safe, but she was proving very helpful.

"So, Veronica learned of the trip from Mullins," Fitz said, "and she learned of the jewels from Gail, somehow. She put two and two together—"

"Maybe she even watched to see if Lena was wearing the jewels when they left," Tabby said, "just to be sure. I wonder if she went to see him that day."

"I could ask him, but…" The thought died a painful death. "He loves his family. If his daughter stole from him—"

"You're gonna have to prove it," Abe said. "Beyond a shadow. That's not exactly a healthy accusation to make against the man's daughter."

"Yeah." Fitz looked at the meal he'd barely touched. He was hungry, but he'd have to wait for the acid churning in his gut to settle before he'd be able to force down another bite.

Telling Ronald Mullins that his own daughter had double-crossed him felt like a very dangerous move.

CHAPTER TWENTY-SIX

"How far do you live from here?"

Tabby's question pulled Fitz from his musings as he polished off his roast beef sandwich. Abe had excused himself to go to the restroom. "About a half hour, maybe a little more."

"I'd love to see it."

He turned to better face her. Things hadn't been exactly comfortable between them since their kiss. They'd held hands a couple of times. But that was no different from how they'd been in Belize, back when she'd insisted they couldn't have a relationship. Now though, she could no longer pretend she felt nothing but friendship for him. The feelings he'd sensed when she'd been in his arms... He might not want to name them, but if he did, *friendship* wouldn't make the list.

And then her quip at Ginger's house after he'd suggested they were in a relationship.

We're still in negotiations.

It gave him hope.

As did her remark just now.

As did the way her cheeks turned pink while she waited for

him to respond. "I mean, if we were near there or whatever." Hedging like a stock trader. She returned her attention to her salad, letting her hair fall between them.

He brushed it back to get a look at her face and felt her shudder at his touch. "I would love to show it to you. When this is all over—"

"I shouldn't have..." Her head shook quickly, and she angled away. "Nothing's changed."

Anger rose at her words, but it fizzled quickly because her words didn't carry any weight. They didn't hum with certainty the way they had before. They didn't hum with finality.

Pushing him away had become her habit, her fallback.

He leaned close, lowering his voice so people at neighboring tables wouldn't hear. "Everything has changed, and you know it."

She said nothing for a moment, then, "I think I'll visit the restroom myself."

Running away. Also her habit.

But Fitz was too much of a gentleman to call her on it. He stood as Tabby slipped past him and watched her until she disappeared down a hallway, wishing he could read her mind. Figure out what she was so afraid of.

Abe settled in his seat. "Should we head to Manhattan? Search Veronica's apartment?"

Fitz dropped onto the bench and forced himself to shift back to the task at hand. "You think she'd have them there?"

"It's a place to start." His eyes squinted and seemed unfocused. "Let's think the timeline through. When was the auction?"

Fitz flipped through his notes. "Almost four weeks ago."

"Assuming Veronica didn't learn about the purchase until after it happened, she'd have had to make some pretty quick plans. She had to get herself to Belize, find a place to stay, case the resort, find a patsy, and get a disguise."

"And find a buyer," Fitz added. "A buyer with enough cash to take all the items, don't you think?"

"That'd be the easiest way to go. She'd get less than they're worth, but it's less exposure than selling the pieces separately."

"Do we think this is something she's done before? I mean, is she some kind of international jewel thief?"

"She sure knew how to crack that safe," Abe said. "That's not a skill they teach in college."

"True. But she could've learned that."

Abe's mouth slid into a smirk. "In three weeks? I don't know. I think she had to already know how to do it. But ripping off her own father... Why him?"

Tabby returned to the table, and Fitz scooted over, giving her the outside. They wouldn't stay much longer anyway, their meals finished, their plates stacked in the center of the table.

"What are we talking about?" Tabby asked.

Abe filled her in. "We're trying to figure out why Veronica would go against her father's wishes."

"And target him," Fitz added.

"You don't think it's because of Ginger's cancer?" Tabby looked from Fitz to Abe and back. "I just assumed she was trying to raise the money for that clinical trial."

"Ginger doesn't want it." Abe rubbed his chin. "But maybe Veronica thinks that, if the money were there, she'd try it."

"I think she's trying to save her mother's life," Tabby said.

"I agree," Fitz said.

Tabby tapped the side of her cup. "I wonder how much she needs. Medical bills can be ridiculously expensive."

Fitz thought about Chris in that wheelchair. Tabby would understand Veronica's motives as much as any of them. Still, though... "Probably not half a million dollars. Who would be able to do it if the price were that high?"

"So she has some leeway on what she needs to get for the stolen goods." Abe was nodding now. "She can sell fast for a deep discount and still have enough to pay for the trial."

"And maybe to make a down payment on a new apartment in the city, if it comes to that," Fitz added.

"But Mullins said he would stop supporting Ginger," Abe reminded him. "Veronica's risking her mother's future."

"Her mother has no future." Tabby's gaze flicked between them. "The woman's prognosis is terminal. You saw her today. That house is the least of Veronica's worries."

"So what do we know?" Fitz let the pieces swirl in his mind. "Veronica has to sell the goods fast. Her mother doesn't have much time, and even if she did, the last thing Veronica wants is to get caught with them. She's had them for five days already. For all we know, they could be gone." And if they were gone, how would Fitz get them back?

And if he couldn't, what would happen to Shelby? To Tabby?

"Let's not go there yet," Abe said. "One obstacle at a time."

"Seems like we need to find her. How do we do that?" Tabby asked.

"I'll check with my guy at the FBI." Abe grabbed his laptop, shoved it in its case, and slid from the booth. "See if she's on their radar."

"Why is he helping you?" Fitz hadn't meant the question to come out so harsh, but he didn't understand how Abe had that connection. After everything that had gone down, Abe should have been discredited. Nobody in law enforcement should trust him with anything.

Abe seemed to hear the accusation in the question. "He's part of a drug task force working to bring down suppliers in

New England. We're trying to narrow down who the true leak was two years ago. He believes if we can figure that out, we can use it to set a trap."

A little twinge of hope, no larger than the head of a pin, pricked Fitz's being. If they could prove another person had been the leak, then his name would be cleared.

He could return to law enforcement.

He could get his life back.

"How close are you?"

Abe held his gaze a long moment. "We're close." The note of warning hummed below the words. Close meant nothing. They'd been close before, and it'd all fallen apart. "Close enough that my contact is convinced you and I are innocent. Because of that, he's willing to help us." He lifted his phone. "I'll make the call."

Abe skirted the tables and stepped outside.

It was twelve thirty, and the restaurant was buzzing with customers. In fact, a number of people were standing along the edges, looking for a table. Fitz felt a few of their glares.

"Let's head to the car."

They took their things and followed Abe's path. Low clouds obscured the little sunshine they'd had that morning. Abe was standing just outside the door, talking into his cell. Fitz didn't want to interrupt him to get the keys.

He and Tabby wandered toward the Lincoln .

Tabby propped her hip against the back door to face him. "You're very good at getting people to trust you."

If this were a cartoon, warning lights would flash around the dialog bubble of her words. Where was she going with that? Was she about to accuse him of manipulating her? But in her eyes, he only saw openness, honesty. "It's a skill I've honed over the years." He spoke slowly, carefully. "It served me well as a cop. Serves me well as an investigator. I try not to use it to my own benefit, but I suppose—"

"That wasn't censure, Fitz."

"Oh. Okay."

"I was just going to suggest that, if Abe can't find her, maybe you can. Why don't you call her? Use your skills to try to figure out where she is. I'd do it myself, but she might recognize my voice from that night at the restaurant. And you're better at asking the right questions than I am, obviously."

Fitz realized what she was saying. "Pose as a potential client, you mean? But don't you figure most of her clients are women?"

The look Tabby gave him—eyebrows raised, small smile. It was some combination of *aren't you adorable* and *what an idiot*. "A lot of women like to shop. People who hire personal stylists do so because they *don't* like to shop but need to look good. They're also people who have a lot of disposable income and not a lot of time. You don't suppose a few men fit into that category?"

She made a point, a point he'd not have figured himself. "You and I make a good team." Before she could argue, he kissed her cheek and whispered, "Don't pretend you don't know it's true."

Abe was making his way across the parking lot toward them, so Fitz backed up a step and called, "Well?"

"He's gonna look into it." But the look on Abe's face said there was more.

He used the key to unlock the door—no keyless entry for this twentieth-century clunker—and hit the button to unlock the rest. The button had probably been a novelty when the car'd been built. They all slid inside. Abe took his time starting the car.

"Tabby had an idea." While Fitz explained it, Abe was nodding along.

"I like it. I say make the call."

Fitz found the number, then closed his eyes and thought through what he'd say. He needed a plausible story. When he had the details worked out, he reached for the door handle.

Abe grabbed his arm. "Stay in the car. We'll be quiet."

He didn't want to, though. He didn't want Tabby to hear what a smooth liar he was. But this had been her idea, after all, and... And he couldn't come up with a plausible reason why he needed privacy. He sent up a quick prayer for success and dialed, half expecting to get voice mail.

But the call connected. "Veronica Dawn." Her voice was similar to her mother's, only slightly higher pitched and much stronger.

"Yeah, hi," he said, sounding uncertain. On purpose. "My name is Jerry." The alias he always used because it could be explained away if necessary—Fitzgerald... Jerry. "I got your name from someone at..." He laughed as if he were embarrassed. "I forget. That fancy department store with all the... I was gonna say clothes, but I guess that'd describe them all."

"Probably Bloomingdale's." Her voice was confident, if a little amused by his bumbling. "I worked there for years. They refer clients to me often."

"That sounds right," he said.

"How can I help you, Jerry?"

"Well..." He started to run his hand through his hair, getting into character even though Veronica couldn't see him, but stopped himself when he remembered Tabby could. "I, uh, I'm trying to get a promotion at work. I think they're leaning toward this woman, even though I'm more qualified than she is. I mean, she's great and all, don't get me wrong, but I have more experience, and..." He was trying to sound like a bumbling idiot and felt he was doing a pretty good job. He wanted to seem like somebody who needed a lot of help. He wanted her to want to help him. "Anyway, one of my coworkers suggested that I should dress the part. She said the way I dress makes it seem like I don't take my job seriously. And she's probably right. She usually is about things like that. And, well, everything."

Veronica's laugh sounded genuine. "It sounds like she's a good friend to tell you the truth."

He was winging this, but what he said next felt right. That was the way it always went with him. Get into a conversation, feel around, figure out what buttons to push to get the reaction he needed. "A friend. Yeah. But, you know..." He let the final words hang in the air.

"I'm guessing you'd like her to be more than a friend?" The intuition, the kindness in her voice... He thought, under different circumstances, he'd like this woman. She seemed kind.

Maybe Veronica was as smooth a liar as Fitz was.

He put dejection into his voice, just a twinge. "She never looks twice at me, though."

"She looked long enough to notice the way you dress."

He brightened his tone. "Hey, you're right. Maybe there is hope."

"There's always hope, Jerry. Is this an office job?"

"I work for an insurance company." Seemed a safe enough bet. There were a million of those.

"And how do you dress now?"

"Oh, you know. Slacks, golf shirts in the summer, sweaters in the winter. But, I gotta admit... I mean, I hate to shop. Most of my clothes I've been wearing since college. The only new stuff I have I got from my mom for Christmas. It's not really my style."

"What would you say your style is?" Veronica asked.

Another awkward chuckle. "Uh, whatever's the least wrinkled?"

That elicited another laugh. "I can see why you need my help." She explained her process and fees, and Fitz made the appropriate responses to show he was interested.

"That all sounds fine," Fitz said. "And it'll pay for itself if you can help me get the promotion."

"The promotion and the girl," she added.

Fitz was nodding as if she could see him. He froze, again thinking of Tabby in the backseat. At least he couldn't see her face. "Yeah, that too. How soon can we meet? I'm free this afternoon and all weekend. I'd like to get going on this ASAP."

"Unfortunately, I'm out of town through the weekend."

"Oh, yeah? Someplace warm, I hope. I'd love to get away from this dreary weather."

"I'm spending a few days in the Keys. I have some business down here."

He met Abe's eyes. "The Keys. No kidding?"

Abe snatched his laptop.

"What's it like down there?" Fitz asked. "No, wait. Don't tell me. Perfect, right? Eighties and sunny, sandy beaches and warm water."

"Pretty much. Except it's supposed to hit ninety today."

He groaned. "I'm in the wrong business. Maybe I should become a personal stylist."

"This from a man who couldn't remember the name of Bloomingdale's."

He chuckled for her benefit. "Good point. I guess I'd better stick to actuarial tables."

"Speaking of dreary."

"Next week, then?"

They set up an appointment, and he ended the call. Slowly, he turned to face Tabby, prepared to see horror or disappointment in her expression.

What he saw surprised him. She looked... impressed. "Wow, you're good at that."

"I try to use my powers for good."

She reached between the seats and laid her hand on his arm. "You're trying to save your sister's life. I'd say that's better than good."

CHAPTER TWENTY-SEVEN

As soon as Fitz hung up the phone, Abe shoved his laptop into Fitz's lap and started driving. "There's a flight in an hour and a half."

Fitz saw the flight numbers Abe had found and dialed Mullins.

He answered on the second ring. "I hope you have good news."

"We think we know who the thief is."

"Who?"

"When I get you the stuff, and when I have my sister back, I'll tell you. But we need to fly out today. You got a card number we can use? I don't have enough cash left to—"

"Where?"

"South Florida."

"And the woman's still with you?"

"Tabby's going to stay with me. She didn't do it."

"What about the other guy, the black guy?" Mullins asked.

Of course Willie had told Mullins about Abe's presence. The last thing Fitz wanted was to drag Abe deeper in with Mullins than he already had. "He's a friend of Tabby's. He didn't know what was going on, just came along to her house because he was worried about her."

"He's not with you anymore?"

"It's just the two of us." Another smooth lie. He'd buy Abe's ticket himself.

"I'll let this play out. For now." Mullins's flat tone didn't foster a lot of confidence. "As long as the Eaton woman stays with you. She's still my number one suspect."

"If she were guilty, why would she still be with me?"

"My guess? She sold the goods, and she's trying to get them back now that she knows I'm onto her."

Unfortunately, his guess made sense. If Tabby were guilty, that would be the best way to handle it. Which meant this was going to be a lot more complicated than just returning the stolen goods. They'd have to prove Veronica did it. Prove to Mullins's satisfaction that his own daughter had ripped him off.

"Your guess is as far from the truth as Pluto is from the sun," Fitz said.

"We'll see."

Fitz didn't have time to try to convince the man. "You have a credit card number for me?"

"Just tell me the flight numbers, and I'll have the tickets booked."

After waiting while Mullins gave the information to someone else, Fitz said, "I need to talk to Shelby."

"Your sister is having the time of her life."

"Nevertheless." He ground out the word, then left it hanging.

Mullins sighed. Fitz expected a promise to have her call him but instead heard him speaking to someone else. "Run and get the girl."

"You're with her?" Fitz's voice rose in the small car. "Is she back in Belize?" The thought of Shelby with this murderous... "Is my sister safe? What's—?"

"Calm down," Mullins said. "We're on the boat. I needed to join them. The crew I hired had to disembark."

The gang was all there. "Is my sister safe?"

"Aside from an unfortunate sunburn, she seems well."

"From your men?" he added.

"Nobody will touch her."

"They'd better not."

An awkward silence settled between them. Fitz certainly wasn't about to fill it with small talk. He watched the miles go by outside the window, praying silently for Shelby, for all of them as they navigated this mess.

"I got your confirmation numbers for the flight," Mullins said. "I'll text 'em to you."

"Okay."

The text came through, and Fitz checked the details. Two one-way tickets to Key West. One-way.

He hoped that little detail didn't portend disaster.

Finally, Mullins said, "Here she is."

And then, "Fitz?" Shelby's voice sounded... off, even with just the single word.

"Hey, sis. How are you?"

"Um. Okay. Just, you know..." But her voice trailed.

"What's wrong? Can you go somewhere to talk privately?"

"Um, like this is Mr. Mullins's phone."

So, no. Fitz forced a deep breath. "Can he hear me?"

"I doubt it."

The uncertainty in her voice concerned him. Where was his happy-go-lucky sister? "Are you still having fun?"

"Sure. We docked in Cozumel yesterday and did some shopping."

Mexico. An entirely different country from where he'd left

Shelby. Fitz had kept her passport when he'd handed her things to Mullins to give to her. Shelby had very little cash and no credit cards. The idea of her floating all over the Gulf of Mexico, stopping at dangerous ports, sent fresh acid to his stomach. If Mullins tired of her, getting rid of her wouldn't be any trouble at all. And he didn't have to kill her. He could sell her at any port on the eastern coast of the Americas and make a tidy profit. And Fitz might never find her.

He set aside those terrifying thoughts. "Mr. Mullins said you got a sunburn."

"Yeah. I was an idiot. It was cloudy, so I didn't even think of sunscreen. But Lena gave me a cream for it, and that helped."

She was talking normally, but she still didn't sound right. "Are you sure you're okay?"

"Yeah, just missing you. Missing home, I guess. I'm sort of craving... oatmeal."

Oatmeal.

The code word for *come get me.*

The code word for *I'm not safe.*

He squeezed his eyes closed. "Sissy." His nickname for her from back when they had a mom and a dad and everything was normal. A nickname that had hung on long after Shelby's baby years. He wanted to warn her, to tell her to keep playing her part, to promise he was doing his best to get her home. But they could be listening. For all Fitz knew, this conversation was being recorded. "I'm with you. A little normalcy will be great, won't it? As soon as I'm done with this case, I'll take you home, and we'll have our oatmeal. I'll even add brown sugar and raisins."

"Ick, no raisins for me."

He laughed, though he doubted anybody would be fooled by it. "I'll light a fire, and we'll have hot cocoa and roast marshmallows. How's that sound?"

"Yeah. That'll be fun." Her voice hitched at the end as if she might be on the verge of tears.

He squeezed his eyes closed, fury and fear mingling.

What was going on? Was Shelby just growing tired of Shawn but didn't want to say so in front of Mullins? Or had she heard something or seen something that put her in danger?

She wanted off the boat, and that fact alone caused his heart to race.

"I gotta go," she said. "Love you."

"Love you, too, Sissy. See you soon."

A pause, and then she muttered, "I hope so," just before the line went dead.

CHAPTER TWENTY-EIGHT

They were nearly to the airport in Providence, but Tabby was having a hard time keeping her eyes open. A teenage girl's life was in danger, and they had no idea how they were going to save her, but Tabby's all-too-human need for sleep wouldn't be denied.

Fitz was in the passenger seat, flipping through his notes.

Abe had his hands on the wheel, expertly navigating the Providence traffic.

Tabby, however, had no way to make herself useful. She yawned, which caused Abe to follow suit, then Fitz.

She nearly yawned again but forced herself to stop lest it travel the car again. "Sorry about that."

Fitz turned her way with a quick smile. "Not a problem. None of us got enough sleep last night." He tapped the laptop resting on his lap. "I have an idea."

Abe's gaze flicked his way. "Spill it."

"Mullins's company owns a house in the Keys. It's listed on a couple of those vacation rental sites. It's rented right now. I wonder if that's where she's going."

"You could ask Mullins if she's staying there," Abe suggested.

"I could." But Fitz's words were far from eager. "I don't want him to know we suspect his daughter until we have more facts. Maybe we can just pay it a visit, see if she's there."

"It's as good a place to start as any," Abe said.

Just like Fitz had said, they got a puzzle piece and then worked to see where it went. Maybe Mullins's property in the Keys would be the perfect fit.

∼

By the time they touched down in Key West, Tabby was struggling to keep her eyes open. The sun had dropped beyond the western horizon. Fortunately, Fitz had found them a cottage.

Tabby and Fitz left Abe at the airport to rent his own car. Apparently, the man had a gift for sleeping anywhere and had caught a couple of hours on the flights, so he would take the overnight watch at Mullins's rental property.

At Fitz's suggestion, Tabby found a place on the island where they'd be staying and ordered a large pepperoni pizza to go, which they picked up on their way.

The cottage was beautiful, with light furnishings and new furniture, and a king-sized bed in her room seemed to be calling her name. But it wasn't even nine o'clock, and as tired as she was, she was more hungry. The tiny bag of pretzels she'd gotten on the plane hadn't done much to assuage her hunger after the salad she'd eaten so many hours before.

She used the restroom, washed the day's grime from her hands, and discarded her shoes, then padded across the house barefoot.

Fitz wasn't in the kitchen, and neither was the pizza. The

back door was open to the sea breeze, which carried in the scents of salt and brine.

She stepped into the doorway and found Fitz seated at a cafe table on the wooden deck. A short fence separated it from the boardwalk that connected this cottage to the others on this strip. Beyond the boardwalk, docks jutted out into the narrow waterway that seemed to act as a road to the gulf. A small pontoon boat was slapping against the side of the dock in front of theirs. She wondered if it came with the rental. She'd have to check, not that they'd have time to enjoy it. But who knew? Maybe, when this was all over, she'd get the opportunity to take it for a spin, explore the canal and even hit the warm gulf waters.

She loved boating. Before Chris's accident, her family had owned a speedboat. She'd learned to water-ski at six years old, just a year or so after she'd first learned to snow ski. That was just one more thing that had fallen by the wayside when Chris had crashed into that tree.

"I fixed you a glass of water," Fitz said, drawing her attention.

He'd set the table with plates and utensils and napkins but hadn't helped himself to any pizza yet.

She sat across from him. "Sorry to make you wait."

"No problem." He reached across the table, and she slipped her hand into his. He said a quick prayer, then lifted the lid of the pizza box. "It smells delicious."

She agreed as she shifted a slice of pizza onto her plate. Oversize, foldable, and dripping with grease. She should probably mop up some of that with a napkin before she ate it, but life was too uncertain to worry about calories and fat.

And she was too hungry to care.

She took a bite, savoring the spicy sauce, the melted cheese, the crispy, curly pepperoni. She couldn't help the little *Mmm* that escaped her lips.

Fitz took a bite himself. "That's good. That's really good."

Faint music filtered their way from a neighboring cabin. Across the water, more houses were lit up, a few people out and about. She'd love to go for a walk with Fitz, do some exploring.

But this wasn't a romantic getaway. She needed to keep her mind straight.

"You've been awfully quiet," Fitz said a few minutes later. "I'm curious to know what's going on in that head of yours."

She swallowed and set the pizza down, unsure how to answer him. He didn't need to hear her self-diagnoses, her regrets, her fears. She told him the truth, if not all of it. "Yesterday, I went to work, did my job, and looked forward to a date with a good-looking guy. Somehow, between then and now, I ended up"—she flipped her hand, indicating their surroundings—"here. It's a lot to take in."

Looking over the top of a second slice of pizza, Fitz said, "I can imagine."

"I'm sure it's no less surreal for you."

He set the slice on his plate and sat back. "I've been running on fear and adrenaline for five days. At this point, I don't know what to think."

"You must be so worried about Shelby."

Though his relaxed expression didn't shift, it seemed to tighten at the corners of his mouth. "I didn't tell you what she said to me. I didn't even want it to be..." He shook his head, turned his focus toward the darkness, the surf beyond.

She waited until, finally, he met her gaze again.

"She told me she was craving oatmeal."

Oatmeal. That meant something. Tabby thought back to the last time it'd come up. The night of their final dinner in Belize, when Shelby and Shawn had found them at the table, Fitz had asked if she was in the mood for oatmeal. The girl had rolled her eyes.

She'd meant to ask about it at the time but had forgotten.

"What does it mean?"

"It's our code word for *come get me*." He swallowed. "What I don't know is if she's just bored or doesn't like Shawn anymore or if there's more to it. What if she's figured something out? Or suspects? What if Mullins finds out—?"

"Oh, Fitz." She reached across the small table and rested her hand on his forearm. "All we can do is pray and trust God."

"I know."

"Your sister is still alive. You're going to save her."

He nodded but slid his arm out from under her hand and resumed eating.

She did the same, finishing almost all of her second piece before pushing the plate aside.

When he was finished, she cleared the plates while he put the remaining pizza in the refrigerator.

She returned to the patio to grab their glasses. Though it had been the longest day in human history, and though she was so tired that she could hardly stand up straight, she was reluctant to go to sleep.

She stood by their table and sipped her water, staring out at the shimmering canal. She needed to go to bed, but a moment to enjoy this—it wasn't too much to ask.

Fitz joined her there. He lifted her glass from her fingers, set it on the table, and took her hands. He looked down at her, his warm gaze holding hers. His voice was soft when he spoke. "How are you doing, really?"

"I'm tired and scared and… I have no idea what tomorrow is going to look like. I don't know what I'm supposed to be doing. I'm just… I feel like… like I'm a fish hanging from a hook, suspended between life and death. Like the fisherman can either cook me for dinner or cut me loose, and all I can do is flop around uselessly." She sounded like an idiot. She blew out a breath and tried to get her thoughts in order.

"It's out of your control."

"Yeah."

"And that scares you," he guessed. "As much as anything else, not having control terrifies you."

"Considering that the guy holding the fishing pole is a murderous gangster, do you blame me?"

"You're not a fish flopping on a deck, Tabby. And that gangster isn't in control, either."

"Sure feels like he is."

"But he's not. And neither am I. And neither is Abe. We're all in the hands of a God who loves us. You know that. You've known it a lot longer than I have."

"Maybe. But you seem to know it better." Tabby loved Fitz's faith. It was new and inexperienced, the kind of faith that still believed.

Wait. That didn't make sense.

Her own faith... what? *Didn't* believe?

Did she really believe God's promises? Did she believe that God loved her, that He was looking out for her, that He was with her? She wanted to, but...

Where was God when Chelsea's father was murdered?

Where was He when Chris crashed into that tree?

Where was He when her mother had descended into anxiety and depression, when their family had fallen into despair?

Where was God now?

How could she reconcile those tragedies with a God who loved them?

She didn't know.

And she'd never tried. Rather than seek God with those

questions, she'd simply decided God wasn't to be trusted, not really, not with the day-to-day things. Sure, she believed he'd forgiven her sins. He'd reserved a place for her in heaven. But it seemed clear that her faith stopped there. If she did truly believe God was involved in their lives, then she wouldn't think it was her job to take care of everybody.

She wouldn't believe her family's well-being was her responsibility.

She wouldn't be so afraid right now.

Here Fitz was, brand new to the faith, yet his faith was so much stronger than hers.

He watched her now, eyes squinted. "I wish I could read your mind."

She laughed, the sound loud and out of place in the quiet night. "Trust me. You don't want to know my crazy thoughts."

The perplexed expression didn't leave his face. "Trust me. I do."

After a moment, his look faded, replaced by something very different. Not confusion or curiosity. "Tabby." His voice was filled with longing.

She started to back away.

Fitz slipped a hand behind her back and pulled her even closer. "Don't do that."

"I don't—"

"What are you afraid of?"

Fitz looked so earnest, so curious. As if her answer mattered more to him than anything else in the world. As if she mattered more than anything else. She knew it wasn't true, but she also knew, in some ways, it was.

This wasn't a game for him.

He wasn't playing with her emotions. All his charms, his easy laughter with his friends, his easy lies when he was trying to get information—none of that mattered. This man watching her so intently, he cared for her. She mattered to him.

He mattered to her.

And any thoughts of brushing off his question or pretending flitted away. The truth rushed out on a gush of air. "I'm afraid my family won't survive without me. I'm afraid I'll fail them. I'm afraid of you. I'm afraid I'm going to fall for you, and I'm going to get hurt. Or you are. Or somebody else is, and it'll all... crash and burn. And I'll end up broken and alone. I'm afraid of... life."

Her crazy words would have had a wiser man stepping back. Instead, his lips quirked at the corners. He lifted a hand to brush her hair away from her face. "Thank you for telling me the truth."

She felt like an idiot. Who was afraid of life?

But the way Fitz was looking at her... She didn't see *idiot* written in his eyes.

She saw something much deeper.

He leaned down until barely an inch separated them. "You don't need to be afraid of me, Tabby. I can't promise you things will be easy. I can't promise you... anything, really. Except that I'll do everything in my power to protect you."

He was talking about Mullins. But didn't he know how fickle the world could be? How capricious?

He did know. Of course he knew. His parents had been killed in a car accident. His own sister's life was in danger because of that same fickleness. And yet, here he was, alive and breathing and living fearlessly.

He held her eye contact. "I'll do everything in my power to protect *us*."

Us.

"But I'm not letting you push me away again," he said. "I'm not willing to sacrifice what we have on the altar of your fears." His eyebrows rose, dared her to argue with him.

But she couldn't find any words.

At that moment, she wasn't willing to lose him, either. To lose this... this feeling of being in his arms. Safe in his arms.

Fitz leaned closer. "I care for you, Tabby. I care enough that I'm going to fight for you. Whatever it takes."

She couldn't concentrate on his words with his breath whispering through her hair.

He kissed the tender skin behind her ear, and her entire body vibrated in response.

The kisses trailed across her jawline. By the time his lips met hers, all thoughts had flitted from her mind. Her hands slid around his neck. Her back arched, and her mouth opened to his.

She could have continued kissing him for the rest of her life. Except kisses wouldn't satisfy. She wanted more from Fitz, more than she'd ever craved from any man.

Desire like she'd never felt blossomed within her, a raging fire warming her every inch.

Fitz abruptly ended the kiss and stepped back. He ran his hand over his hair, eyes wide and bright in the darkness. He swallowed, and his Adam's apple bobbed.

They were both breathing heavily, staring at each other.

"Okay then," he said, as if they'd reached some conclusion.

And they had. She had, anyway.

Because life held myriad risks. She didn't know if she'd survive the weekend—or the night, for that matter. But whatever the future held, she wanted Fitz by her side. She would take whatever time they had together. No longer would she pretend not to care for him. No longer would she sacrifice her life for her family's needs. No longer would she shy away from love.

God could be trusted.

Fitz was worth the risk.

CHAPTER TWENTY-NINE

Fitz took a sip of the extra-large coffee he'd picked up at the all-night gas station on his way to Mullins's property. The cup was almost empty, the caffeine barely doing its job. At least dawn was coming. The light would make it easier to keep his eyes open.

After their mind-blowing kiss, he'd very reluctantly sent Tabby off to her bedroom before taking a lukewarm shower to cool himself off. Not that the night had been hot. But the kiss... He'd needed to put away thoughts of it and Tabby so he could sleep.

Owing to the fact that he hadn't slept a second the night before, he'd drifted off moments after he'd slipped between the sheets of the too-narrow twin in the second bedroom. His alarm had woken him at two a.m., just a little more than four hours after he'd fallen asleep. He'd made the one stop for coffee and headed to Mullins's beach house.

When he arrived, he hadn't seen Abe and hadn't tried to. The less contact between them, the less chance somebody would see and get suspicious. The two had done enough stakeouts together to know the drill. Fitz found a place to watch the house and called Abe to tell him he was there. A few minutes later, a sedan on the far end of the block roared to life and drove away. But not far away. Abe had told Fitz he'd find a place nearby and sleep in the backseat. The man truly could sleep anywhere, and now that morning was approaching, he thought he should be nearby.

Assuming Veronica was even in the house. Abe hadn't gotten a glimpse of the person inside, though after he'd arrived the night before, he'd seen lights go off in one room and on in another. Someone was there. Was that someone Veronica, or were they wasting time staking out an innocent vacationer?

Fitz yawned and stretched, bored. He hated stakeouts.

As the sun brightened the sky in the east, he got a better sense of the neighborhood. The house wasn't as fancy as he'd expected, designed just like every other house on the block. Though he couldn't be sure, he'd guess the places had been built forty or more years before. The bottom floor was more like a garage without doors, open to the air. Beyond the pillars holding the house up, he could see the beach. The living areas must all be on the second floor, which had a deck that wrapped around the whole structure. It wasn't that large—probably not even two thousand square feet. Two, maybe three bedrooms. It was a vacation home, a perfect place to rent out or visit occasionally. A good investment. A place for the kids to enjoy.

It was very... normal, considering the man who owned it.

And Fitz's view of it wasn't great. If anybody did step outside, surely she'd—assuming it was Veronica—step out on the deck near the beach. Now that morning was coming, he needed a different vantage point.

He climbed from the car, slipped on his sunglasses, and jogged between the house next door to Mullins's and its neighbor on the far side, then walked down to the water's edge. He wandered slowly toward the property, passing a few docks.

The one in front of Mullins's property had a bright red speedboat knocking against the side. Seemed nice enough, not that he was any judge. He knew next to nothing about boats. Though he'd grown up near the ocean, and though they'd often gone to the beach, they'd never owned or even rented boats when he was a kid.

He gazed at Mullins's house, trying not to be obvious about it. He went two houses beyond, walked out onto another dock jutting into the calm waters of the Gulf of Mexico, and gazed back toward the east, thankful for the sunglasses that hid his true focus.

He'd brought his coffee and sipped it now. Just a normal guy out enjoying the day. Fortunately, since he'd gone straight from Belize to New Hampshire, he'd had lots of beach attire in his suitcase.

He'd been sitting on the dock at least twenty minutes, mostly ignoring the pretty pink-and-coral sunrise, when the back door of Mullins's house opened, and a woman stepped onto the wraparound deck carrying a mug in one hand, her phone in the other. Long brown hair was pulled back in a ponytail. She was tall and slender. Just like Tabby.

Fitz glanced at his phone, where he'd saved a photograph of Veronica Hernandez. He glanced at it now. He was pretty sure this was the same woman, but not sure enough to bet anybody's life on it. He lifted the cell, hoping people would think he was trying to capture the sunrise, and snapped a few photos of the woman. He lowered the phone and glanced at the screen, enlarging her image.

The woman on the porch... Definitely Veronica.

He sent the photo to Abe. *We got her.*

A moment passed before his phone vibrated with Abe's response. *Good. Going back to sleep. Lemme know if she moves.*

Veronica sat at a small table and sipped from the mug,

focusing on her phone more than the beautiful view. After a few minutes, she went inside. If she were to go out the front and walk away, he might miss it. Probably not, though, thanks to the open bottom floor. If she were to drive away, he'd see the car parked in the driveway move from where he sat.

He decided to stay put for five minutes. If she didn't return, he'd go back to his car and watch the front.

But only three minutes later, she returned and sat again. Maybe she'd refreshed her coffee. This time, she left her phone on the table and gazed out at the view.

The sun was up now, ruining Fitz's excuse for watching the house. A normal person would be oriented toward the water. He stood and walked back the direction he'd come. Just an everyday fellow taking an everyday stroll in paradise.

He should have brought a dog. Everyday guys walked dogs. Alas, he wasn't aware of any dog rental businesses nearby.

He passed the house, continued a few houses beyond.

The slap of a screen door had him turning. Veronica had gone back in.

He walked fifty yards or so, in case anybody was watching, before jogging between two houses and returning to the car. Most likely, if she were to leave, she'd go out the front.

It was eight thirty before Veronica emerged again, this time coming down the stairs that led to the open bottom floor.

Fitz called Abe, who answered on the second ring. "She's on the move."

"I'm ready." He sounded wide awake.

Veronica climbed into a small blue sedan with Florida plates —a rental, no doubt. She backed out and turned toward town.

"You close? She's going south. Little blue car."

"I got her," Abe said. "See what you can find."

Fitz waited four minutes. Then he stepped out of the car and jogged toward the house, going straight into the open bottom floor as if he belonged. An outdoor dining table and chairs were set on the beach-end of the space. Kayaks, life jackets, and other beach toys were stored in a small nook off to one side. Mostly, the space was empty.

An outdoor staircase led to the wraparound deck, but Fitz headed for the steps Veronica had come down. At the top, he was hidden from the view of passersby. He pulled his pocketknife from his sock and worked the lock. It took two long minutes, but finally it clicked, and he pushed open the door.

Unlike the seventies-era exterior, the interior had been updated with a beach theme, all creams and pale blues, glass containers filled with seashells, tabletops boasting sculptures of fish, and walls adorned with pictures of sunsets and palm trees. It was overdone, hugging the line between charming and tacky. Actually, taking in the dirty dish in the sink, which was painted with tiny crabs around the perimeter, he decided the place definitely fell on the side of tacky.

And this from Fitz, who couldn't decorate his way out of a fishing net.

He found the bedroom and searched the drawers and closet. Nothing but clothes and personal items. He was looking for a safe or storage container when he heard footsteps. It sounded like someone was climbing the exterior stairs to the deck.

She couldn't be back already, could she? Why wouldn't she come up the interior stairs?

No, those footsteps were too loud to be a woman's.

Fitz ducked into the master bathroom but kept the door open. The last thing he needed was to get caught in the house. Arrested for the second time in three days.

The footsteps slowed. Beyond the gauzy curtain, Fitz could see the outline of a man. He was moving slowly now.

"I don't think she's home," the man said. His voice was

tenor, on the high side. Young but not a kid. He had a local accent.

Nobody answered him. Must be talking on the phone.

"I never met her in person. She rents the place—"

Whatever words had cut the speaker off, Fitz couldn't hear them.

"Yeah, yeah. Gimme a sec." A moment later, a knock sounded on the back door. "Miss Abbott? Are you home?" Then, "No answer."

A long pause.

"I don't know. She's just a lady." His words were coming faster now. Nervous. "She's never had any parties. She's never damaged anything. She pays. You pay me to manage the place, not to investi—"

Another long pause.

"Yeah, no. You're right, you're right." Fitz couldn't tell if the guy was nervous because he didn't want to lose a client or because he realized his client was dangerous.

Based on the fear in his voice, the second guess felt accurate.

"Every few months," he said. "She always rents through the app." His voice was calmer now. "You want me to go in?"

Fitz tensed. He should've gone down the stairs when he'd first heard the man coming up. But that was dangerous too. Who knew who was out there watching?

Then the sound of jingling. The key in the lock.

The door creaked and the man called, "Miss Abbott? It's Luis, the property manager. I'm coming in."

The screen door slammed.

Fitz pulled his handgun, thankful he'd brought it. Not that he was about to shoot this innocent man, but better to be prepared than not.

The man stomped around the house. "Miss Abbott?"

Silently, Fitz stepped into the shower, careful not to let the curtain slide against the rod.

The man's voice came from the bedroom just beyond the open door. "The place is empty."

"You're absolutely sure." Now, Fitz could make out the words on the other end of the call. That voice belonged to Ronnie Mullins, confirming his suspicions.

"Yeah, I'm sure. There's just a lot of lady stuff. Lady clothes, lady shoes..."

Why would Mullins be interested in who was renting this place? Because Fitz was down here? Did he think Fitz and Tabby were staying here?

No, that didn't make sense. Surely Mullins could have discovered the renter had reserved the place before yesterday.

The manager stepped into the bathroom, and Fitz held his breath and lifted the gun. Not to fire, but to use as a club. If the shower curtain was suddenly yanked open, he'd have no choice but to whack the guy on the head and pray he hit him before the guy got a look at him.

The manager stopped inches away from Fitz.

"And you have no idea what this woman looks like?" Mullins asked.

"I never met her. I leave the key in the lockbox like I do with all the clients."

Fitz heard a cabinet door open and close. "She comes and goes. When she's gone, I inspect and clean." Fitz heard things being shifted around on the bathroom countertop. It's not my job to... to, like, peep on the guests. I'm not a creeper." Despite the fact that he was using the opportunity to snoop. Not that Fitz, hiding in a shower, ought to throw stones.

"Lady toiletries in the bathroom," Luis said.

"Check the other rooms."

The man stepped out of the bathroom. "On it."

Fitz couldn't hear Mullins anymore. Very unfortunate, especially if Mullins asked Luis to keep an eye on the place.

If he did, Fitz would be seen leaving. Not good.

But there was nothing for it. He'd just pray he could get out without being spotted or, if that weren't possible, identified or stopped.

A few minutes later, the door slammed, the keys jingled. Footsteps on the patio boards outside told Fitz the manager was leaving. He wasn't speaking now, so either Mullins was talking a lot—which didn't seem right—or they'd ended the call.

When he heard the man go down the stairs, Fitz stepped out of the shower, taking the first deep breath in minutes.

That was too close.

The second time in a week he'd almost been caught searching a house. What were the chances?

He searched the bathroom, as long as he was there. Veronica had left a hair dryer, a brush, and makeup strewn across the white countertop. In the drawers, he found lotions and the like.

Under the cabinet, plumbing and a toilet plunger.

Just bathroom stuff.

He returned to the bedroom. His instincts told him something was... off, but he couldn't put his finger on exactly what.

He'd figure it out.

He searched the second and third bedrooms, the living area, and the kitchen.

Nothing, nothing, nothing.

He opened a closet near the front door. Empty except...

A suitcase had been stowed on the shelf.

Odd. One person. Three bedrooms. Why hide the suitcase up there? Why not in her own closet? He thought back and realized he hadn't seen one. Its absence—that was what had been off. She was a vacationer, and vacationers always had suitcases.

As he lifted it from the high shelf, he felt his phone vibrate in his pocket. Could be Abe. Veronica could be on her way back.

But he had to finish this. As he swung the suitcase down, he felt something shift inside.

He carried the suitcase to the sofa, laid it flat, and unzipped it.

Outside, footsteps pounded up the steps.

Are you kidding me?

This place was busier than I-95 at rush hour.

Ignoring whoever was coming, he flipped open the bag.

Lying inside and wrapped in bubble wrap was the stolen box. The antique box. The one he'd seen in the video.

The footsteps got closer.

He laid the treasure aside and stowed the suitcase where he'd found it.

He didn't have time to revel in victory, not when defeat was nipping at his heels.

He snatched the box and was nearly to the exit leading downstairs when the door to the deck swung open.

CHAPTER THIRTY

Tabby's phone rang, waking her from a deep sleep. Her eyes popped open, and she scanned the room. White walls and furniture. Turquoise accents. Ocean out the window.

The Keys. It all came back to her.

The phone rang a second time. She didn't recognize the number but answered anyway. "Hello?"

"It's Abe." His deep voice, usually soothing, had an edge to it. "Sorry to wake you, but you need to get up and get ready."

"What's going on?"

"I'm not sure. I followed Veronica into town, and I think I just spotted Lena Mullins, Ronnie's wife. And maybe the kid, Shawn."

"Are they together, Vera and Lena and—?"

"No, no. They seem oblivious to each other."

"What about Shelby?"

"She wasn't with them. If those two are here, it means Ronnie is too. I don't like you being there by yourself."

By herself? Tabby swung her legs over the side of the bed

and tried to clear the fogginess from her brain. "Is Fitz not here?"

"He's at Mullins's beach house. I texted him, but he hasn't answered."

Tabby's heart rate kicked up. She was awake now. "You think something's happened to him?"

"There's no reason to think that." Abe's tone turned soothing. "He's searching the place and probably didn't want to take the time to answer. As soon as he's clear, he'll contact us."

He sounded so sure. She decided to believe him. "I'll be ready in twenty minutes."

"Make it ten. One of us will be there soon." He ended the call.

She didn't waste time pondering what it all meant, just rushed to the bathroom. Whatever they needed her to do, she'd be ready.

CHAPTER THIRTY-ONE

Silently, Fitz slipped through the door and closed it with a soft click. He waited, prayed they hadn't heard.

But the men inside were talking, making no attempt to be stealthy. Unafraid of being caught. Because they were foolishly brazen, or because they believed the place to be empty?

He made out two voices. A third person or more could be there.

Fitz continued down the stairs, considering his options. Above, he heard loud footsteps. Somebody was on the deck. Maybe more than one somebody. If he ran for his car now, whoever was outside and above would probably see him. Fitz might get away.

He might get shot.

He didn't mind being spotted by Mullins's men at the house, assuming they were the ones searching upstairs. It would lend credibility to his story that he'd found the stolen box there.

He did mind very much getting shot.

He slipped in among the kayaks and beach paraphernalia propped in the open storage area, box under his left arm, gun in his right hand, and prayed he'd remain undiscovered.

And he listened. One person in the house. One person on the deck. No third voice, but that didn't mean a third person wasn't there. The two spoke to each other, though from Fitz's place behind a well-used yellow-and-pink kayak, it was hard to make out what they were saying. Sounded more like friendly banter than serious conversation.

His phone vibrated again. He had no room to maneuver and no empty hand to yank it from his pocket. He could only hope that, if that was Abe telling him Veronica was on her way back, the chaos of finding men searching her temporary home would provide enough cover to escape.

Ten minutes passed. Fifteen. They were conducting a more thorough search than he had, maybe being less careful to leave the place as they'd found it. He remembered Willie's search of Tabby's place. Would the goons upstairs be so careless?

He prayed they wouldn't bother with the open area where he was hiding.

It occurred to him that, if he'd left the box in the suitcase, the goons would have found it. If they were Mullins's goons, they'd be able to report back that she'd had it, proving Fitz's theory that Veronica was the thief.

Unless Mullins thought Fitz had planted the box. But how would that explain Veronica's being in the Keys?

Coincidence?

Mullins was smarter than that.

But he loved his daughter. He wouldn't easily believe she'd stolen from him.

If the guys upstairs were Mullins's men, which seemed a fair assumption, what were they doing there? Last Fitz had heard, they were in Cozumel. Could they have made the trip across the Gulf of Mexico that quickly? He tried to picture a map—it wasn't that far from Cozumel to Florida by water. How fast did yachts travel?

He hadn't a clue. But Fitz only knew they'd been in Cozumel at some point. For all he knew, they'd already been halfway to Florida when Fitz had called him the day before. That could explain it.

Assuming the guys searching upstairs were Mullins's men.

Fitz felt like he had fifty pieces of a hundred-piece puzzle, and no picture on the box. But if Mullins was in the Keys...

Tabby. She could be in danger. Would Mullins be able to find her?

He itched to bolt, to do something, but he didn't move. He really didn't want to get caught here, and he couldn't figure a way Mullins's men would have found the cottage they'd rented. She should be safe.

He prayed she was safe.

Twenty minutes after he'd hidden, he heard footsteps on the stairs he'd come down, stairs not fifteen feet away from him. A man yelled, "You search down here?"

Another man responded, "When was I gonna do that? I was lookout, remember?"

The first man muttered, "Useless, lazy..."

Pounding on the wooden steps told him the other guy was coming down. He'd expected more conversation, but the second man seemed to have disappeared. No sound of him.

As the first man walked through the open area, Fitz got a look at him. Marco Novak. Which meant the other guy was the brother, Joey. Tweedle-Dee and Tweedle-Dum. If they were here, that meant Mullins was here. He might've come to get his jewels as soon as possible and pass Shelby back to him.

It made sense that he was in the Keys, but why was he *here*? At his own rental property?

Fitz couldn't see Marco but assumed the man was searching. There wasn't much down here—mostly concrete. It wouldn't be long before he reached the storage area.

Fitz could just step out, hands up, and surrender. Be taken to Mullins, probably. Tell what he knew. He had the box and, he presumed, the jewels. Mullins should be mollified, should hand Shelby over. But without proof Veronica had stolen them, would he still suspect Tabby was the thief?

Probably. And if Fitz tried to convince him, it would only make the man mad. Anything could happen at that point. Shelby would still be in danger. Tabby would still be in danger.

Fitz needed to find a way to prove Veronica was the thief before he spoke to Mullins. It could be done, but he had to think it through, come up with a plan.

And besides, all he knew for certain was that he had the box. It was heavy but felt... empty. Nothing had moved around within when he'd jogged down the stairs. Maybe the jewels were wrapped in bubble wrap like the box was. Maybe that was why.

Or maybe the jewels were gone.

Marco came closer. Fitz lost sight of him on the far side of the kayak. This was the slightly slimmer of the brothers, though both were muscled and dangerous. Fitz heard the sound of one kayak being tossed out of the way.

Fitz would have to come out swinging, catch him with his hands full. One swift whack to the nose with the butt of his gun should make his eyes water. Maybe, hopefully, keep him from getting a good look at Fitz's face. Fitz would have to extricate himself from the storage compartment quickly, maybe take Marco out at the knees in the process. And he'd have to do it all without dropping gun or box.

Easy as canned soup.

Right.

Marco's fingers slid around the kayak hiding Fitz, and Fitz tensed. He could do this.

"Why you wasting time on that?" the other voice said. A moment later, Fitz heard footsteps coming closer.

"He said search the whole place," Marco said.

"You really think anybody'd be dumb enough to store stolen goods in an open storage area?"

"Stay in your lane, idiot. I got this." But nothing happened. Maybe he was considering—

"I finished my job," Joey said. "Just waiting on you."

Fitz had no idea what job Joey would've been tasked with or where he'd disappeared to. He willed Marco to ask a question that would provide the answer.

"Trying to be thorough," Marco said uselessly.

"He told us to make it quick. He don't want us getting caught here. And if whoever's staying here finds his stuff all over the place—"

"Her. It's a woman."

"You think he knows who she is?"

Fitz didn't hear a response. Maybe the man had shrugged.

Joey said, "Well, whoever it is, she wouldn't be dumb enough to store anything down here."

"Yeah, you're right."

Marco backed up. When he spoke next, it was from farther away. "Sucks we didn't find anything."

"Yeah, he's gonna be ticked." Based on the sound of their footsteps retreating, they were headed toward the beach.

When he could no longer hear them, Fitz exhaled a long breath. Almost caught, twice, in the space of an hour. Talk about lousy luck. Though he'd also escaped notice twice, so that was something.

He uttered a quick *Thanks* to the One who'd helped him and was extricating himself from the storage area when his phone vibrated again. He holstered his gun, dug the cell from his pocket, and glanced at the screen. Three messages from Abe. Only the most recent showed.

Get out. She's almost there.

He stifled the curse word that used to be as common coming from his mouth as breath. It was as if the world were playing some cosmic joke on him.

He looked toward the road. Couldn't go that way, not if Veronica was almost back.

The beach was his only choice. Nothing for it but to hope Tweedle-Dee and Tweedle-Dum didn't turn around and see him leaving the place. He hurried that way. Before stepping out from the shelter of the wall beneath the house, he glanced at the goons' backs. They wore jeans and T-shirts and sneakers and looked utterly out of place on the sandy beach. Were they trying to draw people's attention?

Idiots.

But just as the thought hit, one of them glanced behind him.

Fitz backed into the shadows. They weren't as stupid as they looked, though, in their defense, how could they be?

Just as Tweedle-Dee looked forward again, an engine rumbled behind him. Veronica was back.

Fitz strode straight to the surf and turned right, walking at a leisurely pace that defied the thumping of his heart, doing the ordinary-guy routine again despite the bubble-wrapped box in his hand.

He glanced behind him a couple of times, just in case, but didn't see goons or a mobster's daughter watching his retreat.

A hundred yards down the beach, he jogged between the houses and made it back to his car.

Only after he'd started the engine and pulled away from the curb did he grab his phone and call Abe. The man answered with, "What happened?"

"Long story filled with lots of plot twists. But I found the box."

"Good. The jewels?"

"Haven't opened it yet. Mullins's goons are here. The Novak boys—they searched Veronica's place. If they're here—"

"Mullins is too. I caught sight of Lena and Shawn in town."

Acid filled Fitz's stomach. "What about Shelby? She wasn't with them?"

"Sorry, man."

"I'm on my way to get Tabby. I need to call her and warn her."

"Already did. She should be ready when you get there. Lemme know what you find in the box. I'll stay on Veronica."

Fitz hung up and gunned the motor on the stupid four-cylinder, whipping around corners, desperate to make sure Tabby was safe. Could Mullins have found her?

He didn't know how, but it seemed Mullins was one step ahead of him all the time. If Fitz didn't figure out how to catch up, he might lose both the woman and the sister he loved.

CHAPTER THIRTY-TWO

Tabby had gotten ready in less than ten minutes, then stood in the kitchen, waiting. Where were Fitz and Abe?

What was happening?

She resisted the urge to call them. They would let her know what was going on when the time was right. They were busy, unlike her. She had nothing to do.

Frustrating. She wandered through the little cabin, taking in all the details. The furnishings were rather bland, all muted blues and greens.

She found a three-ring binder filled with details on the house, things to do within walking distance, and... Sure enough, the pontoon boat tethered to the dock was available if they wanted to use it. There was even tubing gear in the storage area. Wouldn't that be fun? If this were a vacation...

Tabby heard the sound of footsteps outside. She closed the binder and faced the door, bracing herself. *Please, let it be Fitz.*

The jingle of keys, then the lock turned and the door pushed open.

Fitz stepped inside, eyes wide. They locked on hers, and he blew out a long breath. "Thank God you're okay."

"I was about to say the same thing."

He set something on the table, crossed to where she stood, and pulled her close. "I was so worried."

She wrapped her arms around him and settled her cheek against the soft cotton of his T-shirt. "Me too."

They stood like that a long moment before Fitz backed away. "There's no reason to believe he knows where we are, but I don't want to take any chances. We should get out of here."

She nodded to the thing he'd left on the table. "What's that?"

"I found it at Veronica's."

She realized what it was—the antique box. Considering he'd found exactly what he'd gone there looking for, he didn't look that pleased.

"What's wrong?"

"Bad feeling." He glared at the thing, and his lips slipped into a frustrated smirk.

"Shall we open it?"

"Why not?" He pulled out a chair for her, and she sat. Before he joined her, he got himself a glass of tap water and downed it. He looked her way, must've seen some question in her eyes because he said, "Been a long and stressful morning."

"You want to tell me about it?"

"More complications than I'd expected." He took the chair beside hers and dragged the box close. It was about the size of a loaf of bread with a few slices missing. The bubble wrap had been folded multiple times around it.

Fitz got the packaging off and stared at the top. "Wow."

Tabby leaned closer and trailed her fingers over it. It was dark, aged, and intricately carved. A silver cross was inlaid on the lid as if it had grown right out of the wood. It looked like something that would be displayed in a museum. "I can see why it's valuable. It's gorgeous."

"I agree. Unfortunately, we don't have time for a thorough appraisal."

Right. She dropped her hand away, and Fitz lifted the top. Inside, more bubble wrap. But when he pulled it out and dropped it on the table, her heart fell.

"It's empty."

"What does that mean? Where are the jewels?"

"I searched the house. Mullins's goons searched the house." He shook his head. "Either Veronica already sold them, or she has them on her."

Everything he said after *goons* faded into the background as Tabby considered the man who'd searched her own house. The hatred in his eyes. The threats.

Fitz slid his hand over hers and squeezed. "Different goons."

Not that it mattered. Willie Dunbar was probably near. Willie and Ronnie and two more goons at least, all after her.

She waited for Fitz to offer words of encouragement, promises to protect her. But when she met his eyes, she saw the same fear she felt in her heart.

He swallowed hard. "You should run. Get on a plane to... anywhere but here."

And leave him to figure this out himself? Put Shelby in danger?

"Just for now. Just until we know—"

"No." She shook off the temptation to take him up on the offer. "No. I'm staying with you. We'll figure this out. If I have to trade myself for Shelby—"

"We're not doing that."

"We're not going to let anything happen to her. She's a child."

The look on Fitz's face... For the first time in her life, she understood what people meant when they described someone as looking tortured. That was how he looked now, as if the thoughts in his head were causing him physical pain. Eyes narrowed. Mouth tight.

She didn't know what to say.

Fitz took a long breath. "If Veronica hasn't sold them yet, then we can still do this."

"But the box... the jewels were inside, don't you think?" She lifted the empty bubble wrap and dropped it again. "Why would she take them out before she sold them?"

"I don't know."

"And if she sold them—"

"I don't know," he repeated, louder. "I don't—"

Fitz's phone vibrated, and he yanked it from his pocket and answered, putting in on speaker.

"Tabby okay?" Abe's voice.

"I'm fine," Tabby said.

Fitz said, "Tell me about Veronica. Where'd she go? What'd she do?"

"Nothing, really. Went to a little cafe and sat outside to eat breakfast."

"By herself?"

"Yup. Then she went to the grocery store. Came out with a few sacks and headed back to the house."

"That's it? No meetings? No phone calls? Nothing?"

"She was on the phone once, but I couldn't hear—"

"This is..." Fitz blew out a long breath and ran his hands through his hair.

"What is it?" Abe said. "What am I missing?"

"Box is empty."

Abe was silent on the other end. After a beat, he said, "Okay. I'll stay on her." And hung up.

CHAPTER THIRTY-THREE

Fitz did his best to keep his features neutral as he pushed away from the table. "I'll be right back." He walked at as normal a pace as he could manage to the bathroom. He needed to think.

Too much had happened, and he couldn't make any sense of it.

The jewels weren't in the box, which meant Veronica had probably already sold them.

Maybe... maybe Fitz could get them back. If he could find them and then negotiate for their return, or steal them.

Assuming he could do any of that before Mullins's wrath reached Tabby. Or Shelby.

He didn't want to think about Shelby.

He splashed water on his face, tried to focus his thoughts. First, he had to get Tabby out of there, far away. Once she was safe, he'd focus on finding the yacht and his sister. The jewels might be gone, but Mullins was here. Fitz would have to find a way to rescue Shelby. Then... then they'd all have to run, because Mullins wouldn't stop until he found them.

They were out of options. It was over. He looked at himself

in the mirror and hated the man who looked back. He'd failed. Failed to find the jewels. Failed to protect his sister. Failed to protect Tabby.

He allowed himself a moment to reflect on all the decisions he'd made. From the very beginning, he should have called the police. He should have notified the FBI, alerted the Coast Guard, pulled in every law enforcement agency from Belize to Canada when his sister had been taken. He'd been so sure of his path. Find Tabby, get the jewels, get his sister back.

His arrogance, his refusal to trust others... What a fool he was. What an absolute fool.

It was one thing for his foolishness to cost him. Fair, even. But it would cost Shelby and Tabby. They'd pay with their lives for his stupid decisions.

Far away, a phone rang. His phone, he realized as he tapped the pockets of his shorts. He met his eyes in the mirror. *Pull it together, McCaffrey.* He needed to get Tabby to safety, and in order to do that, he needed to make her believe he had a plan, and her being gone was the best way to make that plan work. Once she was safe, he could concentrate on trying to rescue Shelby or, if it was too late for that, making sure Mullins paid for his crimes.

But he could do none of that until Tabby was safe. Which meant he needed to lie to her. Convincingly.

He knew he could do it. He hated himself for that.

The phone rang again, but the sound was cut off. A moment later, Tabby knocked on the bathroom door. "Abe's on the phone. Says to hurry."

"Coming." He stepped into the hallway, hand outstretched, and smiled at her, a soothing *nothing to worry about* kind of smile.

Her shoulders relaxed the tiniest bit. Before she handed him the phone, she put it on speaker.

He was tempted to take it off, but he didn't want to alarm her or alert her to the fact that he wasn't being honest. "What's up."

"I don't know." Abe's words came out faster than normal for the usually deliberate man. "She's downstairs in that little storage area, and she's wearing a bathing suit. She's up to something."

"Not much in there," Fitz said. "Kayaks, beach toys, stuff like—"

"She's coming out. She's got something. It's some kind of brightly colored bag."

"Maybe she's going to the beach." Why was Abe giving him a play-by-play of Veronica's movements when the woman had almost certainly already sold the jewels? He would have snapped at him if Tabby weren't watching so closely.

He headed toward the kitchen, mostly to keep Tabby from seeing his expression.

"I don't think so," Abe said. "She's crouched on the floor, taking something from her purse. Little black... bags, I think."

Fitz froze in the hallway. "Like, velvet bags? Like bags that hold jewelry?"

"That's it. Yes. She's got the jewels. We can follow, figure out..." A moment passed, and then Abe said, "No. She's headed to the dock."

The dock...

"Fitz." Abe's voice was lower now. Where others' voices pitched up when they were upset, Abe's always pitched down. "I can't follow her. You're gonna need—"

"The boat." Fitz swiveled and focused on Tabby. "Any chance you've seen keys to the pontoon—?"

"I think..." Her gaze flicked around the space. "No, but..." She dashed past him, through the kitchen, and into the minuscule utility room beyond. She came back with a set of keys dangling from her finger. "I read all about it."

Thank God. Thank God for that. He held his hand out for the keys, but she palmed them.

After sending a quick glare her way, he spoke to Abe. "You need to tell me which direction—"

"I'm gonna lose sight of her. You guys need to get out to the gulf ASAP."

"I'll be there." He started toward the door. "Tabby's taking the car and disappearing."

"Fat chance," she said. "I'm going with you."

"I need you safe."

On the phone, Abe said, "Do you even know how to drive a boat?"

"How hard can it be?"

Abe said, "Man, it's harder—"

"I know how," Tabby said. "Been boating all my life." She stepped outside, turning in the doorway. "You coming?"

He didn't want her anywhere near what would go down with Veronica and her buyer, but it wasn't as if he had much choice.

He followed, slamming the door behind him.

Abe said, "Listen, you two. I need to know where you are. Both of you, share your location, and I'll get as close as I can."

"Maybe we should call the police." The suggestion shocked Fitz as he climbed over the side of the small watercraft, mostly because it had come from his own mouth.

Abe seemed a little stymied too. "Uh, not sure that's a good idea. The last thing Mullins wants is his jewels in some evidence locker."

Right. Good point.

Tabby was unwrapping rope from the metal hooks, so Fitz did the same with ropes on other hooks.

When they were disconnected from the dock, she took her place in the driver's seat or helm or whatever it was called and started the engine. She expertly reversed away from the dock, spun the boat in the narrow waterway, and headed toward the gulf.

Posted signs told them this was a no-wake zone, but Tabby either didn't see them or ignored them as she gunned the motor. They passed other houses, other docks. The canal was manmade and had ninety-degree turns. It was as if they were driving streets rather than inlets. She whipped around one, and in the distance, beyond docks and houses and restaurants, Fitz saw open ocean.

Abe's voice barely registered over the motor. Fitz lifted the phone to his ear and blocked the other with his finger. "Obviously, we're on our way."

"She's headed east, toward you. She's in a red boat—"

"I saw it. She's alone?"

"Yeah."

"Okay. I'm gonna hang up and share our location. I'll keep you informed." Fitz did what he promised, then focused on Tabby. "What can I do?"

She glanced his way. "Look around. There might be things we can use. A flare gun or—"

"On it." Fitz found life jackets, an empty cooler, a bunch of trash bags, and a sack full of drink koozies. None of that would be helpful. In the next compartment, he found oars. He pulled them out. They'd make good weapons, if nothing else. At the bottom of the last compartment, he found a handful of little plastic bags with zipper seals and plastic twine for hanging from a neck—lanyards. They weren't much larger than sandwich bags but longer and narrower, almost as if they were for...

Cell phones.

They were clear on one side, brightly colored on the other.

Waterproof and, with that little squishy bit at the back, probably floated.

After he stowed all the stuff except the oars, he grabbed two of the little bags and headed her way. "No flare gun," he called over the too loud engine, "but I found these."

She glanced his way and smiled. "Good find." She unlocked her phone and handed it to him. "Share my location with Abe too."

Fitz did as she asked, then slipped her phone into one of the bags and handed it back to her. She hung the string around her neck and shoved the phone beneath her shirt. He did the same with his own, feeling better knowing that, even if they ended up in the water, they'd have a way to call Abe or the police if it came to that.

Things were working out. So far, anyway.

They reached the mouth of the inlet, and Tabby slowed. The boat roiled and dipped over the incoming surf as they made their way to deeper water. When she'd gotten them past the waves, she glanced his way. "Which direction?"

"I don't know." Where was Veronica? Had she gone by already? Surely not. Her place was a few miles down the beach. But it wasn't as if she had to deal with stop signs on the ocean. And her boat looked fast. Maybe she'd passed, and they'd missed their opportunity.

No. He refused to believe that. He and Tabby had only had a few hundred yards to travel, whereas she'd had miles. She couldn't have reached them yet.

The boat lost its forward momentum, just bobbed on the gentle water as they scanned the horizon in every direction. He looked south. Were there islands out there? Had she turned into the open ocean?

Far as he remembered, the next closest island was Cuba. Surely, she wasn't going there.

But perhaps her destination had been between Mullins's rental and this inlet. Perhaps she'd already made the sale and was motoring back to the house.

He didn't voice any of his fears, just kept his gaze trained to the west. A few other boats were out this morning—leisure boats, ski boats—but not many. Despite all that had transpired that day, it was still relatively early, just after ten a.m. He figured most of the tourists wouldn't start hitting the water and beaches for another hour or so.

Where was Veronica?

The moment felt suspended in time, the waiting more torturous than anything he could imagine.

And then a speck appeared in the west, closer to land than they were, just past the breaking surf. It flew past the beaches and houses faster than any boat should be allowed to go. Long brown hair blew out behind the driver.

"That's her."

Tabby'd kept the boat facing east. Now, she got them moving, though Veronica was still behind them. Could this pontoon boat keep up with Veronica's speedboat?

It would have to.

He kept his eyes on Veronica while Tabby motored on, hopefully looking oblivious to the woman coming up behind them.

When she passed, Tabby gunned the engine, and Fitz lurched against his seat. The boat had more power than he'd anticipated, but it only took a minute to realize it wouldn't be able to keep up. If Veronica was going far, they'd lose her for sure.

The distance between them spread. Fifty yards. A hundred yards. They passed the eastern end of the island where they'd been staying, and Veronica turned north and went under the bridge that connected this island to the next.

Tabby slowed the engine a little but continued to follow. One thing to be caught in the same area in the gulf, but if Veronica turned now and noticed them, she could get suspicious.

Fitz kept up a running prayer for help, never taking his eyes off Veronica as her boat got smaller and smaller in the distance.

She passed the islands on either side and continued north. Little dots of land were scattered across this area. She could be going anywhere. They needed to keep her in sight.

Then, suddenly, she slowed and turned toward a small tree-covered swath of land barely sticking above the ocean's surface. It looked uninhabited.

Veronica motored into an inlet.

Tabby slowed as well.

Fitz never took his eyes off the red boat.

And then it disappeared among the trees.

CHAPTER THIRTY-FOUR

Fitz's already racing heart kicked up as Tabby neared the inlet and cut the engine. It was far too quiet here to think they could get any closer without the woman hearing.

He handed Tabby an oar, and they propelled themselves toward a tiny secluded beach just fifty or so feet from where Veronica had disappeared. No easy task, that. Eventually, the surf helped them, and they reached the shore. Fitz jumped onto the beach, where he sank into the wet sand.

Tabby started to follow.

"No. You're staying here. If you hear any boats nearby, send me a text." He made sure his phone was silenced. "If you hear gunshots or anything, get out of here."

"I'm coming with you."

He ignored the remark. "Once you're safely away, call Abe. But first, get out of here and get somewhere safe. Okay?"

"I'm not leaving without you."

"I don't plan to be seen," he said. Not until the last second, anyway, if he could get those jewels from Veronica. "I'll keep myself hidden. All this vegetation"—he gestured to the thick jungle all around—"hiding by myself won't be a problem. But here, on the beach, you're a bright and easy target. Promise me, Tabby. You hear anything, you see anything, and you get out of here, fast."

"But I want—"

"If you don't, I'll be distracted worrying about you. Distracted is dangerous. Promise me."

She blinked a couple of times, then nodded once.

He hadn't succeeded in sending her away, but maybe he could still protect her.

He turned and fled into the trees. While he jogged along the sandy ground, he prayed for her safety and his own success. They'd wasted five minutes, maybe more, getting settled. How had Veronica used those minutes? She hadn't motored away already. They were close enough to the inlet where she'd disappeared that he was certain they'd have heard her engine.

Was she meeting her buyer? Why here, of all places? One of them had to be extremely paranoid to have chosen this spot.

Well, considering he was following her, maybe *paranoid* wasn't the right word.

The shrubs and trees thickened and slowed him down. Palms and grasses and plants encroached on his route. The air seemed to vibrate with life. Insects, birds, and frogs kept up a steady melody that masked the sounds he made as he picked his way through the vegetation. Wild orchids tucked into the elbows of trees bloomed indigo above hot pink buds on bushes he'd never seen before and had no name for.

It felt as if somebody had turned up the brightness. Greenest greens all around, bluest blues above. Exotic smells and sounds and sights. He'd stepped into a technicolor world.

But not a safe one.

Finally, he could see the shore of the inlet where Veronica had disappeared. The waterway was no more than fifty yards across. Her boat bobbed in the center. She was alone, her gaze flicking in every direction.

Waiting for someone.

Fitz got as near as he could and ducked behind a tree, crouching low. He pulled his phone from the lanyard on his neck and snapped a few photos of her, then sent them to Abe, along with a quick update on what he was doing, just in case.

If he could stop this sale from happening, and if she took them back to the place where she was staying, then he could do a good old-fashioned robbery. Break in, aim his weapon, and demand she hand them over or die.

Wasn't exactly subtle, but he was desperate. The time for subtle had passed.

It'd be better if he could get the jewels now. He could swim the distance, board her boat, and take them by force. Again, not pretty, not subtle. But it could work. He was trying to figure out the best way to get into the water without being seen or heard when the sound of an approaching motor reached him.

It was coming from the opposite direction. Did this inlet have an... outlet?

Wherever it was coming from, Fitz was too late. The opportunity was past.

He traded his weapon for his cell just as a text came in. Tabby telling him she'd heard a motor.

A blue boat emerged, the engine cut, and it floated toward Veronica's red one. Veronica's boat had been fast, but this one—sleek and narrow with a low profile—was obviously built for speed.

There was a man inside. Fitz snapped a few photos of him, a few more of his boat, then lowered the phone. The man had bleached hair a little longer than Fitz's. He was well built, tanned, and wearing board shorts and an aqua T-shirt. Kind of guy who'd be able to sing along to every Jimmy Buffet tune, probably sipping a frozen margarita.

A whole different kind of criminal than Veronica's father.

The man expertly tossed a rope at Veronica, and she grabbed it.

Fitz switched his phone from photo mode to video and started recording the scene.

"I didn't appreciate being stood up this morning." Her voice carried across the water, confident, irritated.

The man sat back in his captain's chair and weaved his fingers behind his head, relaxed as could be. "It's good to see you again, Ronnie."

"Don't call me that," she snapped. "Why the sudden change of plans?"

"Seemed wise after the parade of men in and out of your place this morning."

Fitz couldn't see her face during the long pause. "Were you watching my—?"

"You call me outta the blue and wanna sell me a crap ton of jewelry for a song? Yeah, I was watching your place. I'm not trying to go to prison."

"I would never..." Her words trailed. "What do you mean, a parade of men?"

The man chuckled. "The first one I'm guessing was a boyfriend. Walked in like he owned the place."

"You must've been watching the wrong house."

"It was the place you walked out of this morning. And anyway, I have some fond memories there. It's not like I'd forget it. You 'n me and a bottle of tequila. That night, I thought I was using you for a good time. When you called me about this"—he gestured around them as if that filled in the blanks—"I realized you were the one using me." He shrugged. "Not that I'm complaining. You can use me like that anytime you please."

"That night was a mistake, one I won't make again."

"Ouch." The man dropped his hands and leaned toward her. "What's really going on, *Ronnie?*"

She didn't correct the name this time. "We have a deal."

"Not until you explain all the men."

"I don't know what you're talking about."

"After the boyfriend."

"I don't have a—"

"He's your type." The man's smile was cruel. "Long hair like mine. Sorta looked like a low-budget Bradley Cooper."

Bradley Cooper? Fitz had been told before he looked like the actor, but he'd never seen the resemblance. Low-budget, though. That felt right.

"Obviously..." The man stretched out the word. "He was a stand-in for what you really wanted. All you had to do was call, baby, and I'da been there."

When Veronica turned her face away from the buyer, Fitz could see her expression. Her eyes were wide, blinking fast. Her mouth was slightly open. She looked around, then faced him again. "You're serious? When did you see him?"

"About five minutes after you left. Who was he?"

"Where were you watching from? The houses are close together. Maybe he went to the place next door, and you just—"

"I rented the place next door. Had to make sure you weren't setting me up. Who was he?"

"I have no idea."

In the long pause, the man studied her, seemed to be trying to figure her out. Finally, he continued. "After Brad, the property manager stopped by. He manages a bunch of places on the beach. I've met him a few times."

So, whoever this buyer was, he was a local. If the sale went down, Fitz would be able to find him.

The buyer continued. "At least he knocked before he let himself in. I assume he met your boyfriend inside."

Veronica didn't say a word, but her eyes were wide, her mouth pinched tight.

"He left after about ten minutes. Then two more guys showed up, real goodfellas. They had a *Sopranos* vibe to 'em, if you know what I mean."

By the way Veronica went completely, unnaturally still, she knew exactly what he meant.

The buyer shook his head. "If I hadn't seen you leave, I'da thought you were running a brothel up there. Anyway, they stayed the longest. I actually got bored and made myself some eggs. That's when I called you and cancelled. You can't blame me for being spooked."

Veronica said nothing, but her face was paler than the man's blond hair.

"Who were they?" he asked.

"I have no idea."

His eyebrows rose. "Seriously?" He looked around, all humor gone from his tone. "Somebody's onto you, Ronnie. You think you were followed?"

She gazed back toward where she'd come from. "I didn't see anybody, but..." Her voice trailed.

The man uttered a string of curses. "Let's just do this. Then you go your way, and I'll go mine."

Fitz continued filming as possibilities flitted through his mind. He could try to stop the sale. He could fire at them, hope the guy got spooked and took off. Fitz guessed the beach-bum-turned-thief would do just that, but for all he knew, one or both of them was carrying. He didn't want them firing at Fitz—or at each other.

Too many variables. He didn't want anybody to get shot, least of all himself.

Fitz could threaten to shoot them if they didn't turn the jewels over. He could make the shot from where he stood, take out one of them. If they knew anything about firearms, though, they'd know how hard a shot it would be. They'd likely take off and hope for the best.

And it would be an empty threat. Fitz wasn't about to shoot anybody.

He could swim out there, try to stop it from a closer angle. But they'd have the high ground and all the leverage. If he got shot, he wouldn't be able to save Shelby or Tabby.

All those possibilities flitted through his mind in seconds. None of them stuck.

He continued taking the video.

Veronica opened a brightly colored bag that looked both waterproof and buoyant and lifted the little velvet packets from it.

"Where's the box?" the buyer said.

"I changed my mind, decided to keep it."

The man scowled. "The price—"

"The price is the price. What I have is worth twice what you're paying me."

After a long, tense pause, the man said, "Toss it over."

"Cash first."

He lifted a backpack and opened it.

Fitz didn't have an angle to see the contents, but it was clear from Veronica's reaction that she was satisfied.

The man pulled Veronica's boat so the two were touching, starboard side to starboard side. They traded bags.

The man lifted the jewels from the velvet pouches, one by one. Even from the distance, Fitz could see the spark of greed in the man's eyes. "Nice." Then, looking at the next piece, the bracelet, he said, "Very nice."

"You should make a good profit," Veronica said.

The man dropped the jewels back into the bag. "Why are you letting me make the profit?" His voice was almost accusatory. "Why not take your time, find a buyer—?"

"My mother is dying. The one thing we don't have is time."

The man settled the bag on his lap. "Oh. Well, then... But what about the guys at your place this morning?"

"I can guess who they were. The person I stole these from must've... I don't know how, but he must've figured it out." She made sure the backpack was zipped before shoving her arms into the straps. "We're good?"

"But does that mean... Are you going to be in danger? Am I?" The man's words pitched up at the end, a twinge of hysteria escaping.

"Don't worry. I won't give you away." Veronica's voice remained cool and detached.

"But you—"

"As long as my mom gets treatment," she said, "it doesn't matter what happens to me."

He nodded slowly. "Okay, then. I hope it works out. Give me a call next time—"

"There won't be a next time. Ever."

CHAPTER THIRTY-FIVE

Tabby stood in the ankle-deep water beside the boat and stared at the forest where Fitz had disappeared, willing him to come back. She knew he'd wanted her to stay on the boat, but she'd almost decided to follow him. She'd changed her mind, though, and had been standing in the warm surf for ten minutes, waiting. Praying.

Please keep him safe.

What was happening? She hated not knowing and itched to call him. She'd heard the distant sound of a motor a few minutes back and had texted him. It had come from the direction he'd walked, so he'd probably already known.

There was nothing to do but wait. She'd probably be better off waiting in the boat, though. If they needed to leave in a hurry, she should be ready.

She'd just turned to climb back in when she heard the low, quick thud of something moving across the sand, then a splash. Fitz?

She spun just as a body slammed into her. Hands yanked her away from the boat. She fell back, crashed into a man behind her. He turned her away from the boat and pushed before she regained her balance. She fell face-first. She barely had time to stop the gasp before her head hit the water. She was flipped onto her back, then lifted by a strong grip on her T-shirt. When she broke the surface, she sucked in a breath.

A man was standing over her, eyes wild and bright, lips stretched in a predatory smile.

Wilson Dunbar. "I told you we weren't through."

Willie's words were barely out of his mouth when he punched her in the head.

The blow left her dazed. He pulled her to her feet, but she could barely remain standing, barely force her feet forward as he propelled her toward the boat, which had floated a few feet away. "Climb in."

He was much stronger than she, much bigger. She did as she was told.

Willie shoved her facedown onto the deck. He clasped her hands behind her back and, using the rope already in the boat, tied them together. Then he did the same to her ankles.

He flipped her onto her back. The pressure of her weight against the hard deck hurt her wrists, but that was the least of her worries.

Willie's evil, vindictive face loomed over her. "Seems only fair you get the same treatment I did, don't you agree?"

There was no good response. She wanted to scream, but she couldn't force a sound past the terror that gripped her.

Fair? The man wanted to talk about fair? Nothing about this was *fair*. From the very beginning, she'd been pulled into something that had nothing to do with her. So had Fitz. So had Shelby.

She closed her eyes and begged God for her life, for all their lives. God wasn't about *fair*. God was about justice.

God was about protecting His children.

"Look at me," he said.

She squeezed her eyes tighter.

He straddled her. She felt his knees on either side of her hips. Felt water droplets dripping off his body onto her chest. "I said, look at me."

When he spoke this time, his breath was so close that she could feel it against her wet skin. She opened her eyes.

"Where's your boyfriend?" His ponytail hung down one side of his head, straggly and dripping onto her collar bone.

She stared at it, avoiding looking at Willie's face. "He went to try to get the jewels." Her voice was all wrong, high-pitched and shaking.

"When will he be back?"

"Soon," she said, not knowing if it was true or not. Only knowing that, if Willie thought he had time…

She didn't want to think about what he'd do.

She glanced at his face. He looked more amused than anything else. He leaned closer, whispered, "I guess I'll have to keep you waiting a little longer then," and stood up.

She took a deep breath, trying to calm her racing heart. It was cut short when Willie shoved a bit of rope into her mouth like a horse's bit, keeping her jaw propped open. He secured it behind her head.

"Don't want you shouting out a warning."

He pulled the lanyard off her neck, removed the phone from it, and tossed it into the water.

He yanked her to her knees and sat on the bench seat behind her.

In the distance, a speedboat whizzed by, but as Fitz had promised, this little cove was almost completely hidden from view. Nobody would be coming to save her. Nobody would see what was happening and call the police. The only person coming was Fitz, and when he came...

Something hard and cold pressed against the side of her head. From the feel of it, she guessed it was the wrong end of a gun barrel.

"Now," Willie said, "we wait."

CHAPTER THIRTY-SIX

After Veronica and her buyer went their separate ways, Fitz forwarded the video to Abe and made sure it uploaded to the cloud. It never hurt to be thorough. His years on the force had taught him that.

No jewels, but I know who has them, he typed as he walked. *Headed back to Tabby.*

Fitz shoved his phone back into the lanyard pouch. Abe responded, but Fitz didn't bother to see what the man said. First, he needed to get Tabby somewhere safe. Then he'd figure out what to do next.

He jogged through the forest, unconcerned now about being quiet, and burst onto the beach where he'd left her.

And froze.

The pontoon boat floated in the little cove.

Willie sat on a bench seat.

Tabby sat in front of him on the deck. Based on the way her shoulders were pulled back, her hands were bound. A rope kept her mouth open, kept her from screaming or talking.

Willie's gun didn't stray from her head. "Turn out the lights," he said, "the party's over."

"You been thinking of that line all day?"

His mouth twitched. "You were always on my mind, man."

A jolt of angry adrenaline slid down Fitz's back. He pulled in a deep breath and pushed out the rage on the exhale. "What do we do now? We just gonna stand here and quote Willie Nelson tunes, or do you have a plan?"

"Get in. You're driving."

Fitz splashed across the cove and climbed into the boat. Dripping onto the deck, he crouched down in front of Tabby. "You all right?"

She nodded, but her eyes were wide.

"I'm removing the gag," Fitz said. "There's nobody to hear if she screams."

Willie smiled at that. "You speak the truth. Go ahead."

Fitz untied Tabby's gag, and she gasped for a deep breath. He settled his palm against her cheek and met her eyes. "It's going to be all right. I promise."

"Okay." Her single word held a confidence he knew he didn't deserve. He never should have brought her with him. He should've insisted she stay at their rental.

Or escape to anywhere else in the world.

"While I'm enjoyin' your little reunion"—Willie's voice sounded anything but joyful—"it's time to get moving."

"How'd you find us?"

"Funny story. I was tracking another boat when I came across this one." His finger trailed down the side of Tabby's face, and Fitz noticed a red mark there. The man had hurt her.

Fitz worked to keep his temper in check.

"She keeps claiming to know nothing, yet here she is."

"She's here for the same reason you are," Fitz said. "Trying to locate your boss's jewels."

"Or maybe you just sold 'em. I heard that boat take off.

Now, you're gonna have to explain how you two just happen to be here."

"I guess you'll explain how you never could find the boat you were actually supposed to be tracking." Fitz pointed back to where he'd just come from. "It was in an inlet a couple hundred yards that way, and so were the jewels. But you were here, terrorizing an innocent woman."

"So you got 'em?" Willie asked.

"If we'd worked together, we could have."

Willie chuckled. "You've got an answer for everything don't you?"

Fitz held Tabby's eye contact again, trying to communicate confidence, before he stood and glared at the long-haired man.

Willie held out his free hand. "Your gun."

Fitz unholstered it and handed it over, and Willie engaged the safety and shoved it in his waistband at his back. "Phone."

He slipped it from the lanyard but held onto it, seeing the one Tabby had used empty at his feet. "The information your boss needs to find his jewels is on this. I recommend you don't toss it overboard."

Willie glared at him through squinted eyes. A moment passed. "Shut it down."

Fitz tried to figure a way to make it look like he complied without actually doing it. The phone was their only link to Abe, who was no doubt tracking them.

But Willie was the one holding the gun. Fitz did as he was told, then handed it over.

Willie dropped it at his feet. "You're driving. Let's go."

"Why don't you let her drive?" Fitz suggested. "I've never driven a boat before."

"You gotta be kidding me." Willie laughed. "It's not that hard. Just don't let go of the wheel and stay away from shallow water."

"Maybe you should do it. I'll keep Tabby in line."

Willie almost smiled at the suggestion. "Drive. And don't try anything. You get cute and try tossing me into the drink, she's gonna go too. All tied up like this, she'll sink like a stone."

Not that Fitz had considered it, but the man's words sent fresh fear to his gut. He'd have to be very careful not to flip the boat or sink it. It seemed rather sturdy, though. The bigger danger was the man holding the gun.

Fitz started the engine and pushed the throttle forward like he'd seen Tabby do. The boat lurched, and he pulled back gently. They puttered out of the cove.

Willie shouted, "Turn left."

Left. Like they were on Main Street, not weaving between islands. He did, keeping their speed down. He needed to be able to hear Willie's voice. More than that, he needed Willie not to be jostled and accidentally pull the trigger.

He kept up a steady stream of prayers as he followed Willie's directions. They headed north, passing uninhabited islands, some so small he wondered how they survived high tide. Fifteen minutes passed before Fitz caught sight of a yacht bobbing in the distance.

"Be careful," Willie said. "Try not to bang into it or Ronnie'll be ticked."

Not that Fitz particularly cared if Ronnie got angry, but he slowed.

He'd seen yachts before, but this was something. It was longer than Fitz's house, gleaming white in the bright sun.

The other two goons were standing on the deck, watching their approach. Marco took a few steps down to a low deck at the stern. Joey stayed above, gun drawn and trained on Fitz.

Fitz cut the engine long before he reached the boat.

Marco called, "Toss the rope."

Right. Fitz found one and did as the man asked. Silently, Marco pulled them close.

"Good to see you again," Fitz said. "It's been hours."

The man squinted.

"Though I suppose you didn't see me behind all those kayaks," Fitz added. "Tell Joey thanks for me."

Marco shot a look up at his brother, and Fitz forced a chuckle he didn't feel. Giving off a *nothing to worry about* vibe, as if this were all one big game.

The problem was, the stakes were the lives of the two people Fitz loved most in the world.

Marco tied the pontoon to the yacht, and Fitz attempted to mimic the man's actions on his side. The last thing he wanted was for their only means of escape to accidentally float away.

When he was finished, he faced Tabby. Her eyes were wide. Tears trailed down her cheeks.

Fitz turned his focus to Willie. "You want me to untie her feet, or are you planning to carry her?"

"Untie her. But don't try anything."

Three men with guns, and the closest island a mile or more out. What did Willie think they were going to do? He crouched in front of Tabby and untied the rope around her ankles. She wasn't fully free, but they were getting there.

She muttered a quick, "Thanks."

Before Fitz could answer, Willie said, "Anytime, darlin'." His feigned Southern drawl, tinged with his Rhode Island accent, sounded almost as ridiculous as the man looked. Today, he wore a red bandana around his head. He looked past Fitz. "Marco, this idiot knows nothing about boats. You better check his knots."

"I'll do it when you guys are in." Marco stepped back and motioned Fitz forward.

He stepped from the pontoon to the yacht, then dropped to a crouch, pretending to fix an untied shoelace.

"Get up, man," Marco said.

Fitz ignored him. When Tabby came close, he stood and reached to help her from the pontoon to the yacht. "Easy, there. We don't want you going in."

Her eyes were wide, scared.

He gripped her arm tightly. "I got you. I'm not letting you go." He held her eye contact and tried to add more meaning to his paltry words. "I'm not going to let anything happen to you." He prayed he'd be able to make good on that promise.

She stepped from the pontoon to the yacht's deck.

When she was steady, he slipped his hand down her arm and behind her back, where her wrists were bound. He kissed her forehead as he pressed his pocketknife into her palm. It only had a three-inch blade, but it was sharp.

As far as he could tell, nobody'd seen.

Maybe she could get herself free, get out of there. If nothing else, maybe she could defend herself.

"Up you go," Marco said.

He climbed the stairs and stepped onto the whitewashed deck.

Mullins was seated at a table, casual as could be.

CHAPTER THIRTY-SEVEN

Fitz scanned the boat quickly. The covered deck held an outdoor dining table and six chairs. On one side, a staircase led to the deck above. Beside that, a sliding glass door opened to a living area—couches, a wet bar, a TV. Lots of leather and glass and chrome.

A narrow pathway led around the perimeter of the boat. He couldn't see where the driver would sit. Not that he'd know how to get the thing moving even if he could.

Ronnie Mullins stared at him.

Joey stood just feet away, glaring.

Fitz said nothing as he moved closer to the thug to allow Tabby room to emerge from the short staircase. If it'd been a ladder, Willie would have had to untie her, but she was able to navigate the few steps without her hands.

Tabby scooted to stand beside him, and he gripped her elbow and squeezed.

"I'm all right," she whispered.

Fitz glared at the man at the table. "If you wanted to see us, all you had to do was call."

"This worked."

"Treating us like enemies—you think this was your best play?" His voice rose, the incredulity clear in his tone. "I've spent a week doing your dirty work. A week running around trying to find stolen goods that had nothing to do with me. Nothing to do with my sister. Nothing to do with Tabby. I've done nothing but try to get your stuff back for you, and this is how you treat us?"

Joey said, "Watch your mouth."

Slowly, Fitz turned to glare at him. He held the man's eye contact until Joey looked away. Then Fitz turned back to Mullins. "You need to get some higher quality goons."

"I don't think they like to be called goons." But Mullins's lips twitched.

"Thugs. Punks. Morons. You pick the moniker. Just keep them away from me."

"It couldn't be helped. You couldn't be trusted to—"

"You don't trust *me*? That's rich, all things considered." Fitz pulled in a deep breath, blew it out. In a level tone, he said, "Where's my sister?"

"She's safe."

"I know where your stuff is. I need to see Shelby, now."

Ronnie nodded to Willie, who stood on Tabby's other side. Willie called down to the deck below, "Bring the girl up."

Fitz turned to watch as Marco lifted the floor of the deck to reveal a storage area beneath it.

Shelby was bound and gagged, curled on her side in the small space. Her eyes blinked in the sudden brightness.

Fury colored Fitz's vision, and he turned and took a step toward Mullins with no plan except to hurt him.

Joey grabbed his arms. "Settle down."

He wanted to shake the thug off, but Joey was right. He wasn't in a position of power here. He had to keep his head if they were going to survive this.

"Shelby caused some trouble," Mullins explained.

Fitz's heart thumped wildly. What had she seen? What had she said to land her in that tight spot?

He turned back to see Shelby standing on the deck, looking up at him. "You okay?"

She nodded but couldn't speak past the gag.

"Untie her," he said.

Marco looked at Willie, who said, "Just take off the gag." Then to Shelby, "Keep your mouth shut."

She nodded, and Marco removed the gag from her mouth. She had red marks on her cheeks where it had scraped against her skin. How long had she worn that?

Slowly, Fitz turned back to the monster in front of him. He'd learned all he could about Mullins. He'd learned about the man's criminal exploits, about the men he'd allegedly had killed decades back. But hearing how Mullins had shielded his kids from a life of crime, how he'd provided for his illegitimate daughter, Fitz's impression had become clouded. A little part of him had had compassion. Mullins loved his family. He tried to protect them. Redeeming qualities.

Now, Fitz saw the monster beneath the mask. The monster who distributed drugs to kids, to addicts. This monster who protected his own children while profiting from the addiction of others.

The monster who would kidnap and harm an innocent child for the sake of money and power.

The monster who would kill them all to protect his own hide.

Mullins deserved no compassion, no mercy from Fitz. The desire for vengeance filled his mouth like poison, but he swallowed it back. Vengeance wasn't his to mete out. Vengeance belonged to God. As did mercy. And justice.

And God was there. He saw. He knew. He was a God of

justice. Fitz would trust in Him. His temper under control, he said, "We need to speak in private. You, Tabby, Shelby, and me."

"Whatever you have to say—"

"I know where your stuff is, but I'm not going to tell you in front of an audience."

"I think you'll do as I tell you."

"Trust me," Fitz said, "you'll thank me for it."

Mullins's eyes narrowed the slightest bit, and he turned to Willie. "Take the ladies to Shelby's room and keep an eye on them."

"They stay with me." Fitz took Tabby's elbow again as if that would be enough to keep her close.

"You're not really holding any of the cards here." Mullins nodded to Willie, and Tabby was pulled away.

Fitz watched in silence as Tabby disappeared through the glass doors.

As Shelby made her way to the stairs, Fitz walked that direction. He took her arm as she walked up to join him, ignoring Marco's glare behind them. When she was on the deck with him, he said, "It's going to be okay." He spoke the words as if they were true, as if he had no doubt.

Before he'd seen Shelby trapped in that hidden compartment, he'd hoped maybe, maybe Ronnie would let them all go. But now?

Would Mullins let them live?

Could he, after this?

What had his sister seen?

He swallowed all the questions. "I love you, sis."

"I love you."

"I still owe you that oatmeal."

Her lip trembled, and tears filled her eyes. "I'm sorry. I shouldn't have—"

"None of this is your fault." He kissed her cheek.

Marco yanked her away and pulled her through the glass doors, down the interior staircase, and out of sight.

"Have a seat," Mullins said.

Fitz looked at Joey, who hadn't moved, then back at Mullins. "Alone. Trust me."

A beat passed before Mullins nodded to the man. "Keep an eye on the girls. Anything happens to me, shoot them."

The goon nodded, but before he disappeared inside, Fitz said, "Wait."

He turned back.

"I'm going to need my phone. It's in the boat." He faced Ronnie. "You'll want to see what's on it."

With Mullins's permission, Joey jogged down the few steps to the lower deck, stepped into the pontoon, and found Fitz's phone. He brought it up and dropped it on the table.

Fitz powered it on. Abe had called and texted multiple times. Ignoring the notifications, Fitz navigated to the photos app, then gave Joey a look that he hoped said, *get lost*.

Again, the man waited for permission. At Mullins's nod, he stepped through the glass doors. Only when he went down the stairs did Fitz turn his attention to the man beside him. "Tabby didn't steal anything from you. The real thief chose her because they have similar body styles. She'd sat beside Tabby at dinner the night of the theft." He brought up the photo of Tabby and the woman known as Vera and showed it to Mullins. "We think this is when she stole Tabby's wallet. You can't see her face here, but this is the woman who stole from you."

Mullins looked but said nothing.

"After dinner, she must have bought this shirt"—he tapped the screen on Tabby's blouse—"at the resort gift shop. Did you ever look into who'd made purchases that night?"

"A woman bought the blouse with cash. The clerk only said

she was tall, thin, and pretty. Which describes your girlfriend to a T."

"Except Tabby already owned the blouse—I bought it for her. Why would she buy a second?"

Mullins shrugged. "Trying to throw us off."

"Doesn't make sense and you know it." Fitz took his phone back and set it facedown on the table. He had to be careful, had to lay this out so there was no doubt. "Tabby didn't steal anything from you. Somebody posed as her. We discovered that picture when we were going through photos I'd taken at the resort searching for someone who looked like her. The woman at dinner was the only one who fit the bill—right height, right body style, even similar ages. We decided she had to be the person, but we couldn't nail down who she was.

"So, we took a different tact, as you know. We started trying to figure out who knew about the purchases you'd made at auction. Like you told me, it was a short list. But we found someone. A woman who lives next door to your surrogate buyer, Gail Seder."

"Gail would never betray me. She knows better."

"But the person who stole from you is a thief, and a skilled one. Don't you think it's possible she simply broke into Gail's apartment and stole the information? Or maybe they were friends, and she went through Gail's stuff when she wasn't paying attention. It's not as if Gail's in some high-tech industry. She buys stuff at auctions. She works from home in a secure building. She would've felt safe there."

Mullins's slight nod was the only indication that he accepted the possibility.

"This woman, this neighbor of Gail's, discovered the purchases she made for you."

"That doesn't explain how she knew about our trip to Belize."

This was where it got tricky. Fitz changed direction.

"Why did you have your guys search your rental property this morning?"

Mullins shrugged. "Thought you and the woman might be staying there."

"I was there when the manager came. I was searching the place myself."

Mullins didn't shift, didn't move. But his lips pressed together.

"The man told you a woman had rented it. He told you a woman was staying there—nothing he saw indicated a man was there. I heard him tell you that. Still, you had Joey and Marco come back and search it. Why?"

"I had a hunch."

"So did I." Fitz opened his photos apps again and found the photograph of the antique box he'd found that morning. "When I searched, I found this." He turned it so Mullins could see the image.

His eyebrows lifted slightly.

"It was empty," Fitz explained.

"You admit to having it, though."

"I admit to *finding* it, in your rental property. When your guys showed up, I hid downstairs in the storage area. At the time, I was wishing I hadn't found it so they could have, but it was too late for that."

"Why didn't you just reveal yourself?"

Fitz made a show of looking around. "You keep telling me how you don't trust me. You think I trust you? I needed all the information before I came to you."

Mullins leaned forward. "Do you have it now, all the information?"

"I do, but you're not going to like it."

The man settled back against the chair again.

"Before I tell you anything else," Fitz said, "I want to reiterate... Tabby had nothing to do with this. Her only crime was resembling the real thief. She's still with me because she doesn't want Shelby to get hurt."

"Or you," Mullins guessed.

Fitz shrugged. "In any event, Tabby wasn't about to let a teenage girl get hurt because she protected herself. She's a good person, an honest person."

"So you think."

"So I know. And so do you."

Mullins didn't even blink.

Reluctantly, Fitz found the video he'd taken that day and started it playing. He turned so Mullins could see it.

He couldn't see it himself, but he could hear the audio perfectly. He watched Mullins's face morph from interested to horrified to furious. When the video ended, Fitz set the phone on the table.

He kept his mouth shut.

After a minute, Mullins lifted it, powered it off, and tapped the black screen. "You know who that is?"

"Veronica Hernandez." Fitz paused, then added, "Your daughter."

He nodded once. "She had the box?"

Another quick nod.

"Ironic," Mullins said. "Considering I'd decided to give it to her. Brought it all the way to Belize and then decided not to sell it. She collects boxes, you know. Weird, but... How did you find her?"

"I had a hunch," he said, quoting Mullins's words.

His mouth worked, showing more emotions than Fitz figured he'd wanted. Anger. Frustration. Sadness.

Betrayal.

"Her mother's very sick," Mullins finally said.

"Cancer. We saw her."

His eyes flashed. "Why? Why would you drag her into this?"

"Trying to track down your jewels. If you'd told me about Veronica—"

"She has nothing..." He ran his hand through his white hair. "I didn't know she..." He swallowed hard.

"She knew about your trip to Belize, right?"

"I was going out of the country. I wanted her to know. I wanted to... I always tried to keep in touch with her."

Fitz nodded slowly, letting Mullins come to terms with what this meant.

"You're saying she lives next door to Gail?"

He read the address in Manhattan. "They live in apartments thirteen and fourteen. They're neighbors."

A look of suspicion crossed his features. "This doesn't prove anything," he said. "I don't know what Veronica was doing out there with that guy, but maybe it had nothing to do with me. Or maybe that was your girlfriend pretending to be my daughter. Maybe this is all more lies."

"You suspected Veronica already. That's why you questioned the building manager about who was renting the place. That's why, ten minutes after the manager left, you sent your goons over there to search. When I told you we were headed to the Keys, you knew about your connection to this place, your family's beach house. We hadn't put that together yet. You hightailed it across the gulf to be here. Maybe you thought, even hoped, you'd find evidence that Tabby and I were staying there, but you didn't. And still, you had your guys search it. My guess is that you've brought Veronica here yourself, or perhaps let her use the place. She is your daughter, after all. When I told you we were headed to the Keys, you got suspicious. What other reason—?"

"Being thorough." But his words held no conviction.

"You suspected Veronica. You didn't want to. You wanted to be wrong, but you suspected."

"She's trying to save her mother's life." Again, his hand raked his white hair. "If Ginger would undergo more treatment, I'd pay for it in a heartbeat. She's my daughter's mother, for crying out loud. I'd move heaven and earth to keep that woman alive. She doesn't want it. She doesn't want..."

Fitz said nothing.

Mullins turned to face the sea, gaze unfocused.

After a few silent moments, Fitz said, "None of us harmed you, Ronnie. Not me, not Tabby, and not Shelby. I found out who stole from you. If you want, I can track down the buyer, but not until I know they're safe."

Mullins turned back to face him. His expression shifted from a soft, sad look to something hard and determined. No longer the heartbroken father, he was back to being the hardened criminal. The killer.

For all the times Fitz had been wrong in the last week, he'd have given anything to be wrong once more. But this time, his guess was spot-on.

Mullins schooled his expression quickly. "Let's go get them, and you can be on your way."

CHAPTER THIRTY-EIGHT

After the great big world above, the hallway below deck was narrow and cramped, made worse by the guard looming behind. Willie's hand, heavy on Tabby's shoulder, guided her where he wanted her to go. He pushed her through the second door on the left.

The stateroom wasn't much larger than the hallway. Bunk beds on one side, a small desk and bureau built in on the other. Willie pushed her onto the bottom bunk. It was no easy feat to turn herself onto her back without the use of hands, and without letting go of the pocketknife gripped in one fist—or giving away that she had it. But she managed to flip herself onto her backside and scoot as far from Willie as she could. When she was backed into the wall, she pulled her knees up to her chest to protect herself. Not that it would help.

Willie climbed onto the bed with her. He ran his hands down the outside of her thighs. "Ain't this cozy?"

She squeezed her eyes closed and her knees together.

"Now, now, don't be like that." He chuckled. "Actually, do. It'll be so much more fun if you fight me."

But the sound of footsteps outside had him scowling. He winked at her, tossed out a, "Later," and stood beside the bed.

She exhaled a relieved breath. A reprieve. For now.

Shelby was shoved into the room and onto the bed beside her. She, too, had to fight to get herself into a seated position. She scooted as close to Tabby as she could get.

"You're okay," Tabby said. "It's going to be okay."

Shelby looked at her, the terror in her eyes raising Tabby's heart rate. She wanted to tell her not to worry, that Fitz had it under control, that Abe would be looking for them.

But she didn't say anything. Because maybe Fitz didn't have it under control. And maybe Abe wouldn't get there in time. And nothing felt certain except the ropes cutting into her wrists and the looks on the faces of the men crouching down to leer at them.

Willie and one of the brothers. Marco, Fitz had called him.

"Think they'll be a while?" Marco asked.

Willie met Tabby's eyes. "Maybe just long enough."

Tabby didn't flinch, just held his eye contact. She wouldn't show fear.

But Marco was staring at Shelby with a sick longing, and Tabby realized the only thing worse than Willie getting his way with her would be Marco getting his with this innocent teenager.

"It won't take Fitz five minutes to tell your boss where his things are," Tabby said. "Whatever you're thinking, you're not going to have time."

Willie's eyes squinted the slightest bit, and then he smiled. His yellow teeth gleamed in the dim light, the canines pronounced, bringing to mind a stalking wolf.

"Five minutes," Willie repeated, glancing at his friend. "We can have a little fun for—"

The door banged open, and the other guard stepped in. Joey, if her memory served.

Both Willie and Marco stood and faced him.

"Bad idea," Joey said.

Tabby quickly unfolded the pocketknife and leaned toward Shelby. Her voice was barely a whisper when she said, "Shift your hands in my direction."

Shelby adjusted herself, turning her back slightly toward Tabby. Their shoulders were touching. Tabby felt behind her until she touched the girl's hands. She walked her fingers up and found the rope that bound the wrists. She sawed at the binding, barely hearing the conversation taking place.

"Give us a few minutes," Marco said.

"Not a chance." Joey's voice was all business. "Mullins is already in a crap mood. Let's not make it worse."

Willie took two steps toward the door. Tabby couldn't see his face beyond the low top bunk. "It'll only make it worse if he finds out."

Marco added, "Make yourself useful and step outside. Knock if they come."

"Forget it," Joey said. "And anyway, you know eventually he's gonna turn them over"—his hands gestured toward the bunk—"to dispose of. We can take our time then."

Beside her, Shelby shuddered while the men discussed what they thought Mullins would expect of them. They seemed to agree that bullets to the head would be the most effective.

Tabby tried to drown out their voices. *Don't think about that*, she told herself.

Please, God, get us out of this.

She was thankful at least for the low bunk overhead that blocked the men's view. She furiously sawed at the ropes. Seconds later, they gave, and Shelby started to move.

Tabby grabbed her wrist. "Don't."

Shelby seemed to understand, and Tabby slipped the pocketknife into her hand.

It didn't take Shelby nearly as long to cut through Tabby's rope. When it fell away, Tabby stretched her wrists, thankful for the blood that flooded into her hands and tingled in her fingertips.

Shelby pressed the knife back into Tabby's palm.

Together, they shifted to sit on the ropes, hiding the evidence that they were no longer bound.

The three men continued to discuss various methods of murdering them and disposing of their bodies. Then they moved on, discussing how they'd have their *fun* first—without letting Mullins in on it. Apparently, though the mobster wasn't averse to drug selling and sex slavery and murder, he drew the line at rape.

A meandering line that was indeed.

Shelby scooted against Tabby's side and pressed her head between Tabby's shoulder and neck. Tabby longed to hold the girl, to comfort her, but she wouldn't take the chance of the men seeing that their hands were no longer bound. That and the little knife she held in her grip might be their only hope.

CHAPTER THIRTY-NINE

Fitz walked in front of Ronnie through the glass doors. On his right, a living area with a leather L-shaped couch. On the left, a glass table with built-in benches on two sides, chairs on the other two. Ahead and up a couple of steps, a small kitchen was set off by an island. A cluster of framed family photos hung on a wall. They turned to the staircase where Tabby and Shelby had disappeared.

Below were three armed men and two innocent women. When they had Fitz corralled down there, he'd be trapped, unable to do anything.

Where was Abe? Had he called the police? Did he understand when Fitz didn't answer his messages that they were in trouble? Would they be able to find the yacht?

Fitz couldn't count on rescue.

Just before he reached the staircase, he turned abruptly to face Mullins.

And saw a handgun pointed at his gut.

Fitz lifted both hands and stepped back. "Whatever you think you have to do, you don't. Just let us go. You can sail away, and we'll never have to see each other again. My sister went on this little trip with you, voluntarily. You got annoyed with her and locked her up for a little while. Annoying, but not a felony. There's no reason not to just let us go."

"I don't know what you're talking about." But Mullins's voice was flat, dead. He'd made up his mind.

"You know exactly what I'm talking about."

Mullins took a long breath and blew it out. "I was afraid I wouldn't get my stuff back. I need that money. I had nothing better to do while we waited to hear from you, so I decided to deliver a shipment of goods myself. I usually try to keep my family away from my business, but after having my capital stolen, I thought to cut out the middleman, make a little more cash than I normally would. It won't make up anywhere near what... what was stolen from me."

He seemed to still be coming to terms with the fact that his daughter had been the thief.

"Your sister started snooping around," Mullins said. "She found the goods. She didn't know I knew, but I have cameras all over this place."

Nausea churned in Fitz's gut that had nothing to do with the gentle sway of the boat.

Shelby had seen enough that she had to die. And if she had to die, they all had to die.

Mullins nodded to the staircase. "Move."

Fitz took his time. Surely Abe was looking for them. If he could just drag this out longer, it would give Abe the opportunity to find them.

"I said *move*."

Slowly, Fitz stepped forward, trying to think what to do. He could try to get the gun away from Mullins, and he might not get shot in the process. But then what? It'd be him against three armed men.

And now that Mullins had shown his hand, he was keeping his distance, following four stairs back.

Fitz had little choice but to keep going.

He reached the lower deck and a short hallway.

A door stood open halfway down. Joey hovered in the entry.

Muffled voices had drifted up before, but now all was silent.

Fitz turned again, arms raised. "Shelby won't say anything. She'll keep her mouth shut. We all will."

"Unfortunately, I don't put that much stock in the secret-keeping skills of a child."

"Did she tell Shawn?"

Ronnie's lips pressed together. "She didn't want to make waves, but that doesn't mean—"

"She can keep a secret. She won't say a word. She'll keep—"

"I'm sorry, but"—he shrugged—"I can't count on that. I wish I could. Shawn was devastated when I told him she disembarked in Cozumel."

Cozumel.

Shelby'd been in that tiny storage space since Cozumel?

His horror must've shown on his face because Mullins said, "Relax. We let her out when Shawn and Lena were asleep."

"Let her out *for what?*"

"I'm not a monster. Nobody touched her."

Fitz wasn't convinced or mollified. His hands clenched into fists. If Joey weren't standing ten feet away, he'd take out Mullins right now. Murder him and toss his body into the sea. He could do it. His hands would fit perfectly around that flabby neck. He could practically feel them squeezing Mullins's life out of him.

But then what?

Shelby and Tabby would die.

"Whatever you're plotting," Mullins said, "I wouldn't do it if I were you. I'm the only one who keeps them in line. All the things you worried had happened to your sister, they would happen to them both. Willie might even let you live long enough to witness it."

Fitz forced his hands open. "I'm just supposed to walk placidly beside you, sheep to the slaughter. Is that it?"

Mullins shrugged. "I can promise you it'll be painless that way."

Joey watched from his spot near the door. He had to have heard at least some of that. His hand hovered over the holster at his hip.

Fitz had one opportunity, and it probably wouldn't work. But he had to try. He couldn't stand by and let them all die.

If he got shot in the process...

He would. He wouldn't survive this. But if he could take out Mullins and Marco, and then one of the men in the room before any of them killed him, that would give Tabby and Shelby a shot.

They might be able to fight their way out. Nobody would see them as a threat, tied up as they were. And the men wouldn't so willingly slaughter their play toys. That could work in their favor.

Tabby had the knife. Maybe she'd gotten free. Maybe she could use it. Maybe she could get ahold of a gun. Maybe she and Shelby could escape.

Tabby wouldn't want to leave Fitz any more than he'd want to leave her, but she would. To save Shelby, she would.

They had to survive. If they survived, Fitz would willingly sacrifice himself. Not to protect Mullins's criminal enterprise. But for Tabby and Shelby, he would be that sheep to the slaughter.

For the ones he loved, he'd fight and die.

And trust God to take care of them.

He wanted to get a look at where the girls were, but it would be too risky to stand in front of the door.

He'd have to do this blind.

Joey's gun was holstered at his side.

Mullins had his pointed at Fitz's back.

Three feet from Joey, Fitz twisted and dove at Mullins, knocking him in the knees.

Mullins fired.

Fitz felt a pinch in his shoulder but ignored it as he popped to his feet, jumped behind Mullins and grabbed his gun hand. He shoved his finger on top of Mullins's on the trigger.

Joey'd drawn his gun, but he didn't fire. Fitz was using Mullins's body as a shield.

Fitz aimed and squeezed.

The bullet hit Joey in the chest.

The thug was still falling when Fitz elbowed Mullins in the nose and yanked the gun from his hand. Mullins fell, and Fitz stomped on his head, hard, praying he'd stay down.

Marco popped out of the room and aimed.

Fitz pressed against the wall, and the shot skimmed his back, sharp and blazing.

He aimed and fired.

The bullet hit square in Marco's forehead.

The thug collapsed in the doorway.

Two guns on the floor.

One enemy dead, two down.

One left.

Fitz readied his weapon, flipped into the open doorway, and aimed.

Willie held Shelby in front of him, one arm wrapped around her neck, his gun pressed to her temple.

Her hands were free.

Gone was the smug, arrogant look Willie had worn every

time Fitz had seen him. His eyes were wide. "I'll shoot her. I swear, I'll—"

"And then I'll shoot you." Fitz kept his voice calm. "There's no escape."

He thought of the two wounded men in the hallway, the two guns Fitz hadn't had time to secure. Willie didn't know what a good chance he had to survive this. Fitz prayed he wouldn't figure it out.

"It's over, Willie. There's no way you walk away from this free. But you can walk away, if you put the gun down."

Willie's eyes flicked around the room. He was in full panic.

"I won't hurt you," Fitz said. "Just let my sister go and put the gun down. There's no reason to kill an innocent child."

The man blinked twice, three times, and Fitz had hope he'd listen to reason.

But his eyes darkened, hardened with resolve. "I'm not going to prison."

And Fitz knew the gunshot was coming. He and Tabby would survive, but Shelby...

A hand shot out from the bottom bunk. A knife.

Tabby jabbed it into Willie's thigh.

The man grunted, jerked back.

His weapon fired, and Shelby collapsed.

Fitz shot him. The bullet hit his forehead, and he fell, landing on top of Shelby.

He was dead.

But Shelby...

His sister screamed, "Get him off me!"

Fitz yanked the dead man away, and Shelby skittered onto the bunk, eyes round and wide. Blood splattered across her face. But not her blood. Willie's shot had missed. Thanks to Tabby...

He would thank her properly as soon as this was over.

He would embrace his sister and comfort her. As soon as this was over.

He swiveled to the hallway, peeked out over Marco's body. Joey was alive, his hands pressed to the wound on his chest. The man had moved at just the right second, and Fitz's bullet had missed his heart. He might survive, but he wasn't a threat.

Mullins was gone.

Fitz stifled the curse word. He should've shot the man when he'd had the chance.

He turned back to Shelby and Tabby. They both looked at him with terrified gazes.

"Fitz." The pitch of Tabby's voice rose with horror. "You've been shot!"

The reminder brought back the pain, but he pushed it away. "I'm fine. You know how to shoot a handgun, right?"

She nodded quickly.

"Get Willie's."

He reached down and yanked Marco's from his hand, then shoved it into his holster. Then he grabbed Joey's. He met the man's eyes. "Your only chance to survive comes if I call the police and get you an ambulance. You got that?"

The man blinked terrified eyes, which Fitz took as a yes. Fitz checked the weapon and handed it to his sister.

She knew how to shoot. He'd taught her himself. He wasn't sure she could at this point—she seemed to be in shock. "Keep it aimed at the floor unless someone comes at you. Okay?"

"Okay." Her voice was weak.

He gripped her shoulder, hard. "Shelby. You need to focus."

She nodded, seemed to be coming to her senses.

"Don't shoot me or Tabby, please."

"I'm not an idiot."

There was the attitude he was looking for. There was his sister. He spared a half second for a smile, then addressed

Tabby. "You bring up the rear and walk backwards. If Mullins shows his face, shoot him. Aim for the heart. Okay?"

She nodded. "I can do it."

"Shelby, you're after me. Stay together. We're going up. I'm gonna grab my cell from the table on the deck, and we're gonna get in the boat and get out of here. When we're safe, we'll call the police."

Fitz started the walk down the hall.

Nobody stood in their way. Nobody came from behind.

They made it up the stairs. Fitz peeked, scanned the living area but saw nobody.

Where was Mullins? He couldn't let them leave. They knew too much. His life would be over.

Slowly, keeping low, Fitz climbed the rest of the stairs and stepped into the room.

Movement from the kitchen drew his attention.

Mullins popped up from behind the island and fired.

Fitz dove, yelled, "Down!" and returned fire.

He scrambled behind the white sofa.

He hadn't been shot this time. Mullins had missed.

Had Fitz's bullet hit its mark?

He listened. Everything was quiet. No bird calls. No engine sounds. Only the soft lapping of water against the hull.

And a rattling breath.

"Hey, Ronnie?"

No answer.

"It's over, you know."

Another rattling breath. The man was struggling. Or he was trying to draw Fitz out.

Fitz peeked around the sofa. Mullins wasn't there.

He crouched and made his way to the bottom of the steps that led to the kitchen.

Heard another rattling breath.

Gun drawn and ready, he hurried up the two steps and peeked around the counter.

Mullins lay crumpled on the tile floor, blood seeping from his neck.

"Tabby!" he shouted. "Come out. Call 911."

He snatched a towel from a hook and pressed it against the wound. The towel was soaked in seconds.

A moment later, he heard the heavy pounding of footsteps and stood, gun aimed, ready to take out another enemy.

Uniformed men flooded onto the boat. Somehow, the police were already there.

Mullins moved, and Fitz aimed at his forehead. Mullins reached out, fingers trembling. Fitz's finger hovered over the trigger.

But the man grasped a picture frame that lay on the floor and pulled it toward him.

It was a family photo. Mullins, his wife, his kids, and his grandkids. Mullins grimaced. Was it physical pain? Or perhaps something much deeper than that.

Fitz wondered if a tear might come, but Mullins let out a last breath, and the photo slipped from his fingers.

CHAPTER FORTY

Tabby held Shelby in her arms on the white sofa while cops milled all around them.
Shelby was curled up on her lap like a child, holding her tight. All Tabby could do was rub the poor girl's back and murmur promises in her ear. "It's over now. You're safe. We're all safe."

She didn't mention Fitz's bloody wounds. Surely, they weren't too serious, or he wouldn't have been able to do all he'd done. Somehow, he'd taken out four armed men. How?

She couldn't figure it out.

It had all seemed so impossible. And yet, they were here, breathing, and the bad guys were being carried out on stretchers. Mullins was gone. Willie and Marco had been killed instantly. The other brother, Joey, might survive, but based on the fact that they'd whisked him away in a helicopter moments before, she wasn't sure.

Fitz sat at the kitchen table just a few feet away while a paramedic cut off his shirt and treated his wounds. He'd been shot twice. But amazingly, he seemed okay.

It confused her. Everything felt muddy and wrong. It was

shock. That was what the paramedic had told her and Shelby as he'd draped them both with heavy blankets.

A familiar voice came from the deck, and she looked up just as Abe walked in. Fitz saw him, too, and stood, pushing away the paramedic dressing his wounds. "The cavalry showed up about ten minutes late."

Abe looked like he wanted to embrace his friend, but he got a look at the bandages and dropped his arms. "I lost your location." Abe's deep voice was tinged with frustration. "It's a big ocean. Thank God it came back on just long enough for us to get a read on where you were."

"I was counting on that," Fitz said. "I had to turn on my phone to show Mullins the video. I hoped you were paying attention."

Abe gave him a once-over. "What happened?"

Fitz started to shrug but stopped himself, a twinge of pain crossing his expression. "Grazed a couple of times. It's a miracle it's not worse."

A miracle. Tabby realized how true that word was.

Because there was no way Fitz, Tabby, and Shelby could have defeated four armed men with nothing but a pocketknife. And yet, they had.

Unbelievably, they had.

Fitz left Abe, who turned to address one of the cops, and approached Tabby and Shelby. He crouched in front of them. "Hey."

Before Tabby could think of what to say, Shelby launched herself into his arms. "You came. You came for me."

He held her tight, then lifted her back onto the sofa. Pain filled his features as he did, but Shelby didn't notice.

"Of course I did." Fitz held his sister's face in his hands. "Of course I came for you."

"I'm sorry I'm sorry I'm sorry. I should never have—"

Fitz covered her mouth with his finger. "If you hadn't gone willingly, they'd have taken you against your will."

She leaned back. "Why? What'd I do?"

"Nothing. I'll explain it all later, but it had nothing to do with you—or me or Tabby. This was all Mullins."

"Why would you work for a man like that?"

He held Shelby's gaze. "I wasn't working for him. I was only trying to get you back. All this time, I've been doing nothing but trying to get you back."

Shelby's bottom lip trembled, and she leaned forward and pressed her cheek against his chest.

He held her close and looked toward the ceiling.

Tears blurred Tabby's vision.

When Fitz lowered his gaze to Tabby, his eyes were rimmed in red. "Are you all right?"

And suddenly, everything felt very clear. The men who'd been after her were dead. And she and Shelby and Fitz were alive and well. And it was over.

Somehow, it was over.

She smiled at Fitz, this amazing man who'd saved her life. This wonderful man who'd risked everything for Tabby and his sister. She reached out, squeezed his arm. *I'm alive,* she thought. *I'm safe because of you.*

And both those statements were true.

But what came out of her mouth was, "I think I'll like Rhode Island."

Fitz's eyes popped wide, and a broad smile crossed his lips. He swallowed hard and leaned close. With his arm around her shoulders, he kissed her temple. He said nothing, but Tabby wasn't worried. Fitz loved her. He'd shown her in a million ways since they day they'd met.

And she loved him.

This was right. All the things she'd thought were keeping

her in New Hampshire suddenly didn't matter at all. She could leave her parents and Chris in God's hands and live the life God had for her.

"We'll figure it out," Fitz finally said. "If God can take care of this"—he looked pointedly at the yacht that had nearly been the scene of their deaths—"God can lead us right where He wants us."

That was exactly where Tabby wanted to be—right where God wanted her.

CHAPTER FORTY-ONE

Fitz, Tabby, and Shelby were checked out by doctors and taken to the police station. They were offered sandwiches and coffee and soda, but none of them was able to stomach very much.

The detectives questioned Fitz first. Detective Florence Birch was a heavy-set gray-haired woman. Her many wrinkles told Fitz she was either in her eighties or worshipped the Florida sun. He guessed the second. She had kind eyes, but her no-nonsense demeanor kept Fitz from being pulled in by them.

The other detective, a thirty-something rail-thin bald man named Detective Ehrlich, took the lead with the questioning, but Fitz wasn't fooled. Birch was in charge. The questioning took two hours. No surprise there—it was a strange and convoluted story. Fortunately, Birch and Ehrlich seemed to accept it.

When they'd wanted to question Shelby alone, Fitz had pulled the *legal guardian* card and insisted on staying by her side. He'd half expected her to argue that she was old enough, thank you very much, to answer a few questions all by herself. But she surprised him. She took his hand and held it the whole time.

He kept quiet while Shelby answered Ehrlich's questions. Fitz had been on the other side of that desk enough times to know the wisest thing he could do would be to keep his mouth shut and listen.

And listen he did, horrified, as Shelby recounted what'd happened on the boat while he'd been trying so hard to rescue her.

She'd had fun the first few days, but then Mullins had joined them in Cozumel. He made her nervous. Late one night, she'd watched out her porthole as another boat came alongside the yacht where they were anchored not far offshore. She saw men unloading cargo. She didn't know what it was, but the fact that it was the middle of the night made her suspicious.

The next day, she went exploring and found the packages. "I didn't know what was in them," she told the detectives on the far side of the table. "It's not like I opened any of them up or anything. But I figured it was drugs or something. I mean, what else could it be?"

Neither of the detectives offered other options.

That was the day before she spoke to Fitz and requested oatmeal. Apparently, she'd been in the hole beneath the deck since they left Cozumel on Wednesday. Mullins had had her brought up to talk on the phone while someone made sure neither Lena nor Shawn saw her.

She'd been in the hole for days.

If Mullins weren't already dead, Fitz would kill him.

When the detectives sent them out and called Tabby in to be questioned, he sat in a hard metal chair beside his sister. She laid her head on his shoulder but didn't sleep. They were both too tired to do anything but rest.

Fitz didn't mind the quiet. He needed time to process all that had happened.

He'd never even shot a person, much less killed one. Now,

he'd killed three. Four if Joey Novak didn't pull through. And, based on what he'd overheard from paramedics at the scene, it wasn't looking good.

All he felt was a profound sense of gratitude. Somehow, with God's help and Tabby's quick thinking and his lucky shots, they'd survived.

Maybe guilt and remorse would come eventually, but Fitz doubted it. He might not have done everything perfectly, but he hadn't been the one to start this ball rolling. He could blame Veronica for stealing from her father, but this story had begun long before that. Before Mullins had decided to turn his assets into jewelry and smuggle them out of the country. Before he'd had an affair and made a daughter he had no intention of raising. Long before any of that, Mullins had turned his back on all that was right in the world and had chosen evil. The end of his life felt like a culmination of how he'd lived—in violence and greed and crime.

It was fitting. It was justice.

Fitz was well aware that, while Mullins and his cohorts had received justice, he himself had received mercy. Because he'd given his life to God, his own sins were wiped clean. Mullins had never made that choice.

But the choice had been there, all along. He could've made it, if he'd wanted to. He could've turned to God and rejected evil.

Fitz pulled in a deep breath and pushed it back out. It wasn't his job to figure out the meaning of life or who should get justice and who should get mercy. That was all in God's hands. What Fitz knew was that God was good, and God had been merciful to him and Shelby and Tabby.

Rather than analyze it, he chose to simply be grateful that the ones he loved most in the world were alive and well.

By the time Tabby's interview was over and they stepped

out of the police station, the sun was dipping below the western horizon. His arm was around Shelby. Fitz's other hand held Tabby's.

And he thought about her words. *I think I'll like Rhode Island.*

Abe had been questioned and released hours before. Now, he stood beside his rental car just as he had his old Continental outside the Coventry Police Department a few days earlier.

Or... had it been yesterday?

No. That didn't feel right.

But... yes. Technically.

Fitz needed a real night's sleep in a real bed so he could wake up to a new day and start fresh.

Abe pushed off the car and opened his arms.

For the first time since the rescue, Shelby let Fitz go. She stepped into Abe's arms, and he wrapped them around her and kissed her head. "How you doing, kiddo?"

"Glad to see you."

His low chuckle was amused. "You know your brother couldn't do anything without me."

She backed away and looked up at him. "Obviously."

Fitz growled behind them, but they only laughed. Shelby slid into the car as Tabby offered Abe a hug. "Thank you."

"All I did was show up too late."

"You did more than that. We appreciate you."

After she slid into the car beside Shelby, Fitz held out his hand, and Abe shook it. "So glad you're all right."

"I'm glad they are."

"I was worried about all three of you." The men held eye contact a moment, all the fears they'd both faced unspoken between them. Then Abe said, "Figured you guys were hungry. How does steak sound?"

Back at the little waterside cabin, Abe grilled while Tabby

chopped and roasted potatoes and Shelby made a salad. Fitz set the table and offered Abe helpful advice on how to grill the perfect steak, which the man was careful not to take. There was lots of banter and laughter and fun as they ate dinner on the deck. Nobody discussed what had happened that day. Nobody discussed what would happen next.

That night, Fitz sent Tabby and Shelby to share the king-size bed in the master and crashed in one of the narrow twin beds in the spare bedroom.

Despite Abe's snoring on the far side of the room, Fitz slept soundly.

CHAPTER FORTY-TWO

It was ten o'clock when Tabby woke to the sound of someone knocking at the door. She pulled on a sweatshirt and jeans and walked in bare feet to the door, where Detective Birch stood on the wooden deck carrying a plastic bag.

"Did I wake you?"

Tabby attempted to run her hand through her hair, but it was too snarled. She gave up and shrugged. "No. The knocking woke me."

The woman's eyebrows hitched. "I figured it'd be safe if I waited until ten. I have some information I thought you'd like to know."

Tabby was tempted to tell her to come back later, but the woman didn't seem amenable to that suggestion. Instead, Tabby held the door open. "Have a seat. I'll get everyone up."

It was thirty minutes before they'd all made themselves presentable enough to join the discussion. For her part, Detective Birch had made coffee and set out a container of mini-muffins of various flavors on the kitchen table. "Grabbed them on my way. Didn't know if you guys would be hungry."

Tabby snagged a cup of coffee and a banana-nut muffin and slid into a chair.

The kitchen was barely large enough for the five of them, but nobody suggested they take it outside. In fact, Fitz, Shelby, and Abe seemed as dazed as Tabby felt.

When they were all seated with muffins and drinks, Birch surveyed the table. "Wow, you guys look terrible."

Fitz ran a hand over his wet hair. "It's been a long few days."

Shelby yawned hugely. "I hope this is worth it."

Birch said, "Me, too," and focused on Fitz. "Joey Novak's still in ICU. Doctors think there's a good chance he'll survive. If he does, we'll prosecute him for his part in what happened."

Fitz swallowed hard. "Okay. Thanks for letting me know."

Birch turned to Shelby. "And you were right. Officers found nearly fifty pounds of cocaine in a small cargo hold in the ship."

"I knew it." A twinge of triumph filled her voice.

Fitz squeezed her arm but said nothing.

Birch sat back and addressed them all. "Because the theft happened in Belize, we can't prosecute Veronica for that. We could prosecute her for trafficking in stolen goods, but we'll have to find those goods. So far, they seem to have vanished. The guy you witnessed buying them"—she nodded to Fitz—"was brought in last night. He lawyered up, and we haven't gotten any information out of him. We searched his house, his car, and his boat, but there's no sign of the jewels. We'll keep looking, but..." She shrugged.

"She just gets away with it?" Tabby asked.

Fitz answered. "The items were stolen from one criminal by another in a foreign country. Without the stolen goods, there's nothing they can do."

Tabby's heart raced until she thought it might just pound out of her chest. "She almost got us all killed."

Fitz squeezed her hand. "I know. It's not okay."

"I went to see Ms. Hernandez this morning at Mullins's beach house," Birch said. "I told her about her father's death and the events that led to it. By the time I was finished, the woman was white as a sheet. She didn't confess anything, and I didn't expect her to. But she knows what her actions cost. She knows how close she came to being the reason for the deaths of three innocent souls." Birch let her gaze settle on each of theirs before she continued. "If we can get the buyer to turn on her, we can prosecute. Otherwise"—she shrugged—"I passed her name on to authorities in the US and elsewhere. If she makes a habit of stealing, she'll get caught eventually."

Tabby let that information simmer a moment. Maybe Veronica hadn't known how far her father would go to get his property back. Maybe she had known and hadn't cared. Either way, she'd been desperate to save her mother's life.

"I hope she quits," Tabby said. "I hope that what happened here changes her."

"Me too," Fitz added.

Birch nodded once. "Let's see... Oh, the antique box?"

Fitz stood and disappeared in the house to retrieve it. He handed it over.

She gazed at it a moment, letting her fingers trail over the top. "It's beautiful."

"Mullins had decided to give it to Veronica," Fitz said. "At least that's what he told me."

"Huh." Birch set the box down. "When we're done with it, we'll turn it over to the widow."

"How did she and the son take it?"

"They're in shock." Birch turned to Shelby. "Do you think either one of them knew you were a captive?"

"No." She shook her head vehemently. "They both thought I was just there for fun. In fact, Lena seemed rather thrilled to have me, said she spent all her time with men. She and I had a great time together. After a while, I was having more fun with her than with Shawn. I mean, he's a nice guy and everything, but I got tired of him before I even knew his dad was this crazy, drug-smuggling..." Her voice trailed off.

Fitz tried to hide a smug smile, but Tabby caught it and winked at him. He might not be the girl's father, but he'd stepped into the role well.

"Is there anything else you need from us?" Fitz asked.

Detective Birch stood. "If I do, I'll call you. Otherwise, you're free to go. If Joey Novak survives and stands trial, I assume you'll all be willing to testify?"

"Of course," Tabby said.

"Gladly," Fitz said at the same time.

Shelby just nodded. "If I have to."

Birch shook all their hands and disappeared, and they sat again.

Tabby was reeling.

Just like that, it was over.

CHAPTER FORTY-THREE

Fitz shouldn't have been surprised when he overheard Tabby using his phone to secure a plane ticket to Manchester. Of course she was going home.

He hadn't expected otherwise.

What she'd said about Rhode Island... they hadn't had a chance to talk about it.

Tabby was sure in a hurry to leave.

If she wanted to go back to New Hampshire, fine. Fitz wasn't going to leave her alone. He'd continue to pursue her until he convinced her they belonged together. And if he had to move north to stay with her, he'd do it. He'd sell the house his parents had left them. He just couldn't until Shelby graduated. He could wait.

She tapped her foot and stared out the window. "The four fifteen flight works. Thank you." She rattled off a credit card number. When she was finished, she shoved the card back into her wallet and turned to put the wallet in her purse.

And caught him watching.

She smiled and continued speaking into the phone. "Thank you so much... You too." And she hung up.

"You're leaving."

Her smile faltered. "I have to get back."

"Of course you do. I just thought…"

She cocked her head to the side. "What?"

That they could at least stay through the day. That they could talk about the future. That they could make plans.

She approached, eyes squinted as she tried to figure out what he was thinking.

He smiled his most charming smile. "It's not a bad place to spend the weekend."

Her eyes widened. "Are you staying all weekend? I thought Shelby would be eager to get home. I know she's eager to have you to herself. She needs you more than I do right now."

That was probably true, but still—

"And I have arrangements to make." She closed the distance and held out his phone to him.

He snatched it and shoved it in his pocket, his heartbeat quickening. "Arrangements like…?"

She seemed to realize his fears, and her hands came up to his unshaven face. "Did you think I changed my mind?"

"I had a tiny moment of doubt."

"I need to get a new phone, obviously. I have to put my house on the market and give my notice at work. I have to find a place to live and a—"

He pulled her against his chest and cut off the rest of her words with his lips.

They moved against hers as if they were meant to be together. Just like he and Tabby were meant to be together. Forever.

When he finally released her, she laughed. "Where was I?"

"At a place to live, but you'd better make sure it's a short lease. You won't be there long."

Her eyebrows rose playfully. "Your sister might have other ideas."

"I don't think so. She loves you." He backed up just enough to hold her eye contact. "I love you."

"And I love you."

Her words had his heart bursting.

But she continued to speak as if she hadn't just uttered the most mind-blowing, life altering statement ever uttered by mankind. Womankind.

"But we shouldn't rush anything," Tabby said. "Shelby is going to need time to heal. And you and I might consider, you know, going on a date or something. And not in a resort town or when either of our lives are in danger. Just a regular old Italian-food-on-a-Friday-night sort of date."

"We can do that. We can do lots of that." He lowered his head to kiss her again, but a very irritating sound came from the doorway.

Abe, clearing his throat.

Fitz glared at the man. "Go away."

"I heard you making plans and wanted to get involved," the man said.

"Our plans have nothing to do with you," Fitz snapped. "Go away."

But Abe only chuckled. "They might, but only if you want to get your job back."

There was almost nothing Abe could say to compel Fitz to turn away from Tabby, but the man had found the magic words.

He turned slowly. "What are you talking about?"

"Same thing I've been trying to talk to you about for months. I'm close to proving our innocence, proving the ADA was the leak."

Fitz stepped away from Tabby. "You really think Karen Smithfield did it?"

"No. I think she took her files home, and her son rifled through them. He's an addict. He was arrested not long after you and I left the force. She sent him to rehab to keep him out of prison. Our theory is that he passed along the information to his contacts in exchange for drugs."

"And she didn't know?" Fitz clarified.

"Or she did but didn't confess. But honestly, I think she didn't know."

Fitz took that in. Karen Smithfield had always seemed so authentic to him. He couldn't imagine her being involved with mobsters or even keeping her involvement secret if she learned she was the leak.

"How can you prove it?"

Abe just smiled. "I can't, not by myself. But with you and me and the FBI, I think we can get it done." He nodded to Tabby. "You two make your plans, just be sure to leave a little time for us to work together. And then for you to get back on the job."

Back on the job. Fitz could hardly stand to think of it. After all God had done for him—bringing this amazing woman into his life, saving his sister from the hands of evil—he almost dared not ask for this.

But God had proved faithful so many times. Why wouldn't He prove faithful in this too?

For the first time in two years, Fitz let himself believe he might someday get back to doing what he loved.

EPILOGUE
SIXTEEN MONTHS LATER

Tabby followed Fitz up the steep hill to the rise. Unlike back in Belize, the sounds were as familiar to her as her own face. The trill of backyard birds, the chattering of squirrels, the skittering of rocks against her hiking boots. Everything about this was familiar, but nothing about it was normal.

She'd relocated to Rhode Island a year before, moving into a small apartment not far from Fitz and Shelby's house. While she'd searched for another human resources job, she'd tried to figure out what she really wanted to do with her life.

At first, the answer was anything that wasn't human resources. As luck would have it, she didn't get a job, and in the interim, she started buying used pieces of furniture and refinishing them to resell. And then she learned to reupholster. When she finally was offered a boring office job, she turned it down. Maybe what she wanted to do wasn't practical and wouldn't make her a lot of money, but she liked it. She loved it, in fact.

She was happy in Rhode Island.

Chris had moved out of their parents' house and had gotten a job, which he seemed to like, while he continued working on his degree. Tabby and her brothers had gone in together to buy him a van for Christmas, which gave him more freedom than he'd ever had.

He seemed happy now.

Tabby wished her mother had surprised her when she'd told her she was moving to Rhode Island. Mom had been Mom, though, wailing and carrying on as if her happiness depended on Tabby's never living more than five miles from home.

That had been hard.

But Tabby'd survived it, and to nobody's shock but her own, Mom had survived too.

Dad had been supportive all along.

Over the previous twelve months, Tabby had made frequent trips home to Coventry, sometimes with Fitz, sometimes without. After he and Abe had proved their innocence, he'd been offered his job back. He'd refused, though, instead taking a position as a detective with the Rhode Island State Police, which he loved.

Shelby'd had a hard time sliding back into her normal life. She liked Tabby, though. The two had become like sisters almost immediately. But she'd needed counseling after being kidnapped and nearly killed. No shock, that. They'd all needed to work through what had happened. Shelby was doing better now. She'd just finished her junior year and had already been accepted to a few colleges. She talked about going to Boston or New York for school, but Fitz thought that, in the end, she'd stay close to home, and Tabby tended to agree.

Whatever she chose, Fitz and Tabby would support her. They only wanted her to be happy.

She and Fitz had been dating, taking it slow. As slowly as

two people would take a relationship when they saw each other every day. For Shelby's sake, though, they hadn't rushed. Shelby needed to heal before she'd be able to weather any more major changes in her life, and Tabby was in no hurry.

Fitz reached the clearing and turned back, hand outstretched. She took it, and he pulled her up beside him onto Ayasha Point, the most beautiful vista in Coventry.

He stared at the view. "You were right. This is amazing."

"Isn't it, though?"

He turned to gaze at her. She'd expected happiness on his face, maybe joy. His frown surprised her, as did the way his eyebrows crunched together.

"What's wrong?"

He looked again at the view, the lake, and the little town below. "It's such a perfect place."

It was. So why was he upset?

"You must miss it terribly," he added.

Oh. "I miss a lot of things about Coventry."

"I know. I'm sorry to take you away from your home."

She reached for his other hand. "You haven't taken me away from my home, Fitz. You couldn't if you wanted to. *You* are my home."

His frown faded, replaced by that gorgeous smile that made her heart melt every time. "Okay then."

"Okay what?"

He shoved his hand in his pocket. When he pulled it out, something sparkled on his pinky finger.

She was still trying to put it together when he spoke. "Sweet, sweet Tabitha. I love you more than"—his gaze roamed the expanse all around them—"than the width and breadth and height of this view. I love you more than I ever thought I could love another person. Loving you has changed me. Matured me. You've made me into a man I never thought I could be."

She couldn't seem to come up with a single response.

"I promise to love you every moment of every day for the rest of my life. Will you—?"

"Yes!" She threw her arms around his neck and pressed her lips to his.

She could feel his smile in his kiss. She could feel his love in it too.

After a moment, he backed up. "Did you want to see the ring, or—?"

"Yes, yes!" She giggled at herself, at him, at all of this.

He slid it from his pinky and held it up for her to examine.

It was a square-cut diamond surrounded by rubies in a platinum setting. "Fitz, it's beautiful."

"It was my mother's."

Oh. She looked from the ring back into his eyes. "It's the most exquisite ring I've ever seen. I'll treasure it. But what about Shelby? Won't she—?"

"It was her idea. All of this. She helped me plan it. I asked if she wanted to be here, but she decided this should be just about you and me."

Shelby'd accepted Tabby so wholly into their lives, and now it seemed she planned to accept her even more.

Fitz slipped the ring on Tabby's finger, and they both gazed down at it.

His mother's ring. She could hardly fathom the beauty of it, the depth of meaning.

When she looked at him again, he was beaming with pleasure. "It's perfect, like it was meant for you."

Like they were meant for each other. She would tell him that too. But his lips met hers, and she knew the words would have to wait.

It was all right. They had the rest of their lives.

THE END

I hope you enjoyed Tabby and Fitz's story. I know you're going to love Reid and Jacqui's. Turn the page for more about *Betrayal of Genius*, book 3 in the Coventry Saga.

Betrayal of Genius

Her invention could save thousands of lives...if she can survive to long enough to share it.

Jacqui's research could lead to a cure for Alzheimer's disease, and she's determined to ensure the technology goes to the company with the best shot at creating life-saving products, not just the highest bidder. When her lab is broken into, she realizes her partner is desperate to get his hands on her research and the money it'll bring. Jacqui goes into hiding, planning to lie low until she can find a buyer who lives up to her expectations.

Reid's life is all about protecting his daughter, but when she leaves for a month to visit her mother, he finds himself at loose ends. The pretty new woman in town seems like a good diversion, but he soon realizes there's more to Jacqui than doling out scoops of rocky road. When he senses danger, he's tempted to step away—he won't allow any threat to come near his daughter—but how can he turn his back on a woman in danger, one he's coming to care for?

Jacqui's former partner is closing in and getting more desperate by the day. He'll stop at nothing to get the payout he feels he deserves.

ABOUT BETRAYAL

You're going to love this pulse-pounding medical thriller. Preorder BETRAYAL OF GENIUS today.

ALSO BY ROBIN PATCHEN

The Coventry Saga

Glimmer in the Darkness

Tides of Duplicity

Betrayal of Genius

Traces of Virtue

Touch of Innocence

Inheritance of Secrets

Lineage of Corruption

Wreathed in Disgrace

Courage in the Shadows

Vengeance in the Mist

A Mountain Too Steep

The Nutfield Saga

Convenient Lies

Twisted Lies

Generous Lies

Innocent Lies

Beautiful Lies

Legacy Rejected

Legacy Restored

Legacy Reclaimed
Legacy Redeemed

Amanda Series

Chasing Amanda
Finding Amanda

ABOUT THE AUTHOR

Robin Patchen is a *USA Today* bestselling and award-winning author of Christian romantic suspense. She grew up in a small town in New Hampshire, the setting of her Nutfield Saga books, and then headed to Boston to earn a journalism degree. After college, working in marketing and public relations, she discovered how much she loathed the nine-to-five ball and chain. After relocating to the Southwest, she started writing her first novel while she homeschooled her three children. The novel was dreadful, but her passion for storytelling didn't wane. Thankfully, as her children grew, so did her writing ability. Now that her kids are adults, she has more time to play with the lives of fictional heroes and heroines, wreaking havoc and working magic to give her characters happy endings. When she's not writing, she's editing or reading, proving that most of her life revolves around the twenty-six letters of the alphabet. Visit robinpatchen.com/subscribe to receive a free book and stay informed about Robin's latest projects.

Made in the USA
Columbia, SC
14 October 2023